BREATHLESS

—

Shane Lindemoen

First printing: September 2019, Beacon Publishing Group
Second printing: March 2023, SL Reprints

ISBN: 978-1-7333225-8-4
ebook ISBN: 978-1-7333225-9-1

for kim
we miss you   *1954—2017*

Fenroe tracked Suja's blood through the station to a rec room far from the infirmary where she'd left him—the Russian cosmonaut was there, cradling the gnarled meat-club that used to be his hand.

Suja had dragged himself behind some lockers, behind the showers, and then behind the faux wood benches that were bolted to the floor. He flinched away from the fresh brightness of Fenroe's flashlight as Dunesto—another man, stout and powerfully built— dove for the lock cylinder to manually seal the rec room from the rest of the station, his eyes peeled to their most horrified limit, staring with raw intensity into the preceding corridor. The last thing Fenroe saw before the airlock hissed to the floor was screeching shapes unfolding from the darkness.

Something solid rammed into the other side, and the door jolted in its frame, shaking from a succession of clanging impacts. Fenroe pushed herself back to her feet and searched the module's interior as the things outside brought up a hammering crescendo against the door—unable to think, locked inside the full rhythm of her deep panicked breathing, she looked for another exit but there was nothing.

"What...what is this?" Fenroe stuttered, stepping away from the door. "What's happening?"

Wheezing heavily and trembling, Dunesto aimed the shoulder-lights of his spacesuit at the vibrating aluminum as it formed a new dimple after each forceful contact.

The impact tremors tripped the fire suppression system, and the overhead sprinklers detonated water all over the room. Fenroe backed away from the airlock and stood beside Suja, who was still slumped against the far wall, clutching a dark red draw seeping down his ribs.

Dunesto—bio-suit and helmet now glistening with water— tore himself away from the airlock and frantically circled the room, pulling a light pod away from his chest. He activated the probe and released it in midair, letting its internal magnets take over. Dunesto stepped back as light erupted from the instrument with flat, horizontal beams that methodically swept up and down the surrounding walls, painting the shadows with hard blue waves of contour as it scanned the area for every possible way out. The solid sheets of light between the downpour bent and refracted around the water as if thrown onto the curtain of a cataract.

"What the *fuck* is happening?" Fenroe asked again through fast, deep breaths.

"I don't know," Dunesto stammered, twisting his head back toward the pressure door. "But there's more than one—" and then he started searching the inside of the room again, the sound of his heavy breathing broadcasting over short-burst comms, his face blurred by water cascading down his visor, "—I think it's the crew."

Fenroe clenched her teeth against the adrenaline, feeling sweat drip down her quivering chin. The light-bullet finished its scan and powered down, leaving Fenroe to grope through the fallen darkness. She reached out for Suja and found him still crumpled against the wall breathing heavily. Igniting her shoulder lights, the room took on a reddish hue. In her peripherals, Dunesto bent and dug his hands under an open space beneath the black steel lockers, and lifted. The non-padlocked doors swung open from their hinges and dumped old gym clothes and cross-trainers and ancient, blood-stained towels into soggy piles onto the floor—with great effort, Dunesto hoisted one end and slid his shoulder deep underneath, loading his legs. The thing on the other side continued hammering into the thick door as if it were soft tin—convex, fist-sized divots swelled after each impact.

"That's three inches of plated aluminum," Fenroe said distantly. She was in deep shock, her thoughts flooding with images of living shadows and teeth and eyeless horror.

Dunesto straightened his legs with the lockers braced against his back and dropped them hard onto the pressure door—they crashed at an odd lean to form a rudimentary barricade.

Dazed, Fenroe raked her light across the spreading puddles of water—the drains in the floor clogged with exercise garb and towels—until she found the rectangular outline of a service panel rippling beneath the surface. This was their way out: an access point to the subfloor service conduit underneath the rec room. "I found a panel!"

Dunesto's lights materialized out of the surrounding darkness and downpour like wisps of smoke as he came to her side, and the banging halted. The deeply set metal suddenly shifted under the immense violent force of something monstrously strong—

...and the center of the door began to glow.

Fenroe froze and looked at a rose of molten light blossoming in the middle of the door itself: it was dark at first, like cooling magma, but it grew brighter. In the chaos and panic, she heard a soft hiss of breath escape Suja's lips.

She pulled her eyes away from the melting airlock and bent down, lifting Suja's soaked head away from the wall—the room brightened and rippled with fire glow as if someone ignited a thatch of tinder nearby. Fenroe shook him awake, speaking loud over the sound of falling water, willing lucidity back into his eyes: "Look at me and listen—where's Ulbricht? What's happening?"

"They're eating through the door," Suja whispered through his teeth, wincing against the wound pulling on his side. "They're coming."

ENDEAVOR

1.

FENROE ASCENDED THE LIGHT, feeling as though her dreams had slipped into the seams of what could have been. An outline of sweat darkened the collar of her flight suit—the run through the command module hadn't given her enough time to cool off.

She stared at herself in the glass as the levels passed by in cutting bands of shadow. The reflection was of a young woman with cheekbones that cut into her pale skin, her brown eyes narrow and hooded in deeply sad hollows, her hair of the same color, pulled back into a ponytail, and grim lips set in a permanent look of concern. Not muscular, but carved from hard training and discipline, built brick-for-brick for life in the most extreme environments imaginable. But behind the mask of concealed pain there remained the physical echo of the girl in the woman—the faintest remnants of the untroubled mind, fair skin, and soft mouth which had once belonged to a younger, less cynical reflection. Fenroe looked away from herself and used her sleeve to dry beadlets of sweat on her forehead.

The lift eased to a halt and the doors opened without sound. She walked quickly across the wide control bridge that stretched above hundreds of IDSI Controllers moving with purpose from one terminal to the next on the stadium floor far below, fully aware of the sweat-strands of hair still clinging to her neck. She steadied herself, trying to slow her breathing, and rapped on the glass before moving quietly into the conference room, where she waited for the shadow of a man on the far side to wave her in.

The room itself was dark and empty. A few government chairs and a long glass table. No frames on the walls, no decorations other than the holo-prism showing real time images of the planet Saturn as seen from the lens of the *Pinnacle Observatory*, which flickered as the doors closed behind her with a barely audible *shunk*. Somewhere in Jupiter's orbit, the immense mirrors turned their gaze from the sun, bringing the haloed planet into full view. The shadowed profile standing on the far side—the only actual person in attendance other than her—was Colonel Lee Sitosen, alone amidst near-transparent lighted images of serious men and women in military clothing blinking into existence one at a time as they called in from all over the planet—some even calling in from near-Earth orbit.

Colonel Lee Sitosen was tall and broad—almost tall enough to graze a doorframe with the top of his head—and dressed in a plain black flight suit that indicated no rank or station. He was of mixed Arab and East Asian descent, light tan complexion and obviously fit, knotted-rope lean with cords of muscle showing in the shoulders, forearms, and neck. The Colonel's eyes were crystal-clear-green, but still dark, and as all encompassing as the gaze of a hawk. His face was all angles, carved from granite. His black hair and neatly groomed beard served to highlight the sharpness of his visage as surely as the bevel of an axe head.

Sitosen waited before a wall of light with his hands clasped behind his back, watching the repeating playback of a tiny speck disappearing and reappearing inside saturnine shadow. Without turning to acknowledge her arrival: "Have a seat."

"Yes, sir," Fenroe said, straightening the front of her flight suit. Her heels scuffed the floor as she relaxed and took her chair, nodding at the holograms around the room. She only recognized three of the seven people seated at the table. Sitosen pulled himself away from the projection and laid his hand on the backrest of the closest chair for a moment, and then finally took his seat.

One of the holograms leaned forward—a sharpened man with gray hair, light-brown skin etched with age, his regal and competent frame slightly blurred in the blue haze of feedback, his voice deep and resonant: "Commander, my name is Colonel Ambrose Wren—" he pointed at the hologram seated across from him, "This is Lieutenant Olsen—" and at the darker shadow seated to Fenroe's right, "—and Lieutenant Davis."

"Evening," she said, acknowledging them each with a nod. She tried to keep herself composed, but her shoulders grew heavy. Fearing that something was wrong with the flight schedule, Fenroe felt in the pit of her stomach that her final chance to get out to Jupiter space was somehow slipping through her fingers. She couldn't think of any reason why they would have called an emergency meeting in the middle of the night other than to tell her that something vital had happened to the mission. The sweat around her neck collected the air, and she felt her skin pebble with goose bumps.

Sitosen sat back, regarding her from some internalized distance—she'd known him for years. Worked with him on more missions than she could count, and she had never seen him so unsettled. "There's been a serious situation developing over the

3

past few hours," Sitosen said, trailing off.

Fenroe shifted her gaze from one officer to the next. "Nothing detrimental to the mission, I hope."

"I'm sorry, Commander," Sitosen said, looking her straight in the eyes. "The *Pinnacle* mission's been postponed until further notice—" he held up his hand when she sat forward to protest. "Let me finish, please."

Sitosen waited for Fenroe to settle back into her chair and then studied her, as if he were deciding how to start. "How much do you know about our deep space programs?"

Fenroe stopped, looking again at the men and women in attendance. She shrugged back. "Pinnacle observatory's the farthest—"

"No Fenroe," Sitosen said, "I'm not talking about our orbital stations. I'm talking about deep space manned expeditions."

Fenroe looked a final time at the faces that comprised High Command, trying to understand exactly what was happening. Their stoic expressions gave away nothing. A knot of anxiety tightened in her stomach, sending waves of unease through her thoughts. The concept of deep space had changed over the course of her career as humanity's reach extended each time the current generation of satellites pinged a new milestone. Currently, deep space was defined as the cold, dark expanse beyond Jupiter. The International Deep Space Initiative also had three space telescopes several magnitudes larger than the *Kepler* and *Hubble* observatories—the farthest was attached to the space station *Pinnacle*, a massive wheel-shaped structure currently in orbit around Jupiter's moon Calisto—the farthest any human had ever been from Earth—or so she thought—and until a few moments ago, where she was headed at the end of the month. The *Pinnacle* was supposed to be her last chance at a mission in what she considered deep space.

Fenroe felt a sliver of excitement, trying to wrap her mind around what Sitosen had said, the words "deep space" and "manned mission" not normally uttered by Command in the same sentence. Her thoughts raced with possibilities and she didn't know if he meant the deepest we've ever sent a human, or the deepest anything made by humans has ever been. "I am not aware of any such mission..."

"Commander," the hologram of Colonel Wren cleared his throat. "You have to understand that what we're about to tell you is restricted to the highest levels of Command. Nothing we discuss leaves this room. Is that clear?"

She glanced back at Sitosen sitting with his chin touching his steepled fingers, a new fold of worry knitting into a crease between his brows.

"Yeah," she said, and then quickly corrected herself. "Uh, yes sir. Crystal clear, sir."

The hologram nodded and a block of light materialized on the table in front of her, running down a list of filenames until it stopped at one labeled *IDSIV ENDEAVOR*, and then expanded into a sheet of light containing a manifest.

"Tell me," Wren said, "are you aware of any official reason for sending people to Titan?"

Fenroe's voice caught in her throat and she couldn't blink. She glanced at Sitosen a third time, who was a blank slate, giving nothing away. "I can think of a million reasons for sending people—" she stared back into the faces of the officers gathered around her, choosing her words very carefully, "—but I can't think of any reason the International Senate would fund such a mission."

Colonel Wren nodded his head, as if satisfied with the answer. "There is no reason for the International Senate to allow funding." He leaned forward, "You begin to see why every precaution must be taken to ensure the highest level of confidence. As things stand today, the civil committee is unaware of our Saturn expeditions. Officially unaware, anyway." He cleared his throat and laid the distorted image of a folder on the table in front of him. "We've studied your jacket, Commander. If there's anyone here that can appreciate the importance of this mission, it's you."

"I...I understand." Fenroe wiped her face and unzipped her flight suit a bit, airing herself out, still catching her breath from the run she'd just had. "It's just—it's a lot to take in."

"How old are you, Commander?"

She hesitated. "Twenty-seven, Sir."

"Twenty-seven," he repeated, nodding as if he already knew the answer. "And this mission to the *Pinnacle* was to be your last?"

"Yes, Sir," Fenroe said, not sure where this was going.

"Commander," Wren said softly, "We understand that your crew has been training specifically for the *Pinnacle*. But we have to know—right now, at this moment—if they're prepared for a mission to Saturn."

Fenroe didn't know what to say. She and her crew were preparing for a three-year expedition to Jupiter, followed by a three-month tour aboard the *Pinnacle*, followed by another three month stay in a science station on the surface of Europa, and then it was a three-year trip back home. She had no definitive idea how long it would take to get to Titan, but given how far away Saturn would have to be during launch—assuming her crew's launch schedule remained the same—her rough estimates put the mission into a perspective of a five-year flight plan, one way. Still, at that moment, with the highest-ranking space, air, and naval officers on the planet sitting there expecting her to soldier up, she couldn't wrap her mind around being away from Earth for more than ten years. She'd be nearing forty by the time of her return trip home. But there was no way she could turn down an opportunity such as this—to see Saturn with her own eyes was too powerful a thought to ignore.

"I mean," she hesitated, "I have to speak with them."

"They're ready," Sitosen said, finally coming back from his thoughts. His voice was soft but Fenroe never failed to notice that even the Colonel's silence commanded attention. "They'll do it."

"Your pardon, Colonel," Wren said quietly. "But we have to hear it from her."

She leaned forward and opened the file labeled *IDSIV ENDEAVOR*, forcing herself to relax and think. "Why send people now?"

"This would actually be our second attempt," Sitosen said, brushing invisible dust off the table. He looked at her and shrugged. "We've already sent people."

"There was a crew sent to Titan on an exploratory mission four years ago," Wren said. "A month ago we received a single-packaged message indicating some kind of catastrophic systems failure."

"Then they're gone." Fenroe shook her head, opening her hands. "Colonel, we don't even lose contact with a crew in low-Earth orbit and expect to find any survivors."

"It's not that simple," Sitosen said.

Fenroe straightened in her chair, the initial excitement replaced by a cold sense of worry. "What are you asking me to do?"

"We need your crew to retrace the *Endeavor's* mission, and find out what happened to them."

"With all due respect," she shook her head again, formulating the best words for the right argument, surprising herself with the fact that she was even arguing at all, "we already know what happened. They're gone—"

"We received a transmission from the crew two days ago." Colonel Wren leaned forward and said, "a transmission, Fenroe... After two months of silence."

Fenroe took a breath and tried doing the math—tight beam communication between the *Pinnacle* and Earth was delayed roughly ten hours. Doubling that time would mean a message received from Titan would have been transmitted anywhere within a twenty-four hour timeframe. If they'd received a message two days ago, it meant that at least some of the flight crew was still alive out there.

"What did it say?"

"It was just their flight recorder's distress beacon," Wren said. "No package attached."

"Assuming they're still alive," Fenroe said slowly, "what makes you think they would be able to hold on for the four to five years it's going to take us to reach them?"

Sitosen nodded his head and began ticking things off with his fingers: "They have an onboard ecosystem that replenishes air and water. They had food stocks that could last a crew of nine for twenty-four years. They had oxygenators, recyclers, burners and scrubbers that could pull methane, nitrogen and hydrogen from Titan's atmosphere if need be, and enough solar energy to last an eternity. Assuming there wasn't a catastrophic failure to the integrity of the station itself, they could conceivably hold on until help arrives."

"You know as well as I do the chances of finding anything," she shrugged. "It would be much faster to send a probe."

"We've calculated their odds, Commander. And we have sent probes." Wren's crisp hologram stood and walked toward the wall-screen. "One hundred and fourteen probes, in fact. As soon as anything approaches Saturn at a certain distance, the image goes dark." His hologram touched the screen and the profile of Saturn shifted slightly, revealing a small brown dot moving in the foreground. The shimmering orb was the size of a coin—it flicked out of existence and then reappeared a moment later in the center of the room, spread above the five meter wide table. Saturn had become a refracted blur of patterns on the ceiling and walls; the moon Titan became the size of an automobile.

"And there's another thing," Wren continued. He pointed at the last known image of the Endeavor in Titan orbit. "There's uh...a slight gravitational lensing effect of some kind. We're not sure what it is. You can see Saturn clearly, but when we focus too closely on Titan, the image blurs. We initially thought it was a local phenomenon affecting our telescope, but it's universal. Every single telescope we point at Titan blurs and refracts like nothing we've ever seen before."

"How long has it been like this...?"

"We lost visual of Titan within minutes of receiving the Endeavor's distress package."

Fenroe stood and waded through the light-thrown images until she came to a tiny satellite shaped tube floating several centimeters away from the moon. Sitosen stood near Fenroe and studied her, gauging how close she was to accepting the mission. Fenroe looked up into his serious green eyes. "What do you expect me to do about it?"

"Commander Fenroe," Colonel Wren had the hard manner of a career military man, "this was a mission of exploration. The most prepared mission our species has ever carried out. For some reason, a group of our best and brightest has ended up in dire circumstances on the other side of this solar system. They may yet still be alive, and we are not prepared to leave them there."

"Colonel, I'm not entirely certain I can risk the lives of my men for a lost cause. You've one crew stranded out there. I see no reason to add to that list."

"Leaving them there is out of the question at this point—"

"What was the value of this mission?" she asked.

"Value of this mission? Can you clarify?"

"Why did you send them in the first place?" she asked again. "Why send a manned crew out there if you didn't have to? And why send another? You know as well as I do that stellar law dictates the use of probes for fringe exploration. Gentlemen—" she shook her head and arched her eyebrows. "—this doesn't make any sense."

Wren cocked his head and looked at the image of Lieutenant Davis, a man only slightly younger than him but with much darker skin, who had remained quiet since she arrived. His hologram removed its spectacles and tossed them out of view. "There are certain things that this office is not prepared to discuss at this time," the man said.

"If I'm going to commit my crew to a mission deviation such as this," Fenroe continued, "you're going to have to tell me everything. I'm not walking into a dark spot near Saturn unless I have a good reason."

Davis's hologram considered that for a moment, and then he shrugged. "Five years ago, Command intercepted a transmission from Titan space."

She shook her head and frowned: "What kind of transmission?"

"A timestamp signature," Davis said, leaning forward. "Like what we'd get from one of our orbital installations. But whatever this thing was, it didn't come from anything of ours. This thing was sending us a faked communication code—" he saw the blank look on Fenroe's face, and started again, using his hands to help articulate the words, "—the signal *looked* like it was from one of our ISDI installations, but the code itself was off by a few numbers. The date, specifically."

"And it couldn't have come from our equipment...?"

"The code we received belonged to one of the orbital installations in Jupiter orbit," he said, shaking his head. "There's nothing of ours out there in Saturn space."

Fenroe thought about that and looked again to the other men and women around the table. "Maybe it's one of our satellites bouncing the code back at us."

"It isn't," Davis said. "Before the radio shield went up, we could account for every satellite in Saturn orbit."

"So...what is it?"

The blue projection of Davis shook his head slightly and leaned back into its chair. "We don't know."

"Is it alien?"

He shook his head again and shrugged. "We don't know."

"We sent the *Endeavor* crew to find out," Wren cut in. "And now they're missing."

Fenroe sighed and shook her head, studying the holo-image of the *Endeavor* manifest floating above the table. "I don't recommend sending another crew."

"This isn't a debate of whether or not we should mount a rescue," Colonel Wren said, his flickering hologram turning back toward the image of Titan. "The decision has been made, and we're going. What this conference is about is deciding who gets the job. This is the last known image of the *Endeavor* that we have. Something or someone is now preventing us from observing Titan. We can't even use our telescopes—if we zoom in enough to see, the image blurs, as if there's an optical shield surrounding the planet and its moons. Whether it's a method the crew has employed to signal for help, or some other natural phenomenon, there are now enough questions that the ISIA civil committee may begin to receive inquests from private observatories. We must know what's happening out there. Our probes and telescopes are no longer a viable option, for reasons unknown to us." He turned to Fenroe again and penetrated her with his eyes. His hologram flickered for a moment. "Will you help us, or do we find someone better?"

"Losing another ship won't help with those inquests."

"Imagine if it were your crew out there." Sitosen said, finally looking at her. "The fact is we had an opportunity to send a manned mission to one of the farthest bodies in our solar system. We took it because we could. Because this office believes it's our god-given right to reach as far away from this planet as humanly possible. That crew is now stuck out there."

"And if they're gone?"

"If you arrive and find the crew inoperable," Colonel Wren said, pulling his hand over the black steel-colored brush of his hair, "then you will recover what's left of their bodies, and complete their mission."

"And what was their mission?"

"The *Endeavor's* mission," Wren continued, "was to make contact with the surface of Titan and find the source of that signal."

Fenroe breathed heavily, dizzy from all that had unfolded within those brief minutes. Her dream was within reach, she realized, suddenly terrified. But it was made hollow by the truth of the moment. Most of her life, she had thought about nothing else other than to set foot on terrain unlike anything she'd known on Earth. That hope had been a constant backdrop of her dreams since deciding to become an astronaut. Her entire career—her whole life—was for that one, unattainable moment, which was now suddenly so close she could taste it. Fenroe circled the table again, navigating through the light of Titan. She tried to imagine herself across that black ocean, but failed. There was too much time between then and now for her to remain the same person. If she walked away from this opportunity, she would take that decision with her to the grave. It was a cold, calculated thought. She stopped at the bullet-sized image of the *Endeavor* engulfed by a moon so much like Earth, yet so different. The *Endeavor* flickered for a moment before moving toward Titan, and then back again, repeating the process. It was stuck in an endless looping descent, pulling her dreams along with it. Mesmerized by the possibilities, the explorer in her was powerless to resist.

2.

"Fenroe," Sitosen called after her as she rounded the corner leading back to the After Battery. She turned and waited, numb from the mission brief. He slowed several meters away from where she stood, regarding her with the same respect given to someone who'd just received a death sentence. "It's not about justifying the cost of the mission," he said quietly, after a beat. "Fenroe, it's not even about figuring out what the signal is."

"I know," she replied, shaking her head and turning away from him.

"Commander," he said, more forcefully. He stepped close and looked down at his feet for a moment. "It's about not leaving any of our own behind." He searched her face until he was satisfied that what was said had taken hold. "Do you understand?"

"Understand me, Sitosen." Fenroe said, choosing her words carefully. "If this mission fails—" she looked back into his eyes, "—I won't allow the death of a third crew on my conscience."

He nodded. "I understand."

"Don't come for us, Colonel." She broke eye contact and then started to walk away. "Don't make the same mistake twice."

"I've been added to the mission manifest," he called after her.

His eyes relaxed a bit, which on his chiseled and normally stern face was enough to be considered a smile. "I'll be going with you as support. But it's still your ship. Your crew."

Fenroe studied his lonely profile standing in the center of the hallway, letting the silence grow. The perfect image of a career astronaut—grim, calm, and experienced. Sitosen drew up to his full height, and the light revealed more of the angles of his skin, the shadows around his eyes. "You know why they chose us, Commander?"

She shook her head.

He shrugged simply, finally turning back toward the briefing room, speaking over his shoulder. "Because you and I don't fail."

And he left her there, thinking about the *Endeavor*, and the shadows circling therein.

3.

An unquantifiable number of stars shined in the dark, and from out of that darkness emerged a spaceship: a mechanical pipeline the length of several city blocks that plummeted through the silent vacuum of space. It looked like an enormous satellite in the center of three massive rings that turned gracefully around a main structure. This was the *Crown Meridian*, falling in the foreground of an immovable darkness, in distances so enormous that it would look to a pacing observer as if it weren't moving at all, but the truth was the *Crown Meridian* moved at tremendous speeds.

In the main module—the largest structure inside the gravity pendulum, with its sister modules branching out from each other at equal spacing—Sitosen and Fenroe sat at a table near the Central Post with their arms folded, thinking deeply.

Sitosen sighed heavily, scratching at a couple weeks' worth of beard growth. He then reached for his king, and tipped it over.

Fenroe nodded without a word and sat back, running her fingers through a mane of unbrushed hair. Between the two of them was a chessboard with very few pieces left, bare and in chaos.

"Well played," he said, extending his hand. Fenroe took it into her own and shook.

"Well played," she said, and then checked the bio-clock under her wrist. "Two hours."

Surprised, Sitosen checked his own wrist. "Holy shit..."

She smiled, stretching her neck.

He was quiet for a moment. Then, silently, he reset his pieces and they began again.

Several meters down the corridor, a man in his late twenties who had the name "Ryouichi Dunesto" stitched onto his breast pocket knelt beside a robotic arm that he'd removed earlier from a machine called the Remote Manipulator System—RMS, or *Rims* for short—which was a child-sized robot that the ship's AI would commandeer for most of the spacewalks. Dunesto was built like a linebacker—powerful shoulders and thick back muscles that rippled through his clothing—dark brown eyes and naturally peach skin. His black hair was neatly cropped, and his grim mouth was framed by a goatee that blended to stubble along his jaw. Ryouichi Dunesto was an engineer and a machinist, whose iron-hard hands were always covered with black shadows of grease and small wounds grown over with young callus.

He positioned himself farther beneath the examination table, wiggling a snarl of black cordage that disappeared into the wall. The computer flattened behind a large panel of thick vinyl, but it was easy enough to remove if Dunesto had to get back there.

"Piece of...fuckin...shit," he hissed, moving to his knees.

The dismembered robotic limb extended for a moment before rotating its wrist in a complete circle, and pulled back. The lifeless body it belonged to lay on the workstation.

"Think that's funny?" he asked, huffing back to his feet.

The arm whirred into a ninety-degree angle, as if it were flexing its bicep, and then gave him a thumbs-up. He caught the blur of a tattered orange sweatshirt out of the corner of his eye passing the laboratory.

"Aris," he called after it. "Check this out."

The shadow skipped back and poked her shaven head around the corner—this was the comms officer, Whitney Aris, who had a tendency of staring with such intensity that one could feel the pressure of her gaze even after she looked away. Dark brown skin, she was no taller than Dunesto, but even her loose tee shirt and the orange sweater tied around her waist did not conceal the sleek lines of muscle. Her brows were two black accents brushed horizontally above her eyes, and her nose was long and sharp, intensifying the predator quality of her stare. Aris's mouth was full and expressive to the point of being sensuous, curled lightly in a slight smile that might be sardonic or merely playful. The woman's dark eyes seemed to dare the observer to discover which was the case. Whitney Aris was intimidatingly attractive, and her voice had a husky, stirring quality that could violently seize your complete attention: "Yah—you get it fixed?"

Dunesto stood and brushed imaginary dust from his hands. "Observe."

He opened his arms as if he were revealing the prestige of a magic trick. "Arm, what is your opinion of Communications Officer Whitney Aris?" The arm straightened and rotated its wrist, making a blade of its hand. It smoothly pulled itself into a ninety-degree angle again and gave another thumbs-up. Dunesto clapped once and turned to Aris, who arched her eyebrow, unimpressed. "What about her wardrobe?" He pointed at the old threadbare sweater tied around her waist. The arm flattened the palm of its hand parallel to the ground and made a so-so gesture.

"I'll be in the garden," she said, rolling her eyes.

"I have another sweater." Dunesto said to her back, watching her disappear down the corridor. "I have several you can look at. Clean ones."

"Yeah, but how many of your sweaters smell like home?" she called back over her shoulder.

Whitney Aris walked farther down the hallway, and then turned into another corridor, which extended away from the main habitat to the largest section not directly connected to the station itself, and entered the Garden Module. The warm UV lamps always ran, but a bank of LED's blinked to life as she walked into the room. On the other side of the module, which was roughly half the size of a gymnasium, knelt a pale looking gentleman, thin and slightly balding, lined forehead and the sad, luminous eyes of a well-studied scholar. This was the crewmember everyone affectionately referred to as The Russian, Suja Tsvetkov, the ship's botanist and navigations officer—a man who exuded an immediate and impressive sense of intelligence. Suja always wore black cotton shorts and flip-flops, and one of the many short-sleeved Hawaiian shirts of his collection. Bleary from sitting in the dim light of the heat lamps for so long, he blinked and gave Aris a friendly wave.

"Early start?" she asked.

"Late end, actually." He yawned through his accent. "Can't get this damn nutrient solution to take."

"You had breakfast?"

Suja stretched and rubbed his eyes. "I was going to head down after I finish."

The garden was one of the most visited modules on the station. From outside it looked like a gigantic box, but the dimensions inside were a bit different where the ceiling angled to the main entrance. The garden itself consisted of both soiled and hydroponic troughs planted with an assortment of ferns, vegetables, fruits, berries and thick green flora. It was a microcosm: used water filtered through a purifier, and then through an oyster, algae and large-particle sediment tank, finally feeding back into the garden that fed the oxygenator its supply of CO_2, where the oxygen was stripped and fed back into the crew's supply of life-giving air. The distilled water vapor solidified near the garden's apex, and then ran down the sloped ceiling into a pool, where it was collected and redistributed throughout the rest of the station. It smelled like an indoor swimming pool.

It was the place on the ship that most reminded them all of home.

Suja sat outside of a tented nursery that housed the infant plants on the other end of the module. Besides the Cupola, the garden had the best view on the station—a large, thick portal in the ceiling made of pressure glass. He set down a large dropper containing dark green fluid, and then moved to his feet. "You going down then?"

"Just have to check O-two."

Suja nodded and stretched his back again, then headed for the kitchen. "I'll be there."

Farther down the corridor, at the bow of the station, was the flight deck, which looked similar to most traditional images of a space shuttle. A broad viewport, bifurcated in the center by panels of instrumentation that encircled the flight controls all the way to the ceiling; a seat for both the pilot and co-pilot—there was a large room-like compartment behind the flight controls that contained the *Stellographer*—which was a solar system map of every transiting and orbital ISDI installation and satellite in space—a communications center, and the primary view screen. There was also a small conference table about the size of a restaurant booth, and a refrigerator.

Another member of the crew sat in front of the panel of flight controls—Erika Ulbricht, the ship's pilot. Ulbricht was normally relaxed and easy mannered. College-athlete-lean, with the calf muscles of a powerful soccer player. She had light blond hair—dark at the roots where she parted it, but lighter near the ends, which touched the top of her shoulders when she let it down. Ulbricht had eyes that were narrow and exhausted, a permanent look of fatigue accentuated by alluring shadows and smile lines.

Erika Ulbricht reclined in her seat while playing a handheld video game, very relaxed, her legs resting on an obsidian glass touch-panel that served as the flight controls. Paying little attention to what the ship was doing, she readjusted her position to get a bit more comfortable, and brushed a function on the control panel with her heel. Ulbricht, distracted by her videogame, didn't see it happen.

There were three hundred and sixty four solar arrays fixed to the station's exterior, arranged in a staggered configuration directly behind the light sails. They each led to a system of power converters kept in a compartment near the flight deck. Separated by a thin wall of gold gossamer, Ulbricht sat playing her video game.

The web of photovoltaic fibers within the light sails was enormously complex and mesmerizing. Flowing throughout cooling loops between the solar arrays and power converters was chilled ammonia. Suddenly, a pressure valve began venting gas both inside and outside of the station. As a white cloud of icy dust drifted away from a pressure release valve on the ship's exterior, a toxicity gauge on the flight deck's control panel transitioned from soothing blue to soft purple.

A calm female voice—the ship's artificially intelligent computer, called Eos—spoke to Ulbricht from a directional sound system in the walls: "Caution, ammonia from the solar array heating system has been redirected to the main habitat. A surplus of ammonia in the main habitat may be hazardous to the crew. Advise canceling the redirection and closing the vent."

"Sure," Ulbricht said, still immersed in her video game. "Close it."

"Canceling ammonia venting procedure." The touchscreen beneath her heel deactivated and went dark. Ulbricht didn't acknowledge the ship's AI, but made sure that her foot wasn't covering anything else.

In the kitchen module, Matthew Harris—the crew's behavioral scientist and medical doctor—removed a whistling teapot from the stove, shaking the heat off his fingers and hissing through his teeth. He turned and pulled a baking sheet of leftover red potatoes from an electric oven and slid it onto the center island. He increased the volume to some music and turned back to his work.

Matthew Harris was average height and visibly round, but far from out of shape. The Doctor's face was as mobile and expressive as a chimp. His voice was a penetrating, ironic rasp. There was something almost pleasantly sarcastic about Matthew Harris, with his ruddy cheeks, broad mouth, downturned eyebrows, round ears, and artisan hands sporting fingers with enough definition to serve as a carpenter. Or a grappler. The Doctor's sandy brown hair had grown into bangs messily palmed out of his eyes, and he was in desperate need of a shave.

A comfortable chef, he flipped eggs easily in a frying pan. On a dry eraser board next to the fridge, every crewmember's name had a line struck through it, except Harris. Behind him, Suja Tsvetkov entered with a colander full of berries and vegetables from the Garden module.

On the opposite side of the corridor, in a soundproof chamber that held the crew bunks and personal effects, the ship's physicist and chemist still dozed in his bed, dreaming about zero gravity, and taking his first steps onto Titan. Etched into the bedframe was the name THOMAS BECK.

A photosensitive alarm began brightening from a barely detectable dim to a richer dim, mimicking the summer sunrise at his home in Ohio, until he finally opened his eyes.

"I'm up, Eos," he rasped, and the light mellowed.

Thomas Beck sat up and yawned the sleep out of his head, checking the bio-clock under his wrist. He glanced at his sleepy reflection in the mirror across from his bunk and thumbed a small pink-red blemish on his clean-shaven face, and then he smoothed down his chopped and textured brown hair. A youthful looking man, farm-boy attractive, with permanent creases around his blue eyes from frequent moments of hard concentration. His nose was long and a bit wide at the bridge, suitable for holding a pair of glasses in place—something it hadn't done since he was a kid. Thomas Beck kicked on a pair of sandals, and then headed across the hall toward the scent of caramelizing onions and the sound of music.

The kitchen served as the main social hub for the crew—it was a place to eat, relax, and brief each other on the daily agenda. In the small Mess hall, the crew of the *Crown Meridian* gathered to eat breakfast.

Suja finished rinsing fruits and vegetables and waited patiently while Harris meticulously prepared his plate, finally dusting it with some seasoning. "What do you got for us this morning?"

"Eggs, asparagus, leftover red taters," Harris said. "And whatever else you brought from the garden."

"I don't know what everyone's complaining about," Suja shrugged in mock concern. "I think your cooking smells fine."

Harris smiled. "I figured we could fit in a decent meal before your turn."

Thomas Beck entered the room bleary-eyed, and sat quietly with Whitney Aris and Erika Ulbricht. "Morning."

"Morning," Ulbricht said, doing a double take when she saw the sleepy grin on his face. "Great morning, apparently."

"Meh," he scratched his head and yawned, "Well, actually, I'm curious. How much time do you guys spend in the Cupola?"

"Some," Aris said, dishing up a plate. "Why?"

"Have you ever tried separating the module form centrifuge? Go without gravity?"

Aris shrugged. "Once or twice."

"You have to try it," Beck said to Ulbricht. "It's...it is something else." He crossed his arms, breathing sleepily through his nose, eyes still closed, hair tousled. "You're suspended there, completely weightless, right? Surrounded by nothing but the emptiness of space and the stars." He smiled sleepily again, searching for the right words and then shrugged, lifting his hands helplessly. "Put on some Chopin in the background, a little Nocturne maybe..."

"Chopin? Ah god, here we go—"

"—and you're gone, man. You absolutely lose yourself."

"Lose yourself, huh?" Aris frowned.

"Yah." Beck flicked an asparagus tip at her.

"Like sensory deprivation," Ulbricht suggested, forking some eggs.

He shook his head. "Sense-dep tanks are more like sensory amplifiers. You pick up everything, hyper sound and light awareness...this is different. What I'm talking about is more like...like vertigo."

"The fear of falling," Aris ventured.

"Vertigo's not just about the fear," Beck shrugged, thinking about it while chewing his breakfast. "It's about the fear of falling at conflict with the desire to fall."

"There's a term for that," Aris said, frowning, trying to think.

"The Call of the Void," Beck replied.

"That's it." She snapped her fingers.

They sat in silence for a moment, trying to imagine it.

Ulbricht smirked and arched her eyebrows, nodding thoughtfully: "I'll have to give that a shot."

Commander Fenroe entered and took her seat next to Sitosen and Dunesto.

Aris wiped her lips with a napkin. "What's the good news, boss?"

Fenroe grabbed the peppercorn grinder and cleared her throat. "Good news is we're ahead of schedule."

Everyone looked to Whitney Aris, who set down her fork and shrugged. "We've gotta be close to the dead zone then." She glanced at Fenroe. "The *Endeavor's* distress beacon should be pinging us anytime now—" Aris waited a beat, letting everyone finish chewing their food, "—which means we might be losing comms."

"How certain is that?" Dunesto asked.

Aris shrugged. "Eighty percent?"

"In either case," Fenroe said, looking at Dunesto, "we're entering the dead zone a few days ahead of schedule. Which means Ulbricht, Sitosen and I will be pulling the ship back to a few thousand kilometers per hour sometime in the next couple of days, which also means we may be losing gravity again. Depends on how the sails behave." She studied each of their faces, watching the finality of the moment to sink deep. Four years is a long time to have to wait for something. Everyone was balancing the excitement of Titan, and the hope of getting back home in one piece. And they each looked as if the gravity of it tugged at their thoughts a little more forcefully than usual.

"Eat up," Fenroe said, as carelessly as she could. "Be ready to move in forty eight hours."

4.

Fenroe sat in the dark silence of space, separated from the crushing vacuum by thick layers of armor glass, riding the black sky with thoughts of the lost *Endeavor* mission, and home. This was the observation rotunda, which the crew long ago named the Cupola in honor of the very first space station. The entire room was a two hundred and eighty degree glass bubble, interwoven with high-resolution nano-optics. Saturn was still far off in the distance, its atmosphere no more than a few shades of slightly darker colors of beige. She watched the ringed planet through the glass—unmagnified, massive in the distance—while sitting tense upon a black synth-leather couch, with her elbows on her knees. After a few moments of silence, she spoke quietly to the walls: "Read it to me again, Eos."

"Yes, Commander,"

'But when from a long distant past nothing subsists, after the people are dead, after the things are broken and scattered, still, alone, more fragile, but with more vitality, more unsubstantial, more persistent, more faithful, the smell and taste of things remain poised a long time, like souls ready to remind us, waiting and hoping for their moment amid the ruins of all the rest; and bear unfaltering in the tiny and almost impalpable drop of their essence, the vast structure of recollection.'

"You seem uncomfortable," Eos said. "Can I suggest a more calming passage?"

"No thank you," Fenroe replied. "Once more please."

"Yes, Commander."

As Eos dutifully recited what once was a source of comfort, Fenroe closed her eyes, now unsettled by every word. She always looked to it as a way of coping with the concept of death. Fenroe initially believed Proust wanted the reader to think about how to safeguard the memory of themselves, to preserve it somehow so that it may continue living on long after the moment of physical death. That's part of why she wanted Titan so badly—she was seduced by the idea of immortality, the annals of exploratory legend. But it was the kind of thing she had obsessed over far too long. It was vain, she realized. Narcissistic. It was nothing more than amusing poetry, to lift the spirits. But what if what Proust was actually trying to say was not, as it had been presented over the years, a dreamy assertion but an aggressive and sober dismissal? Fenroe went back and forth in her mind searching for how she got the idea, and when, and why. It was as if she had been staring at a painting far too long, until the images disappeared entirely, leaving nothing behind except strokes of different colored oils. The words were there, in the lines—"Nothing subsists, once people are dead, broken, scattered, and unsubstantial"—and then later in the passage—"amid the ruins of all the rest of us"—vaguely echoing Shakespeare's King Henry battle cry, "this story shall the good man teach his son; And Crispin Crispian shall ne'er go by, from this day to the ending of the world, but we in it shall be remember'd."

At first, Fenroe didn't have a reason to believe that Proust and Shakespeare weren't in agreement: nothing that can be remembered dies. It was now as if Proust refuted Shakespeare, or was at least criticizing his exploration. But why did she think this now?

Fenroe knew the passage was part of *Remembrance of Things Past*, which Proust intended to be about the persistence of memory, or the involuntary nature of our memories, but she also knew that the phrase "amid the ruins of all the rest" was no mere passing comment. Everything Proust put down on paper was both deliberate and integral to a much larger message. So what did that mean? Some dreaming aspect of her suspected that *Remembrance of Things Past* was not written for us—rather, was not written for what Proust thought of at the time as Man—but for "the ruins" we would inevitably leave behind—certainly an end of something, probably his idea of the world, or a semblance of civilization left clinging to history, confused about how it let the past slip away into the dark, unknowable future. With all the time the crew had on this journey, Fenroe spent much of hers trying to understand what Proust meant, because it was very possible that she would never see Earth again. When she really let herself think about it, her self-image had always taken shape in the stars. Away from the chaos of humanity. Away from the heartache of it. But Fenroe still knew that she needed a reason to justify everything, if only for her crew—if indeed the mission failed as the *Endeavor's* had, to make it mean something. That was Proust. That was her passage: a reasonable argument for how their memories would carry on even if they themselves could not. But Fenroe also came to the conclusion, from her bored scholarly pursuits, that such wishful thinking was for children.

As Fenroe watched the distant starlight twinkle in the backdrop of space, she knew that Proust had organized a moral standard in his writing. The "Ruins" and the "Dead" were parables of it. While Eos finished the last line again, Fenroe also suspected that Proust was exploring those forgotten ruins as something nobler than us. They were nobler simply because they would be the things doing the remembering. Whatever it is that he thought about, Fenroe wondered if he meant it to be more fragile and valuable than a namesake, or a legacy.

"Oh—uh, sorry," someone said from the doorway, "Didn't mean to interrupt."

Fenroe glanced over her shoulder just in time to catch Thomas Beck's shadow turning back into the main corridor.

"Wait," she called after him. "I'm all finished in here—that's enough, Eos."

"Yes, Commander." Eos's soothing vibrato responded from the walls.

Beck stood in the doorway, scratching his head.

"Morning," Fenroe said, moving to her feet.

"Morning."

She glanced at Saturn and shrugged: "Thought I'd give losing myself a shot."

Beck stepped into the cupola, smiling. "It is something, isn't it?"

Fenroe nodded, untying her flight suit from her waist. She pulled her arms into the sleeves, trying to set aside the dark place she had been moments before. "And how are your pet photons doing today?"

"Looking good," he nodded. As the ship's chemist and physicist, one of Beck's side projects was to study solar plasma-oscillations on their way to interstellar space. "Relativity still works out here."

"Good to know." They stood for a moment, Beck crossing his arms, taking glances from the viewport.

"Well then," Fenroe clapped him on the shoulder, moving into the access. "I'll leave you to it."

"Fenroe," Beck stopped her. "Can I show you something?"

She put her hands on her hips, looking past his shoulder into the glass module, Proust's lonely words tugging at her thoughts. "Yeah...yeah, sure. Why not."

Beck hopped down the three obsidian steps and stood in the

cupola. "Eos, dial down the reds, will you?"

"You got it," Eos said, and a number of stars disappeared from view—parts of Saturn grew darker, others became a bit white. Beck stepped into the center of the cupola and opened his arms, as if he had taken a giant breath of fresh mountain air.

Fenroe glanced at the stars, each one burning from some immeasurable point on a spectrum of blue. The sky blinked in relation to their destination, like azure diamonds fastened to the inside of a cave wall.

Beck let his hands fall to his sides, talking quietly. "The fascinating thing about all this is that many of these stars don't even exist anymore." He turned in a circle, mesmerized by the lambent blue dots. "You can't see most things quite like the memory of a star." He sat on the couch, transfixed. "You know something else? Many of them can only be seen at the current speed we're traveling. Which means, right now, at this very moment, these conditions can't possibly be more perfect for us— from this room, in the entire span of existence, fifteen billion years, you and I are the only possible things to have ever existed that could and can see the universe this way."

Fenroe sat next to him, falling into his images, losing herself in them. The stars were unmoving lights on the other side of an immeasurably wide river at night. "That's a beautiful thought..."

He smiled at her for a moment and then turned back toward the view, "And you all think I'm nuts."

Fenroe leaned forward, looking at the stars below her feet. "You are unquestionably insane."

His smiled widened and they both sat quietly for a time, like patrons at a museum.

Whitney Aris broke the silence from somewhere else in the station: *Sitosen, Fenroe, come to the mess hall, please.*

Fenroe frowned, the stars instantly forgotten. She keyed the lanyard around her neck. "What's up?"

"*Uh,*" she hesitated. "*Everything's fine now, but there was a fight. I think Suja has a broken nose.*"

Beck and Fenroe exchanged glances. In fifty-three months, not a single crewmember had anything even remotely resembling a physical altercation.

"On my way." She stood slowly, and after regarding the stars for another moment, Fenroe stepped toward the main corridor and stopped, meeting Beck's concerned eyes. "You'd better come with."

5.

When Fenroe and Beck entered the mess hall the crew ceased whispering. Suja Tsvetkov slumped on the floor beside one of the deep-freezers, holding a bloody rag to his face. Sitosen had the chair across from him and sat with his elbows on his knees, instructing Suja not to blow his nose to keep his eyes from swelling. Fenroe looked around the module, clenching her jaw: containers, vegetables and plastic wear had been spilled messily across the floor. When Suja noticed her standing in the module-access, he raised his hand and spoke through a nose full of blood and snot. "It was my fault, Fenroe, I should've—"

"What happened?"

"—paid more attention. I didn't get enough sleep, I've been up all night working on those damn plants. I'm way too tired—"

Sitosen stood and nodded at a sodden photograph on the countertop next to one of the washbasins. "Suja spilled water on the photo."

"I should've gotten some sleep," Suja said. "This is my fault, Fenroe, I apologize, sincerely—"

"It was an accident," Sitosen said to him.

"Completely my fault—"

"That's enough," Fenroe said, cutting off Suja. "Are you all right?"

He exhaled heavily through his mouth and nodded, closing his eyes.

Fenroe picked up the sopping photo: it was a picture of Harris, his wife and daughter, and his twin boys. The colors had bled into each other, turning the images into amorphous shapes of melted wax. The sugar and acid ink used to print photos on the station was very delicate, similar to watered dye on very thin paper. "Where is he?"

"Crew quarters," Sitosen said, lifting his chin toward the main corridor. "I told him to go walk it off."

Fenroe glanced around the mess hall one more time. She pulled her eyes over the crew, searching for emotional cracks. They were stoic, breaking the tension every few seconds to chew a fingernail, or rub away some invisible smudge on the tabletop. Everyone has their breaking point. A psychological limit. And after four years, they were all edging very close to it. She didn't have to remind herself that this was the farthest anyone had ever been from home, the missing crew of the *Endeavor* notwithstanding. Whatever happened—whatever unfolded this far out hinged on conditions no human had ever experienced before. Fenroe set the photograph back on the countertop and stepped over a pile of breadsticks on the floor.

"I'll be back in a minute to help clean this up," she said. "See if you can find anything to set his nose."

Fenroe turned and left the mess without another word. As she was leaving, Sitosen told Suja: "this, my friend, is gonna hurt..."

Fenroe found Harris on his bed in the dim gloom of the crew quarters with his back to the access way, his shoulders hunched. She finished rolling the sleeves of her flight suit above her wrists and sat down next to him, nudging his shoulder with hers. He held a different photo of his family. This one was undamaged.

He glanced up at her, and then back down at the photo. "He all right?"

Fenroe pulled the tension out of her neck with her hand and sighed deeply. "Broken nose, probably."

Harris sucked his teeth and shook his head. "I'm sorry, Fenroe." He looked again at the photo in his hand. "I don't know what happened. We were fine, having a good time," he trailed off, still shaking his head.

After a few seconds of silence, Harris lifted the photo: "My daughter was thirteen when we left. My twin boys, five—" He brushed their faces as he spoke, "—I keep thinking about how long we've been gone—" and he glanced at Fenroe again, hesitant to meet her eyes, "—and then I start thinking about how I'll miss everything. Their whole lives. And you know what it is? What really scares me? I'm afraid they won't recognize me when I get back."

"You'll recognize them," she said. "And that's what matters."

He held her gaze a moment and then nodded, turning his eyes back to the photo.

Fenroe hadn't left any family behind. Most astronauts knew what a career in space meant. Starting a family wasn't normally a wise move. When the first Stafford Tori went up—which were much more spacious, accommodating and comfortable environments than the vessels Fenroe and her crew were used to, like small cities floating in the middle of space—and when mission times stretched into years instead of months, the idea was that astronauts could bring their families with them. But that was ultimately put to rest. There were complications in that scenario, usually in the realm of not only having family members trained for life in a vacuum, but of their inheritances and estate responsibilities. There were ethical standards to think about, such as the possibility of losing an entire family on a single mission, and what that would mean to the morale of space exploration in general. Because of this, most astronauts opted out of homebuilding until the decision was made to stay grounded. It was hard for Fenroe to empathize, because Harris knew the risks—he made the leap, and ultimately chose to see other planets over raising a family. They were well taken care of, financially— the government made certain they would never want or need for anything as long as they lived. Being raised fatherless, however, had its own social drawbacks. Fenroe supposed that's what he worried about—his family needing the one thing they couldn't have. That, and she knew he missed them terribly.

"Are *you* all right?" she finally asked.

"Yeah." Harris rubbed his knuckles and shrugged. "Embarrassed."

Fenroe took the photograph out of his fingers and studied it. "Everyone's hanging on by a thread, here—" she nudged him again with her shoulder, "—but this can't happen again, understand?"

"I messed up," Harris said, lifting his hands, studying the wall and searching for the right words. Failing again to find them, he dropped his fists into his lap. "It won't. I promise."

She handed the photo back and stood. "Take it easy today. Watch a few flicks, play some of Ulbricht's video games. And for godsake, go apologize to the man."

"You're thinking about the *Endeavor*," he said suddenly, staring ahead from someplace deep in the back of his own thoughts. "You're wondering if the time and pressure got to 'em— " He waited a beat, judging himself, and then he shrugged, "—I know that I am."

Fenroe hesitated and turned to leave.

"I want an easy day for you, Harris." She said, pausing in the bright main corridor, speaking over her shoulder. "That's an order."

6.

That evening, Commander Evelyn Fenroe and Communications Specialist Whitney Aris worked together on the flight deck. As Aris nodded off in her chair near the stellographer, Fenroe panned eternity for intelligent sound. She wore a powerful elastomer in-ear capsule called a *Pico*, which canceled natural signals afloat in the solar system's AISM bands. She often picked up radio frequencies from stars and planets that sounded very similar to manmade codes, but the signals Fenroe searched for were easy to separate from the chaff. Messages between deep space structures were encoded with at least one—sometimes two—friendly-identifying algorithms generated from a database of thousands of codes. Fenroe's Pico automatically searched only for familiar cyphers and filtered out everything else.

Whitney Aris leaned back and kicked her feet up on the Comm Center, playing with the patch on the breast of Dunesto's work shirt: her orange sweater was in his custody, held for a ransom of one spin cycle. Although his shirt wouldn't fall quite as well on her shoulders, Aris wore it anyway, only mildly annoyed.

"*Pinnacle Station*, this is the *Crown Meridian*," Fenroe whispered into the air, pulling dark hair behind her ears, fighting to stay awake. "This outgoing package is clocked at twenty-one hundred hours ship time, day eleven hundred and three, communications lag marked at twenty-three hours. You've been quiet for seventy-two hours now, *Pinnacle*, please respond."

A long pause in the background radiation, and Fenroe closed

her eyes, picturing the soft release of her pillow. She listened for a minute, her message funneling away from the *Meridian* through the eons, and then again—

"Repeat, *Pinnacle Station*, this is the *Crown Meridian*. Outgoing bundle clocked at—" she checked the glowing silicon nanocrystals stitched under the skin of her wrist, and gave the time and date, "—twenty-one hundred hours ship time, day eleven hundred and three, communications lag marked twenty-three hours. *Pinnacle Station*, you have maintained three consecutive days of radio silence. Please respond."

She paused, believing for a moment that she'd picked up a soft background hiss, but it eventually blended with the ambience. Fenroe released a deep sigh and shook her head, pulling the *Pico* out of her ear and tossing it onto the Comm Center near Aris's feet. She waited another beat and then rubbed her eyes. "All right, *Pinnacle*. This is *Crown Meridian* signing off." She stood and tapped the other woman on her shoulder: "Bedtime for me."

Aris yawned. "Copy that."

Just as Fenroe turned to stumble her way to crew quarters, the Comm station blipped a strong, muted pop. She frowned, wondering if it was fatigue that had filled in the silence, or if it was something real. To be certain, she reinserted the *Pico* and her heart skipped a beat. There was no mistaking it—a sound contrast to the white static she was used to hearing, almost like a tonal rhythm, similar to a melody. Distant at first, the signal grew and became clearer with each passing moment. The auditory sensation was slow, unusual, and dreamlike. Intangible.

"Aris," she whispered. "I think I may have something."

Aris rose out of her daydream and leaned forward to secure her own *Pico*. What poured in from the other side of nowhere took her breath away.

Radio static, and then a man's voice coming in from some

abstract distance: *"Solar sails still functional, tested in the positive. Garden is over-producing, which is splendid—"* Static, and more distance. Fenroe and Aris exchanged glances and held their breath. There was more static, and then the sound of people laughing, and then—

"Nice try, Jensen." A woman's voice broke in. *"Tell them we're goners—doomed!"* More laughing, then the man's voice again: *"We had to shut down the centrifugal relay. The solar arrays were shaking badly, and we couldn't risk it—one of the converters sustained slight damage, but nothing significant—"*

The voice cut away and slipped back into nothing. Fenroe slowly retook her seat and pressed the *Pico* deeper into her ear, tilting her head toward Aris. "One of their status updates?"

Aris shrugged and turned toward the stellographer—a wide transparent table split down the center by a large vertical view screen, similar to a thin piece of frameless glass: a window standing straight up in the air without a frame. There were images on this screen showing geometric expressions of the trajectories of countless space stations, satellites, comets, asteroids, and planets—the projection on the screen at the moment was of the planet Saturn and its moons. As quietly as she could, Aris frantically searched for something—a light pen, perhaps. "Eos, can you try and clean that signal up?"

"I will try," Eos said.

"You're recording this?"

"I am."

She turned to Fenroe, shaking her head: "I mean, is that them? Is this live?"

"We might have crossed into the dead zone." Fenroe shrugged back, clearing her throat and tapping transmit on the Comm Center, waiting a moment. Collecting her thoughts, Fenroe traced patterned grain in the obsidian floor with her eyes, feeling the nature of their mission teetering on the outcome of this one exchange—from here, this was the point of no return. The Caesar's Rubicon of their objective.

"*Endeavor*," she said as clear as possible. "This is Commander Evelyn Fenroe of the *Crown Meridian*, responding to a call of distress. Do you copy?"

There was no response. Tense and hyper-aware, the two women sat in still silence, consuming every sound. Aris pushed away from the Comm Center and rode her chair back to the stellographer, whispering to the ship. "Eos, show me the signal's point of origin."

"*Pinnacle*," the man's voice broke in louder and crystal clear, startling both Fenroe and Aris. "*We had to drop down to three and a half thousand klicks this morning. Pasco barely detected a comet that came out of nowhere. You have no idea how close we were to crossing paths with it, I can't even begin to describe—*"

"*Endeavor*," Fenroe cut in. "This is Commander Evelyn Fenroe of the *Crown Meridian*, responding to a call of distress. Can you hear me?"

But the man ignored her and continued delivering his report. "*What are the chances of that happening? Two of the most insignificant, tiniest specks in all existence, set on divergent paths from opposite ends of the solar system, where they drifted for eons through the void until finding each other at that precise moment...?*"

He trailed off. No static, no interference. Fenroe thought the signal had gone cold, but then she could still hear the passage of breath on the other end. He was still there, just quiet. Lost in thought, perhaps. Aris snatched a light pen from the Comms Center and tapped a tiny dot on the stellar map next to the planet Saturn, which lit up and began blinking like a beacon. She turned to Fenroe and gave her a thumbs-up, slumping back into her chair.

"Found em. Has to be a recording, you think?"

She nodded. "Maybe one of their activity reports..."

Aris frowned and shook her head. "From five years ago—?"

"*What are the odds?*" The man took a deep breath and continued, "*close to impossible, right? It's gotta be. We dropped to three and a half klicks and paced the comet. We shut down the centrifuge and met in the cupola to watch it pass—this beautiful ball of glass, shooting colors everywhere like a prism right in front of us. I have to say, Pinnacle,*" the voice caught and laughed softly. "*It was the most beautiful thing I'd ever seen.*"

And then he disappeared, replaced by the diaphanous noise of the universe. After an eternity of silence and holding her breath—when she was certain the signal had gone flat—Fenroe relaxed her shoulders and peeled the *Pico* out of her ear again. Both women sat like ancient statues in the darkness, taking it all in. After sober moments staring at the glass, Aris finally stood and shrugged her shoulders, inattentively touching Dunesto's patch.

"They were close," she said, studying the stellographer's hieroglyphic readout. Aris stretched her body and then bent to circle a point inches away from Saturn with her light pen. "Very close."

7.

After breakfast the following morning, the crew quietly gathered at the Central Post. Harris, Dunesto, Ulbricht, Suja, and Beck sat around the conference table discussing the day's agenda with hushed concern. Erika Ulbricht, hunched in her seat, spun her videogame on the tabletop like a dreidel, catching it just before the helix fell apart, and then gave it another spin. Beck double-checked data on a stack of papers, worrying a chip of table plastic with his thumb. Suja absently scraped dirt and chlorophyll from under his nails, stopping every few seconds to flatten the medical tape on his face. Harris, now cleanly shaven, wore a crisp flight suit and his hair was clippered short and groomed—he seemed to be in a clearer state of mind than the previous day, but the jolly, playful look in his eyes was gone.

Fenroe entered, followed by Aris and Sitosen. She pulled her unbrushed hair into a ponytail and waited for Sitosen and Aris to join the rest of the crew. "All right."

She set her light pen on its end, pointing it at the ceiling as internal magnets took over and kept it upright. Eos took a moment to build a holographic image of Saturn space over the conference table. "All right, listen up. As you're probably already aware, we've dropped out of our coast and slowed down considerably over the last eighteen hours."

The crew, knowing that something important had transpired the previous night, exchanged concerned glances.

"This was done to hopefully offer us a few options," she said. "If we decide to alter our trajectory."

Everyone looked nonplussed, but remained silent.

"And you've probably figured out by now that we've lost comms."

The room settled and quieted. Ulbricht slipped the game into her breast pocket and Beck set the data he was looking at back on the stack in front of him. She had their attention.

"I don't mean to be a dick, Commander," Dunesto said. "I'm just having a hard time understanding—and I don't think I'm alone on this—" he waved a hand over his crewmates, "—why we would be changing our trajectory. Titan is our target, is it not?"

Fenroe lifted her chin at Aris, and everybody twisted her direction.

"Right, uh—" Aris stood and pulled a hand over her shaven head, flattening the legs of her flight suit, "—nine hours ago,

Fenroe and I picked up a transmission."

The crew went very still and stole glances from Fenroe and Sitosen, who remained focused on Aris. "It seems the dead zone has been blocking the *Endeavor's* signals from our receiver. Until last night, that is, when we passed into it. The transmission is a bit choppy at first, but it clears up."

Aris looked at Fenroe, who nodded and took her seat.

"Eos, will you play the transmission we recorded last night?" the younger woman asked the ship.

"Copy, Aris."

From the directional sound system in the walls, the voice that Fenroe and Aris intercepted the night before began to speak. Like before, a short melodic sequence could be heard preceding a chorus of laughter, and then the man named Jenson went on to describe an encounter with some sort of comet. Then the voices cut out.

"End of file," Eos concluded.

"A status update," Dunesto guessed.

"Yeah," Fenroe nodded. "The last recorded transmission of the first Titan mission, right before they activated their distress beacon."

"Why are we just getting this now?" Dunesto asked, rubbing his eyes.

"The comsat on this side of the dead zone was stuck in a relay cycle, awaiting confirmation from satellites on the other side." Aris answered. "It cached all the transmissions until another receiver came within range. Namely us."

"What about the crew?" Harris spoke up finally, opening his hands. "Are they still out there?"

"We don't know," Sitosen said, leaning forward in his usual fashion: elbows on knees, hands clasped between his legs. "But they might be. Assuming life systems weren't compromised, they had the food and water to last decades...nitrogen, hydrogen, carbon scrubbers..."

"Question, Fenroe." Beck broke in. "Where are they, exactly?"

"Right," Fenroe sighed and nodded. "Eos, chart a path of *Endeavor's* flight toward Titan prior to losing contact with Pinnacle."

"Yes, Commander."

Light began writing shapes and angles into the air, spilling mixed lambent seams and shadow into the room. Holograms of the lost *Endeavor* mission, the planet Saturn, and a dotted line arcing away into nothing filled the open space above the conference table.

"Man," Beck whispered. "They drifted way off course."

Fenroe stood and paced around the crew, eyes fixed on the dotted line. "You can see where they entered Titan orbit and veered away..."

"That's the question, Beck." Aris said, crossing her arms. "Why the change of direction? Why move away from Titan if that was their intended target?"

"Maybe something happened," he shrugged. "Maybe they were coming home."

"That's not how they would do it." Suja shook his head, staring at the display with two black eyes that gleamed in the light. "If they were aborting the mission, they couldn't just hit the brakes and turn around. They would have used either Iapetus or Rhea as a slingshot. Veering away like that doesn't make sense."

"Unless they were in trouble and couldn't make the slingshot," Beck suggested.

Suja looked back to Fenroe. "Right."

"So," Dunesto asked, "what happens now?"

Fenroe glanced at Sitosen, who cleared his throat and spoke

up. "We go after 'em."

Dunesto crossed his arms. "It's been almost six years—" he shrugged, "—they're gone. End of story."

"This isn't a debate," Sitosen said. "Those are orders. They've been our orders since the beginning. You know that."

"I signed up to be one of the first humans in history to land on Titan," Dunesto said back, now straight in his chair. "Not go wading into space after lost causes."

"Christ, Dunesto," Aris said quietly, shaking her head. "What if that was us out there—?"

"Listen," Dunesto said, raising his thick forearms to emphasize his words. "I hate to break it to you, but we wouldn't have the fuel anyway. Fact is, we anticipated finding them at least somewhere near Titan, not in the middle of nowhere. We can't afford to make such a rapid deceleration, and then go aimlessly searching the whole goddamn solar system. Our projected flight path is that precise. One wrong move and we lose what window we have of making it home. I don't know how to be more clear."

"That's bullshit and you know it," Sitosen snapped, pulling one hand over his black hair with frustration. "We have enough fuel, ion propulsion and solar power for a minor trajectory change like this, and it's not like it isn't for a good reason. Our people could be out there—"

"We are one catastrophe away from needing every single molecule in this ship to get home—"

"Dunesto," Sitosen cut in, raising his voice. "They could be waiting for help."

"Back me up Suja, you're the navigations officer here."

Suja sighed and studied the map, deep in thought.

Dunesto turned back to Sitosen: "You're risking a lot, you know that? Help me understand why. Even without any thrust— say their engines died or something—factoring inertia, velocity, they still could be a quarter of the way to Neptune by now."

"We're not talking about an undesignated search, here." Sitosen stood and put his hands on his hips; his tall, muscular frame suddenly filled the area, making the module seem much smaller. "We have to try, man. We have to give them a shot." He waited a beat, and then shrugged. "All I'm saying is we get as close as we can to the signal and see if we can find anything. That's it."

"What are we really doing out here, Colonel?" Dunesto leaned forward, talking quietly but sternly.

Fenroe arched her brow: "That's enough."

"Hold on a minute. I'm a company man. I know how it works—" Dunesto shrugged, "—Command crunches the numbers and decides, despite a pretty clear cost-benefit analysis, after losing a couple trillion dollars on an unsanctioned mission to one of the farthest reaches of our solar system, they're going to dump another billion or so on the same exact mission—?"

"These aren't questions you had before signing up to come along?" Sitosen asked.

"You are out of line, Dunesto," Fenroe cut in. "You stow that shit immediately."

The younger man leaned back and stretched his thick neck until it popped a couple times, looking off into the main corridor. "I'm just saying that it doesn't add up." He took in a deep breath and let it go, relaxing his shoulders. "We shouldn't be here."

Fenroe stood and pulled more of her bangs behind her ears. She studied the crew—the only one who seemed relaxed, oddly enough, was Harris. Half the crew was either staring at the floor, or biting their fingernails.

"But we are here," Fenroe said finally, meeting their eyes. "And right now we have a decision to make."

"I'd have to check the math," Suja said finally, still leaning forward, studying the holographic map of Saturn space. "But, off the top of my head, I can tell you that their path ends a couple hundred thousand kilometers away from Titan, several more thousand kilometers away from our approach." He passed his hand through the dotted line that ceased a foot or so from his face. "A course correction like that would probably shave off what fuel we'll need for the last third of the journey home."

"That's not a risk I'm prepared to take." Looking at Fenroe, Dunesto said, "we can't, Fenroe. Our lives may depend on every ounce of fuel we have."

"He's right," Ulbricht said, her shadowy eyes passing back and forth between everybody. "I would like to see Earth again."

"Thank you—"

"Can I offer an alternative?" Harris asked. His calm and professional demeanor seemed to cut the tension in the air.

Dunesto rolled his eyes. "Christ, Harris—"

"Commander?" Harris asked again, ignoring him.

Fenroe searched his face for a moment, looking for the parts of him that were broken before, and found nothing to raise concern. He was calm, as if something had been closed off inside since the incident in the Mess. She nodded: "Of course."

"Eos, can you please bring up the trajectory of our return mission to Earth?"

"Right away," the AI pulsed from the walls.

Saturn grew slightly, and moved out of view at the edge of the table, and Eos transposed another dotted line next to the existing one, which stretched all the way back to a golf ball sized blue orb with a single satellite the size of a ball bearing: Earth and its moon, Luna.

"Eos," Harris continued. "You've been paying attention to our discussion?"

"I have," Eos replied.

"You understand what Suja is saying about how a course deviation to the last known coordinates of the *Endeavor's* signal would compromise the fuel we would need for our return trip to Earth?"

"I do."

"Then please plot our trajectory back to Earth, minus the fuel we would use for the course correction."

"No problem," Eos intoned, her rich, soothing syllables pulsing from the walls. The lights threw glare over the table as the blue orb slowly inflated. Saturn disappeared entirely. The path marked by a dotted line floating in the air sheared several hundred thousand kilometers away from the hologram of Earth. "The factored course correction is complete, Harris."

"Thank you."

"That's a hell of a deficit," Dunesto said.

"Commander," Harris said, "Suja and Dunesto are right. It would be a mistake risking the safety of the crew by heading for the signal."

Dunesto leaned back in his chair, extending his hand to Harris. "Thank you—"

"However," Harris continued, "the issue here is whether or not we'll have enough fuel for the return trip. And as Eos has pointed out, deviating any farther from our current trajectory would leave us short. We'd essentially be running out of fuel about two and a half years from Earth—"

"Which is why we should continue panning the emergency bands for new messages from the *Endeavor*, and proceed to Titan," Dunesto cut in. "We shouldn't change course unless we're absolutely certain that they're out there—"

Harris held up his hand for Dunesto to wait. "But there's nothing saying that we couldn't get in contact with Earth on the return trip, and have another crew meet us at the shortfall with some extra fuel."

Sitosen's eyes relaxed, which in his case might as well have been a smile.

Dunesto dropped his worn hand slightly, glanced at the hologram, and frowned.

"Whatever this dead zone is," Harris continued, "it seems to be restricted to Saturn space. There won't be a communication loss on the return trip. Right now, we'll have enough fuel to pass where the trail ends, and then head on to Titan if we don't find anything. And if they are out there—" he shrugged, "—we can head home immediately and have Command meet us at the end of the street with a gas can."

Dunesto looked around the table, speechless.

Aris stared with her powerful eyes at the missing crew's trajectory crosscut into nowhere.

Beck's thumbnail was forgotten, replaced by the cold uncertainty of the moment.

Ulbricht, Suja, and Sitosen each exchanged glances, and then all eyes eventually fell on Fenroe, who studied the star-map.

"All right," she nodded and collapsed her light pen and the holograms, leaving haloes of fading light over the flight deck. Eos brought the atmosphere up from a soft dim. Fenroe stood and clapped Dunesto on the shoulder. "We follow Harris's plan."

8.

Time passed with blurred procedure on the ship, which became less automatic and seamless, as Saturn grew larger in their viewports. Fenroe lay in her bunk, watching the ringed planet from a projection on the ceiling, but she found no rest and her mind raced without destination. Saturn was so near that paintbrush lines of atmosphere could be clearly identified without magnification. She studied it for some time, and then closed her eyes, trying once again to guide her turbulent thoughts into a few hours of sleep.

Someone knocked softly on her bunk's shoji, and a shadow leaned forward on the other side.

"Fenroe," Beck whispered.

She studied the dim outline of his profile for a moment, noticing round shadows in both hands—a container half filled with liquid sloshing inside one hand, and two plastic cups in the other.

"Hey," she said. "Come on in."

"Hey." He slid the shoji to her bunk open and sat at the edge of her bed, lifting the bottle. "I thought you could use a drink."

Fenroe rubbed her eyes as Beck cracked open a half-emptied bottle of peppery-scented bourbon. "How the hell did you get that?"

He smirked. "I smuggled it in a couple of weeks prior to launch."

She pushed herself into a seated position against the bulkhead, making room for him. "Well, then. Have a seat."

"Thanks," he said. "Pleasant dreams?"

She arched her eyebrow and shrugged, "Sure, why not?"

"Let me guess." He poured two fingers of bourbon into a cup and passed it to her, then filled his own. "The *Endeavor*?"

Fenroe didn't trust herself to say anything, but Beck nodded as if the silence was her answer.

"That's all I've been dreaming about," he said. "I keep having this one where we find the crew, but it's not really them, it's...it's another version of us," he trailed off, blinking the dream to the surface for a moment, and then he remembered the cup in his hand. "My clone is just as confused as I am, and then there's an awkward discussion about which one of us is the real Thomas

Beck—" He sighed deeply and shook his head, "—and then I wake up."

Fenroe took a sip of bourbon and rested her head against the bulkhead, watching him. "Maybe you should speak with Harris about it."

"I might." Beck smiled again and lifted his glass. "I just stopped by to offer my support. I think you made the right decision to go after 'em."

"Dunesto doesn't," she said, toasting him. "I don't think Ulbricht or Suja do either."

"But they trust you to do the right thing." He raised his shoulders slightly. "I trust you."

"Trust," she echoed him with self-disdain. Fenroe took another drink and then tilted her head, savoring the rich aroma.

Beck frowned and looked down at his cup. "And they respect you."

They sat in silence for a few minutes, quietly sipping their drinks. Fenroe held the rich, fiery liquid on her tongue before swallowing, thinking of home. She lifted her empty glass: "Who else knows about this?"

Beck shook his head and smiled. "Everyone."

Fenroe kicked him playfully, but more-than-little rough. "You held out for four goddamn years?"

"We didn't know how Girl Scout Fenroe would take it," he admitted, smirking. "Couldn't risk you dumping it."

"Why risk it now?"

"I figure we're lip-deep in this shit pool anyway," he shrugged, the smile melting back into his face. "What's it matter?"

She studied him again, the bourbon warming her stomach, giving her head clarity. "Then you better pour me another. Make up for lost time."

Fenroe passed her glass to Beck, who dutifully refilled it. Still tasting the bite of her last drink—the first in four years—she let herself get lost again inside those images he gave her in the Cupola; she allowed herself to forget about the mission, to forget Proust, to not think about her crew's tremendous heart, to forget the enormity of what lay ahead, and just savor the quiet thing that passed between her and Beck, which was beyond words. She drained the rest of her glass and gave it back to him, and then she returned her head to the pillow, closing her eyes. Feeling Beck start to leave the bunk, she reached out for him, catching the tail of his tee shirt.

"Wait," she said, and he stopped halfway out of the shoji. "Can you stick around for a little bit? Until I fall asleep?"

"Uh, yeah." He whispered. "Yeah, sure...certainly."

Fenroe's body relaxed as he propped himself up with a pillow on the other side of the bunk, stretching his legs out. She heard him open the bourbon and pour himself another drink, and although Fenroe believed she felt more at home in the stars, and although she told herself that she didn't particularly need Earth anymore, she couldn't deny the truth of this one thing: Fenroe needed her crew. She felt the side of Beck's calf and knee against the back of her leg, and the warmth of him. No matter on Earth or halfway across the solar system, or at the very edge of the universe itself, the thought of losing even a single person under her command terrified her. Fenroe loved and embraced each of them with all of her heart.

9.

From some claustrophobic dream, and another place far, far deeper than that, Fenroe sensed a pinprick of light and slowly opened her eyes. Beck was still there, lying on his side and facing the rear bulkhead, dead still and breathing deeply—the sound of his sleep was weightless and tranquil. Fenroe checked the glowing timepiece tattooed under her wrist, and while blinking her eyes back down into sleep again, she noticed a black thread of some kind steadily crawling up the shoji. She frowned and studied it for a moment, as it continued making small movements upward. After a minute of surreal and dreamy observation, she went to touch it—and the partition ripped away from itself. Stunned, thinking that she hadn't fully wakened yet, Fenroe stared at the thread as it ripped even more, becoming something else.

She rubbed the blurriness out of her eyes and leaned closer to inspect the partition—the bedding lurched wildly from under her body. Fenroe's upper back and head smashed hard against the inner wall of her bunk, rocked by a violently building vibration, which ceased as suddenly as it started. White ringing pain exploded behind her eyes. The enviro-LED's flickered for a moment and then died, followed immediately by the crimson strobe of emergency lighting and a series of klaxons. Cold sweat chilled her skin and pebbled goose bumps along her limbs, and her breath came fast and empty—fighting the starry outline of her remaining vision, coupled with a pulsating rush of pain on the back of her head, she pushed away from the bulkhead and reached for Beck in the darkness, feeling his warm and wet shirt covered with what she hoped was bourbon and not blood.

"Beck," she said in a daze, her voice so distant that her words could have been nonchalant, as if she were letting someone know that they'd accidentally dropped their wallet or left their headlights burning.

Unable to see clearly through the red emergency lights, she barely made out his profile staring numbly at his lap. The outline of Beck's head lifted.

"Are you hurt?" he asked.

A brief sensation of falling, and Fenroe's vestibular compensated as hair lifted away from her skull. Dazed in the rhythmic mixed amber and red interchange of light and dark, her body rose lightly into the air, weightless, and she braced herself softly against the overhead. Her sense of direction spun without axis, as the ship lost its gravity in stages—she could actually feel the centrifugal pendulums grinding to a halt, sending waves of vibration throughout the station.

"Eos, I need lights," Beck rasped into the dark. He ripped the rest of the shoji open and pulled Fenroe through space into the crew quarters, toward the red flash of the main corridor.

"Lights are offline," The AI replied calmly, cutting through the state of disorder and panic. "I'm unable to divert power away from the main cargo bay at this time."

"Shut down these alarms!"

Fenroe's eyes rolled into the back of her head, and she desperately fought to stay awake, still reeling from slamming into the wall. Silky warm blood trickled down the back of her neck, and the klaxons cut and faded like a spark, replaced by the distant shouting of the rest of her crew scattered throughout the station. Beck quickly inspected the back of her head. Lines of worry and fear creased his youthful forehead, and Fenroe pushed away from him, wrestling out of his arms: "Get me to the flight deck—"

"Stay still—"

"I have to get to the flight deck." She hissed, clawing out of his arms, and then louder, uncontained, "get me to the flight deck!"

"It's bad—you're bleeding badly," he said, tearing off his damp outer tee shirt soaked in bourbon and folding it flat. He slapped it into Fenroe's hand and made her put direct pressure against the wound. "I have to find Harris. Wait here."

She crunched forward at the waist, making as if she would follow, but he stopped her.

"Just wait here—I gotta find a med kit," he said, and then pushed away, leaving her afloat in the weightless darkness alone.

Shouting bodies and silhouettes could be seen streaking in and out of modules along the gangway. Her blanched skin stuck to the inside of her clothes—panic-stricken, fighting through the fog and nausea until she was finally able to push away from the floor and drunkenly maneuver into the main corridor. The only thought repeating in her pounding head was how a vibration like that would have certainly torn the solar panels to shreds, which would be a death sentence. She propelled herself with a bit more force, but tried keeping her movements controlled—her hand came down on something clammy and wet. A shape tumbled away from her in the dark, and she reached for it, grabbing its shoulder. By the emergency lights of the main corridor, she could tell that the shape was a member of her crew who was knocked out cold. She turned the body around, still hearing people shouting urgently from the flight deck, feeling the build of another violent vibration. The yellow and red strobe closed over her vision, and no matter how hard she tried, she couldn't make out the crewmember's face.

The corridor went dark, and she floated in total blackness with only the sense of touch, nearly without thought except for the slow rhythm of the seconds that she counted in her head. And then the seconds became slower than the beat of her heart. A soundless, massive thud came from somewhere outside of the ship, which she felt more than heard. An even more violent vibration followed, and the klaxons sounded again. In complete darkness, Fenroe searched for something to grab hold of, but she was stranded in the middle of nowhere, afloat in zero gravity as the station oscillated around her like a car collision. She twisted the body of her crewmember around, and a breath escaped her lips. It wasn't a member of her crew at all.

Fenroe studied the dark nimbus mane of hair, the sharp angular features, the pale skin and the piercing brown eyes through a fractured crystalline lens of shock and terror: the lifeless body in her hands was her. Her face, her eyes, her lips. The body was Commander Evelyn Fenroe of the *IDSI Crown Meridian*, and she was dead.

The clone's empty gaze glassed the blinking lights, a dent in the side of its head oozing bulbs of blood that collected on the surface of her matted scalp. Fenroe released the corpse of herself and shoved it away, terrified, a scream building inside her chest. A point of light broke through the inky black and joined the glinting phosphenes in her vision—a recognizable voice called her name. Fenroe watched her corpse float and bump against the wall, sending droplets of blood spiraling away, and then slowly spin in a new direction. Firm hands grabbed her shoulders and hauled her toward that point of light, gasping up out of her dream—he shook her, and she came up even further.

"Wake up, Fenroe."

He shook her again, and she came up, sucking in reality like water, *"Wake up!"*

She opened her eyes.

10.

Beck released Fenroe's arms and she blinked the nightmare away. The first thing she realized upon waking was that the gravity pendulum had in fact ceased functioning—the familiar pull of her bodyweight was gone, which meant something drastic had unfolded somewhere else in the station. And, like her dream, red and yellow lights flashed throughout the main-corridor, accompanied by a system of emergency klaxons. She spared brief seconds checking her bunk's shoji, searching for the rip from her dream, but found nothing. The vibration that woke her pulled at another memory, a more immediate one—the dream of her mirrored self, and the premonition of her own death.

"Come on," Beck said, pulling himself out of her bunk and diving weightlessly into the air.

Leaving the crew quarters, Fenroe and Beck followed twisting shadows and raised voices to the flight deck, where they found the crew exigently working in the dark flicker of the Central Post to keep the ship from tearing itself to pieces. "What's happening?"

"I messed up," Ulbricht said, ashen-faced.

"It's not your fault," Dunesto said.

"It's my duty as ship's pilot—"

"We shouldn't have gone looking for them—" Dunesto glanced at Harris and Sitosen, and then immediately returned his attention to the readout, "—it's not your fault, Ulbricht."

"We veered into some...some kind of a debris trail," she stammered, her eyes moving quickly from side to side, searching for an exact moment to fall back on—a thread she could follow back to her mistake so that she could somehow fix it. "Something large made contact with the mirror shield array and the fragments struck our starboard side like shrapnel."

"Okay, slow down," Fenroe said. "What's the damage?"

"Suja made those last minute course corrections, so I took the data and tried pointing us toward the *Endeavor's* signal, but Eos wouldn't let me."

"What?" Fenroe hesitated. "Why?"

Ulbricht lifted her hands into the air, on the verge of tears. "She said she couldn't allow it. She said we would all die—"

"Eos?"

"I hear you, Commander."

"Why did you not follow Ulbricht's orders?"

"The course correction was ungrammatical," the AI replied. "It placed the crew in unnecessary mortal jeopardy. I'm sorry. My programming can't allow that to happen."

"Did you know that we were headed into debris?"

"Negative. At our current speed, the objects that struck the *Meridian* evaded my detection."

"Then why would you think the course correction was ungrammatical?"

"Be advised: as a result of course correction, fuel consumption is beyond the requirements for our return journey to Earth. Be advised: station *Crown Meridian* has suffered damaging losses of oxygen, hydrogen, and pressure. And be advised: the communications tower has suffered catastrophic structural failure."

Fenroe's heart dropped into her stomach. Breathless, she scanned her crew, her eyes finally stopping on Ulbricht, who was visibly falling apart with the utterance of each new word.

"Someone explain to me what she's talking about," Fenroe spoke softly, almost to herself.

"Eos wouldn't do it, so I had to *manually* input the course correction," Ulbricht stammered. "I checked and I double checked it. The sensors picked up nothing in our path. I swear to god, *nothing*—"

"Enough, Ulbricht!" Fenroe said, "Somebody *talk* to me."

"Eos has manually overridden the *Meridian*," Sitosen cut in, circling his hands through what appeared to be readings of precisely choreographed distributions of gases throughout the station. "It looks like she's currently steering us out of this shit, but like she said, most of the impacts were from objects fast enough and small enough to evade her sensors—I'm now picking up larger objects all over the place, and that's not all—"

"We're losing O-two," Aris cut in. "And we're also venting coolant into the ship. I have several Master Alarms—fires in both the Medical Bay and the main Cargo Bay—and if we don't find that fuel leak, we're going to be running out of breathable air pretty quick here."

"I went over our tangential velocity," Ulbricht said. "Our windows of deceleration, I mean, I knew we were going to be short on fuel, but I thought—"

"Ulbricht," Fenroe interrupted her, biting against the cramp in her jaw. "You have to pull your shit together, understand?"

Ulbricht breathed and closed her eyes. "What do you want us to do?"

"I want Eos to tell us what we hit."

Ulbricht swallowed, and wiped sweat away from her eyes. The crew stopped moving for a moment, waiting for Eos's assessment. Deep breaths and anxiety filled the soundless space, and it was palpable—Fenroe could feel it in the air, those quick and suffocating deaths breathing down her neck.

"I'm sorry, Commander." Eos said, finally. "I'm uncertain at this time—again, it was too small for me to detect at our current speed."

"Okay," Fenroe said, trying to think through it. Each second that passed was crucial, and she bit down hard on the inside of her cheek, letting the rush of saliva rewet her mouth, trying very hard not to appear overwhelmed. She looked around the flight deck a final time and searched the faces of her crew for answers, each of them awaiting orders, or a task—anything that would take their minds away from the crushing moment; anything that would restore a sense of control. Fenroe slowly wiped her face, and stared at the steady rhythm of emergency data flashing across the Central Post, coming apart like a mosaic reflection of her soul.

"Okay," Fenroe started again. "Eos, I'm giving you full control of the ship. I want you to increase our stopping thrust by point-two-five percent, and I want you to keep us away from anything else you pick up in our path. Is that clear?"

"Crystal clear, Commander, I'll do my best." Eos said. "But please be advised: using thrust to slow the station down faster than seventy thousand kilometers-per-hour will consume another eighth of the fuel we'll need—"

"Thank you, Eos." Fenroe cut her off, gripping the handrail next to the accessway, her knuckles bone white and bloodless. "We are aware of the fuel situation. Please increase forward thrust by point-two-five percent."

"Consider it done, Commander."

Fenroe fought the tremble in her shoulders and chest, fought the rising lurch in her stomach, still clenching her jaw. "We're still alive," she said finally, breathing deeply. "So let's figure this out."

"Here's the deal," Dunesto said, controlling the tension in his voice. "It looks like Eos tried rolling us away from something, but her external sensors went offline when we made impact. Right now, she can't read one side of the ship—our starboard side—so it's blind."

Everybody fell silent—each of their hands moving quickly through holograms and control panels.

"Eos, what's wrong with the ship? Tell us how to fix it..."

"Stand by, Commander," Eos said, populating the space over the conference table with more lighted images, and a schematic of the entire station slowly took shape in illusive, transparent pieces. She illuminated three sections, spread across several meters along the *Crown Meridian's* starboard side.

"Be advised," Eos continued, "the primary and backup explosive release devices of the Lander-3 have detonated on impact with the foreign objects. Before my sensors ceased functioning, I detected fire and several punctures inside the cargo bay bulkhead leading to the primary engine compartment, and damage to the wiring trays in the medical bay's thermal insulation blanket. Anti-matter levels are currently above normal capacity, and rising. I've sealed off the damaged areas to maintain pressure, but there's a hydrazine leak near the auxiliary power units, and damage to the piezoelectric alternator, which is currently affecting the station's internal heat. I advise repairing the leak before the remaining aft compartments catch fire. I strongly advise immediately repairing punctures along sectors one and six before the station loses sustainable cabin pressure and oxygen."

"Tell us where *exactly* in sectors one and six we can find the leaks."

"I can't, Commander. I can't see anything on that side of the ship."

"I told you," Dunesto said, raising his hands helplessly. "Her sensors are down—"

"I got it," Fenroe dismissed him, letting out a deep pull of air and closing her eyes. "I'll get dressed."

"Negative," Sitosen cut in. "If anyone's going EVA, it should be me."

Fenroe shrugged. "It's a two man job."

"Fenroe," he said, drifting in close, talking quietly so the others wouldn't hear. "The crew needs you here, on the flight deck."

She ignored him. "Are you volunteering to go out with me, or not?"

"I volunteer," Harris interrupted. "I'll go."

Dunesto's hands stopped moving. After a moment of looking at some distant point through the viewport, he turned to regard Harris. It was as if he'd never seen him before. Like he had suddenly become a new person.

"No," Fenroe said distantly, unable to meet his eyes. She still wasn't confident he was in the right mindset: a single streak of sweat betrayed his newly calm exterior. He shook his head to protest, but she cut him off: "We're going to have to figure out how to get the oxygenator and the atmosphere regulator to strip the hydrazine from the air. And I need someone checking seals one module at a time with the leak detector from the inside. If we can't find anything, someone has to talk us through it." She turned and studied Eos's schematic of the ship before Harris could say anything, and then leaned in Dunesto's direction: "Please tell me the RMS is functional."

"Uh—" he exhaled, shaking his head. "—I'm not—I don't know. I think it is—"

"Get her ready."

He stared at Fenroe a moment, frozen in place, lightly floating near the stellographer.

"Let's go, Dunesto!"

"Okay," he pursed his lips, wide-eyed. "All right, I'll take care of it." He took a deep breath and pulled his muscular frame into the main corridor.

"Eos, shut down these alarms. And bring the lights back up."

Silence gave the illusion that control had returned to the flight deck. Fenroe leveled her gaze on Sitosen. "We don't have a lot of time."

"Fenroe, please," he said, grabbing her arm, "Don't go out there. Harris and I can handle it."

She ripped out of his grip and gave him a long, hard stare. Without another word, she pushed away with her legs and maneuvered into the main corridor.

Aris, Sitosen and Fenroe paced each other through the ship in deadly silence. Dunesto followed, pushing the weightless

Remote Manipulator System in front of him.

"Sitosen, you make for the breaches in the cargo and med bays," she said. "I'll handle the leaks in sectors five and six and check on the piezoelectric generators. If shit gets bad—if we're hit again—hug the hull as best you can until help arrives. I want you talking, Sitosen. No radio silence longer than a few minutes, right Aris?"

"You've got it," the younger woman said, wide-eyed and tense.

"Eos, you take care of the fire in the engine compartments. Dunesto will back you up from the flight deck."

From the walls: "Copy that, Commander."

They pulled themselves into the airlock and Fenroe faced them, measuring their state of readiness. She studied the curves of their faces, and all the memories that came with them, burning their images into her mind in preparation for the inevitable.

"There's no help for us out here," she said finally, meeting their eyes one at a time, letting the moment take hold.

They each looked back at her from separate, unimaginable distances, like Samurai preparing their minds for death—the intensity grew like a cadence behind Fenroe's chest, dumping adrenaline and epinephrine into the collapsed wave of her existence. Each of them had trained their entire lives for this. Time to put that training to the test.

Aris helped Fenroe and Sitosen don their bio-suits, which were in real terms simply smaller spacecraft. Every inch of the suit save the plastic and glass fiber optic visor comprised a system of smart-memory alloy mesh that sucked against their bodies with direct counter pressure. The bio-suit that Aris and Dunesto bolted them into was a closed pressurized system. The suit's skin was matted cream—a latticework of blended nickel-titanium aerogel and a cocktail of thinly insulated polymers. It was functionally light, offering the maximum range of motion, but tear resistant and strong enough to withstand the extreme temperature variations outside of the ship. While the bio-suits were slightly more bulky and cumbersome in Earth pressure, they became like silk when suctioned against their bodies in hard vacuum. Dunesto screwed Fenroe's gauntlet into the grooves of her forearm like the cap of an airtight jar.

"You'll be fine," he whispered to her, wiping the sweat away from Fenroe's face with his sleeve. "You're the most badass person I've ever known, you hear me? You've got this."

Fenroe nodded and twisted her head to look for Sitosen, but Dunesto had already lowered the helmet into place. She felt more pressure against her temples as the suit equalized, and then her ears popped. Blinking lights came to life on her heads-up display, showing her the crew's oxygen and fuel levels, and a positioning mini-map of the *Crown Meridian*, which tracked three dots in a cluster near the airlock—blue for Eos, green for Fenroe, and red for Sitosen.

Dunesto fastened the clamps around the neck of her helmet, locking it firmly into her shoulders. Satisfied that everything was sealed, he pushed himself away and grabbed Eos's RMS by the arms—a small childlike robot with an exoskeleton comprised of stark white polycarbonate plates and a large black faceplate that contained various light and gas sensors. He delicately rotated the android in zero gees and lifted a small membrane covering its shoulder blades, switching it on. Fenroe watched the RMS boot up with a progression of soft blue lights through symmetric veins in its torso and limbs, until it finally flickered to life behind its visor. That light was generated by millions of nanites suddenly coming into contact with one another. Through wireless interlinking, Eos filled the android with her alien consciousness, and slowly, from an indescribable digital scape of immeasurable formulae, she began to move.

With a last check of their bio-suit's integrity, Aris and Dunesto floated out of the airlock back into the main corridor, followed by a series of hollow and heavy clunks. The inner hatch locked shut, and the two suited astronauts and the small robot floated in the still of silence for long, drawn out minutes, waiting for the airlock to equalize.

"You're clear for EVA," Aris finally transmitted over comms.

"All right," Sitosen said, reaching for the pressure release—pulling, rotating, and pushing it back into place. "We're good to go, whenever you're ready."

"Roger that," said Aris. After a thirty-second countdown, the red light above the inner hatch turned green, and the outer hatch depressed with a hiss, twisting and disappearing into the bulkhead. *"Opening airlock."*

The torsion assembly behind the outer hatch released and then pulled away from the center. In one fluid motion, the thick hatch pushed outward and then rolled to the side, exposing the endless night of vacuum. Ice particles sprayed away from the fuselage, and the two cosmonauts and one android stepped out into the vast black of nothing.

"Good luck," Aris transmitted. *"We'll see you in a few minutes."*

MISTAKES

1.

"*All right, Eos,*" Ulbricht said over comlink. Fenroe watched her stretch the tension out of her shoulders and pull her blond hair up into a bun from her HUD. Ulbricht leaned forward and paged through the floating lights of hieroglyphic readout: "*I'll be controlling the ship from here on out, but I still want you monitoring for debris. Is that clear?*"

"*Yes, Erika—of course.*"

"*Okay guys, forward thrusters are cooking nicely, and we're slowing at a pretty good clip—*" Ulbricht took a deep breath, "*—I'll keep an eye open for debris, but be vocal if you see anything.*"

Sitosen replied over comms, "*Roger that.*"

Emerging from the airlock, the only voice Fenroe heard that wasn't spoken over comlink was her own. And through a small corner of the fiber optic heads-up display in her visor, she watched a transparent image of the flight deck, seeing the rest of her crewmates working therein: Ulbricht took her seat in the pilot's chair; Suja and Beck floated at nearby stations, while Dunesto and Harris meticulously searched one module at a time with the leak detector wands.

Moving her eyes to the box below, the blue and red dots of Eos and Sitosen slowly separated from each other at different points along the ship's exterior on her mini-map—each of them separated by distances comparable to a single football field. She began pulling herself hand over hand along the outside of the ship.

"There's a lot of debris out here," Fenroe exhaled. "I can't tell where it's coming from, but there's—" she hesitated and breathed, "—there's a lot of it."

"Copy that," Aris said. *"Are you able to see any gas?"*

Fenroe navigated alongside the hull and stopped. Ice particles cascaded across her visor, giving the distant white sun a spectral ring—and in the shadowed area of the ship, a vast plane of frozen gas tinkled and flashed in the light like pulverized glass from several unseen breaches along its side. A cold blade ran the length of her spine, tracing with its razored edge the margin of just how close to complete annihilation the crew had actually come. With fascinated horror and effort, Fenroe tore her eyes away and forced herself to focus on the next foothold.

"I see gas." Fenroe's dry tongue stuck to her palate, making it hard to swallow. "Coming out of the starboard side. There's a trail of it stretching behind the ship for miles," she transmitted. "It's a bit far from here, but it looks like all of the fuel spheres are intact."

"Copy. What about the hull?"

Fenroe moved herself to the broadest side of the ship where the medical bay's fuselage hung from its module. "I see scarring and some punctures along the cargo and medical bays, and one of the lander modules is completely gone. I'm guessing it's number three." She took a sip of water from a thin straw inside her helmet, looking into the recessed curve and then up around the long cylindrical tensile truss shrouded in blackness, illuminated solely by an arrangement of evenly placed floodlights along both arms of the center pendulum. Sitosen, now a tiny figure on the opposite end of the station, combed the hull of the main habitat with his flashlight, giving short bursts with his thrusters to stay abreast, and then disappeared from view. "It's... it isn't good, guys."

"I'm almost there, Flight-Deck," Sitosen said with a bit of effort.

Fenroe peered over the edge of the station, strafing the hull with light, surveying the damaged sections in broken shadow. She moved to that module's APU control box, untethering a small compound drill from her belt, and went to work removing the panel.

"Flight-deck, I'm topside," Sitosen spoke again through static. *"Uh, yeah—there's a lot of scarring up here. No gas anywhere. Moving to investigate the damaged area."*

"You guys are breaking up," Aris transmitted. From the image in Fenroe's heads-up display, Aris pressed the *Pico* deeper into her ear: *"I didn't copy—getting a lot of static—"*

"God damn it," Fenroe said, drilling the hatch. "Billion dollar installation and we can't get radios that actually work. Eos, can we clear that up?"

She waited a moment, but there came no response. Fenroe glanced at her mini-map—Eos's blue dot pinged near the matter-antimatter engine compartments, unmoving. "Eos, can you clear up our comms?"

"—es, Commander, right awa—" Her normally smooth and rich voice faded in and out. Finally, there was an abrupt pop followed by a stream of fluid static, and Fenroe's comlink cut out entirely.

"Flight deck, do you copy?" She loosened the bolts, which lifted away from the hull for a moment before gravitating back toward a weak magnet on her chest—they each came to rest against her breastplate with gentle, twirling arcs. The seconds ticking by, Fenroe kept waiting for the station to suddenly collapse under the force of its own imploding pressure, instantly crushing her crew: attached to the station, dangling in vacuum by a short rig, Fenroe's mind raced with images of herself snapping into the hull like a rubber ball tethered to a wooden paddle, mincing her bones and organs, rendering the soft insides of her bio-suit into ribbons of meat. "Can anyone—is anyone hearing me?"

More static. She shook her head and opened the control box, trying to keep her breathing steady—the cables inside were scorched and blackened, ripped into sinuous red, blue, green, and copper threads. "Can you guys see this?"

Still no response, and more static.

"Can anyone hear me?" Her voice cracked with thinly contained fear. She looked a final time at the image of the flight deck in her HUD, but it was empty—her crew was gone. Red and yellow lights flashed again in the backdrop, silent and erratic, and she knew that something was wrong.

"Talk to me, Aris." She continued working with speed, waiting, listening to the building frequency of her heartbeat. "Someone tell me what's happening."

She turned and stopped, breathless.

As the station rotated into the light, she finally saw in detail the extent of the damage: that entire side of the passenger and crew chambers—all point five kilometers of it—vented gas from unquantifiable contact points, which froze and coalesced into clouds of ice that extended away from the ship—it looked as if two thirds of the hull had impact breaches of varying sizes, gushing precious, life-giving air and pressure. How Eos was able to equalize everything before the station imploded was baffling.

Fenroe's fingers went numb and she let slip the drill, which pulled taught against a strap attached to her thigh. She couldn't think her way through it. The hull was breached in more ways than they could hope to fix before the station lost all breathable atmosphere. Her crew had mere minutes to live. She closed her eyes and fought back rage and hopelessness. She tried smothering the rising bile of self-pity and failure.

"Flight deck," she whispered, and then again, raising her voice, "say something, flight deck!"

Aris broke into the channel: "*—ou copy, please copy—Sitosen, Fen—please—*"

"Yes! Dear god yes," she fought the hitch in her throat, reaching for the hull as blood rushed back into her chest. "I copy, Aris—"

"*Fenroe, listen carefully.*" She spoke fast and tight. "*We have multiple breach hits in the hull—critical systems alert—*"

"Repeat that?" She frantically scanned the station again, searching through the frozen smoke of ice crystals. "That's a negative, Aris—I'm not seeing anything out here—"

Meteorites suddenly fired directly against the hull several meters away from her position—some particles ricocheted away, but she could see several more fresh penetration points. She grabbed what remained of the APU's fuselage and held tight. Sitosen's broken, exigent words joined the hissing in her ears. He sounded terrified, but she couldn't make him out over the chaff. The distant, off-white blur of his profile maneuvered back over the edge of the station—he was still a football field away. Fenroe leaned toward him, thinking that it would somehow make her clearer—her voice caught again, and she knew this was it—she felt it, right here, right now—she was going to die. "I have visual contact with debris! Repeat, I have visual contact with debris—!"

Unseen and camouflaged by the glare of floodlights, a large

building-sized chunk of something separated from the lens flare in her visor. The object passed through the crystalline dust of vented gas, causing it to swirl and fold into itself—her legs flinched, preparing for the last, split-second moment. The large chunk of debris skimmed the outside of the ship at a distance no greater than the height of a man. Fenroe's entire body went numb. She flattened and pulled herself against the fuselage—smaller missiles shot past her, making devastating contact with the hull. The larger object moved toward her, deceptively slow and majestic, but at speeds approaching a hundred thousand kilometers per hour. It passed mere feet overhead, grazing the station, ripping and shaving segments of the shielding that covered the main truss away at several points of contact, which caused the massive object to tumble on a different axis and push away. Fenroe could see it then—large black industrial letters written large along its side,

IDSI ENDEAVOR

Soundless, without any evidence of its existence other than shadow and inertia, the chunk of spaceship pulled into a new trajectory, propelled into the depths of blackness and eternity by its life-ending contact with her ship.

"It's the *Endeavor*," she whispered, shocked. Then louder, "does anyone copy? We're passing through what's left of the *Endeavor*—"

Ion boosters came to life on the starboard side as Eos's navigation protocol kicked in, triggering evasive action, burning through frightening amounts of fuel in a last ditch effort to clear the station of that Newtonian plane of death. More pieces of debris rocketed by at blinding, near-impossible speeds, seen only by brief flashes of light and flame as each projectile made contact like artillery.

"*We're losing atmosphere*," Aris finally broke over comms. "Eos, get us out of here now!"

"*—es, Commander*," she said, distant. "*Warning: hydrazine levels in-station are almost above capacity—five percent and climbing—*"

"*Fenroe, Sitosen—if either of you can hear me*," Aris started again, breathing fast, trying to talk over the shrill transmission of emergency klaxons in the background. "*We can manually separate the damaged modules, but there are still lethal amounts of hydrazine venting into the ship—we've been tracing the fuel lines in here, but we can't find the breach. Do you copy? Repeat, you have to locate and repair that leak—we can worry about the other breaches later, but that leak takes priority, copy?*"

"Copy, Aris, but there's gas coming out of everything. It's going to take a minute."

There came a high frequency of interference and then Aris disappeared again, leaving Fenroe and Sitosen alone, clinging to the ship's exterior. Fenroe frantically pulled the flashlight away from her chest and signaled to him as he propelled himself toward her position, maneuvering through the shallow layer of evaporating gas, praying that it wouldn't eat away their suits. "Eos, can you still hear me?"

"*Ye—s Command—*"

Sitosen signaled back with his flashlight, and then, out of the static, "*—roe, do you copy?*"

"Yes! Jesus Christ, yes—"

"*Were you able to confirm orbit of that debris?*"

"I saw it. Listen, you have to turn around. The *Meridian* has started losing pressure and atmosphere fast—hydrazine levels in the ship are at five percent, and rising."

"*Shit, that—that's not good.*"

"That leak has to be located, *asap*." She said as clearly as she could, "We don't have a lot of time."

"*Look around, Fenroe—it's all over the place—*"

"I know," she said. "I know that, but there's a hull breach somewhere that's reverse-venting fuel *back* into the station. If we can get that one under control, it'll buy the crew enough time to figure out what to do with the other leaks. We have to figure out a way to find it. They're prepared to separate damaged modules, but we have to confirm whether or not it's a module that contains any life systems."

"*Copy, Fenroe—Flight deck, this is Sitosen. If you can hear this, get into your bio-suits immediately. That'll give you about two hours of good breathing time.*"

"I don't think they can hear us."

He stopped a half kilometer away. She watched him float there, racking her brain.

"*Okay,*" he said. "*All right—Fenroe, we're going to shut down the engines from out here, copy? We have to cut off the flow of hydrazine coolant at the source. That should give us time to think, and give the crew time to jettison the damaged modules.*"

"Okay," she took in a deep pull of pure oxygen, and checked her gauges: oxygen was at ninety-five percent, and ticking lower with each passing millisecond. "Copy that. How?"

He turned and surveyed the station, his light moving back and forth along the hull. "*Eos, can you hear us?*"

"*I can hear you, Colonel.*"

"*I want you to power down all fuel delivery systems and engines—copy?*"

"*Warning,*" she pulsed. "*Disabling engines at our current velocity will leave the station vulnerable to additional debris—I will be unable to steer us out of danger.*"

"*That's a risk we're going to have to take. Shut down the*

engines now, Eos—that is a priority override."

"Voice print identification accepted and noted," Eos replied. *"Shutting down fuel and engines."*

"Good. Now, slow down Fenroe. Breathe. We got time. Let's work the problem."

"Copy," Fenroe said, pressing her forehead against a sponged rim above her visor, wiping the sweat away. She clipped the drill to her thigh and pulled herself farther along the hull, desperately searching for white crystals that appeared to move opposite the rest—the hemorrhage would look like fuel being sucked back toward the ship. But it was like looking for a needle in a haystack—every part of the ship's surface she could see had at least some impact scoring from meteorites that gassed white particle clouds. "There's too much. I can't see anything."

"Copy that, do your best Fenroe. I'm topside again, searching for the reversed breach. Keep talking. Keep positive."

"Eos," she said, struggling to breathe. "How long until the crew loses air?"

"Warning, full loss of breathable atmosphere will be reached in six minutes."

The flight suit sucked tight against her body, and breath condensed on the inside of her visor. She pulled a cylindrical light pod away from her shoulder—the object was similar to her light pen, but larger, older—a bulky handheld computing unit with haptic, holographic, voice, and light-tech, which interlinked with Eos. Fenroe tossed it above the station, where it spun for a moment, shooting tiny streams of gas before finally coming abreast. "Eos, I've deployed a light sensor. I want to see every hull breach on this side of the station."

She looked in the direction of Eos's blue dot on her mini-map and saw the tiny robot a kilometer away, pulling quickly through damaged plates of metal and smoke, working to suction or blast leaking fuel away from the Auxiliary Power Units before anything caught fire and turned the station into a two hundred kiloton compression bomb. Her black oval visor framed in blue light never ceased moving, endlessly panning back and forth, reading as much of the environment as it could.

Green and blue sheets of light erupted from all sides of the cylinder Fenroe deployed, and mechanically painted the station— tiny thrusters pushed it farther away, which widened its line of sight. Fenroe held tight to the ship, searching the darkness for more debris as a grid of light took shape below her hands. Holographic flags in her HUD began shooting away from the hull in staggered, unorganized formation—each flag represented a part of the hull that was in contrast to the ship's original design— these were the recent impacts from meteorites.

"*Mapping complete,*" Eos said.

"Now, I need you to repower the engines and fuel delivery— understand?"

"*That's not a good idea,*" Sitosen cut in.

"I have to see where the leak is—do it Eos, and prepare to shut down engines on my mark."

"*Rebooting engines,*" Eos replied.

"Okay—now Eos, isolate only the mapped hull breaches that are venting gas—copy that?"

"*I copy, Commander—stand by.*"

Many of the flags in her HUD dropped away, but several more remained. "That's good, Eos—really good," she panted. "Very well done."

Fenroe looked again at the tiny robot in the distance, which continued ripping through the burned out fuselage in its sector, giving no indication that a fraction of her attention was on the grid of death extending below Fenroe's body.

"Now. Show me those injuries in which gas particles are

siphoning *back* into the hull."

All flags disappeared, except two.

"Jesus—Sitosen, I found it! I found the leak!" Warm waves of triumph washed over her body, and she fought savagely not to break down or weep. "Eos, map those waypoints onto my HUD, and power down the engines. Priority override, Commander Evelyn Fenroe."

"*Copy, Commander—voice print identification verified. Powering down engines.*"

"*Copy that,*" Sitosen said quietly—she could hear a smile and relief breaking his voice. "*Great news, Fenroe—good job. I'm coming to you.*"

"Can you see it? Aris or Ulbricht, do you copy? We found the leak. The breaches are between the condensation panels in sector six. If you're going to do something, now's the time—copy?"

No response from the flight deck.

"Eos, how much air do they have?"

"*Fatal levels of hydrazine have been reached—climbing at ten percent.*"

"*If they're not in their suits,*" Sitosen whispered. "*They're all dead.*"

"Aris or Dunesto, do you copy? Harris? Does anybody copy?"

"*Keep talking to them, Fenroe,*" Sitosen cut in. "*There's a chance they can still hear us.*"

"Flight deck," she said. "If you can hear me, I'm heading to the damaged area now."

Fenroe propelled herself toward the remaining holograms, pulling a canister of nano-poxy and a needle gun away from her belt. She immediately went to work threading a spool of filament into the gun's loader and unlatched the trigger guard—if she could stitch the broken fuel lines back together with trace amounts of filament, reinsulate them and pack the hull breach with the molecular epoxy, the hydrazine would at least stop leaking into the main habitats, giving the crew more time to decontaminate the ship—which would by her estimation take roughly two hours: almost the exact amount of time they'd have breathable air in their suits. The cold, undeniable fact was that if she and Sitosen couldn't repair the leak in the next three minutes, even with the two hours of extra breathing time in their suits, the crew would be dead anyway: their suit oxygen would run out a good ten minutes before the ship finished clearing itself of poison, leaving them all without breathable atmosphere. She had to work fast. Fenroe pushed those thoughts as far away from the immediate moment as possible, focusing instead on the here and now.

"*Warning,*" Eos said. "*Hydrazine and ammonia at fifteen percent.*"

"Copy, Eos—"

"*God damn it,*" Sitosen hissed. "*It's like the ISS thrust repair all over again.*"

"That's not going to happen," she said firmly. "Don't even think it."

"*Copy that.*"

"Just keep talking to me, okay? Keep me calm," Fenroe said, snapping the filament into her gun, pulling her body harder through space. "What time is it back on Earth?"

"*What?*"

"The time, on Earth—what's the time?"

"*I don't know,*" he trailed off. "*You're going to tell me it's Miller time...?*"

Her laugh threatened to turn into a sob, and she fought it down, despite herself.

"You know," she grunted, reaching for the next handhold.

"Beck told me about the bourbon."

For a long time the only sound from Sitosen was his breathing, and then: *"I'm sorry for dragging you out here. I'm sorry for everything—"*

"Save it."

"No, Fenroe, listen to me. It's important. If I don't make it—"

"Stop. I don't want to hear it."

"Listen—"

"No!" she yelled, cutting him off. "We're making it, you hear me? We're getting *outta* here.*"

Silence, and more breathing.

"I hear you, Fenroe," he sighed, lost in thought. *"I hear you."*

"Hydrazine at thirty percent," Eos cut in.

"Okay," Sitosen cleared his throat, coming back to focus. *"I'm almost to your position."*

Fenroe adjusted her altitude to come about parallel to the hull, and reached the first flag of light. She collapsed the hologram in her HUD and shined light into the breach, immediately setting to work unbolting a burned out condensation panel.

"Flight deck, I've arrived at the breach—repeat, the reverse-flow is coming from a condensation unit." She glanced farther down the hull a few meters. "And it looks like the second leak is coming from another condensation panel a few meters away."

"Hydrazine at forty percent."

"Copy, Eos." Fenroe's mind functioned like a surgical razor—the universe focused and seeped into one static reality. "Opening panel." She unscrewed the bolts as fast as possible—unconcerned about stripping or keeping track of them as they came loose. She saw Sitosen out of the corner of her eye on approach several meters away, flying steadily toward the other breach. "How we doing, Eos?"

"*Hydrazine and ammonia are at fifty percent.*"

"We could use a little help over here."

"*Negative, Commander—catastrophic loss of pressure is imminent. A capacity level of fuel is leaking onto the engines and surplus APU's. I have to put these fires out before there's an explosion.*"

"*Copy, Eos.*" Sitosen said, "*Let us know if* you *need any help.*"

"Battery is non-functional," Fenroe rasped, feeling her hands growing numb from the frantic work. "I'm just going to rip this whole panel out, repair the line, and pack the breach with epoxy."

"*Do what you can,*" Sitosen said, tense. "*But we're going to have to speed this up—*"

"I know," she took a deep breath. "I know—drilling the panel now."

She pulled the panel free and tossed it over her shoulder, sending it tumbling through space away from the structure. She ripped into a film of vinyl netting and pulled the scorched wiring tray aside—she produced a safety razor from a pocket in her chest and cut away the melted wire and copper. "These receptors are shot. The whole board is shot."

"*Lethal levels of hydrazine at sixty percent,*" Eos said.

"I'm pulling the pins now." She reached into the breach with her pliers and ripped the first linchpin away—a corner of the tray beneath the condensation panel lifted, and a hiss of hydrazine escaped the breach, covering her suit—it dispersed away from the station for a moment, and then curled back into the fuel line. "First pin is clear—*shit, shit, shit,* this stuff is on my suit. How much time Eos?"

"*Three minutes until complete loss of breathable atmosphere, Commander.*"

"And the other panel, Sitosen?"

"*Almost there*," he said. "*Thirty seconds. What do you mean it's on your suit?*"

"I have hydrazine all over me."

"*Is it eating through?!*"

"I...I don't think so."

Amber, red, and orange light displaced deep shadow on the hull a few feet away from Fenroe's hand. Too focused on the hydrazine leak, she barely noticed it. And then another bullet-sized hole appeared and expanded, wreathed in flame, which spun in tight spirals away from the station like phosphorescent liquid. Another soft ring of flame materialized not far from that, and it took a moment for Fenroe to realize that debris was striking the station again—

"*Warning, proximity alert.*" Eos pulsed into her ears, "*Brace for impact in twenty seconds—*"

"Oh god," Fenroe whispered. Pellet sized pieces of debris made contact inches away from her position, soundlessly firing through the hull, leaving undulating circles of golden heat. She grabbed the lip of the open panel and pulled herself toward it, trying to decrease her surface area, making the smallest target possible. She looked at the planet Saturn, which was close now, taking up a good seventy percent of her vision, and raked her eyes across its deep corona, searching for shadow or bright contrasts of yellow and orange—

And something massive separated from the light: a two-meter-wide object on collision course with the *Meridian's* mirror shielding.

"Contact, debris at ten o'clock—!"

A pellet made impact next to Fenroe's right leg, puncturing the hull. She felt a little nick of something else very small ricocheting off the back of her suit, and suddenly her oxygen warning started blinking in her HUD. Not alarmingly fast, but fast enough. Her air gauge began to drop, ninety-five percent, ninety percent, eighty-eight percent—

She looked up, watching the larger object slam into the shield, which shattered into a million pieces, creating a chain reaction of interacting metals, inertia, velocity and speed— flaming debris crashed into itself and appeared to rain down onto her side of the station—the largest pieces missed, clearing the structure at tremendous speeds. Unprotected due to the loss of one of their shields, Fenroe watched in horror as another piece of debris smashed into the communications array like a cannon ball, sending more pieces of shrapnel their direction. Gripping what she could of the hull until her hands hurt, she saw Sitosen look up at the towers and mirror shields, which were eroding and falling apart all around him.

In complete silence she watched his thrusters come to life as he tried maneuvering around the hull for cover, but a large piece of debris shot out of the darkness and made impact with his helmet. His body ricocheted against the hull and spiraled away from the station inside a cloud of shrapnel and fragmentation, like a thrown marionette.

Fenroe leaned away from the hull as Sitosen slipped out of her field of vision behind the structure, spinning into the backdrop of Saturn, disappearing into the light.

"Sitosen is hit—!" she screamed, and then softer, clearer, "— flight deck, Sitosen has been *hit*. He is drifting off-structure, and I can't see him. Flight deck, I don't have visual of Sitosen, copy?"

"*Warning,*" Eos said as if from a distance, far in the back of Fenroe's mind, almost too quiet to be heard. "*Hydrazine at ninety percent.*"

Fenroe frantically surveyed the hull around her, searching for fresh impacts, but the bombardment stopped as suddenly as it started. She hooked her tools to a clip near the condensation panel and checked her gauges—eighty percent oxygen, seventy-eight percent, seventy-five—and thruster fuel was at ninety-eight percent. "Flight deck," she rasped. "I'm going off-structure to retrieve Sitosen, copy?"

No response. She pressed a button on her forearm and controls for the Manned Maneuvering Unit popped away from the pack on her shoulders. She pulled the controls into her fists and aimed at the exact point on the hull where Sitosen disappeared, and stopped.

"Eos," she hesitated, breathing deeply, watching Saturn move slowly from one corner of her visor to the other, as the station spun dead-stick off axis—feeling the distance growing between her and Sitosen with each passing second. "How long until the crew runs out of air?"

"*Complete loss of breathable atmosphere will be reached in two minutes. This offsets the crew's two hour reserves of suit air by a margin of seven minutes.*"

Fenroe hung in space near the condensation panel as her heart pulled—ripped with immense force—toward the edge of the hull. But the cold, logical part of her brain locked the rest of her body into place: if she didn't repair the leak within one-hundred-and-twenty seconds, her crew would be forced to hold their breath for seven minutes once the oxygen reserves ran out in their suits: they had exactly two hours of breathing time in their rebreathers, which was the same amount of time it would take Eos to decontaminate the ship of poisonous gas and re-oxygenate the habitat.

She checked her mini-map a last time, watching Sitosen's red dot ping farther and farther away. She released the MMU controls and pressed the button on her wrist again, which snapped the thruster arms back into place behind her EVA pack. Turning toward the panel, she unclipped her tools and punched two minutes into the keyboard on her forearm, which immediately began counting down in the upper left corner of her HUD. Fenroe went back to unscrewing the wiring tray.

"Eos," she said calmly. "I want you to detach from the hull and retrieve Sitosen."

"*I can't do that, Commander.*"

"That is an order. Detach now and retrieve Colonel Sitosen before he drifts too far—"

"*Negative.*"

"Goddamn it, do it now!"

The timer in her HUD passed the ninety-second mark—she thought the numbers counted faster than what the speed of a stopwatch should be.

"*The rest of the crew is in jeopardy,*" Eos said with the calm detachment of a machine. Fenroe looked again, but could no longer see the robot—a cloud of white gas and smoke poured away from the hull where Eos stood moments before. "*Override command of retrieval,*" Eos replied.

"That's a negative, Eos, negative!" Fenroe openly wept, and she fought the tears collecting under her lids in the zero gravity, which blurred her vision: "Detach immediately and retrieve Sitosen. That is an order. The engines will hold—"

"*The leak is spreading into the engines,*" Eos cut her off. "*I'm sorry, Commander, I must contain it. Override rescinded.*"

Fenroe moved away as the wiring tray came free, exposing the ripped fuel lines beneath. She looked around, blinking through more tears and—

...as the ship rotated, spinning out of axis from the bombardment, Sitosen's body cleared the edge: a tiny immovable speck in the distance. Despite her very full heart she watched his body spiral into obscurity, no longer able to make out the details of his limbs—a single white speck afloat in pitch-colored nothingness.

Fenroe turned back toward the fuel line and ripped a manageable length of it out of the hull, and began stitching the broken ends back together with filament. She ripped a small length of aluminum tape away from a roll compartment in her chest, and crushed it around the leak. She stuffed the fuel line back into the breach and grabbed the canister of nano-poxy—a poly-alloy foam used for repairing hull breaches in vacuum. She depressed the trigger and pumped the entire contents of the canister into the breach, watching it fill in the empty spaces around the repaired fuel line. "Moving to the second panel."

"*Hydrazine at ninety-five percent and holding.*"

"Please god, let them be in their suits," Fenroe said under her breath.

She hooked her tools back onto her thigh, loaded her legs to jump, and blasted away from the hull—she pressed the MMU button on her wrist in mid-vacuum, and the thrust controls popped back into position—she gripped the triggers in her fists again and fired thrusters, adjusting attitude to come down on the second panel in a single leap. Fenroe made impact and recoiled off the hull—a quick thrust for adjustment brought her abreast—she reached out, grabbed on. "I've reached the last hull breach, flight deck. Drilling the panel now."

Eos piped in, "*forty-five seconds until atmospheric deficit.*"

Fenroe unscrewed the bolts and tore away the condensation panel—she dug her gloved fingers and safety razor into the vinyl netting and cut away the ruined wiring tray. Fenroe breathed deep, burning through her dwindling oxygen, and ripped the breached fuel line into the open.

"Almost there," she rasped.

"*Ninety-five percent, and holding.*"

"Are they in their bio-suits? Are they—Eos, are they okay?

Can you read them?"

"*I can't read anything inside the station—*"

"Respond, flight deck!"

Fenroe filled the breach with nano-poxy and hooked her tools near the panel: "Punch it, Eos, bring the engines back online."

"*Copy. But be advised, ion propulsion and communications have experienced catastrophic failure. Navigation is limited.*"

"You are *go* for emergency venting and decontamination." She checked her mini-map, "I'm going for Sitosen."

The station came to life beneath her knees and minor traces of fuel began gassing again out of the lesser hull breaches. Fenroe checked her mini-map a second time—the stopwatch flashed a rhythm of all zeroes in the upper left corner of her HUD—and located Sitosen's red dot pinging several hundred kilometers off the bow. She loaded her knees and leapt away from the station again, blasting her thrusters toward his altitude. "I am now detached from the structure, flight deck, headed for Sitosen. Stand by."

She banked and rocketed through a cloud of twirling debris, taking her chances with damaging the suit—thrusters fired in all directions, keeping her level with the distant planet to maintain orientation. "Eos, map my trajectory to Sitosen's position."

"*Done.*" A dotted line of light blinked to life in her visor, stretching a path off into the distance, leading her to an infinitesimal white dot on the edge of Saturn—she could barely make out his profile, which looked like a tiny piece of fuzz slowly blinking in the center of her HUD. It was a breathtaking moment, seeing him there, so fragile, floating within incalculable and awful eternity.

"Sitosen," she exhaled and inhaled short breaths, feeling the weight of her dwindling oxygen supply on her lungs. "Do you copy?"

She fired her jets through the emptiness. Immeasurable expanses of black extended in front of her—the stars changed in her vision as she adjusted and readjusted her trajectory to keep Sitosen's body in the center of her visor. Spinning into the sun setting on Saturn's most distant horizon, much smaller and whiter than back on Earth, she breathed again. She checked her fuel, which continued dropping at seventy-two percent.

"Sitosen," she pleaded.

With one hand on thrust, she used the other to pull the flashlight away from her chest and signal to him: "Can you see? Track my light, come this way—" She checked her fuel again, which dropped below sixty-five percent, "—can you see this?"

A ray of sunlight hit the surface of his suit in the distance, which gleamed for a second, and then went dark again. Fenroe concentrated hard to keep his red dot aligned with her HUD. "Come on, Sitosen." She fought the hitch in her throat again— which was becoming more and more of a losing battle. "Come on," she begged. "I can't—don't make me do this without you— " her voice broke, "—don't, Sitosen!"

No answer, and the white speck of him seemed to move farther away.

"Okay," she said. "Okay, the sun—the sun is at your two o' clock," she hesitated. The red dot on her mini-map flickered for a moment and then disappeared. "Sitosen, talk! Answer!"

The distant sun finally set—the face of Saturn was almost completely in shadow. She kept breathing—the light from her HUD was now the only source of humanity against the dark. She held onto that light, letting it guide her to his gleaming suit, which glinted at less and less frequent intervals. Soon he'd be gone forever, lost in nothingness. Her fuel gauge flashed red as it dropped below fifty percent—she pulled a collapsible mirror away from her chest and held it out in front of her: the *Crown*

Meridian was now a scaled down model of its former self—she was drifting far away. Soon she'd be too far to make it back.

Her oxygen levels began blinking: a row of digital numbers flashing at seven percent.

"Eos, do you copy?" she transmitted, receiving no response. *"Crown Meridian*, do you copy? Aris?"

Powering down her MMU, Fenroe clenched her fists around the thrust controls. She had reached the point of no return with her oxygen and fuel supplies—both the ship and Sitosen continued drifting in opposite directions. With no communication, she finally broke down and wept. A deep, soulful sob.

She was out of time.

"Sitosen," she begged, terrified by the loneliness in her voice. "Can you hear me?"

His suit glinted a last time in the setting sunlight before disappearing entirely in shadow. She looked again at the *Crown Meridian* in her mirror, still shrinking in the distance. The oxygen gauge ticked six percent.

Empty of heart and completely hollowed of all hope, she dropped her chin inside the helmet and turned, pointing herself at the shrinking light of the *Crown Meridian*, and hit the thrusters. She left Sitosen there, in the middle of that ocean of darkness, uncertain if he was alive or dead. She hoped he was dead. She couldn't imagine the torture of that eternal fall, watching the last rung of humanity in this infinite outpost disappear, and disappear, and disappear more, leaving him in the cold dark to slowly die alone.

She continued checking her mirror for him, hoping that he'd glint again, giving her a bearing of some kind. Her oxygen ticked past one percent, and her breath came fast, shallow, and empty. She focused on the tiny scaled model in the distance—the limping strength of the *Crown Meridian*—not knowing if it was pulling away or coming toward her. Fenroe's breathing increased in both frequency and length as the bio-suit lost pressure and her oxygen fell to zero. An alarm sounded somewhere in the back of her mind, indicating that her suit's pressure breached the red. She gave her thrusters everything they had, burning through the rest of the fuel, emptying her tanks—and she merely halved the distance between her and the *Meridian*. She was dead in the water—no fuel, no oxygen—moving solely under the power of inertia, no chance of reaching the ship in time.

Sensing death, she tried thinking about home—about Proust, about her crew. Anything. But she couldn't. All she thought about was squeezing one last gulp of air out of her rebreather, and the immense pressure on her lungs. She lost the rest of her air. Hyperventilating, gulping like a fish out of water, her mouth wide, her throat sucked desperately against nothing. Fenroe tried to speak—she tried to tell the crew her position, but she couldn't. The blackness slowly closed around her vision, and she felt immense weight on her chest, and just before the lights went out for good, she saw the faintest flutter of ion propulsion coming to life, and the *Meridian* turning her direction. Her body flexed into itself, and then relaxed. She spun softly into a carbon dioxide sleep, and the massive ringed planet rose up from the bottom of her visor. Looming over her like an ocean, Saturn nearly eclipsed the universe, so close that she had to stretch her head back to see the curve of its upper most horizons. The morning side of the planet blazed like a forest fire at night—she could even decipher individual particles of dust from the ancient regolith falling within its equatorial discs, which stretched out beneath her forever, like faith.

"Jesus," she said. "Sitosen, I can't...my god...I wish you could see this."

"*I can see, Fenroe.*" She heard him say, calmly, "*Oh, isn't it beautiful?*"

"Beautiful," she whispered back. And she was powerless to look away, her death meaningless in comparison, so close that the planet was static, as if it had never changed in the entire span of existence. And the scale of its bands—its gaseous streams that encapsulated the very essence of her desire for the unknown— reflected the limitless opposite of that eonian black. So close that the backdrop of stars faded away from the seams of a more brilliant light, which moved with detail and beauty and majesty unlike anything Fenroe could have hoped to experience in this life. She was utterly seized by it, hypnotized by Saturn's magnitude, and overwhelmed by its wonder. Black and gray lines moved through immense clouds of different states and colors like a painting of smoke, and for a moment—just a moment—she believed she was looking at the face of God.

2.

Sitosen's reflection hovered in her mirror, following so close that Fenroe could make out the details of his face through the visor: his green eyes glinting with light, the square edges of his beard, and even the contours of veins pulsing along the sides of his neck. Her heart skipped faster with relief.

He was still alive.

But when she turned to snatch his arm and blast off toward the *Meridian*, he vanished. She'd pull the mirror away from her chest, and there he was again, merely feet away, so near that she could touch him and actually *feel* the effect of his gravity. She'd turn again, and again he disappeared. The pattern didn't end. After several attempts, she stopped trying. She swallowed the tears back, staring at his reflection. So close. So very close.

He tried speaking to her: his lips came together and opened, his hands grasped at nothing, adding emphasis to something important, something that she had to understand. But she couldn't. He grew frustrated with her not getting it, and shook his head. He pumped his fists, opening his mouth wider, opening his eyes wider, as if he were screaming something detrimental and urgent. She turned again, and again he was gone. She looked at his reflection. Always behind. Always out of reach.

Then wet coldness stung her throat. And then came the pain in her chest: a distant pinprick of light in the dark, growing brighter and richer—capillaries pulsed at the edge of something red and organic, and then the mechanical wind buffeted her ears, building from a far hush to a close roar, and then that familiar distant light rushed toward Fenroe like a bullet train, opening, yawning, pushing away the quiet dark.

"Breathe," Aris commanded, her voice coming from someplace far away. She tilted Fenroe's head back, holding her lids open with her thumbs, shining light into her eyes. "Come on girl, breathe—"

Fenroe convulsed and turned to the side, retching awake. She took giant mouthfuls of air so fast that it hurt her chest. Some far part of her awareness detected long and fluid shadows moving around her. Aris patted between her shoulders, massaging the blood back into her lungs. Phosphines shimmered out of Fenroe's head, and she breathed in deeply. The world came back with the scent of ozone. She opened her eyes to the Lab's acoustic bulkhead and conduit and recessed LED tubing, which filled the spaces around her vestibular sense of weightlessness, congealing with solidity underneath her body in the form of a stainless steel worktable: the same table Dunesto used for working on Eos's RMS when it needed repairs. Fenroe figured the reason she was in the Lab was because the medical bay had been torn away from the installation or jettisoned. Rolling onto her back, she was surprised to recognize the pull of gravity. Aris cupped her head and brought it up, squeezing water into her mouth from a pouch, brushing the damp and drying hair out of her eyes. "Atta girl, breathe—"

"Sitosen—"

"Breathe, Fenroe—"

She pushed herself up, clawing her hands away, ratcheting her eyes open and fighting Aris's embrace. Through the haze, Fenroe saw her blackened and battered bio-suit discarded in the corner. She followed an insulated hose from the back of her pack to the room across the gangway, where it disappeared inside one of the two remaining lander modules, and she remembered the decontamination protocol. She looked at Aris, breathing it in, drinking the air as if it were water: "h'long was I out?"

"Out of air?" At the sound of her voice, Dunesto let go a deep breath of relief and lifted his head from the table next to her, beads of sweat drying along his glistening hairline. "No longer than a few minutes," he said softly, shaking his head. "But you were out for a little over sixteen hours *after* we got air back into your suit."

Fenroe imagined it—the crew picking her up, unconscious, pulling her into the airlock. Since the station was airless for the two-hour decontamination, and in order to save her life, they had to find a way to keep her oxygenated until the ship finished recycling the deadlier gases back into their appropriate circulations. So they ditched her damaged tanks and connected the lander's oxygen-reserves straight into her suit's CO_2 filter. Without the use of defibrillators and needles, the only thing they could do was administer chest compressions, pump pure oxygen into her rebreather and hope it was enough to bring her back.

Still dazed, Fenroe looked around the lab at her crew— Dunesto was on his knees next to Aris, who leaned against the stainless steel worktable Fenroe had been lying upon; Harris, Suja, Beck and Ulbricht stood near the main corridor access, arms crossed with concern, thinking quietly.

"Where's Sitosen?" she asked again.

Dunesto cursed under his breath and took a seat against the far bulkhead. Aris and Beck exchanged glances. Fenroe's voice broke as she clawed at Aris's shirt, knowing the answer and not wanting it to be true. "Where is he?"

The younger woman caressed the back of Fenroe's neck, hesitating, and met her eyes.

"I'm sorry," Aris said simply. When she couldn't find anything else to say, she just smiled uncomfortably through the tears and shrugged sadly. Fenroe frowned and shook her head, remembering his face in the mirror, remembering Saturn.

"No," Fenroe said, still shaking her head. "No you're wrong, he was there. I could see him, he was *right there—*"

"Eos's OPS lost him a couple thousand kilometers off-structure. We looked, Fenroe." Aris's eyes were swollen and red. "I swear to god we looked. Eos calculated parallax from his last known position, but there's debris everywhere. He could have come in contact with something and veered in a thousand different directions."

"We have to find him."

"We don't have enough fuel—"

"Eos, bring up—I want to see Sitosen's trajectory," Fenroe stammered, out of breath. "Before your OPS lost him—"

"Fenroe—"

"We gotta find his body—!"

"Fenroe!" Aris yelled, gripping her wrists. The sudden shock of their voices retreated with twisting echo down the main corridor. And quietly, shaking her head: "He's gone."

For a while it was only Fenroe's deep quiet sobs filling the silence, as they sat in a daze beneath the harsh light of the overhead LED's.

"Here's the situation," Dunesto said finally, struggling through the exhaustion in his voice. "Thanks to both you and Sitosen, we had enough time to patch up the hull damage and clear the habitat of ammonia and hydrazine. There's a ton of holes still out there, but we're okay for now as long as Eos can keep the right modules closed off and the rest of the ship equalized."

He stared at Harris as he spoke, letting it sink in. After waiting a moment, Dunesto sucked air through his teeth, arching his eyebrows: "But the comms tower was destroyed. In addition to the damage in both the engine compartments and the oxygenators, a lot of our O-two was used up during decontamination, and we burned through most of our fuel in emergency deceleration. This wouldn't have normally been a problem, if it weren't for the leaks." He took a breath, and shrugged again. "As it stands now, we don't have enough fuel or oxygen to make it to Titan. And we're *definitely* not getting home like this."

Beck and Aris helped pull Fenroe into a seated position. A series of evenly spaced, laminated photographs were arranged on the far wall, similar to family photos that lined the stairway in Fenroe's childhood home. These were pictures that the crew had taken to document their journey, interspersed with random photos they'd each brought with them from home. Across from her, staring directly into her eyes was an innocent, clean-shaven Lee Sitosen in his dress blues on the day of his swearing in ceremony. Dunesto smuggled it aboard before launch as a friendly joke, and it stayed there. She couldn't look away.

"Our only chance," Dunesto continued, "is to find the *Endeavor* and hope their life systems are operational."

"That's it?" Ulbricht asked.

Dunesto shook his head. "We don't have a choice. Finding the missing ship is now our only option."

"We flew right through what was *left* of their ship." Ulbricht said softly, the exhausted lines below her eyes made even more severe by the events of the last several hours. "Our emergency beacon's been tripped. I say we hang tight and wait for help."

"You don't get it," Dunesto cut her off, slicing the air with the blade of his hand. "We've lost the capacity to generate oxygen. Our reserves are shot. Any chemicals we have on board that *could* have been synthesized or separated to make more oxygen have all been compromised. We *needed* those oxygen and hydrazine reserves, and now we're solely dependent on what comes from the garden, which is not enough. At the rate we're breathing, we won't last a week. And on top of that, communications are fucked. That debris ripped the tower right off. No way to transmit, no way to call for help."

"The emergency beacon has its own transmitter—"

"Which is jammed by that shielding phenomenon around Saturn space."

"So, what do we do," Ulbricht hissed. "Just sit here and die?"

"That wasn't the *Endeavor*," Fenroe said suddenly, startling the crew. She pulled herself up higher against the wall with Beck's help and rested her head back, closing her eyes. Erika and Dunesto backed away from each other and looked her direction. "It must have been one of her landers."

Dunesto shook his head and closed his eyes. "You don't know that."

"It didn't look like enough debris to be the *Endeavor*. And it passed right in front of me—" she held her hand a few inches away from her face, speaking through her teeth, "—just like this. So close that I could read the designation on its hull."

"All right," Harris broke in, coming back from his thoughts.

"Okay, the way I see it, we have one option. We can use what fuel we have left to get us to Saturn, and ride her out for a slingshot back toward Earth."

"Wait," Aris said, getting an idea. "How much velocity can we suck up from Saturn if we make a couple slingshots around the planet?"

"What do you mean?"

"I mean," she shifted her weight, and grasped her thoughts from the air. "Is there a limit to how many times we can gravity-assist the *Meridian* with slingshots before Saturn stops increasing our velocity?" She looked around the room. "Think about how much fuel we could save by riding the waves of multiple slingshots."

"I know what you're saying," Suja said, leaning against the wall. "Like, uh, a merry-go-round. You're thinking we'll just get faster and faster with each pass around Saturn, and make it home on velocity alone. But yes, there is a limit. If we hit the escape velocity out of Saturn space, we'd have to slow the *Meridian* down at some point to loop back and get another encounter. The amount of fuel we'd need to slow down could be better used during the initial slingshot for an even faster escape. Multiple passes would be a waste."

"What if we string together a series of smaller assists from some of the larger moons?" Harris offered.

"Christ, Harris," Dunesto interrupted. "You're *still* not getting it. For the second time, we have maybe a week or two of air. You understand?" He stepped into him, breathing hard through his nose. "And your plan? Call home and have Ma and Pa meet us at the end of the street with a jerry can or some shit? We'd need comms for that, wouldn't we?"

"Yes, Dunesto," Harris replied, slowly. "We would."

"Right. So it doesn't matter how logical or righteous your

little rescue plan was—" Dunesto looked through him, "—you, Sitosen, and Fenroe fucked us." He looked at them all slowly, and then locked his eyes onto the man in front of him. "You *fucked* us, Harris. We have no way of contacting Earth now, and do you know how long it'll take us to reach home on inertia from the fuel we have left? A whole lot longer than two weeks. And even if we did reach home, without *Command's* help, how do we slow down without thrust?"

Harris looked away, his face filling with blood. "We'll figure out a way to communicate with them by then—"

"Come on, no more bright ideas? Where do we get more air? How do we survive the trip?"

"This isn't helping," Aris said quietly, patting Dunesto on the chest.

"We—" Harris hesitated, now staring back at Dunesto, breathing heavily, "—I'm just trying to help." He lifted his hands, "What do you want me to do?"

"I don't want you to do *shit*," Dunesto hissed back. He turned out of Aris's hands and walked to the rear bulkhead. He grabbed Sitosen's photo and ripped it away from the wall. Stunned, the crew stood still as Dunesto stalked back to Harris and shoved Sitosen's photograph into his arms, knocking him off balance. "For once," he leaned in, speaking quietly, "I just want you to take responsibility."

Harris stood for a moment staring into space. Dunesto shouldered past him and stormed out of the lab. After several long, stunned moments, Harris finally allowed himself to pull the photo away from his chest, and see Sitosen.

"You asshole!" Suja yelled after Dunesto, a newer line of blood trickling out of his broken nose. "Get back here!"

Harris blinked and held Sitosen's photo, looking back and forth between the crew and the picture. Tears welled briefly below his lashes, and he swallowed them down. He shifted his weight awkwardly from foot to foot, and then walked back to the line of remaining photos on the far wall. He looked at Sitosen a final time, and then returned him to his rightful place with the rest of the crew.

"Don't listen to him," Suja said, turning to face him. "It's not your fault. *We* acted on the most reasonable assessment of the situation. All of us."

"Yeah," Harris nodded, looking down at his feet. He turned to Fenroe, and she saw the ghost of a sad smile pass his lips. He nodded to himself again and then walked out of the Lab. Watching Harris intently Suja went to follow, but Fenroe stopped him.

"Don't," she rasped, still feeling the crushing labor of her lungs. Fenroe didn't trust what was happening under the surface with Harris, and she wanted him to have some space. She certainly didn't need him breaking Suja's nose again. "Let him go."

Suja stopped and watched Harris's shadow disappear down the corridor. Aris pulled the tightness out of her neck and took a sip of water, shaking her head. "Dunesto's right. We need to think of something."

"What choice do we have?" Fenroe shrugged. "Like he said, we make for the *Endeavor*. Pray she has something we can salvage."

"If it were possible for them to navigate home," Aris said, "they would have tried it."

"You're assuming the crew was alive to operate the ship." Fenroe said, "The entire crew could be dead, and the ship could still be operational."

Aris, Suja, and Beck each stared at the floor from a thousand yards away, too exhausted to think beyond the moment, at odds internally with the hope of finding the missing ship intact and functional, but dreading the thought of finding nine dead bodies inside.

"In either case," Fenroe continued. "We won't know until we get there."

"It doesn't matter," Suja said finally, wiping the blood away from his nose with the bottom of his Hawaiian shirt. "We have to find a way."

"If we're wrong," Ulbricht said, "if we reach that signal and there's nothing, we'll be stuck out here."

Fenroe pushed the thought out of her mind, focusing instead on her next breath. "We're *already* stuck out here—"

"WARNING," Eos interrupted. "I've lost control of the Lander Module Airlock. Depressurization will be reached in five minutes."

For a long time none of the crewmembers breathed, each exchanging concerned and immediate looks, dreading what this new thing meant after already surviving such a terrible ordeal.

"Explain, Eos," Fenroe said quietly, feeling her heart rate increase. "Is the ship going to depressurize?"

"Negative, Commander. The damage has been isolated within the outer hatch wiring panel, which is frozen in manual control. I've lost connection. Unable to abort EVA sequence. Airlock depressurization will be reached in four minutes and forty-five seconds."

"All right." She leaned her head back again, closing her eyes. "As long as the crew isn't in danger, we're okay with that."

"Warning," Eos pulsed again. "A crewmember is going to die."

Fenroe slowly lifted her head away from the partition. The sweat on her neck went cold. Beck looked at her and arched his brow, which gave him an even younger appearance. Pushing away from the stainless steel examination table, Aris studied the obsidian glass floor, trying to understand what Eos meant.

"Warning," Eos thrummed again. "Unprotected crewman in Lander Module Airlock. Depressurization will be reached in four minutes and thirty-six seconds."

Fenroe couldn't put it together at first, and for a split second some desperate part of her brain thought that Sitosen had somehow found his way back to the station. That he was safe inside the airlock. That he was alive.

"Eos," Fenroe said. "Who's in the airlock—?"

"Be advised," Eos interrupted. "EVA sequence has been manually activated from the inside. I'm unable to stop it at this time. Depressurization will be reached in four minutes and twenty seconds."

3.

They found Harris seated against the far wall in a red wash of light. In four minutes that light would turn green and void the airlock of cabin pressure and air, killing anyone inside not secured in a bio-suit. The lower half of Harris's body cut off at the edge of the viewport, but Fenroe could tell that he was looking down at something in his hands. He was an immovable statue, Fenroe thought, similar to those she remembered from her visit to Greece, in a time far removed from the desolate and hopeless spaces she'd come to occupy. The sculpture from her memory pulled itself out of a block of marble. Something in the artistry revealed a tranquil, determined sense of ease, as if whoever it was modeled after had made up their mind about a long contemplated thought, and it had brought them calm.

With Harris, at that moment, what got Fenroe's attention was the look on his face: a sadly embarrassed clarity in his eyes, a kind of settled somberness that was barely strong enough to recognize.

She could see something there, something warped and hopeless. Fenroe recognized the vaguest obscenity and terror in him, almost like the white sclera of a shark eye.

It was the look of someone who had decided that life was no longer worth living.

When they reached the airlock Dunesto was already pounding his fists on either side of the viewport, spit flecking in the corners of his mouth, fresh tears coming to the surface under his eyes.

"Harris," he shouted into comms. "Harris, open up!"

But Harris didn't react.

"What the fuck, Harris!" Dunesto screamed. "I'm sorry, okay? I'm an asshole. You made your point. Let's just *talk*, okay? Please?"

Fenroe reached the airlock and shoved Dunesto aside.

"He's locked himself in and I can't get the door open," Dunesto stammered, his voice cracking. "Jesus, Fenroe, I'm so sorry, I didn't mean for this—"

"Eos," Fenroe interrupted, staring at the top of Harris's head. "Abort the EVA sequence."

From the walls: "I'm sorry, Commander—"

"Don't start this shit again. We have three minutes of safe airlock access, do it now—"

"I can't do that—"

"Priority override!" she shouted. "Abort EVA sequence, now!"

"Negative, specialist Harris has disabled my access to the outer hatch motor control box."

Fenroe raked her eyes around the edge of the viewport, until she saw a snarl of cable and wire ripped out of a vinyl panel above the outer airlock.

"Airlock release is functioning solely under manual control

from the inside," Eos said. "I can't abort the EVA sequence."

Fenroe quickly studied the airlock on her side. "Is the inner airlock functional?"

"Yes, Commander."

Fenroe grabbed the lock cylinder with both hands and tried pulling it out, but it wouldn't budge.

"Help," she wheezed.

Dunesto snatched the handle in his hands as well and pulled, but it wouldn't move. He readjusted his grip and tightened his hands around Fenroe's knuckles.

"On three," he gasped. "One. Two. Three—"

They pulled and pulled and pulled, but the handle wouldn't give.

Fenroe stopped and breathed, shaking feeling back into her hands. She frantically searched the airlock to see where Harris was. "Eos, open the inner airlock."

"Depressurization will occur in two minutes and thirty seconds."

"We know, open the airlock!"

"Negative, Commander. Specialist Harris has released the outer airlock cylinder. Opening the inner hatch would put the rest of the crew in exigent danger. Specialist Harris needs to deactivate EVA sequence from the inside. Two minutes and ten seconds."

Fenroe desperately clawed at the handle again and, realizing that it was useless, she pressed herself against the viewport and thumbed the intercom. "Talk to me, Harris."

She could see him there looking at his lap, a cold sense of resolution and serenity on his face.

"Don't do this," she said. And when he didn't move she smashed her fist at the glass in uncontrolled rage.

"I need you god damn it!" she screamed. He finally looked

up. Fenroe thought she was getting through to him, so she followed that thread of dialog.

"Please," she pleaded, shaking her head. "Don't leave me here. Don't make me do this alone."

He studied her through the viewport, a deep sadness settling under his eyes.

"What about," she said, smiling through the tears. She felt the vacuum of space outside closing its teeth around his throat, increasing the pressure of its bite with each passing second. "Harris, what about Claire and the twins? What about home? Don't you want to see them again?"

He said nothing, looking back into his lap.

Without realizing it, Fenroe's deep hopelessness and sadness cracked open somewhere inside, and there was a spark. As she stood there listening to Eos count away the seconds, that spark of heartache caught something else and it took, stoking into a roaring inferno behind her chest. At that moment she wasn't sad or desperate or lonely; she was *angry*. She wanted to rip the ship apart with her bare hands and breathe in emptiness and death. She wanted to end it all.

"Coward," she said suddenly, as clear as she could, penetrating him with her eyes. She let the word hang in the air and then she screamed it. "You...you *COWARD!*"

He looked at her, his shadowy eyes full of sadness.

"Go ahead and do it," she said, the feeling of it building in her chest like a molten ball of fire, like a torsion release of tether and frustration and rage. "You...you're nothing but a scared, selfish *child.*" She punched the airlock again, nearly breaking her hand. "*WHAT ABOUT US?!*"

Tears came then without resistance, and she hated the silky sting of them. She hated the way they dropped down her face like icicles snapping clear of an eave. She hated herself, and she hated

Harris even more for hurting her like this. For making her watch. And she *had* to watch; she couldn't look away. Because whatever happened to him was *her* responsibility.

"One minute, forty-five seconds until depressurization."

Harris stood and looked at her. Her heart filled, hoping that he had come to his senses, hoping that he was coming back inside. He stopped at the inner hatch, his face taking up the viewport. Fenroe didn't know how she would contain herself once he was back inside: heat pulsated in her knuckles and yearned to be released hard against his body, yearned to beat the cowardice out of him. She ached to purge all of the pain and fear and hopelessness out of herself. Fenroe looked back and forth between the lock cylinder and his eyes, hoping and praying that he would abort the EVA sequence and open the door.

"One minute, thirty seconds," Eos said.

"*I'm starting to forget what they look like*," Harris said finally, pressing the intercom. He searched her eyes for a moment, and then looked down. "*It's like I've fallen asleep...like...like at one point they were here, as real as me and you...and then suddenly they weren't anymore. It's like I'm dead—*" He hesitated, "*—like I've died, or slipped into a coma.*" His shrug was slow and heavy. Closing his tired eyes, Harris compressed his lips, drawing in a deep breath through his nose. He looked up a final time and shook his head. "*But I'm not in a coma, Fenroe. I'm not dead. And I think that if only I could just...just reach across time somehow...reach all the way back to the beginning, like flipping the pages of a book, I could stop myself from leaving them.*" He wanted her to believe him. In the deep pools of his eyes, Fenroe could see that he needed her to understand.

"*But I can't,*" he said finally. "*I'm on the opposite side of a star, and there's no going back.*"

"We *can* go back," she whispered, searching his face through the glass. "You and me. We can go *home*. We just have to *think* our way back." She pressed an index finger against her temple, still searching his eyes. "We have to *think* our way through it."

"*I'm...I don't want to die without any memory of them.*" He shook his head. "*If you knew what that meant, if you knew what that felt like...you wouldn't try to stop me. I need to preserve what I have left. Do you understand?*"

"Sixty seconds," Eos whispered from the back of Fenroe's mind.

"*I'm sorry about Sitosen,*" he said simply, lifting and dropping his shoulders. "*I truly am. But you're all going to die out here.*"

His face settled, and his eyes cleared. He looked up and pulled some saliva away from his tongue with his thumb, and wiped it against something unseen. He took a step back and pressed a piece of paper against the viewport, blocking himself and the inside of the airlock from view.

"Thirty seconds," Eos said.

Fenroe forgot how to breathe, how to blink—she couldn't wrap her heart around the finality of it. Shocked, watching it all happen, Dunesto backed away from the airlock and came flush against the opposite wall soundlessly, his eyes raw around the edges. He set his jaw and slid to the floor, staring at the inner hatch. Aris grabbed Fenroe by the shoulders and pulled her away from the viewport. Fenroe collapsed into the younger woman's chest and wept, unable to make sense of it all.

The piece of paper was the photograph that Suja had spilled water on in the mess hall. Like before, Harris's family looked melted and warped: his twin boys had blurred together, forming a refracted shadow of a memory; his wife's face was rubbed completely away into whiteness. And then the light above the airlock switched green. The outer hatch opened into the crushing vacuum without Fenroe having to see it, without her having to watch her close friend whom she loved with all of her heart die in front of her eyes.

And just like that, with a flash of green light and a ruined photograph, Harris was gone.

4.

She envisioned a speck of light separating the blackness, cutting through it like a ship at sea. Starry nebulae stilled in the backdrop of this speck of light, moving in the foreground of unimaginable distances, emerging from them. This light, which burned slightly brighter than the lights around it, moved relative to everything else—a teardrop on the face of eternity, a microchip of intention, a stark contrast to the rest of it, until that star finally, slowly, piece by piece, shadow by shadow, took shape and became something else. It became a space vessel falling through the void.

Gold, white, and red lights shone on the exterior of this vessel, as alloy spires tapered into a series of ring structures that slowly—almost imperceptibly—rotated around a pipeline pocked with dormant and blackened scarring. If by some miracle Fenroe could travel close enough without being ripped to pieces on the molecular level, the thrum of emptying ion drives would be felt pulsing in complete silence behind a pair of massive solenoid traps, like the bass of an electronic rhythm. These engines were below and behind two equally immense solar sails, which trapped an infinitesimal volume of photons during the *Crown Meridian's* endless descent. She pictured what was left of her ship trailing through the dark eternal waters like loose rigging behind a skiff.

Fenroe didn't know how long it took her to reach the farthest remaining mid-deck module. Minutes, probably—but those minutes stretched forever, like a river: a never-ending stream of latent, irreversible consequences bubbling through the *Meridian's* dark corridors in a state of endless flow. Her goal was to get as far away from the airlock as possible. To get away from her crew, so that she wouldn't have to speak, afraid that anything she said would come out of her mouth as a raw scream of anguish. And when she did—when she couldn't go any farther, because Eos had sealed off the damaged sections of the ship to maintain pressure— Fenroe found herself where she and Sitosen had finished their final game of chess.

Game pieces had been scattered across the floor, disrupted by the interchanging weight and weightlessness of the ship's gravity. She stared at Sitosen's empty chair for a moment, and then slowly reached for a blanket tucked into the synth-leather seat. She pulled the blanket away and took a few steps back, turning to the side, wanting to see the area from a less oppressive angle. Wrapping the blanket around her shoulders, it still had his scent on it. Fenroe bent to pick up a half consumed water pouch, and she stepped on something solid and dark. Lifting her sandal to inspect the object, she discovered that it was Sitosen's King. For an instant an image of him tipping it over came to the foreground of her thoughts and opened the floodgates of other, more salient memories—the look of his stern gaze. The sound of his voice. The contours of his hands. And then deeper, the light glinting off his suit on the edge of Saturn. Deeper, the crushing pressure of her last breaths before passing out in the vacuum of space. And deeper, what she imagined as the waking nightmare of Sitosen's eternal fall through forever. This invariably circled her thoughts back to Harris.

She closed her eyes, trying to shut away the cold resolution of his words, the look on his face, and once again, as it did each time she couldn't resist torturing herself, Fenroe's heart grew too heavy to hold. She held the chess piece in her hand for a moment, rolling it between her fingers, and then tucked it into her pocket.

Standing in half darkness and numb with regret, Fenroe pulled the blanket tighter around her shoulders and sat on the floor, propping herself up against the opposite bulkhead to stare at the naked chessboard. Sleep eventually came—a shallow dreamlessness that washed away some of the heartache and exhaustion. Somewhere in the back of her mind, Fenroe knew that the temperature had dropped slightly. This confirmed what she suspected while she was EVA—not only did the atmosphere regulator keep their brains oxygenated and their bodily fluids where they belonged, the circulation of those gases helped keep the station warm enough for the crew to survive. The temperature inside the habitat depended on how the cabin heat exchangers equalized outside forces that warmed and cooled the ship at temperatures between negative one hundred and forty, and two hundred and sixty degrees Celsius. This variant depended on the pitch, distance, tilt, yaw, and axis of the station relative to the sun. Under regular conditions, the exchangers compensated the differences in the background, unseen and unnoticed. Now, though...now it couldn't. Lower volumes of gases meant not enough of the air was stirred and circulated, which meant less heat. Fenroe took a deep, cold breath, trying for a moment to catalog this new and terrible variable in the dataset of their looming death. And then she forced her mind to turn off, pushing those thoughts away like a buoy in shallow water.

Fenroe awoke once in a panic, thinking that she was still adrift in space, and had to fight back the urge to vomit. These states changed seamlessly within her for nearly the entire time she'd been alone, moving between sleep and panic and guilt in cycles that she couldn't track nor articulate. She checked the time on her wrist, and although it was correct, Fenroe couldn't remember exactly when she was resuscitated.

Hours, maybe days later, Aris eventually found Fenroe seated cross-legged on a maintenance gantry with her back to the main corridor, ripping apart a small terrain rover piece by piece, and separating each of the components therein. The only light Fenroe had to work with spilled in from outside of the module, but it was more than enough to use. She worked throughout the night, diverting her attention away from undesirable dreams and thoughts. Exhausted and worn thin, Fenroe fought to keep her eyes open, and grabbed a pencil-torch from the floor. Blinking the sleep away, she held a rectangular piece of polarized plastic in front of her eyes and cut plates out of the rover's chassis, shooting sparks into the darkness. Pulling the plates free, she set them next to the copper she'd removed from the rover's wiring.

She slept sporadically, but each time she closed her reddened eyes, ghosts of Sitosen and Harris came to her in the darkness, screaming from behind an invisible wall of silence. And no matter how hard she tried, Fenroe couldn't make herself understand what they were trying to tell her. She finished cutting the plate free and surveyed her supplies again, satisfied with what she'd pulled together.

After some time had passed, she noticed the reflection of Aris in the Lander: the young woman leaned against the main corridor, breathing frozen smoke into the air. She finally gathered a sheet of Mylar around her shoulders in what looked like a fist of tinsel, breathing again, as if waiting for the blood to circulate and bring warmth back into her, but Fenroe knew that it never would.

"Eos, lights," Aris whispered, pushing herself away from the hatch. Fenroe didn't react to the change in brightness, and continued using her needle-nose pliers and phillips to remove a small transformer from the rover's neutron detector. Fenroe knew that Aris would recognize immediately what she was trying to fabricate.

She also knew that Aris would believe it was pointless, even if she wouldn't say so.

"I know what you're going to say," Fenroe said.

Aris stepped around the pile of components, watching her feet. "What?"

"You're going to tell me that this is a waste of time."

"No." Aris shook her head.

Fenroe studied the transformer in her hand for a moment, and set it on the floor next to her.

Aris pulled the gutted land rover close and peered into it, surveying what was left. "Can we talk?"

"Listen," Fenroe sighed, her attention focused on the rover. "I apologize for leaving like that. I needed to get out of there."

"I know. That's not what I'm here to talk about."

Fenroe looked up, studying her. The fatigue in Aris was arrant and crude—days of sleeplessness gathered under her eyes in convex shadow. Her brown skin had lightened and paled, lips shaded with vestiges of blue and purple. Fenroe looked away from her, ashamed by her own fear and smallness that reflected back to her from Harris's suicide, and behind him, much larger and more terrifying, from the gaping maw of darkness that swallowed Sitosen. Fenroe wasn't the only one suffering inside of herself. Aris had also lost friends. Family.

Aris sat down and grabbed the soldering iron. "Suja's wrong, you know."

"About what?"

She shrugged. "There's extra fuel on this ship."

Fenroe looked up into the ceiling, and then nodded. "The methane powered descent assembly in the Landers."

"That's right."

Fenroe turned back to the pile of tools between her knees and grabbed a handful of wire. She put a blue and white one in her teeth and began stripping the insulation away, exposing the copper inside. "I thought of that," she said, setting the copper aside. "It's not enough."

"It might be—"

"It's not enough, Aris."

"Just, stop for a second," Aris hissed, leaning forward. "Suja says that we need to generate enough thrust to accelerate to nine point eight kilometers per second, right?"

"Yeah," she nodded softly. Then again, more sure. "Yeah, and we can't. It would take half a year of acceleration to reach the inertia we'd need to make it home. But we don't have that much time."

"We don't *need* those speeds for a slingshot."

"What do you mean?"

"Well," Aris said, "one gee for one hundred and thirty-three days is a perfectly realistic speed if we wanted to reach home in the shortest amount of time possible."

"Yeah...?"

"Fenroe," Aris said, exhaling a cloud of white air out of her lips. "I don't care if it takes us twenty years. I don't care if it takes us fifty." She shrugged again. "I'm going home."

Fenroe shook her head. "And so we use Titan's gravity to point ourselves toward home, then what? Suffocate three days later? *We don't have any air.*"

"We *will* have air—" she nodded her head, "—from the *Endeavor.*"

"We are out of time, Aris. Come on, you didn't think this was going to happen?" She laughed darkly under her breath, a sickening and desperate sound. "You thought you were going to live forever? Take comfort in the fact that if it wasn't here, it would have been some hospital bed a few decades from now. Or something else." She shook her head again, looking back to her project. "All roads lead to the same place."

"You know what?" Aris gritted her teeth, wringing her fist with the other hand. "It's easy to die. All you have to do is sit there."

Fenroe gestured at the tools and wiring scattered around her, "Does it look like I'm just sitting here?"

"Sitosen and Harris are *gone*."

"I know—"

"Then stop carrying that weight around like they're not. Nobody on this ship cares about your assumed guilt."

"Stop—"

"You might have given up, but the rest of us haven't." Aris sniffed, catching something that might have been the start of a sob, and rubbed something away from her eyes. "We're going to make it, with or without you. It's your choice."

"What do you want me to say? I can't take it back. You make decisions, and things happen. That's just the way it is."

"But you still blame yourself."

Fenroe hesitated and shook her head. "Do you mean I blame myself for us dying out here, or I blame myself for making it my responsibility?"

Aris set the soldering iron down and wrapped the blanket of mylar around her knees. "Maybe both."

"And who do *you* blame?"

She shrugged. "Blame has nothing to do with it. Like you said, you made a decision. Things happened."

"Look," Fenroe sighed, closing her eyes. "I'd like to be alone for a while—"

"Have I ever lied to you?" Aris interrupted.

Fenroe shook her head, exhausted. "No."

"Do you trust me?"

Looking at the floor, Fenroe nodded.

Aris sat forward. "Then listen, because this is important."

Fenroe met her eyes.

"We have *one* option." She held her finger up, inches away from Fenroe's face. "One."

Fenroe thought about that. "The *Endeavor*."

She nodded. "Yeah."

Fenroe blinked, letting her eyes rest for a moment, feeling the alluring pull of sleep. "Can you see it yet?"

Aris leaned back and nodded. "There's *something* out there. But I don't think it's the *Endeavor*."

Fenroe thought back to the mission briefing, and the hologram of the *Endeavor* falling into Titan. She recoiled from the thought at first, as memories of Sitosen brought fresh waves of despair to her chest. That was a line of thinking she wasn't prepared to explore. But the other memory—the image of that lost station—was massive, and much larger than the *Endeavor*.

"So, here's the deal." Aris picked up the transformer and looked at it for a moment, then tossed it back onto Fenroe's pile. "You can sit here, building your little transmitter receiver, or you can *help* us. But I'm not going to stand by while you kill yourself inside your own head like Harris did. You have to realize sooner or later that what he did is not your responsibility." She shook her head. "Hell, it's not even Dunesto's responsibility. It was Harris, and Harris alone." Aris stood and pulled the mylar around her shoulders again. "If you're going to die out here, you'll die fighting alongside the rest of us. Clear?"

Fenroe studied her eyes. An understanding passed between them. There wasn't much point in hiding things from each other anymore. Not this close to the edge. Truth was, when Fenroe thought about it, she had already come to that conclusion anyway: the default state was that they were going to die out here, regardless of how badly they tried to survive. But death comes for us all anyway, sooner or later. And if all paths led to the same place, as Aris said, there *was* no worst-case scenario: she lost nothing by simply trying to make it back home. Death was the ultimate culmination, whether they tried for the *Endeavor* or not. The risk was the same either way, but she stood to gain everything if they somehow succeeded.

"All right," Fenroe said, peeling the insulation away and laying the copper onto her growing pile. "Let's see it."

5.

"You can barely make out the strobe of floodlights on her hull." Beck pointed across the vast but closing distance, leaving the mist of his breath hanging in the cold air. He looked somehow untouched by all that had unfolded. Still youthful and exuberant—hair still chopped like a male model, eyes still gleaming with hope and optimism.

"It doesn't mean anything," Dunesto said quietly, working with Ulbricht to keep the far dot in the center of her viewer. Something had changed inside him. Some part of his heart had closed itself off since Harris killed himself, and he had withdrawn. "Doesn't mean it's alive."

"It means emergency systems are still working," Beck said back, frowning. He shrugged his shoulders. "It's a good sign."

Fenroe stood behind the cockpit, focused on the approaching light. "How far?"

"Five thousand klicks," Ulbricht said. The pilot was hanging by a thread, and it was clear she hadn't slept for a long while— probably the entire time Fenroe was off by herself. Ulbricht's normally powerful and athletically lean body appeared deflated with exhaustion and guilt. Fenroe squeezed her shoulder gently and rubbed her back for a moment, trying to massage away the self-hate Ulbricht was carrying, letting her know that it was okay. That there was still hope, and that they still had each other.

The *Crown Meridian* slowed, closing the empty space and burning precious fuel against the tail end of its own inertia. The light in the distance grew as it drifted towards them, blossoming in their viewports—it seemed to change as they drew nearer, darkening, and bending its reflected light beyond and around them. It settled in the viewer and pulled gently around the center of the docking reticle, rotating onto an equal plane like an emergent eddy in a river. Through great skill and precision, Erika tied both the *Crown Meridian* and the approaching star together with an invisible thread, which moved in front of an ocean of diamonds, infinitely distant star systems, flashing spectrums of nebulae, and obscure mists of eonian gas clouds.

"That's not the *Endeavor*," Fenroe whispered, leaning into the viewer. Their flight path flattened almost parallel with the horizon of Saturn in the distance. A dark blanket of shadow covered most of the planet in view, but majestic pale brown clouds stretching hundreds upon thousands of kilometers seemed to glow at the shadow barrier, quick sparks of friction and electricity painting a beige thinness piquing between the stretched atmospheres—the smaller and distant sun rose again over the brightest horizon, glaring across the surface of its equatorial rings in brilliant white pennants.

The star grew, becoming a massive wheel-shaped structure emerging from the cosmic darkness, now a little more than a thousand kilometers away, locked inside Ulbricht's green and blue grid of readout, which tracked its altitude and flashed measured distances across the stellographer's transparent data viewer. They could see it clearly then—a ring of pure light. And then a hollow, circular space station took form on the view screen, connected by a system of metallic braces and thick ropes of wire and elongated glass cylinders, each large enough to fit an aircraft carrier. The spires connecting the inside of the ring resembled spokes in a wheel rather than a network of halls and corridors. Inside some of these smaller structures were lambent spheres of energy enshrouding rhythmic glowing strings. Other parts of the torus branched monolithic mirrors that extended hundreds of meters across, which deflected white beams of energy onto other mirrors on the opposite side of the station, forming more spokes of light. Fenroe could also see massively torn solar collectors flashing liquid light like an ocean tide made of pure gold—thin sheets of painted photovoltaic webbing, as big and as wide as a small lake—wrapping oddly around one side of the structure.

"My god," Dunesto whispered, squinting at the far object. "Am I seeing this right?"

The object became larger as Ulbricht slowed, eventually closing enough distance for the *Crown Meridian* to drift into its shadow. Pushing away from the flight controls as the structure passed before her windshield, Ulbricht rotated her chair to face a broad view screen on her left. Close now, the approaching space station's hull became more visceral and fractal—angles and stark lines and machinery gave it depth and intentional, circular contour. Fenroe could see how the immense collectors had been ripped and torn into mile-long flaps of gossamer and insulation. Hostile looking and vast, and so close that it eclipsed the planet Saturn in the background, the space station bled flares of blue and orange glare into sheets of coronal spectra, which disappeared behind intervals of purple and red shadow, only to reappear again as they drew closer. It was of the same design and engineering as the ship in which they traveled—which meant it was of human construction—but it wasn't like anything Fenroe expected to find this far into space. Ancient starlight sparkled from between this new shadow like amethyst jewels on velvet. There was no mistaking it at that point, because the crew could clearly see the giant cylindrical lens in the exact center of the installation containing a massive plane of glass. Ulbricht brought the *Crown Meridian* alongside the immenseness of it. Clearly, this wasn't the missing *Endeavor* expedition—and as it moved closer and closer, the *Crown Meridian* became merely a dot in its shadow.

"It's the *Pinnacle Observatory*," Fenroe said.

Beck looked at her, a touch of concern in his eyes.

Dunesto leaned forward, studying the image. "That's not possible. The *Pinnacle* is hundreds of thousands of miles away..."

Fenroe stared ahead, in awe of the complete impossibility of it. The *Pinnacle* was a collection of separate modules that had been constructed and assembled in orbit around Jupiter's largest moon, Calisto: a science station and intergalactic telescope, which had absolutely no propulsion system that could bring it this far into space on its own. The fact that it was pinging back to them at the other end of a missing expedition's emergency beacon made no functional sense at all.

"It can't be the *Pinnacle*," Dunesto said again.

"Look," Aris said, enlarging and sharpening an image on the view screen. The side of the structure had become so big that it occupied the entire observational egress. Aris pulled a small column of light beside the image in a downward motion, reducing magnification. It zoomed out, and immediately began growing again as they continued their approach. The crew's total attention diverted from the egress, now focused entirely on the ghostly images inside the main view screen. Along the side of this structure, panning into the light, a black arrangement of pressed and superheated industrial paint and acrylic scrolled into view, and the designation "*IDSI PINNACLE 17NIU*" could clearly be seen.

"Check that designation," Fenroe said, staring ahead.

"Serial IDSI-17NIU," Eos responded. "Registered *International Deep Space Initiative* science observatory and galactic viewer, *Pinnacle*."

"Check again," Fenroe ordered. "The *Pinnacle* was in Jupiter's orbit when last we communicated with them, was it not?"

Eos pulsed from the walls, "Serial number matches. It is the galactic viewer, *Pinnacle*."

"If this is the same *Pinnacle* that's supposed to be in Jupiter space," Aris said, slowly pushing herself away from the nav-center, shivering under layers of clothing, trying to rub warmth back into her freezing arms. "Who were we talking to before we lost our communications?"

Fenroe looked at the floor and slowly shook her head, trying but failing to make sense of it all. "Eos, I'm aware that our communications are gone, but is there a way to...I don't know, to connect to the *Pinnacle's* network somehow?"

"I may be able to use the *Meridian's* scanners to transmit and receive a signal. But I can establish a LAN connection with my RMS from inside the structure, assuming the mainframe is still operational."

Reflected light from the *Meridian's* floodlights illuminated the *Pinnacle's* shadowed areas. Despite how impossible it was that it had come to be there, Fenroe took in with quiet awe the sight and beauty of the massive star station: humans had made this thing. Great apes from a distant rock on the other side of the solar system. Against all odds, they'd found a way to carry pressure into nothingness. She shivered again, but she wasn't entirely sure if it was because of the cold.

The crew watched as Ulbricht brought the *Meridian* to a slow halt beside the station. A broad viewport drifted into view on the *Pinnacle's* surface several kilometers above one of its docking bays—blankets of darkness covered the only visible corridor within.

"Does she have power?" Aris asked. There were perhaps indications of life inside the structure—at least one emergency light visible, but no signs whatsoever of exterior operations.

It appeared empty. Functional, but empty.

Fenroe passed her eyes over the ghostly exterior for another minute, searching for life, holding onto the hope that her crew would still make it out of this alive. "I wish we could talk to them," she whispered. "I wish there was a way."

"The important thing is that there's air." Beck tapped on the viewer, pulling out an image not far from dock. Inside an observation window, a spray of greenery could be seen crawling across the glass.

"It looks fine," Aris said, awe in her voice. "Other than those sails, there's no wear and tear on the structure at all."

"Someone explain to me how this is possible," Beck whispered, staring into the view screen. The structure was vast, easily the largest space station known to exist. "The *Pinnacle* wasn't designed to travel, correct?"

Dunesto shook his head. "It *isn't* possible."

"Check it out." Aris enlarged another image. A small part of the station rotated into view, held together by sheer luck with meters of slagged hull that had absorbed most of some kind of impact—or, more chillingly, some sort of explosion from the inside. The evidence was blackened and smeared across the *Pinnacle's* exterior.

Ulbricht took a deep breath and rubbed warmth back into her fingers. "We're still going in, right?"

Fenroe blinked, keeping her eyes on the *Pinnacle*: "I'm open to suggestions."

"Okay," Ulbricht said, nodding softly, hesitating. She took a deep, cold breath and turned back to her view screen, pulling low-orbit safety harnesses over each shoulder, strapping herself into the Command chair. She glanced tired eyes over her shoulder at the crew. "All right, shall we standby for dock?"

Fenroe nodded and pushed herself away from the view screen, taking the operator's chair next to Aris. "Eos, can you get a pressure reading of the structure?"

"It looks good," Eos responded. "The *Pinnacle* does have atmosphere."

Fenroe pulled the safety harness over her head, buckling herself in. "It's going to be the same drill as before. So let's do this by the book."

"Copy that," Ulbricht exhaled slowly through her nose again, like a sharpshooter right before pulling the trigger. She made tiny adjustments to the yoke as the *Pinnacle's* airlock fell in line between a holographic crosshair floating at eye level. Ulbricht centered her thoughts, masterfully bringing herself under control, keeping precise authority over the ship's delicate trajectory, compensating with short bursts from jet stabilizers. Fenroe admired the precision of it, as Ulbricht maneuvered the *Crown Meridian* toward the *Pinnacle*. The effort wasn't coming from having to wrestle the ship—the effort came from having to wrestle her own reflexes and impulses to keep it smooth, steady, and surgically precise. The danger was over adjusting for the wrong movement.

Fenroe brought up another angle of the station's exterior, and watched the avionics bay module in the distance—the module that would be sealing the link with the *Pinnacle's* dock umbilical—make slow, incremental movements toward the massive approaching structure. Skilled in her execution, Ulbricht turned and leveled the convex shape of the docking section under extremely meticulous mathematical statements. The action was similar to threading a needle, only the stakes were infinitely higher—one miscalculated move could trigger a series of cataclysmic events that would collapse both structures into a nuclear event horizon.

Suddenly, a bright red light flashed from below, illuminating the underside of Dunesto's face.

"CMD control is locked," Dunesto called. "I'm getting drift alarms from our thrusters."

"Which one?" Ulbricht hissed.

"All of them—I don't know, telemetry's all messed up." Dunesto unstrapped himself and reached up, grabbing a support beam above him, pulling himself away from the flight controls.

"Can we abort?" Beck asked.

"Warning," Eos interjected. "Advise increasing altitude to safe orbit. Strongly advise synchronizing to *Pinnacle* Station orbit. Danger, counter synchronous orbit drift *YO 9987 PS. 89 R205.003*—"

Ulbricht couldn't spare any of her attention, her eyes frozen wide as beadlets of ice cold sweat formed above her lip: "No abort. If we burn thrusters this close, we'll puncture a hole into the *Pinnacle*. Docking is our only chance—"

"I'm on it," Dunesto slapped Suja on the chest, motioning for him to follow. The other man immediately unbuckled himself and stood, and they both disappeared down the main corridor at a run. Fenroe unstrapped herself from Operations and took the pilot's seat next to Ulbricht, resuming orbital keeping.

"Prepare for insertion." Ulbricht took the entire yoke in her grip, her left hand moving rapidly but controlled through a holographic interface, adjusting and manipulating thrust with immeasurable accuracy. "Prepare to capture the hatch on my mark—"

Without warning, the *Pinnacle* dock suddenly pulled hard to the upper right quadrant of Ulbricht's reticle. Her eyes went wide and her face fell—she gasped, wrestling the yoke—emergency systems dropped the flight deck under a blanket of red, and proximity warnings came to life.

"I have gimbal lock," Ulbricht hissed into comms. "Dunesto, you have to hurry."

Reacting quickly, Fenroe reached overhead and pulled a paddled lever out of the ceiling and flipped three toggle switches, preparing for emergency separation as Ulbricht guided the needle back on track, pulling with great effort to keep the *Crown Meridian* from colliding with the *Pinnacle*. The ship tilted slightly off axis—a deadly small movement—and Ulbricht pulled the yoke, fighting to keep the docking module centered. The *Pinnacle's* hull outside flared to life with more emergency lighting as the crew slammed violently into their restraints by heavy gee's. The ship buckled horribly under Fenroe's thighs and then spun wildly, driving her hard forward, and then up, and then to the right. She blacked out for a moment, sight and sound falling away under the extreme torque until reality gradually seeped back into focus. She opened her eyes, groping for Ulbricht to see if she was still conscious—and she was, lips peeled back exposing fierce teeth while fighting the stick, her limbs trembling, muscles bulging out of her neck. The ship started to tip sideways, tumbling into a barrel roll on collision course with the *Pinnacle*. From there, things quickly unraveled.

"Brace for impact," Fenroe called. "Two hundred meters!"

For a few eternal seconds the only reaction was silence and flashing red and yellow lights, then Ulbricht's tight voice emerged from the center of it—somehow, while her body locked itself into the fight of its life, her voice stayed calm, steady and focused. "Prepare for starboard burn—on my mark."

The ship suddenly pitched again and the emergency klaxons

cut away, fading like an echo. Fenroe reached out to steady her self: "We can't do a burn this close—"

"No choice, on my mark," Ulbricht hissed. "Stand by for burn."

Fenroe blinked through trembling shock and terror, held together solely by Ulbricht's insane resolution on the brink of certain death. They would either collide with the *Pinnacle*, or burn thrusters and save the *Meridian*, which came with the risk of punching a hole into the *Pinnacle's* hull and possibly destroying their only chance of making it home. Fenroe reached for the flight controls and opened the starboard emergency stabilizer switch: "One-eighty meters, we're too fast—"

"I know—"

"One-fifty meters."

"Standby—"

"One-forty. Thirty. Twenty—brace for impact—!"

The engine-side of the ship followed its own momentum, but Ulbricht ripped and fought and pulled to keep the two structures aligned—as the station started leveling out, miraculously, somehow still tumbling and twisting on its roll-axis, but it was slowing, easing into position, Ulbricht pulled hard on the yoke and screamed, "Now!"

Fenroe's hands pulled toward the ceiling with centrifugal force. She powered through the resistance and slammed the palm of her hand onto the omni-directional masers, bringing the starboard thrusters to blazing life. She gripped her safety harness as Eos reported that the outer airlock door had been blown away. Near the back of the structure somewhere, either outside the *Pinnacle* ripping itself to pieces or inside the *Crown Meridian*, something detonated and dropped Fenroe and Ulbricht violently against their safety harnesses. The entire viewport became engulfed in white flame—the docking needle snapped into position, plunging downward into blazing planet-ending heat that blasted into the *Pinnacle* against the emergency thrust. In a moment of blinding light and chaos, Fenroe found the strength to flatten the panel above her head—she reached forward, striking the hatch-capture, and with a shuddering drag, the *Meridian's* airlock met the *Pinnacle's* umbilical and slammed into dock. There came the two-note chime of a successful link, followed immediately by alloys grinding together, and then a crushing impact. Everything rumbled to a stop and stilled. They all breathed in stunned silence for a few moments, listening to the cabin hum of the *Meridian's* artificial atmosphere.

"Holy *shit*," Fenroe said, staring at Ulbricht, whose whole body was covered in sweat.

"Piece of cake," Ulbricht muttered, peeling her fingers away from the yoke and slumping into her chair, taking deep, triumphant breaths of relief.

6.

They all cycled through the airlock, and Fenroe switched on her helmet cam. As Beck and Aris stepped into the umbilical, Fenroe approached the RMS charging crèche—opening the compartment panel, she found Eos's vehicle seated in a fetal position. Powered down, the small android curled into a tight ball, gripping its knees. Fenroe pulled her out of the crèche and opened a cover on her right shoulder, checking the battery connections. Certain that everything was operational, she removed a cable that secured the RMS to the wall and then turned it around, opening a membrane between its shoulder blades, where she dug for a switch and then activated it. Sounds of synth booted up from the base of Eos's throat, and soft blue lights poured out of her chest into grooves along her limbs, traveling down her arms, up through the shoulders along both sides of her neck, until they met at the peak of her visor—she flickered to life with soft whirring hums and unfolded herself into a standing position. Fenroe gave her space.

"Commander," the android greeted Fenroe, stepping out of the crèche and rotating her visor around the airlock. Eos immediately crossed to a panel beside the inner hatch and delicately opened a console, inserting her diagnostic spike into the *Pinnacle's* umbilical network bus. A soft flicker of light moved over the surface of her visor: "Network is still offline."

Fenroe turned and moved into the darkened, half-lit docking umbilical. The others followed in single file, each carrying a flashlight that illuminated the corridor with intersecting bands of clear white light shining through motes of dust that brushed the air around them. Ulbricht and Suja remained aboard the *Endeavor*, monitoring the crew from the Control Room—from the small image in Fenroe's HUD, Ulbricht could be seen seated with her legs crossed at the view screen near the stellographer, blanket draped over her shoulders, her entire body hunched around a cup of coffee that steamed into the frigid ship air. Suja sprawled out on the conference table, holding a blanket tightly around his body with one fist, securing a Pico into his ear.

"How you doing over there, Suja?"

"*Nose and cheeks killing me,*" he whispered without opening his eyes, half-asleep. "*The pressure of vacuum...or something...hurts, but I'll be okay.*"

Light from the docking umbilical behind them shone upon two wide bridges that stretched parallel to each other in the warehouse-sized room. The two catwalks were separated by a single-vessel-deep, seventeen-vessel-long shipment and receiving area. They all moved across the two-story height, marveling at the size of the place. Signs of disorder were evident: boxes of paperwork had been hurriedly strewn across the bridge and spilled over the side onto the level below.

There was a damaged data terminal nearby. Aris knelt and studied what remained of it: the glass display had been smashed to pieces. Wiring had been ripped into four separate brushes of fibrous copper and rubber insulation—not cut, but torn—ripped apart by what could have been some kind of serrated edge, almost as if an animal had chewed through it all. Deep gouges sunk into it, as if someone had spent the time digging into the console with a crowbar. Aris touched the claw marks and met Fenroe's eyes, demonstrating how each mark appeared to be no wider than a human finger.

The interchange of their flashlights exposed the immense area in ghostly segments, revealing a spray of blood near a pressure door on the opposite side of the room—piles of scrap metal had been wedged underneath the airlock, propping it open, revealing only darkness beyond.

Fenroe whispered, "Ulbricht, you seeing this?"

"Negative...it's not very clear."

"There's blood here."

"Repeat that?" she transmitted. *"Everything's too dark. I can't see anything."*

"It's old," Dunesto's quiet voice echoed around the space. He bent to examine it.

"Say again?"

"The blood—" he angled his light, nodding to where the trail stretched off into the distance, "it's dark brown, almost black. It's been here a long time..."

They were silent for a moment, each wrestling with internal shadows that filled the hallways ahead. Dunesto stood and found another computer terminal not far from the damaged one. He punched in a few keys, but nothing happened. "Power is gone."

"There's nobody here," Beck said, his light bending against

the far separated walls and the high warehouse ceiling. Smears of black crimson streaked in all directions, dragging fingerprints across the left side of an open pressure door at the end of the catwalk on which they stood, and there was a small amount of splatter on the ground leading away into the darkness ahead. It looked as if someone had braced themselves against the bulkhead for a moment, before making their way inside. Fenroe stood very still and stared ahead, her heart hammering inside of her chest.

When she stepped forward, a bank of wall-screens suddenly flared to life above the doorway in a flurry of light and sound. She flinched reflexively, feeling the sudden pulse of adrenaline shooting up the side of her neck and temples.

The crew let go a collective breath, sending worried glances into the surrounding shadows. If there were any concerns about not leaving a footprint, or not startling any deranged survivors who happened to be stalking the dark corridors beyond, they were now very real.

A man's voice not unlike Eos's filled the entire module: "WELCOME NEW IDSI EMPLOYEES, TO THE PINNACLE OBSERVATORY." The recording broke against the lonely walls, too loud and too sudden after the stark contrast of silence: "THE PINNACLE WAS THE FIRST OF THE THIRD GENERATION GALAXY VIEWERS, AND IS NOW THE OLDEST IN DEPLOYMENT, WITH THIRTY-TWO YEARS OF SERVICE." And he went on, flashing ghostly vestiges of flickering blue light around the docking bay, cycling through a slideshow of stock images intended to summarize the station's history.

They moved ahead, carefully picking their way over scraps of metal and rubbish, ducking under the pressure door, sliding into the shadows of the next module. As they entered the small room, the recording behind them merged with its own echo and quieted, speaking in distant tongues on the other side of the half-open airlock. The light from the media screen still bled unevenly into the next room, throwing and bending jagged shapes and silhouettes.

Fenroe stood still, waiting for her eyes to adjust to the darkness. A stack of carbon fiber supply crates took up space along the right wall, organized into uneven columns atop a long, synth-leather booth—another pressure door lay ahead, with a control interface ornamented midline between the floor and ceiling with a dim plane of light about a half-foot in area—a floating sheet of light and text flickered in and out of existence, indicating that the pressure door was locked. Dunesto's compact shadow moved forward, surveying the strange disorder of everything in the half-darkness—more paper and smashed supply crates lay in the far corner—anything useful inside apparently salvaged long ago. He cautiously approached the airlock and opened it manually—the hydraulics hummed with age, pulling the thick panel of steel into the ceiling with great effort, disturbing a mixture of ice crystals and dust that had collected around the inset frame—and aimed his light into the darkened corridor beyond.

The derelict station invited the first human presence it had seen in what seemed to have been a very long time. Dust swirled in the light, stirred by the presence of life and the passage of stale air. Other than Fenroe and her crew, the ship was empty. Lifeless. Cold.

"I don't like this," Dunesto said, raking his light around the hallway.

Fenroe nodded her head, looking up into the exposed ductwork. She breathed, returning her light toward the forward airlock. "Just keep your eyes peeled."

Dunesto opened the opposite pressure door and they all stepped into the next room, immediately walking into two rows of eight industrial chairs situated in the center, similar to the setup at a bus station or the boarding gate of an airport. Tossed onto a pile near an elevator on the opposite side of the module were several duffel bags of varying sizes. Fenroe shifted her light, searching for any indication of recent life.

"What *happened* here?" Aris asked, her voice traveling slow through the quiet air, addressing no one in particular. She shoved a spill of ancient clothing aside with her boot. "Where's the crew?"

Fenroe knew Aris had asked two questions: one spoken aloud, and one that was not. None of them had misplaced hopes of finding survivors aboard the *Pinnacle* after seeing the state of things. Aris asked it, but each of them wondered about the unspoken half of that question, reading the signs of the long-dormant shadows and dust and darkness...the real question was, *where are the bodies?*

Dunesto approached another airlock on the other side of the room and tried opening it manually like he had the others, but it wouldn't budge.

"Damn," he said under his breath, dropping his hand. He traced the outline of the door with his eyes, and then closed them, sighing deeply. "Something's tripped quarantine."

The crew exchanged looks, shifting on their feet.

"What's that mean?" Aris asked.

He shrugged: "Emergency power only. A lot of locked doors. A lot of inaccessible modules."

Fenroe looked at the floor, taking it in. "What about the Control Room?"

He turned, dropping himself heavily into one of the seats, looking ironically, achingly, very much like Sitosen. He lifted and dropped his shoulders: "I don't know."

"Quarantine," Fenroe said to herself, looking at the locked

doorway. "Was it a hazmat leak?"

"Unknown," he said, closing his dark eyes and sighing out a large breath of exhaustion.

Fenroe approached the door, which had a tetragonal viewport at eye level and a large red cross in the center. It was different from the other airlocks—more reinforced, thicker—and there was another door just beyond it.

"This can't be opened manually," she said. It wasn't a question.

"Blast shield dropped into place after the station lost main power. There are no emergency overrides."

"Two thirds of the station is just beyond the infirmary, Commander." Eos pulsed suddenly, startling them. They all turned to look at the soft blue aura around her small body. "We can't reach the Control Room without accessing this module."

Fenroe turned back toward the door and brushed her hand over a Caduceus symbol in the center of the cross, tracing the entwined serpents with her fingers.

"We have to reroute it somehow," Aris finally said, breaking the silence.

Fenroe's light hovered over a brown teddy bear covered in dust, propped up against a tattered duffel bag. There were no children aboard, which made the toy's presence even more heartbreaking: somebody brought it as a reminder of home, of a child back on Earth.

She thought of Harris.

"We're going to have to split up," Fenroe said.

"Are you shitting me?" Beck snorted, shaking his head. "Screw that."

"There's nobody alive out here—" she sighed, pulling another light from her utility harness and fastening it to her shoulder, "—this place is a tomb."

"You don't know that."

Ignoring him, she tilted her head toward Dunesto: "One of us is going to have to go to the data room, see if we can get this network up."

"I can do that," Dunesto nodded, leaning deeper into his chair.

"All right." She reached into the pack on her hip and pulled out the AM/FM transmitter receiver she'd put together in the Lander module with salvaged rover guts and tossed it to Aris, who snatched it out of the air and turned it over in her hand, clenching her jaw.

Aris sighed and rolled the transceiver in her gloved fingers. "What do you want me to do with this, toss it in the garbage?"

"You want to make for the communications array?"

"Yeah," she sighed, tilting her helmeted head to one side, stretching the tension out of her neck. "I'll head that way."

"Ulbricht, you copy?"

"*Go ahead*," she responded.

"Aris is going to need a parts list if we can't get these communications up. If we have to, we'll rip apart and repurpose the least damaged array to see if we can't re-rig it with pieces salvaged from the other."

"*Copy that*," Ulbricht transmitted. "*I'll get on it.*"

"Beck—"

"I'm telling you, Fenroe, we don't want to go stumbling around in the dark. What if we surprise some crewmate who's been stranded out here for god knows how long?" He looked back and forth between the crew, as if he shouldn't have to be explaining it. "Christ, where do you think all that blood came from?"

"Beck," she repeated, cutting him off. "Are you going to head for the O-two gardens, or go wait back on the *Meridian*? Because we're running out of air and time. We need this station operational *right now*." She waited, knowing that he wouldn't answer, and when he didn't, she met each crewmember's gaze with severity. "I want you all talking, and I want you combing the ship as you go. Check offices, sleeping quarters, the mess, the garden... everything."

Dunesto fastened his own shoulder light and switched it on, angling it toward the floor so he wouldn't blind everyone. "What about you?"

Fenroe opened her mouth to answer, but stopped. A shadow moved in one of the adjacent corridors. She tried not to over expose that she had noticed, but as her shoulder light passed the open door, light shined back from what looked like a pair of cat eyes. She recomposed herself immediately and cleared her throat, resisting the urge to study the shadow directly. Her voice dropped to a whisper: "I'll make my way to engineering. We'll need auxiliary power to open these doors." And then, as though it was an afterthought: "Nobody freak out, but there's someone in that corridor."

Aris frowned and lowered her head to the ground; Beck uncrossed his arms and dropped them slowly to his sides, and Dunesto turned to stone in his seat.

"Right over Beck's left shoulder," she whispered, turning to the side, making as if she hadn't noticed, not wanting to scare them away.

Dunesto snorted and raised his eyebrows: "Serious?"

She nodded slightly, pulling the gauntlet tight against her wrist. Dunesto leaned back and looked—

Something sounding exactly like cables of rebar clattered loudly onto the floor.

Spinning her lights toward the sound, Fenroe instinctively took a step back—not far from their position, a shadow dropped to the ground and quickly pulled away around a corner.

"Wait." Fenroe scrambled after it. Shocked, Dunesto stood fast and faced the corridor—all eyes snapped toward the sound.

"Wait!" Fenroe yelled again.

She ran after the retreating shadow, swinging her lights through the darkness, hearing the slide of something moving quickly away from her. Dropping to her knees on the run, Fenroe slid to a corner that cut to the right. Above her, glowing windows in the ceiling showed only the darkness of space, but the entire structure was still rotating, creating gravity—an edge of Saturn's equatorial ring emerged for a short second, drifting across a line of observational portals above her in pale beige light painting the hallway, and briefly exposed the frantically moving and unquestionably alive shadow jerking violently into another doorway at the end of the corridor.

A voice broke into her comms: *"Fenroe, stop!"*

Beams of light pursued her into the darkness.

"Wait!" Fenroe screamed again at the shadow. Moving back to her feet—her light illuminated a splash of blood on both walls that met at the corner to her right, streaking up the bulkhead to what clearly was a human handprint. A handprint made in a smear of newer blood. Thinner blood. She looked off in the direction the shadow had fled, and moved her lights along the floor—fresh drops of crimson led away from the corner in a tight grouping, but the space between splatter marks grew wider as the blood trail stretched off toward another open corridor.

"There's someone here," Fenroe said. "Someone's hurt, bleeding—"

"Fenroe!" Aris screamed. "Don't move!"

The mellow blue light of Eos's visor stopped in midstride. Dunesto slid to his knees, crashing into Fenroe, violently grabbing her around the waist and bringing her to the ground.

She shoved herself out of his hands: "You saw it?"

"We didn't see anything," he hissed. "There's nothing here!"

"Ulbricht, you copy? You see that?"

"Negative, what's going on—somebody talk to me—"

"There's someone here, I saw him—"

"I can't read that, you gotta speak slower—"

"Sitosen!" She screamed into the shadows, trying to pull herself free from Dunesto's grip, "Sitosen, it's us!" Her vision swam with tears. A weight pressed down on her breasts, constricting the air out of her lungs, shooting needles of pain to all the places in her body connected to the heart. "Come back!"

"Nobody's there." Dunesto tried shaking sense back into her, talking softly. *"Look,* Fenroe—"

She reached her hand toward the shadows, feeling the sting of tears in her eyes. She wanted to curl up into a ball and weep for days. She looked sidelong at Dunesto through brimming eyes, studying him as he frantically scanned the darkness ahead, knowing in her heart that he would disappear too. They were all going to disappear. And there was nothing she could do to stop it.

Her breath misted away from the inside of her faceplate, cleared by the counter-current loop in her helmet, which cooled and heated her outgoing gasses just enough to keep the glass from fogging up. She allowed herself to blink again, slowing her breath, imposing her will upon the moment.

They all waited, listening to the air, but there was only silence—searching the dark corridor, Fenroe hoped beyond all hope that she'd see Sitosen step into the light.

But nothing moved. No ghostly apparitions, no emaciated or malnourished survivor flinching away from the beam of her flashlight...someone behind her angled their lights down the corridor, breathing heavily.

"Nothing," Aris said seriously, eyes wide, mouth open and

sucking air from her brief run. She looked prepared to flee the opposite direction if she had to. "There's nothing here, guys, what are we doing?"

"I saw him," Fenroe whispered, staring ahead into the darkness. "I saw him."

Dunesto loosened his grip, moving to his knees, throwing his light down the corridor as well, trying to locate whatever Fenroe thought she saw. The blood of embarrassment rushed to her face. Dunesto made it back to his feet, staring ahead into the empty passage with his hands up, as if he were preparing to catch her again if she bolted.

"Jesus Christ," he rasped. "What the hell, Fenroe...?"

"He's here," she said. "He has to be."

"*Who's* here?" Dunesto hissed, grabbing her shoulders—he forced Fenroe to her feet, making her look into his eyes—her body and shoulders turned, but her head remained trained in the direction she swore the shadow had disappeared.

"Fenroe... Sitosen and Harris are *gone*," he said. "They're not coming back—"

"Stop," she said, trying to push herself away, but he wouldn't budge.

"Fuck, man—" he said through his teeth, slicing the air with his voice, "—we need you to keep it together. Sitosen and Harris—" his voice cracked for a moment, and he caught the hitch in his throat before it became something else, "—Sitosen and Harris are *dead*." He tilted his head back at Aris, Beck and Eos. "But we're all still here, and we need you right now, Fenroe... we *need* you..."

He bent his head and followed her eyes. "Okay? Help us think our way through this," he said, echoing her last words to Harris before he opened himself into space. "Please, Fenroe, don't lose it in here, okay? Please...?"

And that brought her back. She tore her eyes away from Sitosen's ghost. Seeing the fear in Dunesto's eyes, she nodded softly, and paced her breath.

"All right," she said. "I'm okay."

"They're gone," he repeated more quietly, releasing her arms. "There's nothing we can do." He grabbed her hand in his and squeezed.

"All right," she said again, closing her eyes. She leaned into his arms and refocused. "I'm okay."

"Screw this," Beck cut in, shining his light on the bloody handprint on the wall, shifting uneasily on his feet. "I'm not going anywhere in this station alone."

More sweat wicked away from Fenroe's eyes by the internal pressure as she slowly recomposed herself.

"We stick to the plan," Dunesto said, staring at Fenroe as she traced a whip of blood that led into the darkness. "But we go in pairs. Beck with Aris. Fenroe's with me."

He stepped tentatively away from Fenroe, pulling another light from his harness and fastening it onto the empty shoulder of his suit, angling his beam the opposite direction. "Eos, you head to the mainframe and wait for our signal," he continued. "And then get these computers up and running."

"Copy," the android replied.

"Are you okay?" Dunesto asked Fenroe, sounding like a child who had seen his Mom break down for the first time.

Fenroe regarded her crew for a moment. Instead of speaking, she nodded and looked at her gloved fists, flexing and opening them, willing control. Without checking to see if they would go their own way, she turned and moved ahead into the bowels of the ship. There was some hesitant shuffling, and then several beams of light disappeared behind her. One light remained shining ahead as she began picking over what remained of the demolished, fire-blackened corridor, and then Dunesto was next to her, matching her stride.

7.

Fenroe edged toward the endless shadow, blading the corners with her lights, following the blood on the floor and picking her path carefully over scattered pieces of burned out office equipment. The administrative complex they entered was, like the rest of the facility, completely without power. The only light in the darkness came from what they brought in with them. And there they found more disorder, worse than the places Fenroe had seen so far. The blood trail disappeared near a barricade that blocked access into the next hallway—a hurriedly constructed pile of desks, office chairs, I-beam tetrahedrons, aluminum and steel plates of scrap, ripped conduit and ducting from overhead, and mounds of demolished lab equipment. Kneeling to inspect where the blood dripped over the piled-up metal, Fenroe stopped, catching the glint of uneven lines in her light. Some of the larger pieces of scrap in the pile had been forced away from a spread of deeply set gouges, which scarred all the way through the grated flooring in several different spots. She brushed the slashed and twisted markings with her gloved fingers, tracing her hands over metal that had been torn apart by horrifically strong influences, as if it had been no more durable than wet cardboard. The markings looked very similar to what Aris found near the computer terminal in the shipment module. Returning to her feet, Fenroe stepped over and then under the barricade.

"Man," Dunesto tisked, shining his light. "Look at these markings."

"I saw."

He shook his head and ran an index finger through one of the grooves in the floor. "It looks...*melted*."

When Fenroe reached the other side and entered another hallway that led into a larger open area, she encountered what could have only been described as some kind of last stand. More science instruments had been piled up to form another barricade that would have blocked the next airlock. More scrap and random objects, messily welded together. But the barricade itself had either been torn down by something, or it had collapsed over time under its own weight. Every intention was there to block her path, but nothing succeeded. Everything had been somehow melted down into a mound of amorphous junk.

"More blood," Fenroe announced. The spatter led up the bulkhead to a whip of arterial spray on the ceiling. She knelt and carefully scanned the room, looking for bodies. Anything. "Some kind of fight," she whispered, pointing at obvious signs of struggle—blood stains on the inside of the barricade, scorched medical and scientific equipment, more blood. She couldn't piece it together, and she wondered, given the evidence of how much extended time in space affected the members of her own crew, if the people aboard the *Pinnacle* hadn't lost their minds and attacked each other. She sucked air against her teeth. "What happened out here...?"

"Maybe they went all *Lord of the Flies*," Dunesto whispered back, shining his light slowly across the debris. "I mean, maybe...maybe the isolation got to 'em."

"They've been here a long time," agreed Fenroe. Her blue-white lights moved up from the blood, and she followed the smears as they disappeared into the next doorway, and stopped.

Her service light revealed a bank of scanning microscopes along the far wall. She eased forward, edging into the dark, her pulse thumping along the sides of her neck. Passing the equipment, she entered the next room, holding her breath, half expecting to find an injured survivor of the *Pinnacle* crew cowering away from the cone of her light.

What she found instead was a viewing room of some kind. Smears of dried blood adorned the walls, spattering in tallow thin memories on the floor, ending at the reaching shapes of what looked like a thicket of severed limbs.

Fenroe stood and studied the old, blackened bloodstains on the floor.

"Attention, everybody," she announced over comms. "I have something—" she stopped, slowly panning her light over the macabre scene, imagining the smell of decay and musk on the opposite side of her visor, "—we, uh...Dunesto and I found something."

She raised her light to illuminate the rest of the area, and exposed a breathtaking sight. Beyond the room in which they stood was an observational window looking out into space, and she could see the immense galactic telescope floating within fluctuating polarities in the center of the *Pinnacle Space Station*—looming overhead in the distance, the planet Saturn moved majestically with the slow grace of certain death, distorting everything inside the room with celestial shadow, giving what lay within the appearance of life.

In the cupola, smothered in the midst of falling dust particles, Fenroe and Dunesto found a pile of decayed human bodies. Some were reaching out, blocking themselves defensively; some were curled up in a fetal position like fire victims, and some were lying on the ground, as if they had made a last-ditch effort to crawl under the bodies of fallen comrades to get away from something. They had all become gray dehydrated husks, like an arrangement of granite statues. Buckets of old, dry black blood spread out below them, covering the floor of the entire area.

"God," Dunesto said, ready to be sick.

Nine bodies.

No more, no less.

They were remarkably intact, with trace evidence of decomposition, sucked dry by the effects of still, frigid air and pressure. When Fenroe moved closer to the bodies, they looked fresh, preserved by the deep cold. Their long-dead eyes remained open, flash-frigid and solid gray like lake water welled deep in the sharp outlines of their skulls, and Fenroe knelt, searching their frozen gaze as if she could find an answer inside. But there wasn't an answer, and she reached down and caressed the nametag on one of their flight suits. "You copy, Eos?"

"Yes, Commander—"

Ulbricht interrupted, her voice filling Fenroe's helmet, *"I'm not getting a real clear image here, Fenroe. What ah...what is that...?"*

"Bodies," she said simply, bending to her knees. "Nine of them. I think we found the *Endeavor* crew."

Moments of silence over comlink, and then Aris said: *"Is that confirmed? We know that it isn't anyone from the Pinnacle staff?"*

She reached for the name patches sewn onto their torn and ragged flight suits, checking them one at a time, and said, "Eos, play back the audio file Aris and I intercepted the other night."

Ghostly voices filled the atmosphere, leaving each syllable hanging in the air as billions of separate pieces of data waited to be restored again in the mandibular stimulators of their helmets:

"Nice try Jensen..."
Static, rustling.
"Tell them we're goners..."
Laughter, a man's voice.
"We had to shut down the centrifugal relay mid deceleration.

The solar arrays were shaking badly, and we couldn't risk it—one of the converters sustained slight damage, but nothing significant..."
Transmission break, static.

Dunesto knelt beside Fenroe, brushing his fingers over the names as Eos played through the message. The *Endeavor* crewman named *Jensen* was sprawled backwards over another body that had tufts of long blond hair sticking out of its skull. His neck was exposed, and his hands reached back toward the window as if he were pointing at something through the glass. Fenroe followed his clawed fingers and looked up just as the planet Saturn moved slowly into view, wreathed in the blinking glare of the beacon lights flashing on the outside.

Static, transmission break, intelligible, a man's voice—
"Pinnacle, we had to drop down to three and a half thousand klicks this morning. Specialist Pasco barely detected a comet that came out of nowhere—"

Dunesto shifted to the other knee and angled his light across the display of bodies, hunting for the familiar shape of letters and the raised embroidery of their nametags. His light fell on someone that had been twisted, half covered by the limbs of his fellow crewmates. He reached and ran his gloved hand over the patch.

"Pasco," he whispered aloud, turning the patch into the light so that Fenroe could see it.

Transmission break, laughter, static, a sudden shrill break and what sounded like nine voices screaming at once, transmission break and static, a man's voice—
"I have to say, Pinnacle—"

The sound of breathing, more static.
"It was the most beautiful thing I'd ever seen."

"End playback," Fenroe said, releasing the nametag. "It's them. They're all here."

She heard Ulbricht whisper something to herself over comms, but that was the crew's only response. Fenroe leaned on one knee with her elbow as a quiet sadness fell over the scene. She glassed their milky, frozen eyes with her light as floating dust particles circled themselves in and out of existence, and she couldn't help but see the fate of her own crew reflecting back at her. She saw Sitosen staring through the rictal scream of Jensen's hollowed face, begging her with his eyes. She saw Harris locked in the torment of his quiet insanity, clawing through the air toward the bay window with Specialist Pasco's hands. And somewhere, her corpse was in there too, under the dead remains hiding from the light, buried in the last cold embrace of the only family she had left. And there was a blessing in that, she thought: At least the *Endeavor* crew died together...

Beck's sad voice finally cut in, breaking the moment with a sigh: "*Copy, Fenroe.*"

She spared a glance at his image in her HUD, and saw his point of view: he was leaning against something, staring down at his own gloved hands. She wondered if he was thinking of the dream he told her about back in her bunk. She wondered if, like Fenroe, he saw the promise of his certain future piled atop itself in a tangled, bloodless mess at his feet.

Dunesto shifted back to his haunches, the blue-white aura of his visor joining hers in the dim, ceremonial light cast into the room by Saturn, contrast and stark against the colorless skin of the surrounding bodies. "Almost looks like they were trying to get away from something..."

Fenroe glanced up and watched as Saturn cleared the inside of the *Pinnacle's* ring and became eclipsed. She shook her head and shrugged: "No signs of ebullism. Little decomposition. No blood coming from the eyes or ears, no secretions around the nostrils or mouth. So we know it wasn't a gas leak. And look—" she angled her light down, showing an uneven hole torn into one of the bodies. Dunesto shook his head and averted his gaze, moving back to his feet, but not before observing that each crewman had similar holes torn through their flight suits and into their stomachs, similar wounds under their arms, and on the insides of their thighs. Fenroe moved her light from body to body.

"You think they did this to each other?" he asked.

"I don't know," Fenroe said, briefly touching the gaping wound of one of the closest corpses, and then pulling her fingers back, studying the black dust of old blood left on her glove. "Whatever happened here got way beyond words."

He spared a last glance at the bodies and then turned away again. "I've seen enough here."

Fenroe studied them for a few more seconds and then nodded, moving back to her feet.

"Come on," she said, returning to the moment, regaining focus. "Let's go turn the power back on."

"What about them?" asked Dunesto, nodding toward the bodies.

"Leave 'em," she said, aiming her light away from the *Endeavor* crew, pointing it back down the corridor from which they had come. "They're not going anywhere."

And when she crossed back into the main hall, she was sure that one of the corpses had twisted its head to watch her leave. Like the ghost of Sitosen in the Infirmary hallway a few hours ago, it must have been a trick of light and shadow.

It must have been.

8.

Fenroe and Dunesto continued their search through the dead space station. From a level above them occasional openings of glass had given a clear view of the *Pinnacle's* interior side of the ring and the enormous telescope in the center of it, sprouting cables of hallways and corridors connecting at various points to the larger station. Fenroe could see the slow transit of the *Pinnacle's* rotation, and the moons of Saturn—and the giant planet itself—appeared occasionally at different times, moving delicately across the glass above her—their muted lights painting the ruined corridor and all of the dead chaos around them: the destroyed equipment, the dead plants, the shattered bits of glass, the scattered office supplies and reams of unused paper—and finally exposing the many constellations of ash and dust before disappearing from view again. As they picked their way carefully over it all, the world maintained shape in their flashlights.

Dunesto's voice broke softly into the cold air: "The *Endeavor* changed course and headed here..."

Fenroe considered that and nodded. "They could have picked up the *Pinnacle's* beacon."

"Or the *Pinnacle* could have hailed them directly for assistance," Dunesto shrugged.

"Or the *Endeavor* could have come *here* for assistance," Fenroe countered.

"It's a shit show any way you look at it," Dunesto said, panning his light ahead, stopping to study their route through the corridor beyond. "Their ship should still be docked at one of the umbilicals, right?"

Fenroe looked at him and shrugged. "That'd be my guess."

He shoved a tipped over office chair aside with his foot. "Do you remember how many umbilcals the *Pinnacle* has?"

"Three umbilicals total, and two shipment and receiving docks." She stopped to strategize her next move through the blackness. "Whatever vessel they used to get aboard should still be here somewhere."

"Maybe," Dunesto said. "Maybe not. The *Pinnacle* maintains a constant crew of three hundred people, right? All coming and going several times a year..."

"So where are they," Fenroe said, answering Dunesto's unasked question. "We should have come across someone by now."

"There's still two thirds of the station we haven't seen yet. Two thirds still under lockdown."

"True..."

"Or—" he said, tilting his head to the side, "—the *Endeavor was* docked here, and the *Pinnacle* survivors took it and escaped."

"Three hundred people packed into the *Endeavor*? That's a tight fit."

"What would *you* do? Stay here and die, or take your chances packed into a life raft?"

She nodded. "I'd take my chances on the raft."

"Yeah," Dunesto nodded back, trailing off. He stopped and studied the path ahead.

"We would have heard from them by now," Fenroe said, shaking her head. "We would have picked up their signal on our way out here."

"Comms could be down," Dunesto replied. "They could be floating around out there, waiting for somebody to come find them—" he passed his hand over the destruction spread out all around them, stretching off into the blackness ahead, "—or they're probably dead, Fenroe. I mean, look at this...something *bad* happened out here. Something...something pretty fucking terrible."

Through another pressure door, the corridor opened to a clearing that at first felt like they'd stepped into a part of the station exposed to vacuum. But it was simply enormous, the other side far away enough to remain hidden in shadow. They looked up, stretching their necks back, and traced the arc to the ceiling of an immense domed edifice.

"This is it," Dunesto said, eyes trained on something massive straight ahead. Saturn finished its pass above the corridor behind them and the soft beige light shone for a moment, dragging shadows across the grated flooring before leaving them in darkness. They stepped into the rotunda, first onto a catwalk that circled a vast emptiness that dropped out of sight below, as the echoes of their boots rung in muted, solid insistence. The space was large enough that their light beams couldn't be seen on the other end—they simply coned off into deep nothingness like searchlights at night. Walking along the catwalk, they looked in quiet awe to the center of the room, where an enormous dual-core nuclear reactor rose out of the emptiness below like several upright storage containers held together by braided steel cables as thick around as sycamore, consisting of three immense alternators reaching up out of a large box the size of a small building, which Fenroe believed was the reactor's massive turbine tank—all surrounded by the circular shaped catwalk on which they currently stood. The alternators were dormant—had been dormant for a very long time—detached from the magnet assembly that made them rotate and generate the station's power. As they walked through the half-lit milieu, taking in the solemnness of a thing that should have been alive and blasting with steam, water, heat and energy, an orbed structure took shape in the darkness around the bend. Fenroe could see that it was a control room of some kind overlooking the reactor. Dunesto recognized it, and moved forward with something like relief in his eyes.

"Here we go," he said. "Cross your fingers."

"Ulbricht, you copy?" Fenroe transmitted.

"Go ahead."

"We found the reactor."

"I see it," Ulbricht responded. *"How's it looking?"*

Dunesto's light disappeared behind the corner and bent around the other side, bringing a flurry of shadows to life near the colossal power generator. Fenroe leaned over the guardrail, trying to see if she could find any evidence of damage. "Stand by."

"Fenroe," Dunesto cut in quietly over comms. And then softer, almost sadly. *"I found something."*

She looked up from the emptiness as his light disappeared into the giant spherical building. Fenroe turned back and studied the reactor for another moment and then pushed away from the guardrail, following Dunesto's shadow into the control room.

Rounding the corner, she found Dunesto pointing his light at the floor. It was a circular room with control stations equally spaced below a line of observational windows overlooking the reactor. Seated at one of the stations, a dead body hung out of a chair, its limbs splayed out. A hologram of Saturn flickered in the center of the room, circled by smaller images of the *Pinnacle* space station, and a system of moons—the closest of which was Titan. Above the hologram were three view screens—and in the center of the largest screen scrolled a series of warnings:

HAZMAT Quarantine activated. Authorization: Lieutenant Colonel Ambrose Wren.

Grid [6] through Grid [48] restricted.

Danger: navigational orbital drift Y0.9987 PS. 89 R205.003

Caution: power generation unresponsive (Primary Conduit

offline), (power to Hydroponics offline), (Fuel Delivery Offline).
Emergency Systems Activated (This terminal will remain
active, press Esc to access Administrative Control).

She looked at the body for a moment and then turned her gaze toward the lighted images in the center of the room. She bent forward as the tiny dot of the *Pinnacle* drifted lazily in front of her eyes. "It says here the last data log was made on June 9, 2050." She looked at Dunesto, and then at the floor. "That's exactly two years from now."

"The last data log was two years from now, but the clocks are set *ten* years ahead?" he said distantly, angling his light to study the body. "The system's fried, man. Doesn't make sense."

She shook her head and stood. "What in god's name is going on here...?"

"Fuck if I know," he lifted his shoulders. "Only thing I know is we need to get off this thing. The rest—" he trailed off, pulling his light over the entire room. "The rest I'll leave for Command to sort out."

"I thought you didn't trust Command."

"I don't," he said solemnly. "But I'm beyond giving a shit. I just want to go home."

Fenroe turned her light back on the line of control stations, letting it hover over the limp body in front of them. It leaned out of the chair to one side: its legs were spread out, half mummified by the threads of its own flight suit. One petrified arm stuck to its abdomen, covering a gaping hole.

Angling her light onto its face, Fenroe felt a strap-wrench of unease tighten around her body. She felt the rush of cool air from her rebreather filling her lungs. Kneeling beside the body, she saw how it remained oddly fresh like the others. Very little decomposition. The quiet hallucinatory look of it filled Fenroe with sudden clarity. She reached for the breast of the corpse's flight suit and pulled its name patch into the light, immediately recognizing him. Despite the slow decomposition, his remains had been preserved well enough to distinguish the crest of silver hair, the sharp angles of his features.

"I know this man," she said, feeling the sharp sting of adrenaline, trying to understand how it was that he came to be here in this station, at this moment, in orbit around Saturn. She looked back at the list of warnings scrolling down the center view screen and read again the name that activated the quarantine. A name she hadn't thought about in more than five years.

"Colonel Ambrose Wren," she said, releasing the name badge.

His eye sockets were scarred and hollow, as if something had dug out the eyeballs. The back of his skull had been...*cracked* open, his scalp separated into four parts, his brain missing completely. She looked back and traced the stains of long dead tears streaking beside his dirt-grimed mouth. Her eyes went up at the ceiling, searching for brain matter and blood—evidence of a self-inflicted gunshot wound—but it was clean.

"He's the guy who sent us out here," she said, regarding the weight of those intervening five years as she pictured all the way back at the beginning the flicker of his hologram in the Battery Dome in Earth low-orbit.

"Jesus," Dunesto said, averting his eyes. "Did he shoot himself?"

"They would never allow weapons on-station..."

He angled his light onto the man again and moved back to his feet. "Any idea what he's doing out here?"

Instead of answering, Fenroe carried her beam over the sinuous, gray remnants of muscle and tissue. She probed an uneven wound in Wren's exposed and leathered stomach.

"I have no idea," she started, shaking her head, trying to make sense of it. "He was with Sitosen when they briefed me about the missing *Endeavor* crew. I mean, his hologram was..."

She pictured Colonel Wren's distorted, flickering blue profile standing in front of a wall of light, replaying the final moments of the *Endeavor* over and over again as it fell into the shadow of Titan. The memory of him penetrated her with the sharp eyes of a career military man, *Will you help us, or do we find someone better?*

"So he called in from here..."

"Maybe." Fenroe wondered quietly. "Maybe he sent us out here to rescue him—" she blinked away from the memory and studied the floor, tracing the institutional gray angles and granules of deeply embedded plastic that formed the tiled flooring, "—like you said—a manned exploratory mission doesn't make any sense. It would, however, make much more sense if Wren used his position to authorize his own rescue."

"Yeah, but why not come right out and say it? Why not just tell us where he was?"

She shook her head. "I don't know."

"And what about our status updates?" Dunesto shook his head as well. "We were in constant contact with the *Pinnacle* after we left, all the way up until we reached Saturn space. They said *nothing* about needing help. They said *nothing* about being anywhere near us. And even if they did say something, how is that even possible? For all intents and purposes the *Pinnacle* was printed and assembled in orbit around Calisto with every expectation to die there when funding ran out. It had no navigational capacity whatsoever... so how did it get out here?"

"What are you saying?"

He shrugged his massive shoulders: "I don't think this is the *Pinnacle*. I think it's something else. Maybe an IDSI black project. One nobody was supposed to know about."

Fenroe thought about that: it was the most logical answer. This station was identical to the *Pinnacle*, but definitely not the same structure that was supposed to be in orbit around Jupiter. It simply *couldn't* have been. She stood and studied the crescent of computer terminals on either side of Colonel Wren's body, each numbered in large industrial stencil. Painted on the floor, a message warned AUTHORIZED TECHNICIANS ONLY.

There were four terminals, each displaying the same image: a Y-shaped logic gate, the branches of which pulsed with a dull red glow, indicating insufficient power flow. The monolithic reactor stood beyond the consoles through the observational window. Fenroe scanned the computer terminals and then reached out, grabbing a yellow and black striped lever to the left of Wren's slumped corpse. She pulled to the sound and feel of large machinery coming to life beneath her feet. A hiss of hydraulics came from the generator as an immense augur as big around as a redwood screeched to life and began drilling into some unseen place below.

"That's it," Dunesto said, relief in his voice. He squeezed her arm and stepped out of the control room, shining his light on the awakening reactor.

Fenroe leaned forward and looked up through the window as the magnet assembly rotated around the auger, slowly twisting downward until it fastened into the three alternators with a series of deep resonant *clunks*, and a shower of electricity arced to the catwalk and surrounding machinery. The reactor hummed to life, and a white-blue light erupted from the base of it, as power steadily refilled the engine. Fenroe looked to the control panels one last time and then stepped out onto the metal grated catwalk, looking up with awe at the massive system of machinery. Dunesto looked back, watching her for a moment, then followed her gaze.

The reactor stretched up into the domed ceiling, disappearing far above them. Flashing arcs of electricity touched the catwalk's guardrail without pattern, and they stepped back.

Fenroe patted Dunesto on the shoulder and then jogged back into the Control Room. She finished pulling the last lever, and an automated voice chimed from the console: "*Power diverted to the ADS,*" as currents and braids of lightning wrapped and flowed gracefully around the tower, exploding with blue-violet waves of light that sent minute shockwaves across the rotunda. Fenroe slammed her eyes shut until the edifice darkened, and a thick resonant hum traveled throughout her body. When she could hear again, Dunesto yelled while pumping his fist into the air: "*We have power—*" he said over comms, "*—the crossover just opened up!*"

He pointed back at the direction they had come – lights were coming back to life, and warm air began spilling in from the vents, returning with things that flickered for a few moments until the station's power plateaued with function and sustainability: computers fired up, pressure doors opened, and everything hummed with the arterial flow of gases and hidden machinery. *The Pinnacle's* heartbeat thundered again at full strength.

"You guys seeing this?"

"*Copy, Fenroe.*" Aris said, a smile in her voice. "*We have power—quarantine is being lifted, airlocks are opening up. Lights are good.*"

"*Copy, everybody,*" Ulbricht cut in, her voice crackling over comms. "*Good job guys!*"

Dunesto turned in a slow circle with relief. He looked up at the reactor as it spun within an ephemeral whirlwind of lightning; the massive center stalk twisted imperfection patterns up into the high ceiling. He stood at the guardrail with his arms open wide, taking it all in, and then—

...a series of orange and yellow flashes appeared from the main corridor—more brilliant than the reactor, coming in through the corridor windows. There was a series of muted explosions that shivered the ground beneath Fenroe's feet. Some of the explosions were distant, as if the station had been struck by something far away. Some of them were close.

"What the hell was that?" Dunesto said, bracing himself against the guardrail.

"Is everyone all right?" Fenroe asked over comms, her heart sinking, the bio-suit tightening around her chest. She hurried out of the control room and jogged along the catwalk, keeping her eyes on the far airlock. "Anyone know what that was? Eos?"

"*Some...something*—" Aris transmitted, out of breath, "*—some kind of explosion. We have flashes of light coming in from outside.*"

Fenroe flicked through each of her crewmates visual feeds as she ran, which were all dead, giving black screens with single white lines cutting horizontally across the center. Finding it harder and harder to breathe, that invisible band of dread tightening around her chest again, she spoke into comms, "you copy, Ulbricht?"

Dunesto followed her into the corridor and they leaned to the side, searching through the observational window in the hallway. Two distinct particle clouds of debris expanded away from the station's exterior at different spots, tinkling and flashing with pieces of metal in the distance. Liquid flame spread across the hull like oil pouring into the sky from a burning derrick. And Fenroe watched as the *Crown Meridian* drifted into view, clearing the edge of the *Pinnacle* as it rose away from an obliterated docking station wreathed in flame and venting gas.

"My god," she said, reaching out to the bulkhead to hold herself upright. "They've decoupled. They're drifting."

Dunesto shoved her aside and looked.

"*Ulbricht!*" he screamed. "*Suja, get into your suits RIGHT NOW!*"

Fenroe's heart lurched behind her breastplate, seized by the sudden freefall of the moment.

"Ulbricht," Dunesto spoke fast but clear, reigning control of his voice, pressing the mouth guard of his helmet closer to his lips, trying to enunciate every syllable. "I can see the hull breach, you copy? You have to get out of there..."

Fenroe waited for a signal. Anything. She cycled the dead NVR feeds, all showing the same black screen.

"Jesus," Dunesto stammered. "They're decompressing."

The station rotated slowly up and away from the lowest part of the window, tumbling like a shipwrecked vessel tipping slowly into the throat of the sea. Fenroe froze, heartsick, as she watched her ship burn in and collapse under its own pressure.

"What are we going to do?" he asked desperately.

Fenroe stood locked in place, her mind grinding to a sickening halt. The *Meridian* continued drifting farther and farther away.

"Fenroe," Dunesto said again. "*What are we going to do?*"

When she didn't answer, he tore himself away from the glass and ran down the corridor, which broke the spell.

"Ulbricht!" Fenroe screamed into comms, cycling through the live feeds in her HUD, but still nothing. She tore her eyes away from the burning images and followed Dunesto's shadow, which bolted quickly ahead. Sprinting through the hallways and corridors and labyrinths, she could see split seconds of him cutting around corners. Fenroe ran so fast that her vision and hearing blurred into a single, unconscious experience. Stumbling through the corridor, she couldn't think past the icy slide of terror in her gut. Through every viewport she passed, the *Crown*

Meridian disintegrated in a slow snapshot flux of decompression and flame, with two of her crewmates still inside. She could think of nothing to do except run.

9.

Info-screen light still bled into the docking station. Fenroe ducked under the jammed open pressure door and jogged back onto the gantry. Sparks popped away from the broken terminal halfway down the catwalk, and the massive room filled with sounds of unseen machinery. Looking down fifty feet into the receiving lanes, she saw the powered-up guiding track assembly stuck in place, trying to grasp and move cargo and supplies that weren't there, jerking back and forth beneath a crane that hung in the center. The orientation video still blared into the environment: "WELCOME NEW IDSI EMPLOYEES, TO THE PINNACLE OBSERVATORY. THE PINNACLE WAS THE FIRST OF THE THIRD GENERATION GALAXY VIEWERS, AND IS NOW_"

Fenroe crossed the bridge to another corridor entrance lit from within by distinct moving lights breaking like waves against the shadows, separate from the sepulchral chains of mellow, utilitarian dimness. There was a crewmember inside.

She noticed the adjacent airlock to the docking umbilical flashing a red warning sign, indicating that the opposite side was exposed to open vacuum. The blackened smear of flash-fired electrical smoke spread away from all corners of the door. That might have been there when they first arrived, but she couldn't remember. Knowing the *Meridian* was free-floating away from safety toward imminent destruction, Fenroe jogged to the airlock and quickly looked it over with her light—the machinery was fried, and the pressure door had been welded shut by intense heat. Even if Ulbricht and Suja somehow made it EVA, there wouldn't be enough time for Fenroe to cut the door open: the *Meridian's* coolant only had moments before it made contact with the core and exploded.

She pulled herself away from the umbilical and followed the light. When she entered the corridor, Dunesto stood at a broad window looking out into space beside Eos's dark profile. The small robot searched up through the glass with her visor like a child: both synthetic hands pressed flat against the ballistic glass, which concussed with each silent explosive flash coming from the now sealed and destroyed *Pinnacle* dock umbilical.

Fenroe shouldered through them and looked up.

"It's decompressing," Dunesto whispered to her. He clenched and opened his fists, pacing back and forth like a captive animal.

Beck and Aris burst into the corridor from the other end, both out of breath. Aris spared one look at the ship through the window and continued her run past everyone into the docking station. Stunned and breathless, Beck froze with his hands open, trying to grasp the moment.

"Ulbricht," he said quietly over comms. "Can you hear me...?"

The ship rotated like a dead animal in water. Contrails of debris and chemicals flashed and twirled in every direction between thinning flares that rained against the *Pinnacle* hull like ribbons of smoke.

Aris came back into the corridor, frantic: "The umbilical's gone. The docking hatch is melted shut—"

"What happened?" Beck demanded.

Fenroe looked to the android, but it offered no explanation. The machine simply stared up at the destruction as if she were in a state of shock and despair; as if it were possible she could *feel* something—

A blinding, silent eruption flashed in the distance, and their visors polarized a half second late: the crew flinched and turned their heads instinctively from the light. What Fenroe thought was the last nuclear light she'd ever see, was actually the *Meridian's* engines and engine radiator systems flaring to life with blazes of white-hot orange and red. Four massive thrusters at the end of the linear truss heat shielding lit up with hard, repeating pulses of white-ion flame. Blinking the haloes out of her vision, Fenroe looked back again and saw the *Meridian* shudder and buck as it sped away from the *Pinnacle* on its half-dead spin—soundless explosions continued flashing and vibrating the glass at random intervals.

"What is she doing?" Dunesto asked.

"Piloting the *Meridian* away from us." Fenroe said, stepping closer to the glass, watching the ship pull away on a staggered trajectory.

"Why...?"

"She knows that when the reactor core makes contact with the coolant, the blast could destroy the *Pinnacle*." Fenroe stared through the window, unblinking, attempting to steel herself to witness the death of two more crewmates. Fresh waves of despair coursed through her veins. "She's saving our lives."

There came a sudden breaking of static over comms: sounds of transmission forcing itself through. Fenroe tore her eyes away from the plate glass window and stared into the floor, cycling through the live feeds in her HUD, which were all dead except one—she could see a figure floating in zero gravity from the flight-deck cam—Ulbricht at the Con, in a pool of magnesium fire bursting from the flight controls. She was ablaze—her body wrapped in a spinning cyclone of flame, imprisoning her within it as she was cooked down to sinew.

A voice in the back of Fenroe's mind screamed for her to do something.

The fire looked like phosphorescent liquid in zero gravity: the flames washed up from Ulbricht's shoulders in black-orange fins. The flesh of her arms poured pennants of fire, and they rotated in wild ovals for something to grab hold. As she drifted away from the burning flight controls, her legs scissored the air like a wind up toy cranked to full capacity. Fenroe watched as the liquid flames sucked up into Ulbricht's nostrils and mouth with every breath, seeping into her lungs, consuming them from the inside. Ulbricht curled into herself: her legs kicking softly as she tumbled in midair. Clouds of fleshy smoke orbited her roasted skin like thick gray-black cream.

Fenroe gasped, feeling the nob of her throat sinking into her stomach, a radiating pulse of nausea and panic thumping between her lungs. *"Oh god no—"*

Unmerciful straps of pressure tightened around Fenroe's chest. Her breath came in thin, hitching eruptions. The trauma was such that she could only stare at the images in her HUD, drilling a deep emptiness into it all with her eyes: sheets of burned flesh peeled away from muscle on Ulbricht's shoulders. Her flight suit was either melted off or fused by grisly heat to her skin. Fenroe could see the demolished control panel in front of her like twisted glass and wiring wrapped around crumpled steel. Flames smoldered in her hair, crinkling the ends like plastic.

Suja emerged through thick white chemical smoke and braced himself against the stellographer's glass, blasting Ulbricht with a fire extinguisher. Releasing the canister—letting it float freely away into the darkness—he grabbed a handful of Ulbricht's hair, pulling her yielding body away from the spreading flames. Shielding his eyes, he kicked away from the burning flight controls and sailed through the air until he came hard against the main corridor pressure door, just out of camera view. He dragged her with him, Ulbricht's body trailing ribbons of meaty smoke in their wake.

Fenroe switched views in her HUD and brought up the corridor feed, but the bursts of spreading flame created too much glare—the screen blinked white around a scattering of barely visible shapes. Fenroe, Dunesto, Beck, Aris and Eos watched the last moments of the *Crown Meridian* in helpless silence.

Suja hurriedly raked his fingers through a hologram of warnings that appeared out of thin air next to the pressure door, and then slammed his forearms over his face, releasing Ulbricht's hair as welder's flame exploded somewhere below the camera. White as the sun, its brilliance clearly caused him physical pain. The very oxygen in the air seemed alight, and waves of liquid fire rolled along the ceiling, as sparking white heat popped and collided with itself and shot in every possible direction. In the center of each wave grew smoldering orbs of fire that reached farther and farther across the surrounding walls—each flame pulsating in zero gravity like an artery beneath the skin.

Suja—eyes black and swollen, broken nose free-flowing again with blood, the tail of his unbuttoned Hawaiian shirt drifting behind him like a burning rag—grabbed a fistful of Ulbricht's hair again and started moving out of the flight deck. Clumps of roasted hair came loose in his fingers, so he shifted his grip to Ulbricht's collar.

"He's going for the airlock," Fenroe said. She looked up through the glass, the *Meridian* now so far away that she couldn't tell how much time they had left—things exploded without pattern like heat lightning.

"He'll make it," Beck said, but the hopelessness in his voice betrayed the words.

Fenroe switched feeds to another view in the corridor as Suja's shadow emerged from the liquid smoke and reached an emergency panel, popping it open. He grabbed the lock cylinder and manually sealed the flight deck pressure door, closing the fires off from the main corridor—the airlock slid to the floor, and the hallway darkened instantly—swirling waves of smoke curled inward and crashed against the metal near the floor. His body contorted awkwardly in the weightlessness of zero gravity as he took deep breaths, retching, forcing himself to keep pulling Ulbricht's limp body hand-over-hand deeper into the main habitat.

He followed evenly spaced flashing yellow lights and eventually found the EVA airlock—Suja sailed Ulbricht through the pressure door and then pulled himself in behind her, sealing the chamber. As the hatch lowered into the floor, the feed flickered and died.

Fenroe stood locked in place, stunned, listening to sounds of bending metal reverberate with strange and tortured urgency from her side of the glass. Somber tones, like a sinking freighter: the lonely music of strained and deformed metal.

"Christ," Beck said, looking at the walls. "*Listen* to that..."

All eyes remained on the *Meridian* as it shrunk in the distance, its engines burning with pale red light. Another interruption of static, and Suja's ragged breath suddenly filled their comms. Fenroe went through her HUD's site selector until she saw what looked like a camera spinning frantically in a hundred different directions at once. It was the feed from one of the bio-suit helmets in the airlock.

Suja's seared hand came into view and pulled a pair of bio-suits out of their charging crèches, shoving one through the air toward Ulbricht's limp body floating in the far corner.

The station's alarm system echoed in muted staccato over comms, and the emergency lights momentarily flickered and died—for brief moments, what light there was came solely through the porthole, until another string of fresh alarms burst to life. Through Suja's feed, Fenroe could hear the *Meridian* groaning sounds of distress as the pressure inside continued forcing itself out, buckling the structure under the emergency systems that lost power in stages. Another alarm flashed through the porthole on his side, followed by a louder, more urgent groan, and the *Pinnacle Observatory* beyond the outer viewport shrunk in the distance with each passing second.

"*We've decoupled,*" Suja rasped over comms. "*Does anyone copy? The Meridian is...we're drifting—*"

"We copy," Fenroe said, keeping her voice crisp and readable. "You have to get out of there. The reactor is going to blow."

Suja dove across the airlock, pulling himself against the outer hatch.

The floating helmet twisted in space, tracking Suja as he looked beyond the superimposed reflection of his own face through the window and saw the immense outer wall of the *Pinnacle's* ring drifting away—globes of liquid detritus and massive chunks of debris from the ruptured docking umbilical spun and floated between the separated structures. The *Meridian's* docking system dangled from the *Pinnacle's* demolished umbilical, ejecting clouds of fire and crystalline gas into the void. Metal groaned as the *Meridian* continued crushing itself with its own escaping atmosphere.

"*I can see the hull breach.*" Suja dragged his eyes painstakingly around the edge of the viewport, zeroing in on a massive emptiness near the back of the ship where a large part of the hull used to be.

"Suja, listen." Fenroe's stomach tied itself into knots, and she turned away from the corridor window, numb and terrified, feeling the unstoppable force of what was coming. "You have to eject *right now.*"

Suja turned in the air and snatched the loose bio-suit. He kicked off the wall and crashed into Ulbricht, quickly setting to work maneuvering her unconscious, scorched body into it. The *Crown Meridian* rumbled around him, and he frantically shoved Erika's limbs into the back of her own suit, stammering what he was doing with his hands and arms like play-by-play commentary, reminding himself to breathe—the suit immediately self-sealed around Ulbricht's midsection, and the airlock vibrated in staggered, unending exigency, and Fenroe knew Suja had only seconds. He reached and snatched a helmet tumbling in air nearby, straightened it in his hands, and then set it against Ulbricht's neck-housing—

Suddenly, the inner airlock emitted a drawn out and horribly stressed sound of immense pressure. Fenroe's breath stopped—Suja froze and snapped his head around, waiting for that last moment, that crushing liminal second of still silence before the final violent crack of reality. Terrified to move, he stared at the inner airlock.

When he could breathe again, Suja forced his gaze away from the tortured pressure hatch and worked faster to secure Ulbricht's suit.

"Suja," Fenroe said.

"*I know—*"

"Your suit!"

"*I know—!*"

He grabbed the helmet in both fists and twisted it into Ulbricht's shoulders, locking it into place—loose, melted strings of Ulbricht's remaining hair fluttered for a split second as oxygen filled her suit, and the soft glowing HUD flickered to life and illuminated her raw and unrecognizable face. Suja frantically pulled himself into his own suit then took a spool of filament, attaching it to his utility harness, running it back to Ulbricht's suit, buckling them together with a single karabiner, tethering himself to her. Then came the sound of rushing water and wind.

Something struck the vinyl near Suja's head, spraying flecks of sharp material at his face, and he instinctively threw his head back as a high-pitched whistling filled the airlock.

This was it—this would be the final decompression.

Suja grasped the helmet tumbling in zero gravity and pulled it over his head, hammering it down into place. He reached blindly toward the charging crèche for his gauntlets, screwing them both into each wrist, and his now gloved hand came away wet with blood—thick red orbs of it spun away from the left side of his POV. It wasn't clear where the blood was coming from, but there was enough of it to cloud his vision.

Another high velocity sound similar to a bullet smacking into stone, and Suja's POV swung the other direction—rivets and screws were coming loose and emerging from the fiberglass and vinyl shell that encased the airlock's interior. The growing pressure forced each bolt out of its mooring and fired them into the outer hatch like deadly projectiles—more groaning sounds of bending rebar, but deeper, more imminent—

Something ricocheted and finally made contact with the outer hatch, and Suja let out a deep, shrill scream of pain. Fenroe watched through her HUD as he held his arm into the air, shooting blood in all directions—one of those rivets had fired directly through the hand of his suit, the triweave smart-mesh unable to protect him from that much force at such close proximity.

He curled into the pain and rotated in midair, tumbling into a somersault, his screeching wail trembling with waves of shock. He sucked his scream back into his breath, grabbing his own hand to stop the blood, hissing pain through his teeth and hyperventilating, tears running down his cheeks. *"Gah...it's my...my suit is punctured—"*

He scooped the blood away from his visor with his good hand and grabbed the wrist of his ruined gauntlet.

"Pull your hand into the sleeve!" Fenroe screamed, but he couldn't hear over the rush of air escaping the airlock, his cries getting staggered and raw. "Suja, *listen*—pull your hand into your chest compartment!"

His POV gave a quivering nod, his ragged breath hitching— more rivets fired into the bulkhead, splintering flecks of vinyl and fiberglass in all directions. When his sleeve was empty, he shakily grabbed a titanium cable tie from his utility harness and pulled it over the suit's vacant wrist several inches above the puncture mark, trying to see through the cloud of blood droplets floating in front of his face. He fought through the pain, grabbing the tail of the cable tie and ratcheting hard, securing a makeshift tourniquet, praying that it was enough to seal the breach in his suit: If the hole in the glove wouldn't close, he would only have a few minutes to get to safety after decompression.

One of the rivets suddenly punched through the outer porthole's glass, and there came a more intense rush of air that nearly deafened Fenroe over the crackling hiss of her comms. The inner hatch instantly ripped open as the *Meridian's* atmosphere rushed out of the tiny hole in the viewport. As the airlock decompressed, ice crystals formed on the glass surrounding the marble-sized breach, which started cracking and widening. In a matter of milliseconds, the entire door gave way and ripped apart, ejecting them into space. One moment Suja was reaching toward Ulbricht, and the next he was being fired into the nothingness, careening between two battlecruiser-shaped structures that spun the same direction in his visor.

Pulled taught from the force of escaping air, the cable connecting Suja with Ulbricht whipped them forward, slamming Ulbricht through the narrow hole towards the focal point of pressure—ice crystals, debris, instrumentation—all exploded out of the breach like a volcanic eruption. Everything ejected out of the airlock at once. But the current of the atmosphere was faster than the materials it carried, and the cloud of whirling debris unfolded from itself in a fast disintegrating flurry of kinetic chaos. White blurs and rectangular shapes shot across Suja's POV in the foreground of black space as he and Ulbricht rocketed away from the *Meridian* at breakneck speeds.

Fenroe tore her eyes away from the floor—away from the live feed in her HUD—and looked up through the bay window, searching through the cloud of far debris for their bodies tumbling inside the wreckage.

"They're out," Beck said.

"Where?!" Dunesto panted, his attention welded to the window.

From the feed inside Fenroe's HUD, Suja took giant gulps of air, reaching his good hand out for an anchor of some kind, anything that would slow him down. Fighting the dizzying sense of tumble and drift, Suja reached across his chest and slapped the MMU controls on the wrist of his empty gauntlet—his boosters popped away from his EVA pack, he grabbed one of the controllers with his good hand and twisted, the *Pinnacle* filling his visor—

—and slammed into a large piece of debris that had broken away from the destroyed umbilical. A whitewash of blinding light exploded across his feed. Electric veins streaked down the image and went black, clearing after a moment—he desperately sucked air back into his chest. The impact was so forceful that his back bent to its limit the wrong way. The shock of it knocked the wind out of him, but his EVA pack absorbed most of the force.

Suja and Ulbricht spun away from each other, tumbling in different directions until the safety line pulled tight. It straightened like a rubber band stretched to its tensile limit, and then snapped in half—the force of the break tugged them back together in zero gravity. Ulbricht's limp body slammed into Suja, sliding against his hip—he reached, extending his arm to grab hold with his one good hand, but she slipped through his fingers.

Aris screamed, "The tether broke—!"

"Where are they?!" Dunesto hissed again, pacing helplessly back and forth in front of the viewport, trying to see them in the debris field. "I—I can't see them!"

In their feeds, tumbling away from the collapsing *Meridian*—its booster jets carrying it farther and farther away from the *Pinnacle*—Suja's POV panned the dark void ahead of him, and then the *Pinnacle*, and then the void again, and then the *Meridian*, each structure rolling across his vision as he somersaulted through nothingness. Panting, droplets of sweat and blood falling against the inside of his visor, Suja grabbed his MMU control again and hit the booster jets, but nothing happened. His pack had been destroyed on impact. At one-second intervals, Fenroe watched helplessly through Suja's feed as Ulbricht came into view and hurtled toward the *Pinnacle* at speeds that would crush her on impact.

"On your nine, Suja," she screamed. "Grab her!"

"Ah Jesus—I can't see—!"

Ulbricht's body merged with the other objects spinning in Suja's line of sight and disappeared. *"Christ—oh god, I lost her!"*

"Suja, you have to slow yourself down." Dunesto instructed. "You're heading right towards the *Pinnacle*. You'll be crushed—"

"I can't—" he sucked in a breath, *"—I hit debris,"* he breathed again, *"—my MMU is shot."*

Fenroe searched hopelessly through the tinkling debris floating away from itself in the distance, straining her eyes, unable to separate the details of Suja and Ulbricht's tumbling bodies from the wreckage. And then she remembered the Orbital Positioning System in their bio-suits.

"Eos, bring up their suits in my HUD," Fenroe snapped.

In Fenroe's visor, red and purple dots appeared around a pair of twinkling white specks separating from each other. They were picking up speed, still drifting in the same general direction towards the *Pinnacle's* hull. Ulbricht would smash into the hull if someone couldn't find a way to slow her down, which, if she weren't dead already, would kill her instantly. Same with Suja—without his MMU, the only thing left of him would be a red smear across the *Pinnacle's* hull.

Fenroe racked her brain for an answer—she needed to get outside somehow. The docking station's pressure door motor control box was irreversibly damaged. Even if she *could* use the pressure door, it would take Eos five or ten minutes to cut it open with her plasma—time Suja and Ulbricht didn't have. They had mere seconds to reach minimum safe distance before the *Meridian's* nuclear reactor core detonated.

Fenroe's brows twitched: the muscles flexed and relaxed as if she was trying to blink the stinging air out of her eye. She tried and tried to close her lids, but she lost all control of the muscles in her face.

And like a flash, the memory of Harris clawed its way up to the surface of her mind. He pulled himself up out of the darkness and looked into her eyes from inside the airlock. There was lucid fear on his face: it was the look of someone who'd given up; his mind had shattered like brittle glass, crushed by the airless press of yawning death. She recognized that emotion—his eyes were wide but unclouded, unable to fully comprehend the enormity of their situation. He couldn't understand it, but that fear packed horrifying speculation into the gaps of his understanding. And he'd cracked. Folded under the pressure.

And with that image came the familiar feeling of rage bubbling up from Fenroe's center, drilling through the bone, straight into the marrow: the weight of that rage inside compressed her terror as crisply as an industrial press turned orange-molten metal into sheets of steel. That terror and rage cycled internally as one solitary emotion. But when it burst up against the torrential river of her awareness, it built like a levied river, clawing—*needing*—to break free and flood without consequence. Split seconds compressed that terror, running it through a chopping refinery until it came out the other side as pure, uncontrollable rage. That rage had to go somewhere, and it needed a focal point: if she couldn't find something to target outside of her body, that focal point would *become* her body. She felt it unfolding in her like it did in Harris, like fractals of heartache and madness: if she didn't act—act *now*—*she* would become the target of her own rage. And that was more terrifying than death itself.

She looked at the plate glass viewport and held her hand against it, testing its thick, smooth surface area. She followed the armored glass up into the ceiling where the emergency breach shields were locked in place, safely tucked up into the wall and primed to slam down the moment the cabin lost pressure.

"I need someone to head to the next umbilical and start equalizing it," Fenroe said with intensity. "We're going to be coming in fast."

"What are you going to do?" Aris asked.

"I'm going EVA," she said. "I'm going out there to get them."

Aris and Beck wasted fractions of a second trying to figure out how she planned to do it—they each glanced back through the window at the *Meridian*, and then Aris pulled Beck away by the arm. They were both sprinting by the time they made it to the next corridor.

Fenroe pulled a plasma torch away from her chest and ignited the flame—she gathered a karabiner in her other fist, holding it over the knuckles of her gloved hand, pulling it back. She pressed the beam against the window.

"Jesus," Dunesto swore. "What are you *doing?!*"

"Hold on to something—"

Eos moved on her left, and Fenroe initially thought the android was going to stop her, but she didn't. She threaded her hardened metallic fingers into Fenroe's utility harness and bent her legs, preparing to jump.

Dunesto screamed, "Wait Fenroe—you'll be cut in half!"

"Hold on—!"

Glass surrounding the torch glowed bright orange until it folded under the beam: the softened glass curled wetly into itself like cellophane tossed onto an open flame—

A hole opened, screaming as the air escaped it.

The entire weight of the *Pinnacle's* controlled atmosphere poured into the freshly punctured hole with immeasurable force—without hesitation, Fenroe slammed her karabiner-reinforced fist against the breach as hard as she could, and the glass spider-webbed—

Fenroe's chin whiplashed down against her chest, and there was a moment of blind nothingness—

The weight of Eos's synthetic body pulled tight against her midsection—

And the corridor exploded out into space with an eruption of glass and buffeting silence. The blast shield immediately slammed down silently behind her and Eos as they were pulled through, nearly cutting them in half.

Eos let go of her harness, and Fenroe immediately activated her MMU, which snapped into place—she snatched the controls and timed her ignitions by the pattern of both structures circulating in her visor as she tumbled in zero gravity. When the *Meridian* came into view—when the *Pinnacle* was at her back—Fenroe ignited her booster jets, banking and rolling until the ship took the center of her vision.

Approaching fast, Suja and Ulbricht's red and purple dots centered in her HUD's directional compass, converging in her crosshairs on the opposite end of two winding transparent lines—digital pathways in Fenroe's visor that led straight to them.

"I see them," Fenroe transmitted coolly. She spared half seconds to read which one was closest. "I'm going for Suja."

Eos's rich voice pulsed through the helmet speakers: *"Copy."*

"Fenroe," Dunesto transmitted, breathing heavily. *"Are you guys all right?"*

"We're okay—find us a way back inside the *Pinnacle*," Fenroe said distantly, a detached focus and intensity in her voice. "We can't be out here when the *Meridian's* core detonates, copy?"

"Jesus fucking Christ," he rasped, already on the run. *"I copy."*

She shot in violent freefall toward Suja's dot in her HUD, plummeting into the dark nothing of space at three-hundred miles per hour. She felt nothing outside of her suit—no sensation of freefall whatsoever—and focused instead on the drum of her heartbeat and the slow passage of her sipping breaths.

"Commander," Eos thrummed, *"debris directly ahead."*

"Copy that." Fenroe stabilized with precision, falling facedown along the lighted path in her visor, making hair-raising adjustments between roping gnarls of electrical wire and exposed cable. In the weightlessness of it all, Fenroe's vestibular remained senseless of the unbelievable speeds at which she fell, and the scale of the unmoving space station in the background created a surreal impression of stasis. The only indication she had of travel were the pieces of debris that shot past her like bullets. She activated thrust, banking herself to the right, peeling into a roll directly through a channel of shrapnel and lattices of rebar and bent metal.

Eos instructed over comms: *"More debris—"*

"Got it." Fenroe banked left again and guided herself back on track. A red warning blinked in the top center part of her HUD indicating that she was off course. Steering herself back, something small ricocheted off her visor, and a tiny spidery line split her vision in half. "My helmet is hit—Aris, tell me you've reached the next umbilical—"

"Almost there," the younger woman panted, out of breath.

"More Debris, Commander." Eos pulsed, *"directly ahead."*

"I can see it."

Fenroe adjusted her limbs into a controlled roll away from a fire-blackened chunk of metal the size of an automobile. She banked again, bringing herself down and through another piece of debris.

In the far distance, the *Crown Meridian's* exterior began to explode in a succession of flashing lights at various points. Fenroe squeezed the MMU control in her right fist and rolled to her left, caressing the navigational line in her HUD, and spun directly into the path of debris that she hadn't seen. Adjusting quickly, Fenroe squeezed the thruster in her closed fists and spiraled down until the two larger pieces crossing her path collided in a silent, anvil-and-hammer shower of sparks, missing her by a fraction of a second. Igniting thrust again, Fenroe dropped to her left, rocketing through the immense ribs of a section of detached umbilical. The crack in her visor spread farther across the glass—

The navigational line in her HUD flickered and then died.

All visuals disappeared.

She saw only darkness—no waypoints, and no dots

indicating the crew's position.

"My display is dead," she said. "I'm flying blind."

Part of her HUD was still working—she could still see Suja's POV in a small, cracked screen in the upper left corner of her visor. It panned onto a large burning shadow coming into view, veering into the path of something massive. Unable to maneuver with his damaged MMU controls and thinking fast, he created a split second short burst of thrust by ejecting his EVA pack, which shot away from his back and nudged him into a divergent trajectory, creating just enough space to avoid being smashed to smithereens against a larger piece of debris—tucking his knees into his chest, the missile grazed Suja and obliterated the ejected EVA pack in a short, brilliant flash.

"*Fenroe, I can see you,*" he mumbled, dizzy from blood loss. "*Approaching on your eleven o'clock.*"

"I don't have a visual—"

INSTABILITY DETECTED IN VISOR, flashed across Fenroe's vision. ADVISE EMERGENCY RETURN TO HABITAT.

Flashes of light manifested on Fenroe's left, and flaming ejected segments of the *Crown Meridian* made contact with the *Pinnacle's* hull—the micro explosions blossomed in silent, flashing patterns of white light, and she could feel the shockwaves of gases pressing against her bio-suit.

Another large object shaped like a cylinder rolled into her trajectory—Fenroe couldn't tell if it was something that had broken off the *Pinnacle* or the *Meridian*—and she tried slowing with her pack, rolling to her left, timing it as the object rotated and eclipsed the universe. She gripped both jet controls in her fists, committed to her flight path, and angled her body to drop into the cylinder like a dart at just the right moment, and as she passed into it, feeling the inside of the cylinder rip by at a hair's breadth, she was consumed by a split second moment of pitch darkness, and then her body instantly cleared the other side. Fenroe realized she'd been holding her breath: she had passed through the eye of a needle, and survived.

Another piece of debris—the largest so far—spun immediately into position on the other side of the cylinder. Fenroe gasped, falling through space too fast, her mind reacting too slow. There was too much surface area on either side to navigate clear of it. Unable to move, she searched the center for a similar opening to the one she'd just passed through. Another eye of a needle. And she found it—a slight bending of light; an empty hole punched all the way through to the other side. She made herself into an arrow and blasted forward, accelerating, banking slightly down and to the left, and finally into a half barrel roll. She rocketed head first through the opening, and after what felt like an eternity of pitch-blackness her body ejected from the other end.

She had a clear shot straight to Suja.

Two needles down...

Still alive...

With blood rushing to Fenroe's temples, Suja was now close enough to see. Because she couldn't just intercept him at their opposing speeds—the force of crashing into each other would be enough to seriously injure or even kill them—she kept her fists on the thrust, tracking Suja's shadow with her eyes as he shot past above her in a permanent state of acceleration, heading straight for the killing ground of debris she'd just passed through. Fenroe followed her own momentum at an arc so that she could come about directly behind him as he passed. When he lined up, she burned thrusters and fell toward him, closing the distance, reaching—the larger piece of debris that Fenroe passed through moments before was far enough not to be an obstacle, but the flaming cylinder structure spun back into their path. Suja saw it and pulled his knees to his chest again, sensing a collision—

Fenroe banked to avoid it—

The piece of debris missed Suja by mere inches—

Fenroe reached for him again—

And a sliver of metal hanging off the back end of the cylinder clipped her right shoulder and a good portion of her EVA pack, knocking her out of trajectory—

Suja's fingers slipped from her grasp.

Stinging fire shot down Fenroe's right arm, and she lost all sensation from her shoulder down.

She was spinning out of control, tumbling wildly into a new trajectory.

A pair of jets fired from out of the darkness, twirling and dancing between the spinning chunks of debris like twin missiles tracking a heat signature. Recovering quickly, Fenroe used her good arm to make small adjustments in order to keep clear of debris as much as she could. The *Pinnacle's* hull took up increasingly more space in her visor. They were dropping into it at a lethal velocity. The killing impact was mere seconds away.

The twin missiles fell in behind Fenroe—spinning and banking with immaculate precision—and as they pulled away to avoid another large wayward segment of the obliterated umbilical dock, Eos's exoskeleton appeared at the top of two streaming rails of flame shooting out of booster jets opened up from within her calves. Hanging like loose rigging in one mechanical fist was Ulbricht's limp body. Eos rocketed into a position to intercept Fenroe with her free hand, closing the distance, reaching out to her.

"Grab Suja!" Fenroe hissed, coughing and hacking the pain out of her lungs. *"Not me, SUJA!"*

Eos barrel-rolled back into place directly behind Fenroe and extended a hand.

"Grab Suja, Eos!" Fenroe screamed again, coughing, sucking air, "Not me, *god damn it—he's right there!*"

She knew the android wouldn't listen. Fenroe knew that it operated under a hierarchical system of logic. Eos couldn't assign feelings to any of her crew—to the AI, each of them were nothing more than a list of point variables and value—commanding officers occupied the highest priority. She knew deep in her heart that Eos was about to let Suja die. And she'd have to watch it happen all over again to another person she loved with every piece of her heart—a person that she was supposed to protect, who expected her to fight with everything she had to bring him home alive.

A tight, nauseating presence filled Fenroe's chest and her body went numb, tumbling and spinning off-axis through space, hurtling toward certain death, and she raged inside.

Eos banked closer and came abreast, maneuvering to overtake her before impact, and Fenroe was powerless to stop her. Rocketing, tumbling, falling toward the *Pinnacle's* hull, Fenroe accepted and embraced that the death of people she loved was retribution of some kind. The blood of her crew dripped from her fingers. If she hadn't asked them to trust her, they wouldn't have come out here. She shouldn't have *let* them come. She could have saved them all.

But in that moment, something else happened. At the sound of Fenroe's desperate voice, Eos broke away and dropped from view. The contrails erupting from Eos's feet changed direction, and Fenroe knew immediately what that meant.

The machine had listened to her. It obeyed.

For once it had defied logic, and decided to follow her orders.

Eos dropped back for Suja, leaving Fenroe to hurtle faster and faster toward the *Pinnacle* hull, which blazed toward her like a bullet train.

She forced herself to relax, wondering if she would feel her body splatter in an instant, scattering across the *Pinnacle's* hull—if it would be a flash of pain followed by gradual pulses of nothingness, or if she would switch off like a light. She slowed her breathing and counted back from one hundred to zero, thinking feelings of *peace*, *comfort*, *calm*—spelling the words, picturing each letter in her head, preparing herself for death—

The twin blazing lights came back, rolling and reflecting off a railcar-sized segment of the docking umbilical tumbling parallel to Fenroe's flightpath. And then—

...she felt her body slam against the *Pinnacle's* hull.

She felt herself rip in half as something struck her midsection, and it wasn't so bad. The pain wasn't nearly what she imagined. But the universe stayed in focus somehow, and Fenroe held onto consciousness, watching the *Pinnacle* station fall down and away—and instead of coming at her head on, the hull suddenly shifted and passed in front of Fenroe's face, blurring by at a tremendous speed, forming streaks of ephemeral gray light.

That's when Fenroe realized she was still alive.

She felt her body ratchet against something mechanical and hard, and a hand was clutching the front of her bio-suit. She followed the wrist and arm, and the steady glow of Eos's visor blazed against the darkness. The android banked and spun, avoiding pieces of destroyed airlock, climbing upward, clearing the *Pinnacle's* hull. Eos passed the edge, where she banked again and leveled out, sailing far above a massive sea of glass in the center of the *Pinnacle's* immense ringed body. The lake-sized telescope tilted toward the planet Saturn in the distance, beautifully calm and immaculate.

Fenroe went numb, powerless to fight the tears of relief that had been tears of resigned acceptance and failure a second before. She looked, not wanting to see, afraid that Suja wouldn't be hanging in Eos's other hand. And her chest decompressed of its air, her mind uncomprehending the truth of it.

Swaying gently in Eos's other fist, enshrouded in blackness, Suja hung from the empty sleeve of his bio-suit like a rain-soaked fabric sheet in the wind of a storm.

And Ulbricht's limp body trailed behind him, held tightly in his good hand.

She couldn't believe her eyes.

Eos had saved them all. Somehow, the *Meridian's* AI had found a way.

Angling down toward the *Pinnacle*, the android towed them into the open center of the stadium-sized structure. When Eos cleared the inner edge, a blinding light erupted somewhere behind them in the distance. They continued past the lip of the *Pinnacle's* radiation-shielded hull at the exact moment the *Crown Meridian's* reactor core detonated, and nuclear light from the spacecraft that had been their home for half of a decade broke against the edge like a wave of white glass pressing the shadows away.

Noiseless, everlasting, and unsound.

10.

Dunesto carefully leaned Suja against the wall and helped him slide slowly to the floor. With an empty sigh, the injured man settled and curled his whole body around the arm pulled into his chest compartment. His bruised-black eyes within the visor held the thousand-yard stare of barely contained agony, two thin lines of blood leaking down both nostrils.

Aris lifted her ear away from Ulbricht's face and shook her head. "I can't feel a breath."

Fenroe grabbed Ulbricht's bio-suit again in her fist and dragged the woman's body into the infirmary with Eos, trying her best to see a path through her shattered visor.

"All the umbilicals are gone," Beck stammered. His brown hair was wet with sweat and his youthful eyes were wild with the shaky comedown of adrenaline. "The only thing we could do was disable one of the docking bay's blast shields and decompress the entire module—"

"*Why* are they gone?" Suja cut in, wheezing through pain. "How did this happen?"

"It must have something to do with turning the power back on," Beck said, lifting his hands helplessly. "They were all destroyed. Every single one of 'em. There were too many barricades for us to make it to the next docking module, so we had to circle back to this one—"

Ignoring them, Fenroe and the android Eos each grabbed handfuls of Ulbricht's singed flight suit and dragged her lifeless form onto one of the four trauma pods that lined one side of the room. Fenroe dug out a pair of scissors from her utility harness and the rest of her tools spilled, chiming prettily as they skittered across the obsidian floor. She pulled the unconscious woman's suit away from her scorched throat and cut the triweave metal-infused fabric down the center of her chest. Fenroe leaned over Ulbricht and listened again for breath, feeling the slightest caress of air on her ear.

A thin line of blood seeped down the woman's face from an opened knot just above what was left of her hairline—Ulbricht's melted forehead was swollen and pitted with bits of shattered glass. Her burned eyes had swollen shut, disappearing deep inside her puffy flesh to become thin horizontal slits. Her right ear had fused to the side of her cauterized temple. Her skull was badly swollen.

Fenroe finished cutting the flight suit away from Ulbricht's body and peeled it from her limbs with shaking hands, fighting to keep her fingers delicate as they moved over pieces of fabric that had melted into the skin. She pulled the med-pod's glass lid down over Ulbricht, sealing her behind a clear enviro-shield while pure oxygen flooded the capsule. Struggling to stay on her feet, Fenroe reached up to her own suit's neck housing and popped the locks away. She unscrewed her helmet and dropped it onto the floor with a clatter, and then fell to her knees, sliding her gloved hand across the med-pod's touch-screen, bringing it out of sleep mode.

The screen blinked with a list of commands. Fenroe stabbed a red icon marked *EMERGENCY*, and the pod's surgical system rotated into position above Ulbricht's body, panning a sheet of soft green light back and forth down her peeled and blistered skin. Readout streamed across the side of the enviro-shield, giving a slow heart rate, a bottomless blood pressure, a staggered pulse and a stream of hitched, uneven respiration data.

Suja clumsily ripped his helmet off with his uninjured hand and breathed deeply. Aris knelt by his side and peeled the bio-suit away from his shoulders—much of his body below the neck was sticky and gummed with dark red blood. As she gently pulled his injured arm out of the tied sleeve, his hand formed a club of gnarled, shattered meat with a ragged hole through the center of his palm. Aris searched for dressing in the cabinets, but everything had been ransacked and rifled through. She reached for a safety razor that Fenroe had dropped onto the ground with the rest of her tools and cut strips away from his Hawaiian shirt to use for bandages.

"Come on," Aris said under her breath, reaching to pull the battered man to his feet. "Let's get you in a pod."

He held up his good hand in protest, breathing deeply with beads of sweat dripping down his face. "I just need to sit for a minute...just one minute."

Suja stared over Aris's shoulder in a daze, and watched as the bedding below Ulbricht molded itself around her body, foam raising her neck slightly, tilting her head back; her deformed jaw opened naturally from the movement and the angle. A plastic tube came out of the surgical apparatus and threaded itself into her mouth and throat. Another long tube suspended above dropped down smoothly, inserting itself into one of her nostrils, as *AIRWAY OEDEMA, EMERGENCY RSI* flashed on the outside of the pod. An orange mist dispersed and fell on her body, and then small wires came up out of the inside of the pod as the bed self-rotated Ulbricht's arms and inserted needles into her veins—dosages of Saline, Succinylcholine, Norcuran, Pavulon, Zemuron, and Nimbax scrolled across the bottom of the pod.

"Okay, let's go—" Aris grunted, pummeling her hand around Suja's chest, pulling his good arm over her neck, "—come on."

When the med-pod began humming and working under its own direction, Fenroe backed away and looked around the dead room. Nauseous, she clenched her jaw to keep from vomiting. Drained of emotion, overloaded with sensation, Fenroe backed away until she felt her shoulders come against the opposite wall. Staring at Ulbricht, Fenroe let her body slide listlessly to the floor. Whatever kept her going until that point had deserted her. She sagged against the wall, dropped her head forward, covered her face with her hands, and sobbed uncontrollably.

For every moment she sat there—in the infirmary, watching Ulbricht suffocate, with Suja bleeding to death right next to her—Fenroe had kept control because that's what was expected of her. Because she was their Commander. The truth was, all their blood was on *her* hands. Because Titan was the seat of the unknown, and her exploration-obsessed mind wouldn't allow itself to abandon any attempt to understand its secrets.

Beck knelt and put a comforting hand on her shoulder.

"It's all right," he said gently, masking his own pain.

"Everything's going to be okay."

Fenroe shook her head, lost and defeated: "We're all going to die."

"Don't," he said, shaking his head, and Fenroe saw that his face had aged years in the past few hours. Old man eyes, weighed down by all that he'd lost. She got the sense that he couldn't psychologically afford Fenroe giving up right then. He just couldn't summon the strength to deal with it. "Don't even dare say that."

"It should be *me* in that pod."

"But it isn't—"

"I shouldn't have brought you here," she said, taking her hands away from her face and meeting his eyes. "We shouldn't *be* here."

He frowned and sighed and looked back at the crew. He said nothing.

"I keep asking myself why," Fenroe said, turning her head from side to side, pinching her eyes shut like she was trying to force the memory of something shameful out of her thoughts. "You know? *Why* did this happen—?" she lifted her hands, "—all this—Sitosen, Harris, and now...now...this—" she looked around the infirmary, "—this *fucking* place. All of this happened for a *reason*, you know? For a single, stupid, unforgivable, arrogant reason—" She felt the sting of tears in her eyes and wiped them away, feeling ever more embarrassed for losing her composure, "—because we were too *arrogant* to admit that leaving the planet might not be a good idea."

Beck sat back on his haunches, unresisting. Letting her purge.

"Which is another way of saying," she continued, sniffing the tears away, forcing herself to calm down, "that this is *my* fault."

Beck's frown deepened, and he shook his head sadly.

"I did this to all of you," she continued, "Because I was too selfish to tell Sitosen *no*. This mission doesn't make any *fucking* sense. It's too dangerous, too *wasteful*—" she shrugged helplessly, unloading it all while she still had the courage.

Beck pushed himself to his feet, offering a hand. Fenroe sat unmoving, staring into space. After a moment of breathing and collecting her thoughts, she looked at the floor and nodded once softly. Instead of taking his hand, Fenroe pushed herself up onto her feet.

"Suppose that's all true," Beck said, bending to pick up her discarded helmet. "It doesn't negate the fact that we're stuck here, and that we still have to find a way home."

Fenroe nodded again and took several more breaths, taking the helmet from his hands. She raised her head and closed her eyes, feeling the soreness in her neck, breathing calmness back into her lungs. When she opened her eyes again, her attention drifted onto a smear of blood beyond the med units that disappeared into the shadowy glow of another doorway. There was a liquid aspect to the pale yellow light that spilled into the infirmary, as if the room beyond contained an aquarium of some kind. Curiously drawn to it, she found herself walking numbly around the med pods, studying the bloody handprint on the bulkhead. Beck turned his head and followed her gaze as she traced the blood around the wall and stepped into the next room.

It was a high-ceilinged chamber lined with monitoring consoles, cables snaking across the floor and connecting to a whole series of standing glass tubes filled with yellow fluid lined up in the center of the room—a line of bloody fingerprints streaked all the way across each tank, like somebody walked by dragging their wounded hand. She stepped over ropes of cable, gazing at the technical and medical equipment—and stopped, staring with complete brain lock.

The overheads detected her presence and blinked to life, and Fenroe finally began to grasp just how far beyond her understanding this reality had become. In the fluttering new light, her pattern-seeking brain immediately recognized the shape of a face in the yellow liquid. Parts of the face were still anatomical and proportioned, but everything else that would make a human face had been replaced by a shadow-severed visage carved just below the neck in ragged strips of flesh and muscle.

It was staggering to take in; a complete and utter distortion of structure. And from the uneven tufts of hair floating dead in the liquid, to the ragged flaps of fibrous and sinuous human tissue, it finally sunk in with horrifying detail.

Fenroe put her hands on her knees and retched. She spun away from the tanks and dropped to the floor, vomiting onto the deck. She closed tight her eyes, hoping she was wrong, hoping it was all a bad dream. Because in each tank—at least thirty of them on the farthest side of the room—floated a severed human head.

Eos came quickly to her side, finding Fenroe on her hands and knees spitting bile off her lips. The small android placed a comforting hand on her back, and then looked up toward the horrific site before them.

The severed heads were wrong. Misshapen and...and *wrong* in some way that Fenroe couldn't immediately process. When she had the courage—after moments of simply passing air in and out of her lungs—she forced herself to look again.

Instead of a forehead, instead of a pair of eyes and a nose, it appeared as if the inside of a car engine had exploded outward from the base of the severed head's skull. Each human head still had a lower jaw and a tongue flopping out of place. But everything above the tongue was transformed, replaced by what looked like a nest of wires and cords of copper, folds of plastic, shavings of gold and silver, each interspersed with different sized buckles and plates of different kinds of metal fused to the skin. As if the tops of their heads had blossomed like a flower made of scrap metal. Almost as if something had scalped them, hollowed out their skulls, and jammed slivers of metal and plastic rubbish into the empty cavity, like machine parts were growing out of the bone.

Fenroe shook her head: "What is this...?"

She wiped the puke away from her face and moved to her feet. Eos took a step back and watched as Aris, Beck and Dunesto came into the room. Fenroe followed the line of tanks with her eyes. The tank on the very end had been knocked over. What was left of it lay shattered in a million pieces on the floor. What must have been twenty gallons of clear yellow fluid formed a standing puddle around the exploded tank. Fenroe followed the stream until it came flush against the pressure door on the opposite side of the room. She met Dunesto's shocked gaze, searching his eyes. "One of the heads is missing."

Eos took a step back, staring at the liquid, moving her face slowly back and forth over the broken glass and fluid, reassessing this new information.

"Don't touch anything," Dunesto warned.

Ignoring him, Fenroe reached down and picked up a clipboard covered with a sheet of plastic, and read: "*Removed after sporification. Placed in stasis during procedure.*" She pulled a plastic sheet up and scanned the next page. "Report is dated two years from now." Fenroe flattened the first sheet and held the clipboard out for Dunesto, who hesitated a moment before taking it from her hand.

"Two years," he read to himself quietly. "Same date the quarantine was activated by your friend in the reactor, Colonel Wren."

Fenroe knelt beside the standing stream and studied pieces of metal left behind by whatever was in the tank.

"They cut his head off while he was still breathing," she whispered.

After another stunned moment of standing in place, Dunesto squatted beside Fenroe. Eos stepped over the puddle and bent down on the other side. The light in her visor flashed and became a thin horizontal line, which traveled to the top of her face and then scanned downward. Fenroe watched as the beam of light passed slowly over bits of wet, fleshy-looking chunks on the floor and then flicker away. Eos extended an arm and then flattened her right hand—a tiny needle emerged from her wrist, and she surgically inserted it into one of the largest pieces of metal-fused meat.

"Anomalous secretion detected," Eos hummed. "Carbon eighteen percent, Hydrogen ten percent, Phosphorus one percent, Calcium two percent, Potassium point-three-five percent, Magnesium point-zero-five percent," she trailed off, removing the probe. Eos stood and turned, facing the darkness ahead, following the stream of liquid that had drained into the unlit corridor beyond. "The remaining sixty-five percent is an equal distribution of Copper, Cobalt, Iron, Lithium, Strontium, Aluminum, Silicon, Lead, Arsenic, and Bromine."

Fenroe stood and stepped back toward the intact tanks, studying the floating severed heads within. Between shards of metal protruding out of where the faces should have been—other than the remaining tongue and lower-jaw—the entire heads were repetitive patterns of metallic shards filled in between with granules and flakes of different colored minerals. Mixed in with the blood was an opaque grayish fluid squishing between the spokes. The lights on Eos's shoulders flared to life and painted the darkened corridor beyond.

"What *happened* to them?" Beck asked.

"It looks like—" Aris started, and then leaned in to inspect it closer, "—like...like this metal is growing out of the skin."

"Commander," Eos thrummed. "Advise replacing your helmet immediately."

"Yeah," Fenroe said, nodding her head. "Yeah, of course." She wiped the muck away from her face and went to return her helmet to the neck housing, but stopped. The visor was cracked beyond repair. "Is the air clean?"

"Unknown," the android Eos said. "I'm not reading any contaminants at this time."

"Was there a contagion?" Fenroe wondered. "Maybe the *Endeavor* crew *did* make it to Titan. Maybe they brought something aboard."

"Why *remove* the heads?" Aris asked.

Beck sucked his teeth, leaning to inspect the ghastly contents floating inside the tanks. "I don't think anyone went to Titan," he said quietly. When he realized everyone was now watching him, he stood and shrugged. "We're certainly not going."

At first she thought he was just being hopeless, but there was something in Beck's voice. Something certain. Something that meant something else. Fenroe straightened and looked at him.

"There's something you need to see," he said.

PINNACLE

1.

THE BULK OF SATURN'S NORTHERN hemisphere drifted behind Beck through a transparent wall-screen above the dusty blankets of its equatorial rings. When he moved his hand through a block of light hovering above the terminal, the screens clouded over and then cleared as a far off scattershot of moons orbiting thin dust-like planes of trapped comets and pulverized asteroids rotated in their statuesque movements around the distant planet. Beck moved his hand again and the image pulled back even farther from the outer ring system. Saturn filled the window, its giant beige and off-gray orb nestled within a perfectly flat disc system of rings.

"As soon as you and Dunesto restored power, this switched on," said Beck, nodding toward a curved view screen taking up the module's entire far side wall. "We didn't really have time to look at it too much, because the *Meridian* decoupled within minutes of this coming back online, but I did find one thing."

"What is this?" asked Fenroe.

"This is recorded data from the *Pinnacle's* optical deep space telescope," replied Beck, moving his hand across the control panel until a small segment of Saturn's atmosphere filled the curved window. A quarter of the gas giant was in sunlight. Vestiges of beige supercells undulated under thick bands of dark brown and off-red oceans of cloud cover. A slice of the great pentagonal hurricane at its northern pole could be seen coming into view. The image was utterly, unquestionably one of the most beautiful things Fenroe had ever seen, and the vividness of it all nearly caressed the breath right out of her chest.

"It should be coming up," Beck continued, pulling everyone back to the moment. The planet rotated faster than normal. Flashes of light and smaller orbs of tiny entangled shadows streaked across the surface clouds. "There," he said, slowing the image down. A collection of smaller star-like objects blinked into existence one at a time as their orbital paths led them into the light of Saturn's foreground. "You see?"

"Moons," Fenroe said, nodding softly. The stars that did move away from the shadow became clearer. Some were perfectly spherical, others were oval shaped. Some were indescribable. Fenroe leaned forward, studying the images drifting across the view screen.

"Yeah, but look here," Beck continued, pointing at the first light. "The moon Phoebe—" he pointed at the next light, a smaller one, "—Hyperion," and then the next, calling them off one at a time. "Iapetus, Rhea, Dione—" and his hand stopped at the smallest light, which became clear only for a moment before it was eclipsed by one of the other moons. Fenroe could still make out its outline, but the shape was opaqued somehow, barely visible, obscured by the smothering darkness.

"And Tethys," he finished quietly.

"This is recent," said Dunesto.

"Yes," Beck nodded. "It's the past thirty hours at roughly thirty-two times normal speed. I wanted to show you a couple of full cycles." The young physicist's fingers wavered over the lit interface again, bringing up another pulled back particle cloud image of the other sixty-two moons and the varied shapes of their ring revolutions around Saturn. Many of the objects were dark gray—almost black—some blue, some the color of enriched uranium, others silver. As beautiful as they appeared in the thick light so near the planet, they also looked ominously vacant and ancient. "You'll see the shadows of lesser bodies come around. Right here—" he pointed at another disc forming on the right, "— Enceladus, Janus...some of the smaller moons."

Fenroe glanced at Aris for a moment, who looked back with deep concern filling her intense eyes.

"And there," Beck said finally, crossing his arms, looking away from the view screen.

"Phoebe again," Fenroe intoned, just as the moon Hyperion began its stately movement into the light of Saturn for the second time. "One full cycle."

"Now, watch this." Beck approached the console and moved his fingers over the interface. The playback slowed considerably, nearly stopping altogether, and zoomed into a small quadrant off Saturn's eastern hemisphere.

"You mind telling us what we're looking for?" asked Dunesto.

A streak of small white light shot out of nowhere into the outer most E-ring.

"Hold it," Fenroe said. "What was that?"

"That," Beck said, dumping a metric ton of resolution into the station's bandwidth, slowing the playback down considerably, "was a communication satellite."

He reversed the playback and dragged a graphical box

around the blurred object with his hand, upping the resolution even more—the image inside grew and crystalized. As the pixels cleared and shrunk to more detail, two octagonal solar panels and a mirrored disc took shape amid the blackness. And then, moving forward frame by frame, the satellite inexplicably disappeared. It was there one moment, and gone the next.

"Watch," said Beck. His voice was subdued, calm and carefully articulated. Fenroe and the crew were silent as the shadowed outline of the moon Hyperion in the background filled the image—massive in its own right, like the silhouette of a blue whale emerging from deep water—and then another silver blur shot into view. It streaked toward the center of the screen like the last one, inching forward one frame at a time—

...and disappeared.

Then another streak, and another, all coming from different directions, all disappearing at the same exact spot in the image.

"Satellites." Fenroe said aloud. "A lot of them."

Beck pushed away from the interface and stepped down onto the platform.

"It's *eating* them," he said finally. "That's why we haven't been able to send or receive messages out here. This point in space is *eating* satellites."

Fenroe looked away from the view screen and tilted her head toward Beck staring ahead, clenching his jaw, wearing a mask of deep intensity and concern.

"What do you mean?" she asked, "*What's* eating them...?"

"Aris and I decided to sweep the labs," he said. "While we were making our way through the telescope control room, the viewer lit up when the power came back online." He pointed at the screen. "First thing I saw was that the *Pinnacle* telescope had been tracking this exact spot near the edge of Saturn's E-ring, following this...this empty space around the planet itself." He touched the screen where the beige overlay of obliterated moon dust gave way to the utter darkness of space. "Right here," he continued. "Someone *programmed* the telescope to follow these coordinates specifically." He waited a moment, letting it sink in. "What's so special about this spot? It's just an empty pocket..."

"It's apparently eating satellites," said Dunesto.

"You notice anything specific about these coordinates?" Beck circled the console and leaned against the partition wall just below the view screen. "Or about the rotational sequence of Saturn's moons?

"Titan," Fenroe said finally.

Before the rust blanket of Saturn's boundless surface, the frozen image of a satellite with ribbons of solar sails a few kilometers wide connected to a convex mirror-disc. Commanding and enormous in the backdrop of the satellite, Saturn's northern hemisphere could be seen as clear as the grains of faux veneer in the flooring aboard the *Pinnacle*, but there were also strange optical distortions around the image. Cream-colored clouds gathered and coalesced across the sunlit quadrant of Saturn, and bright shafts of deflected sunlight shone a swirling hurricane onto the planet's dayside beyond the fine edge of the Cassini division. Fenroe could see the hurricane begin to circle south of the Huygens gap, following a century long trajectory around the globe.

"During that whole moon cycle," Fenroe continued. "I didn't see Titan once."

Dunesto frowned and looked up at the view screen.

"That's because it *isn't there*," Beck said, as if he were a teacher speaking to a student who showed some promise. Then his voice sharpened, taking on the edge of despair. "That's because it's *gone.*"

"Bullshit," said Dunesto. "You're not reading it right."

Beck didn't bother responding. He stared at the recording.

"There's gotta be some...some interference," continued Dunesto. "Some optical pushover from another moon, or from the planet itself. Hell, it could be the *Pinnacle* lens for all we know."

"I was able to get through three Saturnian days of data before the *Meridian* decoupled," Beck said. "And not once did Titan come into view."

Dunesto shrugged: "It could be its prolonged orbit relative to the other moons. It could be a *million* different things—"

"The coordinates," Fenroe cut in.

"Right, the coordinates." Beck nodded, turning back toward the view screen. "The telescope is set to follow the exact coordinates of where Titan *should* be. I checked it and double-checked it, Aris triple checked it. The *Pinnacle* has been tracking Titan's orbital path for the last *ten and a half years*. But Titan, as you can see, is *gone*. There's *nothing* here."

"This space station has been here for ten years? That's just not possible." Dunesto shook his head, irritated. "We linked up with the *Pinnacle* before hitting the terminal bowshot toward Saturn space."

"Impossible," Fenroe agreed quietly. "Yet here we are."

"So you're telling me that the *Pinnacle* somehow developed the ability to fly all the way out here," hissed Dunesto. "Where they spent ten years watching Titan, then figured out a way to magically fly all the way back to Calisto to meet up with us, and then, after we left, miraculously beat us *back* out here?"

"I'm not saying it makes sense," Beck said seriously. "I'm merely telling you what you can clearly see with your own eyes. Look around you—" he opened his hands, sweeping the inside of the room. "Impossible, yeah, but this is the *Pinnacle*, and the data logs say it's been orbiting Saturn for the past decade."

"What is the data storage like here?" asked Aris before

Dunesto could say anything else.

Eos answered, startling everyone: "The telescope's hard disk has six zettabytes of space. At the right settings, this can be anywhere between ten and twenty years of recorded video data."

Aris nodded and then looked toward Beck. "And you say that the viewer has been tracking Titan's coordinates the entire time?"

"Yeah," Beck nodded, lost in thought, glancing at Dunesto. "Yeah, that's right."

"So track it," Aris shrugged. "Review the playback. Find out how the *Pinnacle* got here."

"Commander," Eos cut in. "I've taken the liberty of triangulating the *Pinnacle's* origin of travel based on its current speed and trajectory."

The crew looked at one another for a moment, and then stared at the little android, who stood perfectly still.

"We're not in a fixed orbit?" Fenroe asked finally.

"No, Commander," Eos said. "The *Pinnacle* is currently traveling away from a fixed vector through vacuum at approximately three hundred kilometers per hour."

"This station is not a space traveling craft."

"The *Pinnacle* is not moving at thrust, rather, it's been accelerating along an orbital path under the power of its own inertia."

"...set into motion by what?"

"Unknown," Eos hummed.

Fenroe glanced back up at the screen and traced the outline of a newer satellite pulling toward an invisible focal point at the exact spot where Titan should have been. "And you can retrace the *Pinnacle's* trajectory back to the moment it was set into motion...?"

"Negative," Eos said. "I can only retrace the *Pinnacle's* movement back to the exact moment it was set onto its current trajectory."

"Okay," Fenroe said quietly. "Okay, do it."

"Already done." The little android raised her bladed chin toward the view screen. "The trajectory's point parallax is the spot Beck has referenced."

"Those coordinates?" Beck asked, raising his eyebrows. He pointed at the center of the empty quadrant on screen, the exact spot where all the satellites vanished. "The *Pinnacle* came from right here? This empty space where Titan should be?"

"That's what the data states," Eos replied.

"All right," Fenroe said, regarding Eos for a long moment. "I want you to show us."

Eos took position at the administrator console, and her delicate mechanical fingers stroked the control panel. The screen trifurcated and projected three-dimensional images near the front half of the module. Shapes built themselves in the center of the room with holographic light.

Fenroe joined Beck on the floor and waded into an amorphous, illuminated mirage of something taking shape. One of the images transposed a thin sheet of tiny particles of light rising out of the flooring until they coalesced and became an orb. Eos's hands danced over the panel in a stream of fluid movements, and Saturn's larger orb took form in the backdrop.

"What is she doing?" Fenroe asked.

"She's rerouting the video recording through the holo-prism," Beck answered, in quiet awe.

Light of all visible spectrums burst across the room like ejected particles of a campfire, giving the sensation of floating untethered through an ocean of stars. Eos slowed the high-speed playback just enough for the crew to take in what they were seeing.

An orb of light that represented our sun circled in the distance at an arc across the room thirty inches per second, which vanished as it reached the edge of the holo-display, only to rise again on the right side of the room and continue its orbit around Saturn and its moons. The elliptical repeated endlessly, speeding up as Eos rewound the recording back to the beginning.

Despite the knowledge of it being wholly intangible, Fenroe couldn't help but feel the immense speed and vertigo of the illusion. She saw Dunesto out of the corner of her eye grab hold of the nearest terminal as the choreographed ballet of sun, planet, rings and moons unfolded before them in a dazzling display of color and reflective patterns.

The space within the coordinates that the telescope had been programmed to track suddenly peeled open like a black curtain, and intense shimmering light poured out of a perfectly formed black sphere—which seemed to appear out of nowhere—in a reverse spiral that joined the stately dance of the other planetoids following their orbital paths around the room.

"What the hell?" Dunesto said.

"We're watching this in reverse, right?" Aris asked. "She's rewinding it?"

"Yes," Beck said under his breath, nodding to Aris, his tired gaze fixed to the black star that appeared out of nothing.

"Slow it down," Fenroe ordered, unable to wrap her mind around what she was seeing.

The spiral tail of white light and the black orb halted slightly in its orbit, but reversed at a speed that was easier to see. During each revolution around Saturn, more and more light poured out of the black orb like white paint. After several rotations, the ejected material took shape in the form of a much larger orb made of light not far from the dark black circle that trailed behind. An explosion of light materialized and then sucked together, spinning around the black star's edge like a splash of milk, and then finally joined the larger, growing ball of pure light that looked as if it were being rebuilt as a planetoid.

"Titan," Fenroe said, looking to Beck for confirmation. "That spiral of light is what was left of Titan."

"The black sphere must have ripped the entire moon apart," Beck said, his mouth agape, looking up at the lighted images reversing themselves around his body. Fenroe hadn't noticed at first, but the view from the telescope had been drifting closer to the black sphere as it regurgitated more of Titan back out into space.

The characteristics of the sphere were awesome to behold. It looked as if there were three coronae overlapping each other: the very outside of the sphere's edge appeared to rotate and spew light like waves of gravity, and there was another edge just beyond it; a borderline of different light, bent like an oblate ergosphere that flattened just at the very top and bottom of the primary sphere.

The planet Saturn, the perfect black sphere, and the giant ball of light grew in size after each passing second as the telescope's POV reversed closer and closer. The images grew, filling the room with even more light, building to something grand and inexplicable. The light intensified as the black orb continued vomiting Titan back into orbit, the ejected colors that elevated and changed from a deep dark red to bright white all came together like an explosion in reverse. Beck circled the images and carefully drew an invisible line with his hand between the spiral and the black orb.

"This black sphere," he said, walking beside the disk, "must have collided with Titan."

"What *is* it?" asked Dunesto, searching up through the display. "An asteroid...?"

"I don't know," Beck said, awe and wonder in his voice. He shook his head slightly, lost in the formulation of his thoughts. He swept his hand around the edge of the black orb where the white tail smeared around the focal point: "This almost looks like what the accretion disk of a black hole would look like."

"Not possible," said Dunesto, without much certainty.

"Look at how the moon is *smeared* like that, almost like it's spiraling down a drain," Aris cut in, pulling her hand over her shaven head—a thoughtful movement, meant to stimulate her thinking. "And then how the tail of what's left slingshots the opposite direction..."

The black hole reversed closer and closer to the head of the tail of light until the two bodies touched, and a brilliant flash of even brighter light burst out of nowhere and began sucking back toward the moon like colored smoke. Closer now, the images still rewinding back toward normality, the *Pinnacle* drifting nearer to the cataclysm, the moon Titan became as big as Saturn had been when Eos first started the playback. Saturn's massive presence in the background bent oddly around the walls and instrumentation.

Closer still, the black hole disappeared as the last parts of Titan spewed out of it and collected back to its original shape. The moon was whole again—the black orb and the reconstructed moon moved majestically away from each other, the liquid rippling dot of pure blackness becoming an invisible contact point that disappeared altogether, as if it never even existed in the first place. The tiny sun and planet Saturn made their paths unaffected by what in astronomical terms was considered a relatively small event, but what in Earth terms would have been apocalyptic. And when there was enough space between Titan and the invisible black hole that destroyed it, something else appeared, this time as a flat, white disc erupting ion cones of light from its center.

"This can't be a black hole," Dunesto whispered.

"He's right," Aris said, joining Beck by the platform as the unfolding ring of light followed Titan along its elliptical. "Look at the way the light bends around the center. I have a pretty good idea of what an accretion disk looks like, but I don't know what you would call this..."

"Even if you're right," said Dunesto to Beck, "Every man, woman and child on the planet with a telescope would have seen this. A black hole would've screwed with the elliptical of every single object in our solar system as it passed into it. There's no way this could have gone undetected."

"Unless it just appeared here," Beck countered. "Unless it popped into existence *right here*. If that were the case, it wouldn't have affected anything. Nobody would have been able to see anything unless they were looking for it."

"You don't think we would have noticed Titan being ripped apart?" Dunesto asked.

The telescope continued reversing toward the ring of light as it separated from the now intact Titan, until the moon itself had moved out of frame and was no longer visible.

"The *Pinnacle* wasn't tracking Titan," Fenroe said, lifting her chin at the screen. "It was tracking the anomaly."

The *Pinnacle* gravitated toward the newly formed orb of white light, and the image began to vibrate and oscillate in a surreal way, as if it were a mirage baking over the blacktop of a highway. The ring of light disappeared entirely, and the image blurred out of focus. With one last explosive flash, the three dimensional images that had given the viewing room life blinked away, leaving the after burn of fiery orbs hanging in the air. The lingering feeling was hushed, like the sudden stop of an engine. The crew was silent for some time.

"Please play back the recording frame by frame from the beginning. Forward this time," Fenroe said.

Eos moved her hands over the terminal with the purposeful care of a surgeon, and the holo-prisms lining the room flickered back to life in a flurry of multicolored light beams. After a few moments of nothing, three-dimensional shapes began to once again take form among the crew.

"Right there," Fenroe said, holding up her hand. "Freeze it."

For a split second the deep, endlessly black orb became a blinding light farther away from the center of the image. In that fraction of a moment, the evidence of an immense hurricane the color of rust could be seen through the other side of it, stretching off to the right, swallowing the edge of something else. Fringes of billowing, thick bands of beige smoke surrounded the apocalyptic storm as it traveled across the image, where it came in contact with another hurricane that was off-white in color, and a third of its size. Slowly—very slowly—Fenroe focused and concentrated, taking in the detail of the image: the dark and light curls of atmosphere, the slant of parallel gas bands cutting out of view. In the center of that ring of light—which they saw would eventually collapse and become a black hole that would eat the entire moon Titan—those details organized in a way that Fenroe had seen a hundred times before—a *thousand* times before. These were details hammered into her memory by a life spent dreaming about what conditions were like on other planets.

"My god..." Beck said, seeing it clearly now, the image through the black hole shifting like an enormous vortex of atmosphere and finally coalescing into an ovoid disc of planet-ending weather and truth.

Somehow, through an impossible rip in the fabric of space-time—for a split second—planet Jupiter's Great Red Spot could be seen in the center of the hole.

In orbit around Saturn, through a massive hole in space, Fenroe and the crew of the IDSI *Crown Meridian* could see the planet *Jupiter*. Immense spirals of cloud-wave spread beyond the edges of what the viewer could show, rust and beige and dirt-brown lines moving slowly across the gas giant's swollen horizon. But only a part of the massive planet could be seen through the rift, and Fenroe looked up beyond the rip in space, toward Saturn, which appeared only a mere several thousand kilometers away.

Dunesto was right. This wasn't possible.

Jupiter and Saturn were separated by hundreds upon hundreds of thousands of kilometers of empty space. Yet, she found herself gazing upon the surface of both planets at the same time. One where it was supposed to be, and the other through a rip in the fabric of reality.

"It's a *wormhole*," Beck said finally.

"Wormholes are...just theory," Dunesto whispered in awe, uncertain of everything that unfolded before him. "Mathematical abstracts."

"Yeah," Beck agreed. "So is gravity."

"Last I checked, wormholes aren't supposed to *eat* planets."

Beck didn't respond to that. He stared ahead, thinking deeply.

"Wormholes don't occur naturally," Fenroe said slowly. "And in over three hundred million documented star systems, we've never recorded anything like this." She lifted her head, meeting Beck's gaze. "What makes you so certain?"

"I'm *not* certain," he said, shaking his head. "But I don't know what else you'd call—" he looked back at the image, "—*this* thing."

Eos resumed playback. The view from the *Pinnacle* suddenly manifested out of instant darkness some distance away from the ring of light, and Jupiter's red spot swirled for what passed as seconds on playback, but in actuality occurred over the course of years at regular speed. The scene played out again, only forward this time. The view from the *Pinnacle* telescope drifted away from the wormhole that connected Jupiter and Saturn space, until

Titan came into frame on the left side. When the *Pinnacle* had cleared far enough away from the rift, the hole curled into itself and shrunk drastically in size—pinching closed the tear in space—and became a single dot of starry light. It drifted for a moment, a tiny speck of light, and then popped out of existence, leaving only blackness.

The telescope remained trained on the empty space as Titan panned into frame, and once the center of the image reached the penumbra of Titan's edge, a vast and black sphere-shaped emptiness wreathed in smears of light appeared out of nowhere and made violent contact with the moon in a brilliant, spectacular display of radiation and light.

"I can't believe we're actually seeing this," Beck whispered, passing his hand through the shower of sparkling light that exploded across the room. "The rate of consumption is just..."

"Just what?" Dunesto asked quietly, staring into the images frozen in air.

"It's *terrifying*," he said, trailing off.

"What *exactly* are we looking at?" Aris asked.

"I have no idea," Beck responded, shaking his head. "This thing is behaving like a black hole, but it's clearly *not* a black hole—" he shrugged, "—wormholes don't transform into black holes. Black holes just don't come from nowhere."

"I mean," Dunesto sighed heavily and pinched the bridge of his nose, "what does all this *mean*?"

"I just don't know," Beck said finally, looking back at the images. He nodded softly, speaking more to himself than the others, thinking it through. "The *Pinnacle* must have been pulled through this... this wormhole. Maybe it collapsed into a singularity somehow. Then it...it started eating the closest thing within reach."

"And then it began *eating* communication satellites?" Aris

asked, shaking her head with lost confusion.

"Which is why we haven't been able to send messages home," Fenroe spoke finally, turning away from the light show. The crew fell silent and exchanged attentive looks, and then all eyes fell on her. She sat at the nearest terminal, staring into space, stunned by all that she had seen.

"Okay," she continued, her tone low, but her powerful voice echoed through the silent room. Fenroe lifted her head and opened her hands. "Here's what we know. The *Crown Meridian* is gone, along with its lifeboats and methane landers. The crew of the *Endeavor* is dead. The *Pinnacle* crew is dead. There is... something... in orbit around Saturn eating its moons, and this something is preventing us from contacting home." She trailed off, unable to think of anything else to say. Fenroe eventually closed her jaw and said nothing more.

"What about the *Endeavor*?" Aris asked. "If its crew made it aboard, the ship still has to be here."

"I told you," Dunesto said. "All of the umbilicals were rigged with some sort of dead-man trigger that switched over when the power was restored." He shrugged. "If it *was* docked here, it isn't anymore."

"We don't know that," said Aris. "You've only seen two out of the three docking stations. The other one could still be intact." She turned to Fenroe. "The *Endeavor* has to be here. It has to be, or we aren't getting off this station."

2.

"We've marked six corridors and three service tunnels leading into the other modules," said Dunesto, his hoarse and eroded voice echoing in the large space as it retreated down the many branching hallways. His face had become more gaunt than before, from the extreme hormonal-chemical differential of the past thirty or so hours. The crew's very dire circumstances moved frequently between ninety percent tedious boredom—sitting around in the frigid cold, worrying, planning, inventorying, fixing helmets and equipment, mapping—and ten percent mortal terror. And that shift from boredom to terror seemed to happen in an instant. This had an effect on Ryouichi Dunesto, whose eyes had sucked back into his anxious skull, his goatee spilled into the stubble of five o'clock shadow that was growing into a patchy beard. This was Fenroe's observation. Depleted and worn thin herself—her brown hair snarled and limp, stuck to her neck and chin, her eyes of the same color raw and swollen, fighting desperately not to collapse into a deep, powerful sleep.

"But it looks like most have been walled up pretty tight," Dunesto finished, staring down at a blueprint table, his face alight with soft violet dimness. He pulled a map of lines that hovered just above the terminal every so often with his hand. Gridlines swiped beneath his fingers as he searched for a route to *Docking Station-A*, where he hoped the *Endeavor* spacecraft was still moored.

"How long would it take for Eos to cut through these barricades?"

"I'm...I don't know, a couple of hours," he pressed his finger on an intersection of glowing lines, and then raised his chin toward the blockage piled high in front of the corridor access over their shoulders. "There are two airlocks at this end leading into the next module—one on this level, and one on the level above— which would take us right through the control deck's head-end. The first thing we have to do—" he pulled up the relevant corridor on his map, and zoomed in, "—is decide whether or not we want to focus our efforts on the corridors above, or cut a pathway through the station down here."

Once the exhausted crew split into separate groups, Fenroe and Dunesto navigated through the dark corridors to a quiet whisper of ventilation and machinery. While power to the entire structure had been restored, there were still damaged junctions that left much of the station in darkness. They occasionally found half-dead flickering lights, but many of the rooms and hallways leading out of the main corridors were still without power.

Fenroe's shoulder lights illuminated another barricade that had been scramble-welded with pieces of rubbish like the others—a pile of office desks, work chairs, filing cabinets, repurposed pressure doors, and bags of luggage all bolted and melted together to block access to the next module.

"I'm thinking down here," she said. "Some of this stuff doesn't look welded together. We could pull most of it down."

After hours of exploring and mapping corridors, Fenroe and Dunesto lost communication again with the rest of the crew. The last she'd checked on everyone, Eos and Aris were crawling over some obstruction in the darkness, having switched on their infrared filters and dropping their POV's into shades of off-green and white chaff, carefully making their way toward the mainframe. Beck stayed behind in the labs in hopes of figuring out where exactly the black hole in orbit around Saturn came from, and whether or not it was a danger to them.

Suja slept in a medical unit next to Ulbricht, both injured crewmates deep in a muscle-relaxed oblivion, unaware of spidery hair-like fibers threading into their flesh, pumping them full of antibiotics and painkillers. Ulbricht was still alive, but...

Fenroe didn't think she was going to make it. The med-pod was doing Ulbricht's breathing for her, and her skull had swollen to an obscene size, which put a lot of pressure on her brain. Fenroe's stomach dropped again—for the millionth time—and again she had to force the thoughts of Ulbricht back down into her heart, storing them there for later so she could focus on the task at hand. So she could concentrate on bringing these people home.

During their search, Fenroe and Dunesto were forced to double back several times as some hallway or pressure door stopped at a dead end or another shoddily constructed barricade. Most of the barricades they'd come across had been defeated by something—as if the best the builders could do was flash-weld piles of junk with a torch, none of which appeared to hold very well. A couple times they surfaced into wide hallways only to walk into a dead end or a barricade far too difficult to push through, sometimes crawling on their hands and knees through tunneled openings beneath the wreckage. When they could go no farther, Fenroe and Dunesto backtracked the *Pinnacle* corridors toward *Docking Station-A*, and entered another passageway that eventually, after a number of twists and turns, opened to a large commons area and the data terminal.

In dark light overcast from Saturn, several automated food kiosks fanned away from a seating area at equal spacing in a crescent shape—like what you'd see at a mall—open patios, stairways, elevators and social areas extended out from a series of balconies on three levels, which were only half visible in the darkness. This room—rivaled in size only by the reactor core—exposed the most breathtaking view they had yet come across. The sloped ceilings were open pressure glass, showing the clearest cosmic vista of Saturn that Fenroe had seen so far. Wild plants and overgrowth crawled up the vaulted ceilings and spilled over the balconies above. Soft light from the ringed planet and his moons poured in from above like the amber glow of streetlights back home.

The sprawling openness and immense size of the structure was a stark comparison to what they were used to in the

Meridian's cramped quarters. The *Pinnacle* would have seen a constant rotation of researchers all arriving, leaving, and staying for extended periods of time. It was an immovable island in constant contact with Earth, and it was normally very close to the *Variant Space Station* near Europa, which kept them pretty insulated from emergencies: there was always someone close enough to help if need be. Or so Fenroe thought. She wondered where exactly a wormhole incursion fit into the *Pinnacle's* emergency action plan.

The *Pinnacle* crew could afford the luxury of open space, in other words. The *Crown Meridian* and the *Endeavor* spacecrafts, on the other hand, were precise instruments designed specifically for traveling as fast as possible to the outermost reaches of space, and depositing a small contingent of astronauts onto the surface of a terrestrial moon. And then get back just as fast.

"What about this," Fenroe pointed out a series of thin lines and right angles in the grid of light that made short turns until coming against a thicker line stretching all the way to the third docking station module.

"These are no good," Dunesto rasped, shaking his tired head. "They look like service conduits of some kind running below the first level here—" he pointed at a thicker line that passed by a box labeled *INFIRMARY*. "—I vaguely remember something about access ways beneath the subfloor—that they were wide enough for crew to use—but it's been so long since I've studied the *Pinnacle's* blueprints to know how accessible these tunnels are."

"How confined are we talking, here?"

"Well," he shrugged, "it could be just full of pipe, ducting, and cables. Like I said, it's been a long time since I had to think about the layout here."

"If that's our only option, we'll have to make it work."

"That could be a quarter-mile belly crawl."

Fenroe sighed, studying the blueprints. "Granted most of the barricades have been torn down, but we have to assume that the other areas ahead are also blocked. At least here," she indicated a series of junctions beyond the barricade on the far side of the commons. "Whoever put these up hit every intersection all the way from *Docking Bay-C* to the labs. They wouldn't have risked missing anything—" she shrugged, "—I wouldn't have."

Dunesto shook his head, looking up and around the commons area. "Yeah, but why? Why barricade anything at all?"

"I don't know," she said. "I'm not even sure if I *want* to know."

Dunesto collapsed the light-table. "Wanna head back?"

Fenroe didn't respond. She didn't have to respond—he knew her answer when she shoved away from the light-table like a zombie and shuffled back the direction they'd come. Dunesto raised his chin, trying one last time to bring up the crew's video feeds in his HUD, and followed her into the half-lit gloom of the corridor ahead.

Not far from the commons area, Fenroe felt the texture of the ground change beneath her feet, and she realized that she walked upon coils of ripped and blackened cables that snaked away from the closest wall, and she followed it with her eyes up to the ceiling. A destroyed control panel hung in pieces from the next pressure door; documents and folders had been scattered in panicked randomness; desks and chairs were turned over, and what looked like evidence of some kind of explosion gathered detail in the circle of her shoulder lights. Constellations of dust floated through the air as she walked toward the opposite end, and the polished obsidian floor and severed cables gave way to something grimy, layered with some kind of dust, like a soft film of spider silk covering sand. Fenroe's bio-suit tingled, loosening as external air pressure normalized.

"There's some kind of—" she hesitated. "Some kind of secretion on the floor. It's like...little...grains of rice or something, like dead meal worms..."

"Try not to step in it," Dunesto said softly, more to himself than to Fenroe. "It could be what triggered the quarantine."

Fenroe strafed her light across what she recognized as some kind of freezer unit—they had entered a food prep area behind the line of kiosks in the Commons. The space was filled with boxes of food and large industrial tubs of condiments. She circled her light around the long room for a moment, and then took a few steps toward a washbasin and squeezed a handheld faucet—a constant flow of water shot out of the tap.

"There's water," Fenroe said under her breath, releasing the nozzle. "Food, water, and air...but no crew."

"They're here somewhere," said Dunesto, intense but low, as though he feared being overheard. He slapped the shoulder of her bio-suit and nodded her along, aiming his light around the corner into the hallway leading back toward the infirmary. "In some capacity, anyway..."

They carefully pushed back into the shadows, their lights moving from one bulkhead to the next, the corridors choked with half-burned litter and debris that hadn't been disturbed for the better part of a decade. Ambient planet glow crept up through straight-edged hallways into branching offices and waiting rooms and laboratories: anywhere that opened up to a window looking out into space. The entire path back to the infirmary drowned in shadow, and the invasive darkness pushed more and more against Fenroe and Dunesto's dimming service lights. Now and again the darkness parted to reveal floating dust or another corridor, or rooms off to the side that still received power. The hallway they were in extended arms of longer, darker hallways every few meters, humming power quietly in from the walls around them like the station's low-pitched heartbeat.

The flashlight trembled in Fenroe's hand, exposing most of the destroyed area with a continuous rain of light; although they'd spent a great deal of time mapping everything out, and since the network was still offline until Eos could get it back up and running again, and since the station's blueprints could only be accessed at specific data terminals around the installation, it was still very possible to get turned around in the twisting, labyrinthine layout that was made worse by the chaos of things. There was no telling where they'd end up if they strayed too far from the main corridors.

Far off in the back of her mind, indistinct but relentless—distant voices cycled endlessly and obsessively within—the shades of her dead crewmates pulsated to the surface: spectral shadows of the living. Always there, always calling to her in the distance.

The main corridor in the science and medical wing was an immense cavern of shadow, striped with moving beige gridlines shining through the broad, rectangular windows by the planet light that came in from the outside. Fenroe stepped through the hallway, her boot heels echoing against the walls. She'd lived in spacecrafts for more than half of a decade, but seeing this place welded messily together in dark lit shadow—and the decayed smell of old death...

Most IDSI vessels had an unusual smell of their own: the enclosed scent of ozone and freshly watered soil from the oxygen garden half captured by the sweat of primates packed into close quarters, recycling the musk permanently into the station's airflow. That mixture of Earth and the smell of living sweat of unwashed humans had always been, for Fenroe, the smell of space exploration.

Now the *Pinnacle* smelled only of decomposing plants, and

ancient mildew.

During a routine supply dock a few years before their slingshot toward Saturn, Fenroe remembered thinking about how the *Pinnacle* had been this miracle of human willpower: this impossible object of unrelenting force of reality, created solely through the expression of human dreams. Here scientists would step into and embrace the unknown and purify themselves in it, empowered by the need to learn as much about natural law and the cosmos as possible. Though explorers no longer worked in these rooms, the *Pinnacle* remained.

Now it was a tomb.

"Up there," Dunesto said. He stopped ahead in a pillar of starlight that rained in from the outside, gesturing toward a small rectangle of working lights spilling into the corridor from the infirmary ahead.

They could see shadows of crewmates bending around the walls inside. Fenroe instantly felt a weight lift from her shoulders, having been out of contact with them for more than two hours. She hurried to put the dark behind her for a moment. As they neared the infirmary, the first thing they encountered through the door was a slick line of dark red blood pulling around the bend of the next pressure door. Blood that hadn't been there before.

Stunned by the sight, Fenroe traced the red path with her light on the floor as it disappeared into the dark network of hallways ahead. Dunesto hesitated, and Fenroe could see in his eyes that he was also trying to make sense of it. They followed the blood trail as it smeared back into the infirmary.

Fenroe edged carefully into the room, her pulse thumping along the sides of her neck. She couldn't breathe, hoping to find the rest of her crew talking in hushed silence as Ulbricht and Suja rested in their dreamless, healing sleep.

But what she found instead collapsed the breath right out of her chest: smears of fresh blood adorned the walls and pooled all over the floor. The glass shielding of the medical unit closest to the door had been smashed open—shards of glass scattered around the frame on the floor, and more broken glass collected in piles upon the bloodstained mattress—blood and sweat had soaked deep into the white bedding, leaving a brown outline of a body.

Ulbricht was gone.

Suja's medical pod was also open and empty, but Fenroe could see no signs of forced entry. After stunned moments of standing very still, Dunesto brushed through the shards of broken glass and stepped into the next room with the fluid tanks of severed heads, throwing his light around frantically, his breath picking up in ragged, panicked rhythm.

"Suja!" His alarmed voice carried into the darkness. "Ulbricht!"

Fenroe stumbled directionless through the infirmary, trying to piece together what she was seeing. From some far, far place in the operation of conscious thought, Fenroe stood in a circle of blood and destruction with glass crunching under her boots, looking for a sign.

"More blood," Dunesto called back to her, pitching his voice to carry more clearly.

Numb, Fenroe followed his shadow into the laboratory, and her light strafed the tanks of floating severed heads, until it found Dunesto on the far end, aiming his lamp into the doorway on the opposite side of the room.

She stopped next to him, forcing deep controlled breaths, taking care not to step into the river of blood flowing out of the room. Dunesto continued forward silently, following the trail stretching farther and farther into the dark unknown ahead. They moved cautiously, Fenroe's senses on high alert.

There was a locker area, and through the door the shape of a man took form in Dunesto's light; his crumpled body slumped against a wall directly ahead. His legs spread out, half covered by sodden red towels and an upturned bench. The man was Suja, holding up his hand in the sudden light—he lowered it after a moment, too tired to keep it raised, clasping his other hand weakly against his stomach, clutching the oozing source of blood. His face was relaxed, ashen, and distant, teetering on the precipice of death. He was trembling and terrified.

Angling her light away from his face, Fenroe thought he seemed too exhausted to acknowledge her presence. Dunesto quickly gathered a handful of towels and started cutting one of them into long wide strips with his safety razor.

Suja wheezed, the ghost of a sad smile passing his lips. "I couldn't stop them..."

The quiet, hallucinatory sound of his words cleared Fenroe's thoughts like a winter storm. She touched him, gripping his shoulder with one hand, trying to bleed comfort into him somehow. Trying to soak up all of his fear and pain so that he didn't have to feel it anymore. His eyes had glassed over, very close to never seeing anything ever again.

"Couldn't stop who? What happened?"

"Ulbricht...she's...she's hurt," Suja said distantly, not knowing what else to say. He slowly opened his eyes, as if something came together for him. Deep concern and panic gathered between his brows and he looked at Fenroe, searching her face—she could see tears forming and spilling onto his dirt-grimed cheeks. "Fenroe," he whispered, trying to shove her away. "You have to go—"

"Suja, *where is Ulbricht?*"

"No, no, no," he said, shaking his head weakly. Dunesto knelt on the other side of him and wrapped two layers of towels around his midsection, which immediately bled through. "It's coming back. You have to go, now, get out of here," Suja stammered.

"We will," she said, touching his shoulder softly, easing him into silence. He stared at her, wide-eyed and distant. "Just relax...it's okay...calm down—"

"You don't understand," he mumbled, slipping away.

"What's he talking about—*what's* coming back?" Dunesto asked apprehensively, passing Fenroe a strip of cloth so that she could help tie off the dressing.

"Stay with us," Fenroe said, shaking him gently. "Stay with me, Suja. Tell us where Ulbricht is."

But he continued to fade. Dunesto finished cinching an end of the dressing, which kept seeping blood at an alarming rate, and then met Fenroe's eyes. He nodded, and they bent to lift Suja up to carry him back to the medical unit—

...and a high-pitched whine erupted from someplace close behind them.

Something organic, and primal.

Something near and broken, like the screeching tymbal song of a cicada, or the high-gain buzz of an electrical wire—the sound echoed off the walls, coming from the network of corridors behind them. Fenroe and Dunesto's heads snapped in that direction. The sound built until Fenroe had to cut the receivers in her helmet. The injured man winced awake, pressing his palms against the sides of his head. Dunesto stood and turned toward the doorway.

"*What is that?!*" Fenroe hissed.

Dunesto gave Fenroe a hard stare and then rushed out of the locker room toward the sound, his light quickly disappearing back into the maze of branching tunnels and corridors behind them. Fenroe hesitated. She wanted to follow, but didn't want to leave Suja. After one last look at the broken man crumpled on the cold floor, Fenroe stumbled to her feet and tripped out of the locker room as Dunesto slipped into the opposite hallway. "Dunesto!"

His lights snapped out of view just as he disappeared around the corner. Fenroe jogged after him. She rounded the corner, stumbling over burnt wreckage and debris, around another corner, until she saw Dunesto's white light reflecting off the wall opposite the infirmary door.

Fenroe found Dunesto standing with his back to the doorway and skidded to a halt—he was aiming his shoulder lamp at a slithering shadow that scrabbled through the darkness away from the light. Fenroe looked to where Dunesto's beam had ended, and on the opposite end of the room, skittering across the floor on spidery fingers of metal, a severed human head flopped unevenly toward the med-pod room, whining loudly like a centrifuge coming to life.

"Rrreeeeeeeeeee!!!! Rrrreeeeeeeeeee!!! Rrrreeeeeeeeeee!!!"

The tongue extended up out of its mandibles like an obscene tube of meat: a severed piece of lower intestine propping itself up onto insectile legs sticking out of its face. A scream erupted from its throat-hole, rasping like long planks of wood dragging against one another: a whine building into a screech so powerful that Fenroe instinctively reached for her ears. A chorus of distant, similar sounds responded from the darkness.

The severed head spidered upright until its legs found purchase. It shot awkwardly into the opposite hallway, its screams reverberating against the walls. Dunesto made a stunned movement to follow, training his light on the grotesque horror—

...and stopped dead in his tracks.

Living shadows squirmed into view ahead. Limbs too long and too thin scrambling fast around the corner, oozing around starlight spilling in from a bay window far away. Dunesto staggered back, reaching blindly behind himself for balance. Two steps. Three. Four steps, and then reality snapped back into focus. He wheeled around and sprinted toward Fenroe, snatching her arm with a look of sheer terror in his eyes. His gloved fingers sunk tight into the arm of her bio-suit and pulled her back into the hallway, back toward the locker room where they'd left Suja.

In that split second Fenroe saw something claw into the infirmary, gliding over the med-pod's broken glass like a sightless serpent. It was much larger than the head-thing that had skittered away a second before.

Through the feedback of enviro-mics in her helmet, Fenroe heard the hollow *fiiip* of bone on metal over her own breathing. She inhaled a gulp of filtered air that now stunk of rotten fruit. She saw a creature sliding between slats of light pouring in from Saturn: a thing stitched together by starved angles and loose skin, the tender flaps of its open scalp sucking against an empty brain-case: ragged triangles of bloody skin opened in four slices on its face like the meaty petals of a desert lotus. The thing had no brain that Fenroe could see, just a hollowed bowl lined with gore. It was a mirror of what she'd found in the tank of yellow liquid, except this severed jaw and tongue and metal was still attached to a body. Fenroe clawed after Dunesto, squeezing him tight as they stumbled back, taking giant sucking breaths.

The thing pulled itself through the corridor in some kind of pain: a living corpse pushing up out of wet burial-earth. Fenroe thought it had been skinned: it was a sliding, pulsating heap of sinew trying to grab her, sliding forward with amphibian thirst.

Fenroe couldn't breathe. She couldn't blink.

A forceful voice screamed from the back of her mind to *RUN!* to *GET OUT OF THERE NOW!*

Another shape filled in behind it just as grotesque, just as emaciated. Then another. And another: a writhing knot of corpses, like a nest of serpents rooting through a pile of severed human limbs.

Dunesto and Fenroe's boots slipped in the red paintbrush-swipe of Suja's blood as they stumbled back through the maze of modules and side corridors toward the recreation room. Several human-shaped shadows poured in after them like a wave of uniformed flesh, screaming and clicking like a squirming mass of deep sea parasites. These shadows closed in on them fast, crawling hungrily over each other, reaching for the sound of their boots scraping and squeaking on the floor as they fled.

Dunesto twisted and dove for the lock cylinder to manually seal the rec room from the rest of the station, his eyes peeled to their most horrified limit as they stared with raw intensity into the preceding corridor. The last thing Fenroe saw before the airlock hissed to the floor was screeching shapes unfolding from the darkness.

Something solid rammed into the other side and the door jolted in its frame, shaking from a succession of clanging impacts. Fenroe pushed herself back to her feet and searched the module's interior as the things outside brought up a hammering crescendo against the door—unable to think, locked inside the full rhythm of her deep panicked breathing, she looked for another way out, but there was nothing: a single pressure door, some benches, sinks and mirrors, a few showerheads and a wall of lockers.

"What...what is this?" Fenroe stuttered, stepping away from the door. "What's happening?"

Wheezing heavily and trembling, Dunesto aimed the shoulder lights of his spacesuit at the vibrating aluminum as it formed a new dimple after each forceful contact.

3.

The impact tremors tripped the fire suppression system, and the overhead sprinklers detonated water all over the room. Fenroe backed away from the airlock and stood beside Suja, who was still slumped against the far wall, clutching a dark red draw seeping down his ribs.

Dunesto—bio-suit and helmet now glistening with water—tore himself away from the airlock and frantically circled the room, pulling a light pod away from his chest. He activated the probe and released it in midair, letting its internal magnets take over. Dunesto stepped back as light erupted from the instrument with flat, horizontal beams that methodically swept up and down the surrounding walls, painting the shadows with hard blue waves of contour as it scanned the area for every possible way out. The solid sheets of light between the downpour bent and refracted around the water as if thrown onto the curtain of a cataract.

"What *the fuck* is happening?" Fenroe asked again through fast, deep breaths.

"I don't know," Dunesto stammered, twisting his head back toward the pressure door. "But there's more than one—" and then he started searching the inside of the room again, the sound of his heavy breathing broadcasting over short-burst comms, his face blurred by water cascading down his visor, "—I think it's the crew."

Fenroe clenched her teeth against the adrenaline, feeling sweat drip down her quivering chin. The light-bullet finished its scan and powered down, leaving Fenroe to grope through the fallen darkness. She reached for Suja and found him still crumpled against the wall, breathing heavily. Igniting her shoulder lights, the room took on a reddish hue. In her peripherals, Dunesto bent and dug his hands under an open space beneath the black steel lockers, and lifted. The non-padlocked doors swung open from their hinges and dumped old gym clothes, cross trainers, and ancient, blood-stained towels into soggy piles onto the floor—with great effort, Dunesto hoisted one end and slid his shoulder deep underneath, loading his legs. The thing on the other side continued hammering into the thick door as if it were soft tin—convex, fist-sized divots swelled after each impact.

"That's three inches of plated aluminum," Fenroe said distantly. Her thoughts flooded with images of living shadows and teeth and eyeless horror.

Dunesto straightened his legs with the lockers braced against his back and dropped them hard onto the pressure door—they crashed at an odd lean to form a rudimentary barricade.

Dazed, Fenroe raked her light across the spreading puddles of water—the drains in the floor clogged with exercise garb and towels—until she found the rectangular outline of a service panel rippling beneath the surface. This was their way out: an access point to the subfloor service conduit underneath the rec room. "I found a panel!"

Dunesto's lights materialized out of the surrounding darkness and downpour like wisps of smoke as he came to her side, and the banging halted. The deeply set metal suddenly shifted under the immense violent force of something monstrously strong—

...and the center of the door began to glow.

Fenroe froze and looked at a rose of molten light blossoming in the middle of the door itself: it was dark at first, like cooling magma, but it grew brighter. In the chaos and panic, she heard a soft hiss of breath escape Suja's lips.

She pulled her eyes away from the melting airlock and bent down, lifting Suja's soaked head away from the wall—the room brightened and rippled with fire glow as if someone had ignited a thatch of tinder nearby. Fenroe shook him awake, speaking loud over the sound of falling water, willing lucidity back into his eyes: "Where's Ulbricht, Suja—*look at me and listen*—where's Ulbricht? What's happening?"

"They're eating through the door," he whispered through his teeth, wincing against the wound pulling on his side. "They're coming."

The brightest part of the circle in the center of the door melted and ran down to the bank of lockers wedged against the bottom. The bright red parts broke down to the consistency of tallow, quickly turning pale amber. In seconds it had become white hot and began to smoke. Fenroe grabbed handfuls of Suja's collar and pulled him through the water to his knees.

"We have to move," Fenroe rasped, dragging Suja's heavy frame. "*Come on, move!*"

Grabbing Dunesto's shoulder as she passed, Fenroe stumbled away from the airlock while holding Suja's weight draped across her neck, tripping over his feet. "They're eating through the metal!"

Dunesto stood frozen in place, staring with detached shock and horror at the melting pressure door. "*What* is eating through the metal? What the fuck—?!"

"Dunesto!" Fenroe tugged harder at his arm. "We've gotta move—" she pointed below the shallow waves of the growing puddle, filling up deeper and deeper over drainage grates clogged with wet paper and trash and gym clothes. "There's an access-panel in the floor."

Reaching the panel below her feet, Fenroe dumped Suja into the standing four inches of water, and ripped a hand-sized impact drill away from her chest, praying to whatever god that might be listening that the square panel in the floor wasn't a storage compartment of some kind, and hunted beneath the water with trembling fingers for the sink of a screw. Molten metal popped and hissed behind them as it made contact with the water. A red hot bubble with tiger stripes of black and gray formed in the center of the door and burst—an inhuman arm forced its way through the blazing hot center, and uncurled into a steaming claw that trailed strings of smoke into the air.

"Hurry," she said to Dunesto, as another claw pushed itself through.

And then another.

"I'm trying—"

"They're almost through."

"I'M TRYING!"

"You—you can't," Suja whispered, eyes flinching against the falling water raining down from the fire suppression system. "You can't stop them."

"We don't have to." She nodded at the panel, grunting with effort. "We just have to not be here when they push through."

The wounded man craned his head to see, and the deep fogginess cleared from his eyes. Fenroe and Dunesto finished drilling the small panel and lifted it up from under the water weight, which immediately began pouring into the compartment below. The space around drained the standing water and left only slick tile. Fenroe pulled herself across the slippery floor and grabbed Suja, who moved to his feet, now fueled with the sudden hope of escape.

Fenroe breathed heavily: "Hold onto me—"

"*Fuck—*" Dunesto hissed, his voice breaking with panic, "— the goddamn bit broke!" He frantically searched below the water with his drill, stealing terrified glances from the melting airlock. "I think the last two screws are stripped—" he fumbled his slippery, gloved fingers along the part of the service panel bolted to the floor, hopelessness rising in his voice, "—I can't get it open."

The upper torso of something roughly human in shape forced itself through the newly liquefied center of the pressure door— the shape blindingly groped down at the glistening floor with strangely clawed arms streaming ribbons of smoke into the air. The nubby fingers cooled to a dull reddish glow, like recently ejected volcanic rock.

Fenroe bared her teeth and grabbed the loose end of the panel with both hands, digging into the wet tile with the rubber heels of her boots, and yanked it up, bending the metal until there was enough space to fit a leg. Dunesto grabbed hold as well, adding his strength in hopes of opening enough room for them to slide through.

"Suja," Fenroe wheezed, holding the panel open, her forearms burning, her grip failing.

At the sound of her voice, the wounded man crawled onto his hands and knees and then slid on his stomach into the opening, clinching the wound on his side against the pain, and dropped into the wet, splashing darkness below.

"Go, Fenroe," Dunesto hissed.

Behind them, a smoking figure fell onto the lockers and rolled clumsily to the floor, rising to its feet covered and dripping with cooling metal, just as another form began pushing itself through. The new shape took one step forward and slowed to a halt, freezing in place by the quickly hardening metal.

"You first—"

"*Go, GOD DAMN IT!*" Dunesto screamed with rage.

Fenroe released the panel and dropped to her knees. She tried forcing herself into the dark opening, but her helmet was too broad to squeeze through. Ripping the clamps away from her neck, she tore the helmet away and tossed it onto the ground behind her. She pulled herself near the edge, and then dropped into the conduit. Her body hung in utter darkness for long moments until she splashed hard into a puddle that spread in both directions of a long tunnel—scrambling to her feet, she looked up, feeling the cold ship air on her exposed face. Four separate waterfalls spilled into the conduit from above and met at right angles all around her: a boxed cage of cascading water forming sheets of liquid glass distorting the tunnel on both sides.

One hand wedging the panel open with the help of his knee, Dunesto frantically tore his helmet away from its neck housing with his free hand, and then bent down, squeezing himself underneath the thin sheet of metal. Shapes of obscure living smoke blurred and poured into the room behind him. Fenroe reached up and clasped his scrabbling hands. She pulled with everything she had.

Dunesto heaved a high-pitched whine, as if the wind had been knocked out of him. His eyes went wide and his hands tugged hard away from Fenroe's grip. She held on tightly, the soles of her boots squeaking against the flooring as Dunesto's whine built from a squeal to a gurgled scream, pushing thick bodily fluids up into his throat. In the soft orange glow spilling in from above, ropes of blood poured out of Dunesto's lips and nostrils, spilling across Fenroe's arms and face. His lower, unseen half tugged again, but Fenroe held on with all she could—his body jerked sideways to where the remaining bolted half of the service panel met with the floor. With one last violent tug, Dunesto's body had become pinched between the panel and the opening, and his torso came free from his legs, spilling his unraveling intestines all over the floor. The sound of his suit and flesh coming apart was similar to the tearing of cotton fabric and burlap.

Dunesto's eyes went distant and hemophilic, his tortured, liquid scream cut suddenly by a throatful of thick fluids. His lips parted silently as his torso slid oddly through the opening without resistance—Fenroe pulled—his severed trunk bounced against the subflooring like freshly butchered meat. Dunesto slipped an arm out of Fenroe's grasp and his fingers carefully searched the extent of his fatal wound, this immense yawn that separated him from his hips, exploring the braids of his insides unraveling onto the glistening wet floor with his fingers, his face perfectly blank. The service panel bit and chewed away strips of flesh from his abdomen as it slammed back into place, sealing the passage off from the horribleness above.

Numbing ice spread across Fenroe's chest, and she staggered backwards through the puddle grasping one of Dunesto's twitch-firing forearms with both hands. She dragged his torso away from the service panel as something massive howled above them with triumphant hunger and rage. Dunesto's mouth popped wordlessly, blood rising out of his face like a wellspring, his expression going slack, his eyes growing vacant. He was still present for those last seconds, still aware—a brownish green paste mixed with blood spilled out of his bowels, smearing across the dark floor as she dragged him through the standing puddle of sprinkler water.

Suja cried out in soul-anguished despair and retched, stumbling down the dark passage ahead. He reached for something to brace himself and disappeared into one of the branching tunnels, leaving Fenroe alone with Dunesto splashing his hand weakly in the shallow water.

Dunesto looked up, blinked and cored into her eyes. She kept dragging him away from the ceiling panel with jerking bursts of strength. He was still alive, a look of horror and shock and revulsion on his face, the life leaking out of him like a punctured carton of milk.

Fenroe dragged herself through the tunnel with one hand, rowing Dunesto's body one jerking pull at a time. The metal panel above began to glow with pale light. After several breathless meters of darkness, Fenroe realized she had been dragging half of a corpse: Dunesto's empty eyes pointed unseeingly toward the ceiling.

Numb tears trickled down her face, and she released her grasp on his arm. Fenroe couldn't help herself: she broke into a freshet of halting sobs. She tried to hold them in but her body shivered and trembled without control; it sung at a register far beyond panic, far beyond visceral horror. It was the register tuned to a frequency of basic thought, dialed solely into the rat part of her brain: the process of her consciousness that thought only about voiding its waste onto its own meat to make itself unappetizing to the predator. That register of indescribable panic filled her nostrils with each fast breath; it poured into her mouth, seeped down her heaving throat, and settled heavily into the pit of her stomach. She felt that feral panic move inside, trying to claw itself out. She felt it tickle her guts like the dusty wings of a million moths. And she couldn't rein it in. She couldn't even try. The rat part of her—the survivor part—assumed control, and she was powerless to stop it.

She turned and scrambled on hands and knees into the infinite midnight of the service conduit, feeling the cold air stinging her exposed face dripping with salted tears, taking in giant mouthfuls of the stale oxygen.

By the time she rounded the first junction, her gloved fingers blindly groped and clasped around Suja's ankle, who was sprawled out on his stomach, breathing heavily: a small line of blood seeped through the bandaged stump of his injured hand. Trace stains of darker crimson oozed through the fabric of his Hawaiian shirt from an unseen wound on his torso. "We've gotta move—"

"It tore him in half," he said, his face blank with horror.

Fenroe raked her teary eyes through the darkness behind them: the lambent orange weld-light rained into the tunnel from the locker room above. The sparks of metal fragments glittered onto what was left of Dunesto's body. She turned and straddled

Suja and gathered two fistfuls of his bloody, sweat-soaked shirt – the fabric tearing as she hefted him to his feet. Fenroe grabbed the wrist of his good hand and pulled his arm over her neck.

"Get up," she ordered, pulling him to his feet. "We need to move now—"

"He's gone—"

"*GET UP, GOD DAMN IT!*"

He moved as she commanded, sliding his vacant, half-dead body against the curved inside of the tunnel at a crouch. He wheezed hard, and she felt in the weight of his body that he was beyond the edge of collapse. The glowing red-orange light faded behind them. Metal scraped loudly, and the ceiling dipped with a flimsy rolling *ka-chunk*.

Something massive *wuffed* slow and deep into the breached service panel like it could sniff Fenroe's sweat-terrified hormone trail out of the air. The burning light intensified, raining particles that popped and smoked when they landed on Dunesto's twitching torso.

"They're coming," Suja rasped, his lips trembling. Fenroe pulled as hard as she could and moved as fast as the four foot height of the conduit would allow, ripping and dragging the injured man around the corner.

She turned her head one last time, and something formless and dark dropped into the newly melted opening, trailing smoke and fire like an asteroid breaking the Earth's atmosphere. It plummeted and splashed into the puddle that fed from the fire suppression system above. Melted aluminum made contact with the water below in an explosion of black smoke that engulfed the corridor and spread toward her. Something alive moved inside, clawing to its feet.

Fenroe pulled Suja into another tunnel that narrowed with just enough space to crab-walk in a low crouch. She released the injured man's wadded shirt collar and slid her back against the tight space, knocking her head against the ceiling and clattering her bio-suit against the narrow walls.

"This way," Fenroe gasped, emerging into another conduit on the other side. She turned to help Suja through, supporting his weight until he was clear. Her lower back and neck screamed with pain from having to maintain a constant hunch in the cramped tunnel.

They staggered through the passage—the dark maze of hallways passing like highway pylons—crawling through side passages covered by louvered panels, stumbling blindly beneath ventilation ducts that ascended to other levels every few meters. She gripped the first rung of the first ladder they came across, preparing to climb into the vent, and stopped: a mass of shapeless limbs appeared in Fenroe's light, clawing down at her from above. She retreated down the ladder and pulled Suja back in the direction they'd been heading.

The beam of Fenroe's light wavered hypnotically in the tunnel ahead. She blinked, seeing what looked like another dark shape sliding out of a deeper darkness: a glinting obscene form moving toward her and Suja from the opposite end, filling the entire tunnel at the very edge of her light's reach. The whispering chitter of ripped vocal cords came from the moving shadows ahead.

"Go back!" she hissed.

Suja stumbled in reverse, tripping over his own exhausted legs. Behind them another dark mass of shapes exploded and spilled through the narrow opening, closing the route off like a wall made entirely of decayed human flesh—the things that tore Dunesto in half were close enough to distinguish individual forms in the mass: separate sets of arms and legs reaching through the dim light.

Suja bumped hard into Fenroe and knocked her off balance. She frantically searched the conduit ceiling with her light for something—anything—that would lead them out of the maze of tunnels. Thick black pipes ran in both directions, and Fenroe could see a bundle of braided data lines tucked between the cables. She grabbed Suja's slumping body and pulled him to the side, reaching through the widely set piping until her hand found the wire, and followed it.

A chorus of tortured screams erupted just beyond the edge of their light, almost human but higher pitched, distorted behind a dial tone of pixelated breaks coming from everywhere at once. Each low frequency scream gathered with and behind a sickly deep rhythm of stridulation. It sounded like the scream of a machine that realized it had a soul: a deep, aching shriek of an infinite number of circuits firing at once. But it was strangely prehistoric, like it could have been coming from something that hunted large jungle prey.

Fenroe focused on moving quickly down the dark, low-hanging veins of the conduit, the bundle of cables overhead sliding through her panicked fingers as she stumbled to keep her balance. She prayed it was a wire run that could lead them out.

Sliding in her hand, the rope of wiring led Fenroe and Suja into another tunnel and then joined with a much larger bundle that stretched off into the darkness ahead. She ran, sucking in deep, watery breaths while pulling Suja's staggering body toward what she hoped would lead to the network's Head End and the mainframe, where Eos had been headed before they'd all lost contact. Suja's mouth hung open, his face slack from exhaustion and blood loss. His lips drooped with lines of spittle. She kept pulling him by his shirt, forcing him to move his legs. All they had to do was follow the thicker braids of blue cable until it reached the end, and hope the path was clear.

Fenroe and Suja stumbled around the corner of a T-junction, throwing their lights into the emptiness ahead—she looked up, feeling more than hearing the sound of exposed bone on metal: a large dark form fell toward her through a narrow vent from above. It dropped into the tunnel like a stone, slamming hard onto Fenroe's left side—a whitewash of light forced breath out of her lungs, and she sprawled to the smooth, black flooring, scrambling to her stomach. She instinctively kicked the thrashing shape away and braced herself, picturing the thing mounting her chest and vomiting its sickness into her open, screaming mouth.

The thing that uncurled itself in her light was a man.

But it only barely resembled a man.

And it was wearing the tattered rags of a *Pinnacle* uniform.

The man-thing slithered on all fours in her twitching shoulder light, and raised its dead face toward the ceiling. It lifted its head as if it were inviting Fenroe to slit its throat, as if it were preparing to release a bloodcurdling howl of triumph—Fenroe kicked away from it hand-over-hand in the dark, trying to get back to her feet, slipping, awash in soul-sucking panic—and the thing unfolded itself from the darkness, reaching with wiry white limbs, uncoiling itself like a deformed crab ready to feed.

The thing looked starved: its limbs were long, its stomach bulging in the center from years without protein. Its skin was semi-transparent and spidered with giant purple varicose veins crawling all over its body. Its arms and legs were nothing but bone sheathed in a casing of intestine, like a limp sausage filled with milk.

She saw an insatiable need in its movement, swaying its body with a quivering hunger. Its bony ribs stuck out like the teeth of a bear trap. Massive handles of flesh oozed gray ichor over its shoulders; ulcerated boils popped all over its skin: needles and screws of different colored metals stabbed out from underneath the yet-unbroken skin of its face.

The corpse's head inflated in the shadowy light, yawning its mouth farther than any human could—like a snake dislocating its jaw to feed—its scabby black tongue flopping out into the dead air. Its rotten skull with patches of mangy hair inflated until it reached capacity and mushroomed into a flower of exploding needles—flecks of glinting metal sparked off the tunnel walls and ceiling as white organic flachettes bounced and ricocheted around the walls.

Fenroe felt a stabbing pain at the base of her thigh and she screamed, instinctively wrapping her hands around a glistening ivory barb that had pierced her bio-suit and plunged deep into her flesh: one of the blunt, bone-colored fingers that had been ejected from the thing's sporified head.

She fell against the wall, howling at the pain, and clutched the white nub sticking out of her leg. Fresh blood oozed between her gloved fingers. Biting down hard against the white-hot fire, Fenroe kicked away from the now headless corpses still writhing on the floor: the melon rind of its head was peeled open and pumping ropey orange fluids out of its bloody throat-hole. The headless body still lived, pulling itself forward with mindless hunger.

The ivory-colored barb sticking out of Fenroe's thigh went from the solidity of an iron spike to a thick rubbery finger as soon as it broke the skin, and she could feel it burrowing into the flesh. She could feel the thing writhing with life, digging into her meat, sending tendrils of electric fire that blurred her seared vision with red shapeless bands of starfire shooting down her body.

Hearing Fenroe cry out, Suja turned and stumbled back to her: he still held the bloody stump of his right forearm against his ribs, wheezing deep and hard like an old man. Holding her own leg, Fenroe desperately kicked herself away from the headless corpses still groping at them through the darkness. Suja fell to her side and grabbed her utility harness with his good hand, fighting through the pain of his own wounds, and pulled Fenroe away with everything he had. She grabbed hold of his shoulder and leaned her weight against him. More creatures poured into the conduit behind them.

The blood from each of their wounds ran together and smeared to form a single trail on the floor, and the tunnel suddenly lit up with a series of powerful explosions as more barbs were deflected by the walls.

"Where are we going," Suja hissed through his teeth, now bearing her full weight, blood seeping steadily out of the stump of his right hand. More blood came from an unseen wound above his hip.

"Follow the data line," Fenroe said, clutching her bloody leg. "It'll take us to the mainframe."

They fell and staggered around narrow corners and junctions, limping and running on and on through the darkness until everything became a directionless blur.

"I can't go any more," Suja wheezed distantly under Fenroe's weight.

The pain in Fenroe's leg had become unbearable. She stopped him for a moment and leaned against the wall to pull a flap of her ripped triweave fabric over the wound in her thigh, tucking it into the leg strap of her utility harness.

"There's something in my leg," she said, fingers trembling, threads of terror squirming in her stomach as the thing swelled inside her thigh. Fat drops of sweat oozed out of her brow and tumbled down over her quivering lips. "It's moving," she finished tightly. "I can feel it."

"You're going to have to go alone," Suja said forcefully, sliding to the floor, his bruised eyelids dropping like hammers.

"I'll catch up, jus'need to ress frr minute..."

Fenroe's leg had already begun to swell. It throbbed with intense red heat that reached up into the center of her chest. "I'm not leaving you."

"Fenroe," Suja hissed, summoning the last bit of energy he had to shove her away. He peeled his injured, sticky hand away from his side, revealing just how much blood he had lost: slimy and thick, his Hawaiian shirt had soaked through with blood from under his armpit all the way down to his hip. His face was bloodless and white, and his lips had paled to the color of rotten fish. "I can buy some time, but you haveta run—"

"There's no fucking way—"

"Harris died because of me," Suja said with intensity. He stopped as the fire left his voice, and his face relaxed in complete exhaustion. "You and me have been friends long enough that you have to feel some kind of commitment to me." He sagged against the wall, talking softly. "Please, I won't let anyone else die because I wasn't strong enough. So go, please god, Fenroe make it easy for me and *just go*—"

"*You* listen," Fenroe said forcefully, scanning the dark passage behind them. She could feel the shadows moving closer and closer with each passing second. "I'm *not* fucking leaving, all right? You wanna die? Die on your own time."

"Fenroe, please—"

"You and me?" she asked, cinching tight the improvised bandage around her thigh. "We're getting out of here."

Suja opened his eyes and took several deep breaths, the muscles along his jaw clenching and flexing like gunfire. "God...god *damn you*, Fenroe...you're gonna die you fucking idiot..."

"Everyone dies," she hissed, reaching down to grip his arm like a vice. "*NOW GET UP AND MOVE!*"

He cursed and pushed himself away from the wall, pulling Fenroe's arm over his neck and grabbing a handful of her bio-suit at the beltline, lifting her up. In one bone-skirting flash, a lightning bolt of fire seared down her thigh just below the hipbone. She grasped hard around the ragged, gummy skin of her leg and felt a sluggish outflow of blood running with alarming speed through her fingers, which glued the fabric of her flight suit to her calf.

Needles of agony blurred her vision, and Fenroe fell against the conduit wall, clawing at the writhing worm that twisted its rubbery body deeper into the meat of her thigh.

"*Ah god, get it out!*" She howled, the guttural sound grating up out of her throat. She couldn't think, couldn't understand anything but the alien presence inside of her leg, forcing its way up toward her reproductive organs.

Suja begged, "Just tell me what to do—"

"*Get it out,*" Fenroe screamed through her clenched jaw, which had welded itself shut with so much force that she could feel her teeth crack. "*Ah god get it out of me!*"

Suja pulled her a little way down the conduit, the living shadows thinning out behind them, their piercing screams growing wider and thicker and closer. Fenroe fell to her good knee, needles of red cutting into her vision. The pain was so intense she couldn't move.

Suja ripped the flap of her toolkit away from her chest, and all that was inside were a pair of pliers, one plasma torch, and a couple of titanium zip ties. He peeled the pliers away and groped in the shadow of her service lights for the hole in her leg with his good hand. He pinched the flap of her bio-suit with the pliers and tore it away, exposing the pulpy rubber tubing of muscle and flesh. Some of the blood vessels were so inflamed that Fenroe could actually see their throbbing, severed tips squeezing blood into the air. In the center of the wound was a nubbed finger of some kind. It moved when Suja stabbed at it with his pliers, sucking deeper into her skin like a startled earthworm.

Fenroe screamed in agony.

The clawing shadows poured into the conduit from the other end. Suja dug the pliers into the wound and opened the flaps of skin, staining her flesh the color of cowhide beneath the ceaseless flow of blood bubbling up in rhythmic cadence with her pulse: Fenroe's heartbeat chugged in thick viscous bursts.

Her screeching voice ripped into the air once more, but not because of Suja; she screamed because she could *feel* the thing twitch inside. It moved as if it knew that something on the outside was threatening to pull it free from the warmth of her skin; the thing stuffed its blunt head deeper into her leg, and all Fenroe wanted to do was grab something sharp and hack her own leg off.

"Oh my god," Suja hissed, staring into the seeping hole in her leg. "*I can't do this, please Fenroe oh my god!*"

Fenroe rolled her head toward him, his mouth hanging open beneath the bleached parchment of his face and completely washed of pigment. His eyes were dilated like a shark's mouth.

Which is when Fenroe felt something reach out of her skin.

Which is when she looked down at her leg.

She'd seen the white meat of its body for only an instant. It was thicker than Fenroe had imagined: fat as a piece of intestine. The part sticking out of her leg split into four separate appendages. They looked spongy but deadly, too, like the leathery flesh of an elephant ear. It flinched like an insect suddenly exposed to the light; its body had snapped madly as it pulled itself deeper into the safer layers of her skin.

She wanted to dig her fingers into the wound and rip it out with her nails. She felt the bare stump of her femur—cold as glacial ice. Suja's pliers closed around the waxy parasite and the separated labia of Fenroe's wound were rubbery and slick, gummed with the blood that flowed freely like a faucet.

Suja twisted the pliers and scooped into the muscle beneath the thing, grasping it moving inside with mindless warmth, and forced his hand deeper into the wound. A spurt of gray pus bubbled around the ragged lips of the hole like oil.

Fenroe felt a species of fear penetrate her heart. But the fear she felt now was adolescent, languid. She had no precedent for it. It was the deep, incomprehensible terror of a child: something was *inside* of her. It was *eating* her from the inside out. Her mind recoiled at the perversion of it: everything was wrong in ways she couldn't really understand. She'd never been in any sort of accident before. She'd never seen her own insides pulled out like that. She'd never been under the surgeon's light as people with masks frantically worked to save her life. And that gap of experience—that deep chasm of understanding—was more terrifying to her than anything she'd ever experienced before.

The creatures poured closer, the flaps of their toothy skulls flagellating the dark like the tentacles of a man o' war, and Suja held on and stared down out of Fenroe's field of vision with revulsion, a thick unblinking body-horror in his eyes.

She felt the pliers close on something solid and rubbery, like an extension cord writhing beneath the skin, in the muscle, around the bone. Red-hot fire spiked down the side of her blood-soaked knee.

Suja tugged hard.

And the pain...

It was too much, like a sawblade of fishhooks raking her gums.

Suja ripped the thing free and Fenroe's skin made a wet sucking sound. It separated like the final purge of birth. It was the color of old bloodstained ivory, twisting and turning in her service lights like a giant maggot, stabbing its free half repeatedly toward Suja's bare wrist. The thing writhed inside the jaws of the pliers with the slippery sound of earthworms flopping around in a bowl of milk.

The infected crewmen were feet away, screeching with the intensity of a train wreck.

The cord-like maggot responded by opening the leafy flaps of its translucent shell like a starfish, the thing's organs pulsating underneath its clear skin like digestion, flat meaty appendages quivering like the sucking mantle of a squid.

"*Throw it!*" Fenroe screamed, clawing away.

Suja whipped the squirming thing into the throng of rotten limbs reaching for them through the darkness, just as it opened up like a flower and peeled back over itself to attack the pliers still clamping its body.

Suja pummeled his shoulder under Fenroe's armpit and hoisted her up, dragging her deeper into the tunnel, away from the frenetic sound of sliding flesh. Sucking in thick air, feeling the effort of each breath weigh on their heaving chests, Fenroe and Suja supported each other through the low passage, aiming their light back at the trail of their own footprints outlined in blood. As Fenroe's leg stiffened, she limped hard enough to realize that the parasitic thing had taken out a small chunk of her muscle when it was pulled free, and each step of her right boot squished blood out like a sopping wet rag.

They groped their way through the access passage, the darkness coarsening and texturing with insect sounds and deep, canned breathing. They followed the bundle of cable with Fenroe's light as it led deeper and deeper into the cold darkness. The grated walls brushed against Fenroe's numb fingers as they limped forward. If she were less exhausted, if the frigid air on her slickened skin hadn't been so harsh on the unbearable pain of her bone-deep fatigue, she would have stopped and laid down with Suja right there and just let herself die.

Pieces of white electrical tape ticked off every meter-length of wire as they approached the penumbra of their own shadows. All the pain and loss finally broke the levee of exhaustion in her lungs, and it all became a seamless mirage of bone-deep anguish, a distant dream, a rabid desire to let her knees drop so that she could be taken by the strange creatures pouring in from all directions. But she knew Suja wouldn't leave her side. He'd die right there with her, fighting off the tide of death with every last drop of blood in his body.

This was the only reason Fenroe kept moving.

Leading her deeper into the tunnel, through places that narrowed so tight that they could only pass by turning their bodies to the side, the hem and bluish glow of her service lights gave just enough illumination for them to avoid stumbling into the curved walls and low ceilings—their silhouettes spread out behind them like smeared ink. Following the chain of ghost-light around a curve, Suja stopped in his tracks and took several deep, shuddering breaths.

The way was blocked. The tunnel sheered in the glow of an unnatural wall.

The route would have taken them to a service panel near the mainframe's Head End. Assuming they had been following the right wire-pull, Fenroe and Suja might have found the server hub, and they might have been able to get Eos's attention if she was still there working on getting the network back up. They could have found one of those floor panels and banged on it until the android opened it from above.

But the tunnel ahead of them had caved in as a result of some explosion in the hallways above. There were thick I-beams twisted like barbed wire, crushed by the immense weight of collapsed permasteel concrete and armor glass. The network cables they had been following had ripped during the collapse: the wires twisted and disappeared into the obstruction. Fenroe and Suja were cut off. Trapped.

Her eyes closed in defeat, her breaths coming in hitched, shuddery gasps as she fumbled around to aim her light at the sounds of rotten skin sliding through the darkened tunnels to finish it. She collapsed against the wall, and clutched the hole in her leg.

"What now?" Suja was hoarse, and his breath had a wet quality to it, like his lungs were filling up with liquid.

Then she heard what sounded like a nest of cockroaches scuttling and rubbing together beneath a slat of cardboard. Saliva squirted into her mouth, bitter and tangy as a copper penny. She felt faint with fear. Her stomach flooded with cold lead.

They were going to die.

Right there and then.

The rat part of her brain that she'd become aware of earlier gnawed out through her skull with the cold teeth of survival. Her legs went numb: the bones felt as if they had been liquefied. The sickening sound of moving corpses invaded her mind, creating a carnival of nightmare images: visions of deep-sea creatures with slurping mouths large enough to swallow a tractor tire. Skulls that had been sucked dry of their meat with feelers of scalp-flesh, huge white tentacles sliding out of the tunnels enlarged by the horrifying selection of abyssal pressure. Long, tube-like hands groping out of the shadows, reaching for her. A shuddering groan escaped her lips. She put her hand over her face, her back sliding against the bulkhead as she bit down on her lip.

Behind them, not ten meters away, what looked like a wet burlap sack of severed human limbs clawed into the tunnel. There were so many headless corpses writhing in unison within the cone of her shoulder lamps that she couldn't identify where one body ended and another began. They were packed so tight in the tunnel that each visible limb was attached to something glistening with blood, which somehow—through a complex knot of rotten shark skin—attached to an exploded head similar to what she'd found in those yellow specimen tanks in the Infirmary's bio-lab. Only these heads were still attached to their bodies.

Some of the corpses had intact skulls that were still bloated with parasitic needles. Others were peeled open like eyeless, briny fungi of shaved metal and teeth. A nest of a hundred headless tongues probed the air, wriggling and licking like the limbs of a sea star, searching for them.

The sound of metal blades chewing wood filled the tunnel with their screams as each deformed head snapped toward Fenroe and Suja's position, tracking their movements. The two injured astronauts moved painfully to their feet and staggered away as the writhing mass came to frenzied life, invigorated by the sudden movement. Countless bodies packed into the enclosed space, floor to ceiling, wall to wall, squeezing through like sludge.

Fenroe summoned strength and held herself upright against the wall. She pulled the hand torch away from her utility harness and opened up an eye-piercing beam of pure energy, bathing the inside of the low tunnel in irresistible plasma. The filter-shield had been smashed to pieces, so she averted her eyes and sliced into the wall, guiding the beam by feel. The metal liquefied in seconds and popped as it made contact with her bio-suit, filling the space with colorless strobing light and white smoke.

Between a pattern of flashing sparks, the entire tunnel brightened long enough for Fenroe to see in broken freeze frames just how close the things had come: a horde of bloated human corpses covered with splotches of glistening minerals and metallic spores growing out of their flesh crawled towards her through the light, packed so tightly in the narrow tunnel that they could only seep forward by the force of the masses pressing in from behind. Living corpses with hands that had twisted into gnarled arthritic claws, some stiffening as hard as rock, still covered in cooling metal from the locker room pressure door they'd melted through above. The ones that hadn't yet ejected their salvo of worms had blood and metallic fluids leaking from their clouded, unseeing eyes. The gold and silver liquids came out of their nostrils and mouths, soaking deep into their ripped and faded gray uniforms—crusts of granulated streaks of thick ichor dribbled down their dead chins, rimmed with ancient flaking blood, their lips peeled back, mouths hanging open showing long black and cracked tongues like the surface of a dried-up lake bed, necks so swollen with blood and squirming parasites that they couldn't turn their heads.

The plasma of Fenroe's cutter plumed and sputtered out before the wall could fall completely free from itself. Bracing herself against the opposite side of the tunnel, Fenroe pulled the boot of her good leg back and stomped hard onto the loosened metal, violently kicking it open just enough for her and Suja to squeeze through to the adjacent conduit. She twisted to the side and ducked into the opening that her cutter made glisten like uncooled glass, and then turned to find Suja's arm, enshrouded in welder's steam, clawing through. Ripping him into the new tunnel with her, Fenroe fell hard against the opposite wall with his weight, and they both immediately scrambled to their feet. One direction led back the way they'd come, and the other end was cut off by a wall of piping, gauges and meters.

Another dead end.

Suja grabbed Fenroe's reaching arm and helped her limp and stagger in the opposite direction. Coming to a separate junction, more corpses burst into the tunnel ahead, blocking the conduit with their bodies, crabbing forward with headless necks blossoming like orchids of viscera and tongues and blunt human teeth.

"Back," Suja hissed, nearly out of breath. "Go back!"

Fenroe and Suja skidded to a halt and stumbled back toward the dead end. Returning to the hole she'd just cut with her plasma, they backed into a thicket of decayed arms clawing through. Fenroe couldn't breathe, and she didn't have the strength to keep moving; she was carrying too much weight.

She frantically peeled her bio-suit away from her shoulders and slid it down past her waist, kicking her legs out. Her navy blue flight suit had become black and soaked through with blood and sweat. The first of the corpses pulled itself through the opening, flopping hard onto the smooth floor, boxing them in. As soon as it hit the ground, the creature started probing the air with its headless black tongue. Between the light cast from the discarded bio-suit lying on the ground and the thrashing, oozing dead limbs clawing up the tunnel from the only possible escape route, there was only a vague ring of orange light leaking in from the seared hole in the wall for illumination.

"What now?" Suja's voice was hollow and dead, his words spoken through a slackened jaw.

She sparked her plasma cutter again and reached it toward the ceiling.

Biting into the smooth surface directly above her head, Fenroe dragged the stabbing light of her plasma across the metal, which in a matter of seconds began to melt and drip onto the floor.

"How do you know that's a way out," Suja said, unable to take his eyes away from the emaciated human remains clawing towards them, the skin flaps of their opened heads moving and reaching out like individual appendages. "That could be a foot of permasteel..."

Fenroe reached the first arc of her new opening as flecks of hot metal dropped onto her temples and the back of her neck. The cut side of the ceiling sunk slightly under its own weight, showering her with orange sparks, and a thin line of light broke through and cast onto the floor.

"There's light!" She called over the sound of blasted phosphorous, focusing on not thinking about the shadows growing larger and larger in her peripherals.

They had only seconds.

The first infected crewmember through the opening crawled to its hands and knees, vomiting sheets of greyish gold and red liquid out of the orifices in its face. Small, wriggling things moved inside the vomit.

Suja shouted, facing the threat. "Hurry—!"

The creature stood and guided itself as if it didn't know how its legs were supposed to work. It stumbled toward Suja with its arms outstretched, its headless black tongue skinned out over the lower teeth of its jaw. The thing shambled into a broken run—more and more of them plopping through the welded opening with every step. Fenroe spared a glance over her shoulder—she was almost there.

Dragging her cutter around the first arc, the two-inch thick metal sunk even lower into the conduit. Within reach now, Suja brought his knee to his chest, and kicked out hard as the bottom of his bare foot smashed against the soft underside of the nearest corpse's chin. He kicked its thrashing, bloated body back into the clutching, groping creatures behind it.

The thing arched its back as it hit the floor, bridging its chest into the air, and its midsection expanded like an overinflated lung. Through the sound of cracking ribs, its stomach burst like a wet sloppy fart, firing a salvo of ivory parasite-barbs in every direction.

Suja let out a grunt of sudden pain and then waded back into the wall of death, kicking and stomping at anything that moved with one last ditch effort of survival.

Finishing the molten circle of cut metal, the ceiling swung down, nearly crushing Fenroe's skull. The panel hadn't completely separated from the ceiling, but she cut away enough so that a person could climb through.

"It's clear. Let's move!" She tossed her cutter up through the opening and grabbed the back of Suja's sweaty, blood-soaked Hawaiian shirt, yanking him away from the sucking shadows— their open skulls unfolding and closing like the circular jaws of a lamprey, their severed esophagi bubbling and coughing up golden bloody fluids—

He turned with her, tears streaming down his battered and dirt-grimed face—she reached up and clutched the red-hot lip of the floor, burning the soft flesh of her palms. Pulling herself up and through the opening with the help of Suja below, Fenroe slid across the floor into a dim office space. The hole in her leg dragged heavily over the edge, which delivered intense bursts of pain into her chest strong enough to knock her out cold.

"Fenroe!" Suja raised his good hand up into the light—she scurried around and grabbed it, reaching back down over his shoulder to get a handful of his black cotton shorts, feeling his fast breath blow onto her shoulder—moving to her feet, Fenroe dug her heels into the smooth ceramic flooring and ripped Suja up and out as he kicked furiously at the dead bodies below that had completely overrun the tunnel.

Once he cleared the cut metal, Fenroe released him and climbed to her feet. She stumbled toward the only pressure door in the room, expecting it to open. She instead crashed into the metal hard enough to rattle her own teeth. To the right of it, where there should have been the pale blue glow of a holo-pad, there was nothing. And it wouldn't respond to her frantically waving hands.

"*No!*" Fenroe struck the door with her palms, trying to will it open. She looked up at the flat rectangular panel above the airlock—six square inches of metal: it had been ripped open and blackened by long dead fire; it dripped strands of melted wire and copper from the motor control box like creeper vines reaching toward the floor.

She slumped against the cold metal and drew some of the chill out of its smooth surface. It was much thicker than the floor panel. It would take more time to cut through with the plasma. Time she and Suja didn't have.

Suja collapsed his back against the door beside her and gasped in huge gulps of thick air. He held his bloody hand to his side—the bandage had ripped loose and become tangled around his wrist, soaking through with dark brown and coppery blood—and let his exhausted body slide to the floor.

The spidery creatures pushed up through the dark orange light and the electric glow from the white hot fire-flashes of Fenroe's still-burning torch cutter lying on the floor nearby. Their thick flaps of scalp opened up around tentacles of blood-cracked tongues that licked the air. Their brainless skulls were hollowed eggshells squeezing into the room like worms pushing up through sodden mud; their bodies folded at the waist as they cleared the lip of the hole in the flooring, coming down onto their stomachs like slabs of meat on a butcher's block. One by one they pushed up into the module under the strobe of her flickering plasma cutter, seeping up like overflowing wastewater. Their bodies appeared blistered and scalded, and they had the rigid swollen look of boiled pork.

With her hand pressed hard against the puncture wound in her thigh, Fenroe followed the curve of the wall with her eyes until it ended somewhere near a long, sleek soffit that concealed a line of fire-pole-thick cylinders like track lighting. There was frost on the wall behind the cylinders. She squinted into the light as her vision adjusted to the white neutron star of welder's flame still burning against the darkness on the floor—the fish-gut eruption of corpses clawed out of the hole and spread out in all directions—her cutter scorched the ceramic, a ring of blackness spreading away from it like the embers of a slow-moving brushfire.

Fenroe pushed away from the airlock—Suja's nails taking some skin as she pulled her arm free from his grasp—and dove for the cutter. Grasping the solid weight of it in her hand, she lifted the cutter into the air, and the smooth shell of the compressed gas cylinders behind the soffit shimmered back at her with reflected plasma light, bending like an intimate sunset on an ocean only she could see. The creatures latched onto her body, pulling themselves up the back of her legs with bone-thin fingers, and she reached up, dragging hard against the writhing, gnawing, living quicksand sucking her back down, and stabbed the burning plasma cutter between the two frosted gas cylinders.

She dove to the side, pulling herself out of the groping dead hands, the corpses' jawless tongues threading up her legs, wrapping around the insides of her thighs—

Suja's voice was a half-smothered scream. He reached for her, and his hand snatched a belt loop around her waist, pulling her away from the eye-piercing light. When the luminous zone of her plasma flame touched the cold cylinder, reality itself let out a high volume shriek, as if Fenroe had stuck a knife into its stomach. The module brightened and sucked all the air into a flash-funnel siphon that pulled from the gas cylinders out into the main corridor. Fenroe felt her body rip away from what had become a dead-gentle caress as the canisters detonated, and slam violently into a blurred solid mass on the other side of the room. For a moment, the muscle-knots of anxiety and panic that had tied themselves into her body disentangled and fell away; awareness and fight-or-flight responses eased down from her shoulders and slid off her back as unconsciousness began to take hold. And just as suddenly, the blackout moment passed, and the pain rose up through the very core of her, through her hands, her shoulders, her legs. The pain went through and through until it reached her heart, and blasted away the universe.

4.

The sound of fast, terrified breaths trickled in from the distant clanging and bending of heat-contracting metal. When awareness crossed into the universe once more, someone with agonizingly strong hands crushed Fenroe's wrists as they dragged her deeper into the bowels of the space station. She didn't know where exactly: there was intense heat and a pulsing whiteout of memory fragments stabbing into the back of her eyelids like a paintbrush of needles. She peeled her lips apart to speak, but instead puked up the small contents still left inside her stomach. The clear vomit splashed across her left arm, her left hand, and she made a fist around the metallic fingers clamping around both of her wrists.

She felt herself moving through a tunnel of fire, and then through a cyclone of smothering smoke. There was a distinct pattern of white artificial light passing by above her. Then darkness for a time.

When she could open her eyes again, she saw Eos's blue visor light shining through the blackness: the android's insectile limbs flashed across the walls with unbelievable speed, her body sliding down the corridor with frightening lethality and purpose as she detached from the ceiling on the run and twisted in mid-air, the rivet cutters on each of her forearms opening with blazing orange-blue heat.

How the android found them didn't matter to Fenroe. Eos was there, she'd grabbed them, and she'd pulled them away from the horde of parasitic corpses coming up from the service conduit beneath the subflooring.

Fenroe saw only hitching snapshots of sputtering darkness, and the separate ballasts of her mind rebooted in stages: her nerve endings flickered back to life one at time, starting with her sense of sound, then touch, then sight. Coming up out of the dizziness, she felt herself gulping mouthfuls of air. She thought she was drowning, barely holding her head above the water.

With the oxygen came the faraway bagpipe sound of inhuman screams; screams that were muffled and distant in ways that had nothing to do with proximity. Those first breaths, Fenroe drank in thick choking air like it was water, making broken *hhk, hhk, hhk* sounds with her throat. Darkness expanded out from within her vision, closing the firelight of the distant explosion to a depleting mass of deafening black.

It felt as if somebody had dumped a bucket of ice cold images onto her body, each one running down the contours of her brain like an ocean tide breaking against the rock face of a cliff.

Crash, a tidal wave of breath.

Crash, a tidal wave of images.

Crash. Suja stumbling through the strobing light, bruised face and broken nose covered in viscera, lips peeled back over his bloody teeth, eyes wide, pupils gaping open like sinkholes.

Crash. Eos leaping over Fenroe's body from the very edge of awareness, her heat-simmering arms flashing into a cloud of red smoke, cutting things in half that were afire and screaming with tortured, inhuman voices.

Crash. The air changing from smothering hot to a deep, frigid cold.

Crash. The scrabbling, rubbery, floppy sounds of alligator flesh mucking away from the whispering hum of hidden machinery.

Up until that moment Fenroe felt as if she had been standing at the edge of a cracking glacier. And now it had cracked. The blade of ice on the very edge of it had snapped free, and it was now plummeting toward the cold water below. The frozen sea rushed up at terminal velocity and filled every degree of her vision, the hallway in the *Pinnacle* beneath her sliding body became the tumbling blocks of glacial ice, and the inhuman screams of hunger and rage became the roar of crashing waves swallowing her up. For a time, there was only darkness.

5.

Fenroe was running in place. Her legs moved, but her body didn't. The fire burns from the explosion that she thought had happened to someone else covered her arms and legs. Her eyes had become thick, swollen slits, and her lips skinned back, away from the gums. The control panel sparked and burst into liquid flames as she fought the stick. The Pinnacle *rotated in dizzying concentric circles inside of her viewport. The flames caught the trace remaining amounts of hydrazine on the fabric of her flight suit, and her hair started melting together like wax. She tried breathing through it, choking, gasping, inhaling thick liquid contrails of heat that streamed through the smoke of her own burning skin, the flames coursing through the paper-delicate vessels of her lungs like thermite dust. And she fought. She steered the* Crown Meridian *through the searing pain as far away from the* Pinnacle *as she could before the core went critical: if she was going to die, right here, right now, she would die fighting. She could make her life mean something. She could save them all.*

Suja kicked out of the thick white smoke and sailed toward her through the weightless air. And in that dreamy moment, Fenroe realized that she wasn't herself. She wasn't Commander Evelyn Fenroe anymore. She was Ulbricht, and when Suja reached her, at that moment, pulling her body away from the electro-kiln of fire, ripping her limp body away, her head separated from the cervical root nerve and tore away from her flesh. Outside of her body now, Fenroe watched her head, Ulbricht's head, pull free and spin in midair, tumbling softly against the wall behind the stellographer. A spray of thick, bloody droplets showed where it had smacked into the vinyl. And then—

She opened her eyes and found herself sitting across from Sitosen, her legs folded beneath her in lotus, hair still tousled from the short sleep she'd had a few hours before. Sitosen's brow folded in deep concentration, a glint of atonement in his eyes. He slid his Knight from c6 to d8 and edged to the front of his seat. "Check."

They could hear Harris cooking in the Mess, hear music echoing in from someplace near the flight deck: the smell of onions and olive oil diffused in the morning light of Saturn. Fenroe studied the board and saw her move immediately, but decided to draw it out. She plucked her bishop with her ring finger and thumb. Sitosen cursed under his breath and smiled knowingly.

She took his knight, h4 to d8.

"Shit," he laughed under his breath.

"Check," said Fenroe.

"Be honest," he searched the board for an escape, glancing at his pieces lined up like the victims of a firing squad. "You did this competitively. On a team or something."

"Nope." She shook her head, leaning back, "but my dad was

a chess guy, so..."

Sitosen looked at her for a moment. He sucked his teeth and nodded, arching his eyebrow. "We've known each other how long? Ten, eleven years?"

"About ten years," she said.

"Ten years," he said slowly, looking at her as if she had suddenly become someone else entirely before his eyes, as if he had finally chipped away some of that iron hard exterior. "This is the first I've ever heard you say anything about your family."

"Yeah, well..." Fenroe shrugged and glanced toward the sliver of starlight through the doorway a couple modules away. "I'll try not to make it a habit."

"And you decide now," he smiled. "Today, of all days, to say something."

She shrugged, returning her attention back to the board, and then palmed a lock of her brown hair away from her face.

"Tell me about him," he said.

"What?"

Sitosen shrugged. "What kinda guy was he?"

Fenroe shook her head. "I don't think so."

"Why not?"

She smiled. It was a sad, uncomfortable line.

"Tell me about *your* family," she deflected.

Sitosen shook his head and let the misdirection slide. Somehow, he knew—Fenroe could tell by looking at him—or he at least felt suspicious that getting her to open up about personal things would be a fragile and delicate process. Because it was something he could get wrong. A sudden question, anything that seemed too eager, and the opportunity would be lost.

"My family," he said, looking at the board, settling back into himself to let the memories clear away the smoke of the moment. It was his turn to smile, and he seemed to remember something.

A deeper, more cherished moment that might have been too intimate to share.

"I'll tell you my favorite memory," he said finally, softly. "One I hold close. On the condition you tell me something in return."

She thought about it, and nodded. "Let's hear it."

"All right," he said, glancing at her to make sure she was paying attention, and then settled deeper into his chair. "I grew up on a farm. We had goats and some ponies, a few potatoes. Not a whole lot, but there was this school nearby, about two miles away. A forty minute walk on most days. Now, it was the only school for fifty miles or something, and we only had one shitty car that barely worked..." he trailed off, letting the memory in all the way. "It was very important that my brothers and I went to school. My father didn't want us to grow up to be dust farmers like him, stuck in the same place all our lives. So he made sure we went, because he knew we hated it. He knew we'd veer off into the hills and get into trouble. He'd walk with us every single morning. Without fail. Never missed a day. And we'd talk girls, soccer, stuff like that..."

Sitosen quieted for a moment, teasing the details out as if the more he talked, the more real the memory became. The tone of his voice was warm and pleasant and sad all at once.

"He'd pat us on the back," he continued, "and pull us all into his big arms, and he'd say *'ta na surguuli, little men! Go to school and make me rich!'* and we'd wrestle him to the ground, my brothers and me. *'Khuuchin khun,'* we'd say back, *'forget you old man, we'll make ourselves rich!'* And he'd pick us all up on his shoulders and stomp around, *'make me rich little men, so I can relax and eat all day long!'*"

Fenroe smiled and closed her eyes and let the warmth of Sitosen's memory carry her away. She imagined his father—a farmer with hands so eroded with callouses that they would scratch your skin. A lurch of pain fingered the inside of her stomach, and an iron band tightened around her heart. She didn't know why, but she somehow knew that he'd never make it back to his father and brothers again. She wanted to be wrong so badly that another kind of pain nearly snuffed the air right out of her. It was something indescribable, and distant. Something looming.

"Your turn," he said.

Fenroe opened her eyes. "Huh?"

"Tell me something."

She shook her head and went back to studying the board. The pain subsided. The finger in her stomach brushed away in an instant; the band around her heart loosened, and the dark cloud of dread hanging over her head peeled back like the moon drawing the tide.

"Come on," he said, moving his king to b5. "We had a deal."

Fenroe tried to think of something, but even the good things she could remember were anchored to the bad ones. Even chess. But she wasn't completely powerless. She had this game where she relived the bad memories the way they *should* have happened. She took that memory of her and her father in the dark midnight light, each of them scraping wooden pieces back and forth, the scent of stale alcohol and old coffee settling on everything while they concentrated, and turned it into something else. Chess wasn't her father's game anymore; it was Sitosen's. And this is how she did it. Simple, salient, and complete. This is how Fenroe took control of her past. She held all the bad memories under the waters of time, and cleansed them with the present.

Fenroe leaned forward and moved her other bishop to g2.

Sitosen smiled at how much peril she'd put him in, but he was more interested in Fenroe. She got the impression that although he didn't want to grasp too hard and shatter it, now that he had chipped away a tiny crack into her well-guarded exterior, he was determined to finally get a glimpse of what may be lying beneath it.

"Check," she intoned, her mind drifting to a dream of a memory. Fenroe eased into her seat, tucking her legs back into lotus.

Sitosen looked down at his king, and a shadow passed over him. When he met her eyes again, he glanced over her shoulder and raised his chin. That's when she heard someone speak her name.

"Evie," she heard from over her shoulder. An older woman's voice. "Evie, come here please."

Sitosen's eyes went from whoever was over Fenroe's shoulder back to her. "You better go see what she wants."

She turned to look, but no one was there. "Who is it?"

His face hardened. The muscles along his jaw flexed and his lips compressed into a grim line. He raised his chin again toward the shadow, steeling himself for something she didn't really understand. And the world had changed, like the sudden drop of a curtain. She looked back again, expecting to see the soft cold whiteness of Saturn's gas bands and equatorial rings.

What she found instead was a meadow of uncut grass.

6.

Floating outside the *Crown Meridian,* Fenroe looked at the house therein and marveled at the infrangible madness of it all. There was detail: striking, endless, *staggering* detail in the landscape painting itself all around her; a patchwork of memories stitched seamlessly to one another, all of the images dragging together like beads of mercury that formed a single half-coherent shape.

And yet.

Even with all of that detail, she couldn't remember how she got there. When she tried to think about how she came to be EVA without her bio-suit, and when she tried to wrap her mind around how she was able to still breathe in the vacuum of space, her memory clutched at the air for balance, and it dropped to its knees.

Fenroe thought that maybe she was in a dream. Or maybe it was just a higher plane of existence. After all, until that moment all she'd ever done in a dream was observe it. Like a passive rider watching things unfold without any real power to affect them. Observation was the easiest part of a dream, as natural to it as our senses are to waking life.

At some point it occurred to her that she was in serious, serious danger.

From outside the *Crown Meridian*, which rocketed through space at nearly half the speed of light, Saturn looming in the distance like a river stone worn by the patient friction of time, she looked at her childhood home inside the ship's O-two gardens: an exact replica of it, all the way down to the last detail. It was a brown brick two-story with white slatted windows and blood red mulch around the curtilage. It was almost the same, almost exactly as she remembered it. She swum through vacuum and stretched her arms out like the wings of a hawk. If this were really happening, she knew she wouldn't have been able to steer her body toward the ship like that. She had a strong feeling that the point here was not deciding what was possible and what wasn't.

The point was to observe.

Fenroe shut her eyes. She listened to the sound of birdsong on the summer wind. Through that sound, she heard a woman scream. Then came the leafy friction of a hundred flapping wings. Opening her arms, she sailed through the glass viewport as if she were a spirit, into the gardens, her feet coming to rest gently on the grass.

Suja Tsvetkov was on the far side, oblivious of her presence. His nose was healed, his eyes unbruised and bright with clarity. His Hawaiian shirt clean of blood and grime. He sat cross-legged on the sleek white floor, meticulously dropping nutrients into egg cartons filled with tiny cups of dirt, each sprouting small green shoots. She left him to his work, and moved to the center of the module.

It was clear that the house had been abandoned for some time because the yard had overgrown like a field of hay, and the windows were dusted with thick age and peeled shavings of old lemon-green paint.

Fenroe knew immediately that something was wrong. The house itself had never been this worn by time when she had lived in it: uncut grass and old paint. Empty flowerpots that once held bubbling wellsprings of color were now cracked clay vessels for old dirt. On the front sidewalk weeds grew over broken concrete, and crabgrass erupted through the cracks.

This was where she'd grown up. And little details about the house were returning, like the opening of a lock. She knew that when she pushed open the front door, it would swing unresisting of its own weight and bang against the closet if she didn't catch it; and Fenroe knew that as she stepped through the doorway, flat cream-colored wooden slats would scuff loudly under the soles of her feet.

Another dream played out behind her. A simultaneous one. While she remained focused on the house, Fenroe could sense the *Crown Meridian's* engines rumbling to glowing life in the backdrop, carrying it away from the *Pinnacle* space station in the distance. When it had reached a certain distance, she knew, it would crack with a moment of blinding light. The light would suck back into itself, giving way to a brighter light that would spread in waves for millions and millions of years, all the way to the edges of eternity. Another part of her was living *that* moment as well, using her plasma cutter to puncture the glass to get EVA, so that she and Eos could rescue Ulbricht and Suja...

But here.

Right now.

She stepped inside her childhood home.

The door did open easily and she caught it before the handle banged against the closet, like she'd anticipated. The wood did scuff, and there was a higher degree of intimacy in the walkway's quiet and dormant air, and the *snick* of the door shutting behind her.

There was something else, too. Something elusive. It was a thin shimmer on the floor, as if everything was getting a little brighter. It was the feeling of waking in the morning light after a deep sleep; the feeling that your eyes would automatically drift toward shadow to maintain an even keel.

And Fenroe could feel that something had shifted inside. In the cloth of her thigh, as if, relative to the yard and the house and the space station in the background, something was eating deeply into the muscle. She ran her fingers over the fabric of her leg, and expected to see ragged flaps of bloody skin, as though her flesh and bones had been replaced by something tender and thick and rubbery...

Instead, she simply saw her leg. But that bone deep ache remained. Whether she was or was not, Fenroe *felt* as if she were being violently penetrated by something. It took her several moments to put the sensation aside, which lingered until a part of her found a compartment where the weight of her dream could curve that feeling toward her desire to let go, to release, to be happy, to forget the pain of memory, and to fall into a deeper state which would smother that pain, until she could finally feel a different sensation take its place.

Despite the daylight pouring in from the mired windows, every lamp was switched on in the house. She could hear the soft murmur of voices coming from the living room. One voice was cold and sharp; the other was warm and soft.

"Evie," a woman's shrill voice blurted. "Evie, come here."

In the living room, she'd find the flat screen and the furniture and the lamps. If she followed the stairs directly ahead, she'd go up to the second floor. There she would find her and her brother's bedrooms, and the master bedroom.

She wanted to follow the voice, but it also seemed that the stairway pulled her with a kind of gravity she couldn't resist. She longed for the safety of her childhood bed, which tempted her by pulling in its direction with the delicate current of a stream. But she didn't ascend. She couldn't.

Following the voice into the hallway, Fenroe saw her mother's shadow on the wall, hanging long from a sharp point stabbing out of her clenched fists. Although the room was filled with piercing, inescapable light, it was what transpired that blinded Fenroe.

She rounded the corner and her mother pulled a kitchen knife the length of her forearm out of her father, and then plunged it back in. She did this several times. Her father's body flinched lightly after each impact, but the rest of him didn't move. It was too vivid. The fabric of her father's shirt fluffed with air on each impact of the blade, a pool of bright red crimson spreading around him, covering the chessboard, the pieces scattering all over. She could still hear him whimpering. A sad and terrified freshet of tears.

Her mother pulled the blade out of his skin, ripping a line of arterial blood across the ceiling, and stumbled backward, crashing into a boneless heap in the far corner. She settled, eyes wide and insane with shock, blood dripping from her fingers like thick warm paint.

Fenroe slowly backed away.

She turned quietly and left the memory alone, letting it all unfold again and again by itself without her. She didn't need to see this part. She saw it a thousand times in a thousand nightmares. Retracing her steps, she reached the door and walked outside, turning to stare up at her old bedroom window.

All of this had happened before they'd told her that a neurological disease had eaten away her mother's nervous system, corroding her mind in small, undetectable ways until that final explosion of homicidal madness: a secret battle had been waging inside, between sanity and a chorus of voices that whispered endlessly—every waking hour—about her family's non-existent devious plots.

Her mother never spoke about her internal struggles. In that way, she and Fenroe were alike: they'd rather deal with things on the inside than endure advice from people who couldn't fully understand what they were going through.

Fenroe heard the slide of skin against skin, and she opened her eyes.

"Jesus, I'm...I'm sorry," Sitosen said, passing his hand over his face. "I didn't know."

In the *Meridian's* main module, Sitosen and Fenroe still sat at a table tucked into a corner near the Central Post, arms folded, thinking deeply.

"It's all right," Fenroe said, crossing her arms over her knees. "My brother and I bounced around foster homes after that. Never staying too long in one place. Never *rooting* in anywhere." She was silent for a moment. "I think that's why the stars were so appealing."

Sitosen nodded his understanding. "No need for roots out

here."

"Right," she said sleepily, unfolding her legs. She stretched her neck and nodded again, remembering where she was. Between the two of them was a chessboard with very few pieces left, sparse and disorderly. After a short evaluation, she moved her last knight to b2.

"Checkmate," she said.

Sitosen sighed heavily, scratching at a couple weeks worth of beard growth. He then reached for his king, and tipped it over. Fenroe nodded without a word and sat back, running her fingers through a mane of brown, unbrushed hair.

"Well played," he said, extending his hand.

Fenroe took it into her own and shook.

"Well played," she said, then checked the bio-clock under her wrist. "Two hours."

Surprised, Sitosen checked his own wrist. "Holy shit..."

She smiled, stretching her neck again. "Intense, isn't it?"

"Yeah, it is," Sitosen said quietly to himself. He looked up, choosing his words carefully. "I once thought that I understood why you wanted to be an astronaut. I believed that you needed to prove to yourself that you could be part of it. The great human adventure. From out here, you can see where our species began—" he nodded at the small blue star through the viewport, and then tilted his chin down toward the floor, "—and the heights that we've achieved. I mean, the contrast is astonishing. Yet it seems to give you no satisfaction."

"What do you mean?"

"I mean, in light of everything you just told me, maybe what you're looking for isn't out here. Maybe what you're actually looking for is a state of mind. That feeling of arable land, where you *can* have roots. Where you *can* let yourself grow."

Fenroe focused on arranging her side of the board for the next game. She didn't need to see his face to know the expression he'd been wearing: a mask of polite interest both intense and tolerant. They were friends. That much was true. Best friends. But they were friends who hardly knew a thing about each other. Work friends, who bonded through their shared utility, driven by the mission.

"That's not the only reason," Fenroe said.

She looked around the sleek, wise curves of the *Crown Meridian*. She took in the flat, hidden, thin instrumentation with soft blue diodes glowing into pockets of glare. She passed her eyes over the viewport inside every visible module, filled with crystal starscape cleansed of Earth's light polluted watermark, over the door that led to the lab, where she could see Dunesto's muscle-lined shadow stretching into the main corridor as he worked on Eos's dormant vehicle. She saw Whitney Aris making her way to the Mess, the arms of her threadbare orange sweater hugging themselves for warmth. The younger woman caught Fenroe's eyes and gave a two-finger salute, yawning the sleep out of her head.

Fenroe lifted a hand and waved, dropped it again. It was a brief flick that encompassed the entire station. "I came out here to be alone."

Sitosen snorted. "That's pretty fucking bleak."

"Yeah," she nodded. "That's why I don't like bringing it up."

Sitosen leaned forward, a hint of concern in his eyes. "What happened to your brother?"

Fenroe shrugged and sat back. "He got into some bad things. Ended up dying a few years before we left Earth."

"I'm sorry to hear that," he said. "It must have been hard."

She didn't say anything; just stared, emotionless. He studied her for a long time and then shook his head.

"You know," he said easily, "I've dreamed of beating you at

this fucking game. It's the only thing I think about nowadays—" he shrugged and lowered his head to examine the pieces, "—but if I ever do, it would probably depress the hell outta me. I would have nothing else to dream about."

"Hmm," she said, a hint of a smile reaching her eyes. "You need better dreams, man. Need to aim higher."

"I find more and more that I'm leaving the past behind, you know?" He sighed. "Which is a good thing, I think. Because Earth gets farther and farther away every day, and I'm becoming more comfortable with the thought of being out here. Because—" he shrugged, "—not thinking about home is the only way I *can* get comfortable. This stuff—" he nodded toward the chess board, "—keeps my mind right here, right now, where it needs to be."

This cut a little too close to the bone for Fenroe's comfort; she slid her first pawn to c3, thinking about Proust.

"Don't you—" She began slowly, and then started again. "You ever think about just staying out here?"

Sitosen looked at her for a long time.

"No," he said finally. "What are you talking about?"

She shook her head. "Never mind."

"You'll get used to it," he said, reassuring her. "It just takes time."

"It's been four years," said Fenroe. "If I haven't gotten used to it yet, it's not going to happen."

"Are we talking about dealing with being out here, or getting comfortable with the idea of going back home?"

"I don't want to go back," she said quietly, sitting back and wrapping her arms around her knees again. "There's nothing for me there. Nothing but shitty memories and an empty house."

"There's nothing for you out here, either." Sitosen clamped his mouth shut; he appeared to study her from a new perspective. "Look, we're gonna find the *Endeavor*. And if we don't—" he shrugged, "—we go on to Titan. And then it's home. It's that simple."

"I know."

"Maybe you should talk to Harris."

"Maybe you should move," she shook her head with irritation. "It's your turn."

Sitosen glanced down at the board and then checked his wrist. He closed his eyes and frowned, pinching the bridge of his nose. "We should probably call it. I have to get some breakfast in me. I feel nauseous."

"Look, I'm sorry," she started, lifting her hands. "I didn't mean to—"

"No, it's not you. It's just..." he placed his hand over his heart, and winced. Beads of sweat formed on his forehead. "I'm not feeling too good. I think you wore me out..."

At first Fenroe thought he was looking down at the chessboard: his chin tilted, almost touching his clavicle. And then—

...he started wheezing heavily. His eyes ratcheted closed, and then popped back open. He lifted his shocked gaze to meet hers.

"Something," he rasped weirdly, like his throat had closed on him. "Something's not right."

His pectorals ballooned up and down with effort—it sounded as if the breath leaving his body was being drawn by something else altogether. Something deep inside.

Sitosen jerked to his feet, knocking chess pieces skittering across the floor. Fenroe's body went numb with terror, as the top of his head seemed to give with an incredible pressure. He shrieked, a deep existential howl spilling over with gurgled revulsion and terror.

His head inflated, elongated, and then split open, separating into four flaps of hairy scalp. His hands groped and clawed out to the sides of his body without purpose, like a recent corpse that had taken a grenade directly into the face.

Fenroe's arms flinched up from the blood spattering into her eyes. All thought slipped into a torrential, split-second jolt of terror. Her breath stopped, overwhelmed by the sudden dumps of adrenaline. When her vision cleared, she followed the blood up Sitosen's flight suit, and it was as if a cold metallic snake had wrapped itself around her heart, and constricted.

Sitosen's tongue emerged from his pulsating brain, up out of the flaps of his skull, and drooped over his chest like a massive feeler. A parasite of some kind swelled from the collar of his flight suit, zippering back the top of his head as if it were simply a garment of flesh. His tongue had drained of blood and become the oily off-red of a bloated maggot. Toxic silver and copper liquids oozed out of its strangely erect taste buds, drooling down to form a frothy buildup around Sitosen's flexing neck.

"IT'S NOTHING," he rasped again, burping up through the bloody viscera and muck of his exploded neck. Fenroe scrambled back over her seat, feeling as if she were being shoved over the edge of a cliff, believing she could hear Sitosen's voice harmonize with something else deep inside the trembling throat hole behind his tongue—she thought she could hear his eternal scream trapped somewhere below the harmony of that other voice.

"IT'S JUST," he screeched, *"NOW YOU HAVE TO WAKE UP."*

The other voice clawed up from the sphincter in the center of what was left of Sitosen's head: curved and unspeakably soft, like the air in a nursery. The sphincter was lined with a million tiny razor sharp teeth pulsating like bristles of fine hair lining the inside of a water pipe.

Sitosen's tongue pulled back like a cobra ready to strike. It tracked the heat of her breath, and then shot out, latching onto her face with blinding speed.

It pulled her into Sitosen's hungry arms: the four flaps of his scalp sucked onto her face, and the tongue forced itself down her throat.

Blind now, clawing and scrabbling at his scalp, trying to push him away, smothered by his exploded face, she felt her body go down with his on top of her. She screamed around the meaty tongue filling her insides, and then she saw the light.

7.

Fenroe jolted awake.

Blurry shapes drifted above her like shadowy smoke threading under her arms, under her legs, and under her back. The smoky limbs were solid, and Fenroe half realized from deep inside her head that she was being carried somewhere. At first, Fenroe couldn't recall where, or even who, she was.

She had dreamt of...of *something*. Something powerful and smothering, like a thick coagulant of a memory that gurgled to the surface but thinned before it could be contained. The sudden darkness from the loss of power gave no clue, and the filthy stench of the service conduit still ratcheted her brain tightly into her skull.

Fenroe's eyes fluttered open to see Suja collapsed against the far wall, his face blackened by a mixture of ventilation dust, surface blood and deep bruising around the eyes. His Hawaiian shirt had become an unidentifiable tattered rag hanging from his shoulders. His left hand was a swollen club of dark meat granulated with chunks of black-cherry blood, fingers gnarled and twisted into his hand, blood soaked through the bandages that were stuck all over his body.

Aris came to his side and ripped strips of cloth apart from

something she had salvaged and packed more layers of dressing onto his hand. "Where are the others?"

Suja couldn't speak. He was slipping from consciousness, his chest rising and heaving as if he were drawing his last breaths. He tried to answer, but he shook his head instead and wilted in her arms, breaking down into uncontrollable sobs. Aris raked her eyes over his body as blood dripped and pattered out of wounds too numerous to count, afraid that the merest touch would send him into an irretrievable shock.

Fenroe's brain crackled like bad transmission, a strange pressure seeping to the surface. An uncomfortable needling in her stomach, like a runner's side ache. She raised her head, fever sweat making her brown hair stick to the glass viewing table they had laid her on, a deep ache pulsating in her thigh. She reached for her leg instinctively, and probed the cauterized seal—someone had burned and glued the wound shut, but it still hurt badly. Her knee had stiffened considerably, and she winced at the pain.

Beyond the icy blue fog of the server room through the next pressure door, Fenroe saw something—a shadow dropping to complete blackness. Past the pressure door beyond the mainframe, the lights at the far end of the corridor flickered and switched off. A moment of dreamy pause, and the server room switched off. Then went the control room, each going out like a line of dominoes.

The darkness stalked them. Fenroe watched the shadow fall nearer with each plunge of light, numb and half conscious, and the room on the other side of the nearest pressure door behind them finally went dark... until they were all in the last remaining cone of overhead light in the Server Hub.

"We're losing power again," Aris said.

Beck peered out of the bay window and studied the station's exterior as it curved away from them at a distance, still flickering with power and light. "It's just this module—" he made pulling motions with his hands, instructing them all to the center of the room. "—get away from the door!"

And with one last axle-grinding *chunk*, all the overheads went out, leaving them with only the glowing terminal in the corner for light.

The fresh blackness was everlasting and heavy.

"It's them," Suja said from the floor, startling them all. Fenroe raised her head and followed the weightless echo of his voice, which hung in the cold air like an oath. She found him there, a black glistening smear of pale flesh in the corner: he was no more than a wasted shell, and the only thing that differentiated him from the creatures in the tunnel was the blazing fire of life in his eyes. Those eyes were looking right at her, piercing the darkness. She held them for what felt like an eternity, and something passed between the two of them that was beyond words. He reached his good hand up and pressed it tenderly against two holes near his left shoulder, and she knew instantly what that meant: In the service tunnel, after he'd kicked one of the infected crewmen back into the shadow, he had grunted in pain.

Fenroe didn't think anything of it at that time, but without a doubt, she knew that thick rubbery maggoty things were eating deep into the meat of Suja's chest, heading straight for his nutrient-rich heart. He saw the spark of understanding in her eyes and looked away, letting his head fall back against the cold hard wall. He was just so, so tired. He shifted his weight on the floor and eased into it, relaxing his body, a cold acceptance settling over him. Turning his head, Suja focused his eyes in the direction of the distant screams, and waited.

8.

"We have to go back for them," Aris said, tears collecting under her fierce eyes. Her shaky hands packed the wound on Fenroe's leg with strips of fabric that looked as if they had been salvaged from a piece of furniture. A caustic reek overshadowed everything: an edged, nasal-burning flavor not unlike burnt rubber.

"We can't leave them," Aris hissed again, a slight panic in her husky voice. "We have to go back—"

"They're gone," Fenroe said weakly. She wanted to say more in the following silence, but she didn't have the strength. She closed her eyes and focused on pushing the images of Dunesto's spilling intestines out of her thoughts. She wanted to dig her thumbs into her own eyes and tear the retinal after burn of his shocked, uncomprehending face dragging through a river of his own fluids out of her head. Her whole body was numb, and her heart was nothing more than a solid malignant growth nestled between her lungs. "They're dead."

"We don't know that," Aris shook her head. "Their comms could just be down—"

"I was there." Fenroe's voice broke, hard as stones. "I saw it."

Aris lifted her hands helplessly and shook her shaven head, unable to find the words. With a heavy sigh, she closed her eyes and slumped back against the wall, dropping her hands into her lap—she fought something internally for a moment, searching for answers. Like a river breaking its levy, she collapsed into a string of quiet, weeping breaths. The sound—the racking, choking gasps of her crying—was more than Fenroe could bear.

Fenroe stared up into the dark ceiling, following the slow crawl of light arcing through the room via a bay window above her head. Saturn rolled slowly into view, penduluming the darkness before disappearing again. She couldn't bring herself to look at the younger woman, or impose any more on her anguish than she had already. The weight of it was too much—the bone-deep, hollowed-out space in her heart where she housed the memories of the people she'd lost had become too stretched and too vast and encompassing. She focused on everything but Aris, shoring up that pain, building the walls around her heart to keep it from breaking to pieces right then and there.

Three sources of light shot through the ovoid room, mostly coming from the window above Fenroe's head, all bleeding and intersecting with each other at different points on the spectrum: the Saturn light and ring light and starlight coming in above her slumped body, the delicate blue-green glow of the airlock's holo-pad, and the midnight television glare of the computer terminal in the far corner. Although the main power seemed to have gone out, these three things kept them from having to endure complete darkness.

The sharp, tangy stench of decay, she realized, was coming from the wound in her leg.

"There!" Beck rasped over the liquid, inner-ear roar of her pulse. She raised her head to see him pressed against the bay window, swaying unsteadily on his feet with fatigue, looking distantly across the *Pinnacle's* inner ring. He leaned his hand against the window for support, blood smearing the glass around his fingers. "There," he said again quietly.

It took a moment for Fenroe to realize that the blood wasn't his. She looked down and saw for the first time a deep black shadow spreading out around her body. The stain lay out like smoke from her right thigh. She underestimated just how badly she was hurt.

Turning quickly away from the window, Beck hurried to the

corner terminal and activated a shield that whirred to life and pulled back into the wall like an iris dilating to an even wider view of the *Pinnacle's* interior side. The station was still turning, creating its centrifugal gravity: the interior array of cable struts rotated slowly beneath the colossal observatory's forward shell like the spokes of a wheel, and Saturn rose slowly on one horizon of the structure, arcing softly across the starscape in the distance like a zeppelin.

From the outside one could hardly tell that anything was wrong with the *Pinnacle* at all.

Fenroe stretched her neck to see over the edge of the window, following the direction of Beck's intensely focused eyes. On an exterior under-block nearly two thousand feet below the lower curve of the *Pinnacle's* hull, Fenroe could just barely make out the dormant artificial gravity pendulum of the *Endeavor* spacecraft docked at the last remaining umbilical mast.

"My god," she whispered, staring through the window. "I thought...I thought Dunesto said all umbilicals were destroyed."

"I guess not all," Beck shrugged. After quick moments of putting it all together in his mind, he turned his back from the bay window and leaned over the terminal nearby. "That's our ticket outta here."

"How far?" Fenroe asked, propping herself up with the help of Aris's shoulder. She dragged her eyes around the window, down along the curve of the hull, measuring out a quarter, maybe a half-mile distance. Any other day that'd be a ten-minute stroll. Now, the *Endeavor* might as well have been docked on another space station entirely.

"One level down. Two, maybe three modules away," Beck whispered, his hands moving fast over the lighted interface. "The reactor is still online—" He glanced up at the ceiling and inspected the dead lights, "—they must be eating through the local cable."

"Eos," Fenroe rasped, propping herself up against the wall. "You analyzed the samples back in the infirmary."

"Yes," the android replied.

"What exactly are we dealing with here?"

"Nothing I've seen before," Eos pulsed. "It's a hyperviral lithoautotroph of some kind, which gets its energy from mineral compounds found in its environment."

"Hyperviral," Aris said under her breath. "So it was a contagion."

"A parasite," the android continued. "Some appear to be egg carriers, others appear to seek, consume and replicate mineral compounds found in the host's body."

Fenroe's stomach dropped, and her fingers brushed unconsciously across the sealed hole in her right thigh. "The metallic liquid they bleed..."

"Secreted from minerals harvested from your bodies," Eos thrummed. "Along with everything else it eats. Walls, doors, equipment...everything. It draws resources from available compounds to replicate more of whatever mineral they happen to be feeding on. Presumably this is why many of the infected appear to have metal-infused skin."

"How did they get aboard?"

"Unknown."

"How are they able to eat through walls?"

Eos pulsed again: "Over time the body's organs, skin and water content seem to become converted; using the trace amount of minerals in the host's body, blood may be changed into a more potent conductor."

"So they heat themselves up," Aris said. "They create enough internal amperage to melt down the metal—"

"Listen," Beck interrupted, looking back down at the

terminal, his fingers drifting away from the console. Confusion and concern settled deep behind his eyes. "There's a message here."

Suja stirred on the floor and listened, moving himself painfully against the wall; his head fell back lifelessly, but his eyes stared at Beck through the darkness, watching intently.

Light blinked back and forth over Beck's face as he read silently. *"Infected have been isolated behind the radiation shielding, which appears too thick for them to eat through, and they have gone dormant. Do not lift quarantine. Contagion immanent. Do not leave station."*

"They must have been released when we restored power," Aris said quietly.

"There's a video file," Beck continued, data streams pouring across the screen. His fingers moved again over the display. "I'm putting it through the prism."

Light ignited and poured in from the walls and built blocks of several three-dimensional images in the center of the room, making everyone blink away from the sudden shift of brightness. Strafing bands of light carved the blocks into harder shapes, until a massive machine took form that looked like a long, sideways drum container set deeply into the wall of a large, man-made cavern.

"That's the particle collider," Beck whispered. And for an instant, there was something in his eyes—a spark of some kind, as if something had clicked in his mind. There was a brief moment of understanding and knowledge that faded just as fast as it had appeared. He pulled himself together and pointed at the large magnet assembly. "That giant cogwheel is one of the six or seven magnetic detectors," he said softly, shaken by the thing he had seen, unsettled by some connection he'd made in his head. "That hole where all of the piping and conduit is being fed is the particle tunnel."

Fenroe followed the images of gnarls of wire, metal piping and plastic conduit extending out from the detector, which comprised its parallel beamlines that wrapped around the entire outside of the station. The cavern was the collision point for high-speed particles. Photons were fired from opposite ends, and they raced through beamlines seeded in the walls around the entire facility until they smashed together mere fractions of a second before reaching light speed. The idea was, if a few million photons hit each other hard enough, fragments of even smaller particles might break off. The goal of this experiment was to learn more about what makes the physical universe possible—to peel back reality's curtain and find the glue that holds everything together. The *Pinnacle* was one of three orbital installations in the solar system built with its own particle accelerator.

"Look at the equipment," Aris whispered over Fenroe's shoulder.

The exposed part of the detector was intact. And so were the hundreds of cables and bundles of wire and cryogenic pipes pouring out of its center.

Everything else had been warped. Fenroe couldn't tell if she was seeing distortion in the playback, or if everything around the detector had been smashed by some unknown force. The damage pattern radiated outward in all directions from the base of the collider itself, as if everything within reach had been pancaked by an invisible curved surface. Like a violent shell of energy had formed around the machine and expanded outward.

The side of a trundled data rack closest to the detector had been compressed like an accordion. Dollies and servers and equipment all around the platform had been flattened and bent over the surrounding guardrails. Little bits of holographic glass fused in place where they'd been flash-melted together. Fenroe followed the curve of everything to the overlay of cracks in the grated flooring, which all resonated away from the collider's platform slab. The three stories of scaffolding on all sides had collapsed.

A ghost appeared near the collider, shimmering with broken light. The image flickered and fizzled, blurring around the edges as if the playback had been aged beyond normal function. The very walls rumbled suddenly, and at first Fenroe's stomach dropped, thinking the infected corpses had found them and were beginning to breach the airlock, but then she realized that the rumbling sound wasn't coming from anywhere in the room at all.

It came from the recording.

A holographic clone of each smashed object reappeared in thin air at their respective places of origin. And because of the long-neglected flaws in the holo-prism, the recorded voices that spoke to them across a decade of silence were unearthly and demonic, broken into a thousand uneven fragments that couldn't remember how to fit back together entirely. It was the indecipherable, guttural murmurings of the dead.

It sounded very alien, like an old radio broadcasting a pirated frequency from deep beneath the ocean's surface. Beck glanced at Fenroe, but her attention remained focused on the pale, lucent figures with empty eyes floating around the room.

One of the ghosts stepped toward the collider and reached out, and the entire playback dropped from view and disappeared with a seethe of interference and electrostatic. They all sat in stunned silence. Eos's blue visor was brightened in contrast by the playback's sudden fading light. The sounds of pressurized atmosphere behind the walls filled in the silence until, after sharp drawn out seconds, Beck lifted his hands to see if he could get the recording started again. The directional sound system in the walls rumbled back to life with more intensity, and the holographic ghost reappeared in the center of the room, stepping toward the collider, reaching out to touch it.

Fenroe's brain had to wrestle with the images to make sense of everything. The playback sputtered, losing power as the ghosts fluttered in and out of existence.

After that, the image changed entirely. Just as Fenroe's vision began adjusting to it, she was immediately blinded by a brilliant display of blueish-green light.

It was just a flash—a brief moment between the ghost's movements—but in that instant Fenroe saw something spherical pulse outward from the exact center of the collider with vibrating light, like a doorway, or a portal that spasmed open and shut like the whipping blades of a helicopter. In that strobe of light—which fluttered at the steady, ripping speed of automatic gunfire— Fenroe could see a strange night sky. Constellations that she didn't recognize. An alien star map of a dying galaxy.

The stars on the other side of that portal darkened quickly from bright blues and whites to a dark red in a single second. Amid those quickly dying stars, a dull swirl of galaxy could clearly be seen at the very top of the portal...and a planet with a distinct pink tinge that Fenroe had never seen before.

"What's happening?" Aris asked sharply. "What are we looking at?"

Beck stepped away from the terminal, pulling his hands up to show that he was no longer in control. He didn't speak. He didn't breathe, his eyes darting between the terminal and the holograms in the center of the room.

Another split second, and another pulse of light expanded away from the collider; the holo-display glittered and fired a stream of iridescent colors in all directions, twinkling prismatic fragments of light across their faces—there were visible stars on the other side of that portal, which stretched in a wide belt above the expanding shell around the particle collider, and the strange planet that Fenroe saw through the opening dimmed just like the stars had a moment before, and grew dark, and then darker still, until it looked as if it was starting to break apart and disintegrate.

The playback sharpened suddenly, and the ghost fled from the expanding orb of light: an older, military-looking man with gray hair and a squared jaw, tall and broad shouldered. The man wore an acid-gray *Pinnacle* uniform with a single patch of a Colonel's star on his shoulder. She knew him. What remained of his body was currently decomposing in the reactor's control room with its hand still clutched to the station's HAZMAT quarantine.

Fenroe stared at the image. "That's Colonel Wren."

The light display flickered for a moment, and then finally died for good. The room was dark again, and Fenroe's eyes readjusted to the soft planet light leaking in through the window for the third time. Beck waited to see if the playback would start back up again, but it didn't.

"That looked...a lot like the black-hole-wormhole thing we saw in the playback of Titan," Beck said quietly, reeling from what he'd seen. "And it looked as if it had come from the particle detector."

It seemed like hours that they'd sat in place. Fenroe realized she had been digging her fingers into the blood soaked fabric of her flight suit above the knee.

"I don't—" Aris finally passed her hand over her face and shook her head, breaking the silence, "—I don't understand what I just saw."

Beck was quiet for some time, thinking deeply. He focused his attention back on the terminal, and moved his fingers again through the light. "The recording is dated two and half years from now."

"We know that already," Aris said, shrugging helplessly.

"The station clocks are messed up—"

"There's something else," he said, reading more, his face a mask of intense focus. "I've found the reason for the *Endeavor's* distress beacon. There's apparently a panic relay that triggers if the onboard AI experiences catastrophic systems failure." He looked at Fenroe. "Did you know about this?"

Fenroe shook her head briefly then stopped, closing her eyes, the delicate motion almost enough to put her out again.

"I had no idea," she said, knowing instantly what that meant.

Beck turned to the android: "Is this true, Eos?"

The android didn't answer at first. Lines of data panned down the length of her visor. She twisted her head and looked to her Commander, almost as if she were hesitant to answer. "All ISDI vessels are preprogrammed with the same protocols. In the event of catastrophic damage, I'm to immediately trigger emergency response."

The world crystallized into focus, and Fenroe felt that sinking feeling in her stomach begin to regurgitate back up into her throat. Sharp invisible needles pricked the skin of her neck.

"Listen to me Eos, this is important," Fenroe said sternly. "Did you trigger the *Meridian's* emergency beacon before we boarded the *Pinnacle?*"

"Yes, Commander," the little android nodded. "Immediately after we encountered the debris field."

"Oh no," Fenroe said, closing her eyes, the needles stabbing deeper into her neck, the heavy presence of nausea rising higher in her chest. "Did the message get through the comms anomaly? Did anyone receive it?"

"I didn't receive confirmation."

"Tell me you've contacted Command and turned them away. Tell me you have some protocol for contagion..."

"I have no such protocols," the android hummed.

Every hard breath Fenroe took sent deep aches resonating down her hip and thigh. "If Command sends another crew for us, they will all die. They'll track your beacon to these coordinates and find the *Pinnacle*."

"I understand," Eos said, lowering her hands. The data ceased streaming across her visor plate.

"We can't risk letting this thing off the station," Fenroe said. "We can't let it get back to Earth."

"What are your orders?" Eos asked.

"I want you to cancel the emergency protocol."

"We're assuming that the communique made it through the anomaly," Beck said.

"Wait a minute—" Aris cut in, "—what do you mean *cancel* it? They need to know what's happening out here."

"They will when we get off station," Fenroe replied. "But this thing has to be contained *here*. If they intercept the distress package now, they'll receive no information on what we've found. They'll come into this blind just like we did, and more people will die."

"I'm going home, Fenroe." Aris said, clenching her jaw. "I'm not dying in this place."

"I know that," Fenroe nodded. "But we can't rely on them coming for us—"

"Why *not?!*"

"We have to figure this out on our own," Fenroe said, trying to stay calm. "We'll make contact once we've made it to the *Endeavor* and cleared the observatory."

"How do you know they won't come looking anyway?"

"They won't."

"Yeah, but how do you know?"

"Because," Fenroe said, catching herself. She thought about not answering. For one long eternal second, she even considered lying. "Because I told them not to."

Aris stood still and cored into Fenroe with her eyes. "What do you mean?"

"I mean," Fenroe said, "part of the condition of my taking this mission was that, if we ever went offline, they wouldn't waste more lives coming to look for us."

"What?" Aris asked, shocked. "You had no right..."

"I had *every* right." Fenroe said with intensity, the always-present rage bubbling up through the pain, giving more breath to her voice. "I *will not* put other people at hazard because of our failures. If the *Endeavor* crew had thought the same way, none of us would be out here."

"And you think Command didn't just say what you wanted to hear?" Beck said, dismissing them both. "They'll come anyway. You know they will."

"God damn you," Aris said, more tears filling her eyes. She smothered a curse and clenched her jaw, sitting very slowly onto a swivel chair near the window. She couldn't look Fenroe in the eyes, and stared instead at her hands cupping the starlight. "You've killed us...you know that?"

"How was I supposed to know?" Fenroe asked, her voice grating like barbed wire, begging Aris to give an answer. "How was I supposed to know we would be walking into something like this?"

Aris's last words cut deep. Deeper than anything that had cut before. It was enough to suck the will to continue fighting right out of her, to crush her with the weight of unrelenting shame and guilt.

"Fenroe's right," Beck said softly. "It's up to us. We can't wait years for a rescue. We won't last a *week* with those things roaming the station."

Aris opened her mouth to protest, but was cut short by the

sound of something heavy ramming into the pressure door behind them. All eyes snapped onto the sound, and the air went very still.

After a pregnant pause, Eos's rivet cutters unlatched and opened away from her forearms, heating and powering up like a centrifuge. The android turned and stepped between them and the far side pressure door as the center of it began to glow in soft orange circles spreading out like ripples in a pond. And then a stream of molten metal began dribbling down to the floor, hissing into spectral wisps of rising smoke from the crack.

9.

Fenroe slammed her fist against the airlock control as she staggered into the frigid server room, and it fell to the floor with an airless *shunk*.

"Unauthorized Access to Tech Servers," the computer said. *"Security Lockdown Initiated."*

The room's interminable glow of blue ice dropped into total darkness, followed by the flashing of red and yellow emergency lights.

Eos deactivated the station lockdown and pulled her spike out of the nearest server. "Mainframe is back online," she hummed. "Doors are open."

Eos stood and offered her compact vehicle to Fenroe to lean on, and the little android supported her weight as they dragged themselves deeper into the circular-shaped server room one blood-squishing step at a time. Their legs plowed the heavy, knee high ice fog like ships at sea. Frozen clouds of icy mist congealed just above the floor, breaking like waves against the massive rectangular server towers bolted to a simple four-rail track system that ran around the room's exterior. There were maybe fifty servers as tall as the room itself, nine feet wide and three feet thick, each with a three-handle crank on its side, which allowed technicians to slide them back and forth on the track assembly.

"Prep the *Endeavor* for separation," Fenroe said to the android. "And backup all *Pinnacle* files to its hard disks."

"All files have been saved," Eos hummed, the blue lights in her visor pulsing with each syllable. "Prepping the *Endeavor* for dock separation."

"If we get separated," Fenroe said to the rest of them, "we'll meet in the *Endeavor's* umbilical dock."

Beck moved past and eased Suja down against the side of a desk in the center of the room. The injured man wrapped his bare and black-smeared arms around himself, shivering heavily. His tired eyes had retreated to some deep place, his tattered and blood-slickened Hawaiian shirt and cotton shorts offering no protection against the server room's freezing cold temperature.

"You've gotta leave me," Suja breathed. "I ca...can't go with you...jus slow y'down...too tired—"

"We're almost there," Aris said, cupping his head gently. "You just have to hold on a little longer, okay?"

"No...no, you don unner-stan—" he shook his head, lifting his hand weakly, his accent coming through more thickly now, "I can't...yer all at risk...infected...I'm infect—"

Something moved behind the walls, thrashing like thick slabs of meat in the ductwork.

Fenroe looked back through the window just as something crashed into the pressure door, spreading the flaps of its scalp over the glass viewport with wet sucking thuds.

"Beck," Aris pitched her voice over her shoulder. "We've gotta move, now!"

Beck ran his hands frantically over the wall of servers until he found a small, red light breaking through a crack between two of the towers. That light belonged to the terminal of another airlock that was blocked by the positioning of the servers on the track.

"I found it," Beck rasped, then louder, "I found an exit!"

Aris eased Suja's head gently against the desk and then moved to her feet, jogging to the server at the very edge of the track, and the pressure door behind them began to heat up in the center, shooting tendrils of white smoke into the frozen air. Aris forced herself to slow down in order to steady her shivering hands, and cranked the server, sliding it around the circular room until there was enough space for them to reach the exit on other side of the track assembly.

Eos stepped through first with Fenroe's arm still draped over her neck, and manually opened the lock with her free hand. The door slid into the ceiling and opened to a wide corridor, thick clouds of icy fog spilling out into the darkness. Beck and Aris gathered Suja and pulled him painfully to his feet, leading him into the dark hallway ahead.

Something large and heavy crashed through the ceiling behind them, screeching like an emergency brake system. Fenroe could hear the wet burping fart sounds of its stomach exploding, shooting parasite barbs in all directions. More alien screams returned from deep within the darkened tunnel to their left, and the shadows of corpses began to stir and pull in their direction.

They ran, staggering away from the sliding skin sounds toward a light at the end of the corridor. They passed through another pressure door and crossed into a wide quarter-landing stairway overlooking a massive curved window that stretched all the way up to the top level, and all the way down to the level below. The runoff of planet light seeped in from the skylight above, and Fenroe stopped, temporarily blinded by the sudden brightness.

She blinked the glare out of her eyes just as something thick and rubbery came out of nowhere and crashed into them all, sending her and Eos sprawling across the floor. Fenroe rolled painfully to her knees, and looked—

A large corpse scurried toward her through the bright orange and beige-white glare with the twitchy fast movements of an arachnid. Its lower jaw hung by strips of skin from what remained of its quartered skull flaps, like a python preparing to feed. Vomiting its tongue out of its exposed throat hole, the tubed organ stretched to an impossible length, exposing rings of tiny, razor-like fangs poking up behind its blunted human teeth. Fenroe pulled herself across the floor, just as several more corpses dropped from the ceiling and poured in from the tunnel behind them.

Tumbling farther down the stairwell, Beck and Aris scrambled to their feet.

Eos unfolded herself lithely from the floor with the quick precision of death, and lunged with shocking speed at the disfigured body scuttling on all fours toward Fenroe. The android punched her metal fist deep into the top of its head, shoving her arm down its throat up to her elbow. Fenroe saw the light of Eos's rivet cutter glow through its skin, saw the shadows of a million parasites writhing around inside of its gut, and then watched in detached horror as Eos stood and lifted the thing into the air with both hands. The rivet cutter of her one hand ignited from within and slagged the corpse clean in two, spraying buckets of thick, foot-long worms squirming inside a pile of cooked guts onto the floor. Eos tossed the twitching halves back toward the hordes piling into the stairway from above.

Suja was sprawled against the bulkhead on the other side of the pressure door, just out of reach. He was barely holding on, his hand leaving splotches of baby footprints in blood on the floor beneath his legs as he tried pulling himself up. Red arterial lines poured out of his ears, carving a trench through the grime to the tip of his chin.

Fenroe met his tired eyes for a moment, the shadows closing in on him, and then she looked up at the sound of human weight moving and bending the ductwork and metal overhead. The ceiling glowed bright yellow and sagged, trickling particles of melted vinyl until it finally gave way, dropping more infected human bodies to the ground between her and Suja and the pressure door.

Suja moved to his knees, wincing and grinding his teeth through the pain, and crawled desperately to the airlock controls. The first of the corpses grabbed hold of his leg, unfolding the flaps of its skull as it prepared to feed. He reached his hand into the air, brushing the holographic light controls with his outstretched fingers—

Eos grabbed Fenroe and pulled her away—

Fenroe screamed, trying to wrestle free from the android's arms, reaching out and take Suja's hand, to save him, to pull him into the light—

His tired eyes closed, and he hammered the control panel hard with his closed fist. The airlock slammed down like a guillotine, sealing Suja off with the corpses pouring into the corridor behind him and clawing up his outstretched body—

More of them flooded into the stairway from the ventilation ducts.

Aris tried climbing back up to reach Fenroe, but she was cut off by the sheer volume of living dead meat threatening to overtake her.

"*Go!*" Fenroe screamed over the rising din. "*GET TO THE ENDEAVOR NOW!*"

Aris's mouth was open in a silent scream, tears streaming down her face. Beck reached her side and grabbed hold before the things were close enough to rip her apart and drag her back up the stairway. They reached the lower level and disappeared quickly into a branching corridor. Hundreds of parasite-filled bodies swarmed after them into the darkness.

Eos and Fenroe were boxed in, surrounded by a mob of bodies.

Fenroe clung to the small android and took a deep breath, waiting for the moment she would be ripped to pieces. She closed her eyes.

"What's your primary directive?" Fenroe whispered. She didn't know why she asked this question. Perhaps she wanted to feel like she wasn't dying alone, and that Eos, for all of her lifeless programming, was still some kind of person. Someone who could help bear the weight of what was about to happen. "What's your purpose?"

Without hesitation, Eos thrummed: "To protect the crew—" and she turned her head, stepping between Fenroe and the nearest corpse, shielding her commander with an arm blazing with red fire. The dead bodies crawled over each other from all sides, pouring down the stairway, through the vents, crashing down from the ceiling, "—to make the crew safe."

"Make the crew safe," Fenroe echoed with total mind-lock, looking for a way out, finding nothing. "Protect the crew—"

"I will, Commander," Eos pulsed. "Just stay beside me."

And Fenroe realized that the android mistook what she said as an order, and she looked down, feeling the simmering build of intense warmth radiating from Eos.

The android opened her hands as if she were inviting the dead bodies in, and she activated the unresisting heat in her forearms, the soft blue lights of her visor blushing suddenly to a deep, warlike red. Eos's plasma cutters grew so hot that they shot sparks of energy into the bending darkness, her arms cooking with heat—soundlessly, with the cold dispassion of a combine, the android launched itself into the horde of infected bristling human corpses, and cut into them like a scythe made of pure red light. She sliced her plasma-bladed hands into the grotesque wall of dead flesh as if it was nothing, and proceeded to rip a bloody path straight through them.

10.

The re-animated bodies of nearly a hundred *Pinnacle* crewmen flooded into the stairwell in howling thirst and soul-anguished pain. Fenroe scrambled down the landing and steeled herself, waiting to be torn limb from limb. She desperately searched for a path to the lower level, listening to the horrible sound of agony and demise as human fingers and tentacled limbs scrabbled across the floor, wriggling with unidentifiable organs protruding out of bloody stumps that tore into the strobing blackness centimeters away from her face.

But she was still alive, still breathing, still moving with one dead leg.

Fenroe heard Eos's cutters buzz and whine in the darkness each time they came in contact with bone. Twisted human limbs reached and clawed at her face to tear her head off and pump it full of worms as thick as sausage. From every direction, terrible heavy shrieks buffeted her like a hurricane of panicked, dying animals. Eos held the wall of infected corpses back with sheer will, shoving Fenroe down toward the lower level by inches.

The android gleamed black-red in the strobe of her plasma cutters, spinning so fast that she appeared to have doubled in size, and the valleculae through which her MMU's nanites coursed and distributed her power changed as well—they burned with a bright, eye-piercing shade of red, matching the light of her visor. The infected bodies packed onto themselves, piling onto that wall of powerful, starving, gnashing teeth and scalp flaps all the way to the ceiling—all reaching for Fenroe—and Eos struck from a thousand different angles at once, her crystal-white carbon glinting in the orange plasma, the decayed flesh and bone offering no resistance.

Eos had become death, a walking combine of mathematically precise destruction, chopping her way down through the fog and bone of Oppenheimer's worst nightmare.

Fenroe could no longer make out the interior of the stairwell—wherever she looked, rippling flaps of rotted flesh and macabre bristled with thickets of headless tongues, probing a way through the indestructible battle tank that had once been her ship's AI. Eos slashed and dissected them all, ripping everything to pieces.

Fenroe turned back toward the lower stair, shielding her eyes, and she caught something else in her peripheral vision—a lighter shadow moving into a darker one through the window that took up the entire far wall and ceiling. That's exactly when she heard the sound of electrical wires again—the corpses screamed in unison, the sound growing and building until it was so loud that Fenroe instinctively reached for her ears. Something ripped at her leg and pulled her down the stairs toward the lower level. There was pressure on her shoulders, and she was forced away from the window by a nest of grease-slickened limbs. The closest crewman's skull flaps unfolded, drooling its tongue way out, reaching it toward her clamped lips—

And Eos dropped to the lower level from the landing above, coming down hard on the corpse's skull in a three-point stance plasma first, crushing its head like a watermelon. The android lunged from one side of the corridor to the next, vaulting over the twitching bodies scattered in loose groupings all around her, and landing, rolling, she came to her feet in a devastating rush of death.

With her last fiery reserves of battery power, just before the gruesome swarm of snakelike organs pulled Fenroe back into their howling open mouths, just before she was violated with a million tubes of meaty parasites, Eos obliterated everything standing in her path. Severed heads came free in blurs of orange light and landed in puddles of parasite-laced blood. Some of the parasites were small and threadlike. Some were massive, as long and as thick as a python: they slapped onto the floor and opened their strange, squid-like mantles, exposing a wormy mouth of tiny teeth, and wriggled with disgusting, glistening energy in the light. Many of the arms and legs Eos had hacked off came to life themselves, sprouting legs of their own as they scurried away from the android to safety—it was as if the parasites were using the host's organs the same way hermit crabs use a conch. Eos stalked into the nearest open pressure door, dragging Fenroe with one arm, and spraying undead blood and metallic ichor onto the walls with the other.

Every other step made Fenroe's leg scream, and when she shifted her balance, a knife of agony stabbed into her right thigh. She hoped to god she could run. Flinching at each lunging shape, averting her face from the disintegrated mist of mutant flesh that sizzled in the aura of Eos's inescapable cutters, Fenroe felt the deafening howl of the infected piercing the soft spot behind her jaw, and she kept moving, fueled by a deep body terror, hunted by alien tongues threading for her throat to fill her mouth with the taste of raw meat.

Everything darkened. Fenroe felt the floor beneath her legs vibrate, and when she looked back at Eos crossing into the next module, the small android blazed with energy. Red-hot light burst from every diode on her body, her limbs chopping like the blades of a jet engine. Eos caught a lunging corpse in mid-air and whipped its momentum into the wall on the other side, simultaneously crushing its head and rendering it down to a mixture of metal, flesh and blood with her blazing hot plasma cutters. She dropped the carcass into a pile and whirled around just as another corpse slithered across the floor. This one dislocated its human jaw, opening the feelers of its skull—the android timed it and dropped the blade of her knee onto its head before it could launch itself through the air—she pinned it down and sliced it in half at the torso with her plasma cutter, its arms and legs flopping and thudding uselessly on the floor.

Fenroe was losing it, her brain was shutting down from sensory overload—all the blood and guts and viscera had closed something off in her heart.

The window through the pressure door brightened again, as if the station itself were falling into a star—the vacuum outside burned like an asteroid skidding into the atmosphere. Fenroe twisted her head back toward the airlock, and the light grew brighter. The intensity of it increased until it felt like her eyes were being burned out of her skull, and the light through the window finally leveled out like a sine wave across the swarmed stairway—through the bay window, looking out into the blackness of space, she saw a massive hole in the universe drift into view, and it took Fenroe a half second to realize what she was seeing.

Horrific things moved in the foreground of Fenroe's vision, and Eos pivoted on her feet, sprinting to the side. In one fluid motion, the android leapt and dove into the wall, using it as a springboard to vault and pierce into the torso of an infected corpse with her whole body—she made a flaming arrowhead out of her red-orange glowing fists and rolled to her feet before the creature's remains collapsed onto the deck in quivering chunks.

Covered head to toe in blood, dodging and weaving between

the flailing limbs of the surrounding bodies in a complex ballet, Eos sliced and tumbled and rolled to her feet, cutting intricate streams of fire and blood into the air with her fists. Wherever she struck, things came apart in bloody wet streaks of mist.

But this was all peripheral. Fenroe's mind was locked onto something else. Outside of the station—through the massive window that stretched all the way to the ceiling—the colossal hole in space wrapped an accretion disc of immense galactic measure around the body of a planet, and Fenroe felt the meaning of it all before fully understanding it. It clicked, coming together like the tectonic plates of a fault line.

In the fraction of a second she'd been pressed against the wall—as Eos cut to pieces everything that moved, dispassionately separating the meaty, fleshy particulates of all the things that meant to rip Fenroe's flesh off her bones and skewer her organs— while the android melted the infected bodies that reached to pull Fenroe into their open insectile mouths, it became clear: the planet-sized hole in space was the very same black hole that had consumed Titan.

She knew that. It was right there. Inescapable.

It was the same celestial phenomenon, only bigger.

Much, much bigger.

The hole's cataclysmic edge blazed like a molten sawblade, spewing Hawking radiation in all directions for hundreds upon thousands of kilometers, stretching to an astronomical distance too far for Fenroe to see.

It had grown far larger than the hole Beck had showed them in the viewing room, far larger than the Earthlike moon she had seen it eat.

It had grown to the size of a thousand Earths.

And Fenroe could no longer see Saturn's equatorial rings.

Because they were no longer there.

This rift in space-time had *eaten* them. It had eaten the rings. They were just...*gone*. Completely gone. And it had become so large that Saturn began ripping itself apart, tearing itself to pieces in a slow snapshot flux of dilation as it was fed upon, which stopped Fenroe's breath.

Eos was at her side again covered in gore, pulling Fenroe to her feet as countless seething shadows poured into the corridor behind them. The android dragged Fenroe deeper into the darkness, away from Saturn's remnants, away from the monstrous tear in the universe that consumed them, and whipped her spinning through the next airlock.

Fenroe came back from deep inside her head, and sprawled heavily onto the floor. She twisted her neck and located the flickering glow of the airlock controls and scrambled forward on all fours, reaching up and slamming her fist onto the lock capture, dropping the door into place. More shadows stretched ahead of them, cutting them off from the new corridor they'd just entered.

Without breaking stride, Eos turned and waded into the wall of bodies with her plasma cutters, which broke against her like a tidal wave—corpses dropped to the floor in twitching piles, still pulling weakly at the android's legs, their quartered skull flaps opening and closing like the jaws of a dying cobra.

Behind them, a fist smashed through the airlock's transomed window, clawing the air wildly. Fenroe stumbled back, covering her face from the spray of glass.

Eos vaulted onto the door and hung from the shattered fanlight, bracing herself with her feet, grasping the lip of the broken window with one hand. The android chinned herself up and shoved her free hand through the window, igniting the plasma. The infected crewman's arm came loose on the other side and Eos ripped it through, tossing it over her shoulder, where it flopped onto the floor and shot spidery limbs from its gray skin and scrabbled out of sight.

More glistening shapes poured into the corridor from unseen ducts, and crashed through the ceiling from the upper level.

"Move, Commander," the android pulsed, guiding Fenroe deeper into the darkness. The arcs of her limbs exploded with heat, and everything within reach came apart in bloody pieces. Although removed from the body, the dismembered remains continued grasping with mindless hunger, some of them popping like bog marsh, shooting ivory barbs into anything that would stick. Eos pivoted, slicing out at random, and instead of a constant beam of plasma, the android's arms began burping like the muzzle of an automatic rifle, firing in short controlled bursts as she rationed her lithium power cells.

Eos dragged Fenroe's limping body by a fistful of her soaked flight suit, her bare feet slapping onto the cold floor. They reached through the dense mist of the corridor's suffocating half-light and passed through another pressure door. Eos shoved Fenroe inside the new corridor and slammed her metallic fist against the lock— it dropped like a hammer, hissing to the floor, sticking, grinding—

And it froze in mid-descent.

The drive motor box sputtered. One hideous shadow rose up in front of the android, its headless tongue flicking back and forth in the glint of Eos's red warlike glow.

Eos shoved her fist against its throat beneath the chin, and blasted its head clean off with a single phosphorous burst. The corpse stood headless in the darkness for a long second, swaying on its unsteady feet, reaching out blindly to its sides with its arms, and then collapsed: the reanimated bodies may have not had any brains in their skulls, but they must have had some remnant of a nerve cluster at the base of the neck. And Eos keyed in on that in-stride, focusing her fire at the brainstem.

Eos lifted her arms and grasped the service handle at the

bottom of the pressure door, and hung from it until the friction gave. The flood of infected bodies had already eaten through the prior airlock, and they swarmed over each other, the closest of them trying to belly-slide under the gap.

Eos lifted her legs and dropped her weight repeatedly, the door giving whole inches with each pull. And the friction eased some more, and the door finally gave, sliding hard the rest of the way like a guillotine, severing a thicket of arms that tried clawing underneath.

Fenroe scrambled to her feet, feeling needles stabbing down her right leg, and pulled herself under a desk in the center of the corridor—infected bodies scurried and bounded over the top of its steel surface from the other direction, and lunged onto the small android like ants swarming an invader.

Eos spun herself into a buzz-saw of plasma, slicing everything around her in half, but there were too many. Tucked under the desk, Fenroe braced herself as the things leapt blindly over her. Eos's arm shot out and a spray of dead blood teeming with millions of maggot-sized worms slashed across Fenroe's open mouth. The salty fluid wriggled against the soft flesh of her lips and tongue like half-cooked grains of rice. She spat and wiped frantically until she could no longer feel the granulated muck, and twisted away from the frenzy.

Bodies scrambled over the top of the desk, rippling the surface with frenetic weight as each one leapt onto Eos. But the android was still on her feet, whipping and elbowing and burning and cutting everything that moved.

Fenroe crawled hand over hand through what was left of a defeated barricade, blindly threading through the objects littered around the corridor under the cover of Eos's last stand, and groped until she found a ventilation hatch several feet above the floor. She stretched and slammed the palm of her hand against the access panel, and it dilated open with the sound of wet metal on stone. Fenroe reached up and pulled herself scraping forward headfirst into the pitch-black vent.

She thought she heard something move heavily through the ductwork ahead, but she couldn't see beyond her own outstretched hands. The vent itself was thickened with darkness.

Before the hundreds of infected bodies turned her direction and crammed themselves into the ventilation duct to follow, the small android dropped to its knees and disappeared beneath the waves of that terrible sea—blue flickers of light trailed up the base of the corpses' spines, and they began to conduct electricity from within, distributing it through their collected scalp petals, burning hot enough to melt through Eos's exoskeleton. In one last burst of energy, Eos ignited her cutters to full capacity, and sliced several of the corpses to pieces as she was dragged down. A remaining body had softened one of Eos's arms and ripped it free while it was still firing. The final jet of plasma arced toward the vent hatch, and the feeding frenzy of infected *Pinnacle* crewmates tore Eos's exoskeleton in half, spraying lambent red ichor and nanites into the air.

Fenroe crawled as fast as she could deeper into the vent, the last burst of Eos's plasma engulfing the open hatch and catching the soles of her bare feet just enough to burn the skin. She screamed in searing agony, desperately pulling herself away from the blistering needles of fire. Crawling until the metal beneath her body had cooled, Fenroe curled into the fetal position, trembling with shock.

Fresh tears burst as she tried to force air past the emptiness inside her chest. She wanted with all of her heart for the darkness to blink the world away this final time, this terrible dream, this last moment.

Leftover phosphenes fired across her black vision, and

Sitosen's body falling through the void was suddenly all Fenroe could think about. She wanted to think about the good things before her death, about the rust colored canyons of Mars, the breathtaking ice eruptions of Europa...but all she saw were Dunesto's intestines spilling out onto the floor of the service conduit.

She wanted the good parts of her life to flash before her eyes, but they didn't.

In her mind was her mother and farther. Her brother. And her crew.

All looking back at her with sad, confused eyes from across those dark waters. Waiting for her to come join them.

Something cracked inside, some truth that left her shivering. It was her crew...

Fenroe was supposed to protect them. She was supposed to die for them. And she failed.

The weight of that truth crushed her. It pulled her down into the swallowing darkness, ate her whole, chewed her up until there was nothing left. It was so seductive to just let it all go, to simply lay there and die. She felt her bones give under the weight of all the people she'd left behind, and it was too much.

Her eyelids peeled back as far as they could go, hungrily pulling in trace photons so she could make out the vague angles of the vent's interior. A sliver of light suddenly bled in from behind her prone body, and for a split second she could clearly see the vent stretching off and dipping down to more darkness up ahead; she followed that light, twisting her head back until she found its source: the infected bodies that ripped Eos apart had followed her. They were melting through the access hatch, and the metal began to glow pale red.

They just kept coming, like the ticking seconds of a clock, like the slow flames at the base of her pyre. Fenroe turned her back on the hatch and wrapped herself around that light, hugging it in, letting it fill her up until it felt as if she would burst.

She gathered her knees under her body and forced herself to push deeper into the vent, and she carried that light with her. She took up the weight of it, because it was the only light she had left. The monstrous echoes in the dark followed her closely, lusting for her light like the dead lusted for a way back.

EIGENGRAU

1.

LEANING AGAINST THE NEXTEL and foam-softened wall beside the ventilation duct from which she had emerged—blood soaking through her fingers where she'd pressed a hand firmly into the glue-sealed wound on her thigh—Fenroe wiped her filthy sleeve across the cold sweat dripping down her face. An open door farther down the passage poured in frozen white light, flashing with the slow movement of something unseen, cutting back and forth in the corridor in a rhythm of darkness and light like the turn of a half-dead fan blade. It made the long corridor look as if it were a train car passing through a tunnel. The effect was disorienting, flickering in freeze-frame snapshots like a reel of broken film. When she reached the open room, Fenroe slid carefully to the edge of the door and peered inside, holding her breath, and searched the darkness for movement.

It was another control room, but this one had a low ceiling. Two control chairs were stationed before a tri-grid observational window with its blast shields lowered. But they were half-ajar, open just enough for a thin sheet of light to stab through. That light *cut...cut...cut* in pace with something outside, interchanging with bands of shadow. Fenroe maneuvered around the seats and bent over a circular shaped stellographer canted at a forty-five degree angle. She reached forward and passed her fingers into a plain of holographic light hovering just above the center console, and the blast shields whirred to life, peeling open slowly, widening a view of the telescope lens in the center of the installation. Fenroe staggered back and gazed up into the abyssal horizon, a cold sense of awe and horror squeezing her stomach with iced fingers.

She'd found the source of light.

Through this window, the planet Saturn was completely gone.

In its place was a cataclysmic, star-like vortex swollen almost as large as the missing planet, maybe even larger. Saturn's corpse had become smeared across the vortex's fiery accretion disk, stretched upon the edge of the black hole's perfectly spherical event horizon far in the distance, dragging space-time along into its crushing maw.

Fenroe could only stare. The black hole had grown astronomically since last she saw it, devouring everything in orbit. All that remained of the planet Saturn and his moons was an obliterated tail of white light swirling and dragging in an arc far behind its new orbit around the tiny sun in the distance. The sight of it—the sheer immensity and cataclysm of it—twisted her guts with nausea. It was like looking over the edge of the world, staring down into the cloudy chasm where the earth fell away to endlessly deep shadow. To scale it, planet Earth would have been a small blue speck of glowing dust on the edge of this thing, and the immensity of that comparison terrified her beyond anything she'd ever experienced.

Forcing her eyes away, Fenroe held the wall so she wouldn't faint. She studied the deck below her feet as if it was a thin sheet of paper, imagining the forces of oblivion tearing it to shreds from underneath and swallowing her whole. The very walls made her nauseous, because the only thing separating her from being eviscerated by those unfathomable gravitational forces was a thin layer of aluminum. Pushing the cold terror down into her gut, she turned her attention back outside and scanned the ship's hull, following its interior side with her eyes up to the top levels. The installation was clean from the outside, a facility blinking with red and white lights like a landing strip at night. She staggered forward and bent her head to see if she could find the *Endeavor* still parked in dry dock, but the hull curved out of sight.

As she turned to head back toward the main corridor, she caught the movement of an off-gray shadow inside one of the closest bay windows on the level above, gliding out of sight with the deliberate grace of a leviathan returning to the deep. Fenroe blinked and squinted her eyes, but the shape had already disappeared. She pressed her forehead into the glass, feeling a twinge inside of her chest, a sudden sensation of sharp prehistoric triggers pulling along her spine. The movement was too fast, like the snap of a curtain, or the crashing spread of a wave: she couldn't tell if she had seen the flash of one massive thing, or a seething group of several things moving together as one. Whatever it was, it moved like liquid, changing direction like an emergent flock of birds or a school of fish. The fact that it was above her, on a separate level, didn't make her feel any better.

A spoke of light needled the corner of her vision from the left. It was a softer light than what came through the observational window. Blueish, like the muted glow of a data terminal. She located the source of it, and found another doorway tucked in shadow that had been melted and torn inward.

Squeezing through the rent metal, Fenroe stepped into the dark milieu of the next module, and once inside, she made her way down a slightly sloped walkway that opened into a rotunda the size of a stadium. She reached out and grasped the handrail, tilting her head back to take in the scale of this place, everything bristling with machinery and lab equipment. Thick chains hung from the tall, domed ceiling suspending large platforms and scaffolding that were set upon columns several meters above the dark unseen floor below. On the largest open platform directly ahead—which glossed like smooth concrete in the half light—was a massive slab of neodymium alloy in the shape of a cogwheel the size of an Olympic swimming pool, positioned deeply into the center of a cavern. As she looked around the immense area, she noticed that all piping and conduit and wire funneled back toward this machine.

She had found *Pinnacle's* particle detector.

The narrow walkway sloped down to a small three-stair veranda, which then ascended to the network of aluminum-grated girders and platforms that wrapped around the gigantic magnet assembly directly in the center. Hanging half over the catwalk, one leg and one arm tangled in the railing, a solitary body in an aged Faraday suit lay prone and unmoving.

Fenroe carefully made her way down the walkway, stepping over a handful of thick canisters of hydrogen coolant that had fallen off their racks. She pressed her hand against the bandage on her thigh and pulled the knot tighter, securing it as best she could.

Mounting the stairs to the raised main platform, she pulled herself up carefully next to the body. Fenroe could see that the person had died long before the parasite had spread and consumed the crew. The person wore a *Pinnacle* uniform, their limbs and helmet showing no puncture wounds anywhere that Fenroe could see. She knelt and studied the scene for a quiet moment, and gently pulled the body away from the handrail, rolling it onto its back until it came to rest fully on the platform.

Wiping away a thin, glittery layer of metallic dust from the person's faceplate, Fenroe discovered that it was the body of a woman. She was well preserved by the low pressure and coldness, her skin only slightly off-gray, her lips only slightly blue and bloodless. Fenroe's eyes drifted down over the body until she found the woman's nametag.

"Mia Caraway," she whispered aloud, the sound echoing throughout the cavern, shocking her senses: it had been so long since she'd spoken anything. She almost didn't recognize the sound of her own voice, which had become stringy and rasped. Brushing the nametag with her bare hand, Fenroe looked around the body for a sign.

"You're one of the ghosts we saw in playback," she whispered, reaching down to gently tuck Caraway's arms against her sides, trying to give some semblance of rest.

Running her icy fingers along the stiff fabric of Caraway's Faraday suit, Fenroe searched for signs of trauma, but it was clean. She palpated the suit and found a large split in the top of Caraway's helmet, old blood and dark gray bone fragments dried into the cracks: evidence of blunt impact. Fenroe craned her head and measured the distance to the collider, and decided that Caraway must have been blown back against the guardrail hard enough to crack her helmet.

Fenroe was suddenly struck with a nauseating and horrible fear, and grasped at the handrail to her side to keep from falling over. She wanted to get out, to run from that immense place back into the main corridor, to find the *Endeavor* and escape, to suck out the venom of hopelessness flooding her veins.

It was the state of this particular death that shook her. It was so...so *restful*. It was like Fenroe could see back through time into the moment, and in the minutia of it, she caught a brief glimpse of Caraway's last breaths. She could picture the woman clearly, watching her let go and fall deep into those waters, letting it spread over and cover her body. The urge to lie down next to her was powerful, the aching need to let her bones relax and sink deeply into the cold metal and close her eyes...

Fenroe stood and stared down at the peaceful scene. Caraway could have been in a deep sleep. She had to focus on something else, because the desire was too powerful. She forced herself to look away, panning her eyes across the darkness, taking in the detail of the entire room, until her focus drifted back toward the detector.

That bluish light sparkled again in the corner of her vision, and she followed it. There was a slight gangway, almost like a ramp, and Fenroe could see an arrangement of tiny lights blinking below the scaffolding, still glowing and flickering with waves of blue upon the walls.

Fenroe inched closer to the dormant machine, and noted how pristine it looked. It was the only thing in the cavern without a single mark on it.

Grasping the rail, she pulled herself up with careful effort, her leg clamping down with dull, pulsing aches after each step, and the coldness of the metal stung her hands.

Like the hologram Beck had found in the Server Hub, everything within a twenty-foot radius of the detector had been pancaked outward and smashed to pieces. Bits of glass had fused to the ironwork, and shards of exploded equipment spread out in all directions. The damaged area stretched away from the machine in a perfect sphere, the wreckage ending at the exact same distance in every direction. From somewhere below in the darkness came the tangy dirt scent of blood, and something else—

dense and fleshy and bitter and fetid: the sour shit of a meat eater. It was hard to tell in the dimness of the rotunda, but Fenroe thought the gory smell emanated from the collider itself...

She sidestepped over a litter of dumped equipment boxes and paper. This massive rotunda was once the nexus of all work done in far orbit, all directed and collated from here; now it looked like a crypt, its black rafters scavenged and cleared of anything useful, its contents spilled all over the platforms and the ground below.

But the machine was still operational.

It was powered down but still on standby, locked in stasis after the very last event.

A Newton's cradle knocked steel ball bearings back and forth atop the console not far from the main gangway. An inexplicable presence pulsed from the shadows with incomprehensible purpose and meaning, as if the room itself had suddenly opened its eyes to study her. She got the feeling that everything had been set upon the hair-trigger of a deadfall, waiting patiently for someone to come along and trip it.

She limped around the open space and knelt, brushing her fingers across the machine, willing her frozen hands to grasp a datapad lying near Caraway's body, as if it had been cast from her dying hands to that very spot. The pad blinked awake, and soft white-blue light shined from its badly cracked screen.

Sitting carefully on the floor, Fenroe pushed herself up against the console and leaned into it, stretching her legs out with the painful slowness of an old woman. She gritted her teeth and cinched the dressing on her thigh again, its white fabric gone rusty black, and then paged delicately through the dark blue screens, leaving tiny fingerprints of blood on the glass.

Most of it was particle physics she couldn't summon the mental strength to deal with, but there were half-coherent notes typed into the margins, highlighted by different shades of color:

chat boxes attached in random places around an experiment report, as if it were a discussion between two of the *Pinnacle's* researchers. It could have simply been a quick way for technicians to communicate to each other in a manner that wasn't monitored by Command, or it could have been nothing. Fenroe glanced up at the particle detector once more, isolated somehow from the desolation spread out before it. Returning her gaze to the datapad, she focused her eyes until the letters and words and sentences became clear enough to read:

RANDALL: Spin-2 particle reacting with SM at TeV...is this what a graviton would look like?

CARAWAY: No chance. Gotta be misreading, but better retest.

RANDALL: Kaluza-Klein and ADD models coincide with data: massive spin-2 decay detected as resonance. That's looking like confirm graviton, but I also have a side observation I need you to check: sensors detected presence of higher particle accelerating opposite of applied force after graviton decay.

CARAWAY: My results have validated. Confirmed higher object with negative inertial mass (???) Is this real? Heading off station for a few days. We'll talk more when I get back from Calisto outpost. Keep this off-channel for now.

———

RANDALL: That is again confirmed weird particle. Have validated your data: unquantifiable number of objects with negative inertial mass that appear immediately after what I believe is the manifestation and rapid decay of gravitons, which show positive electric charges accelerating away from other unseen objects with (presumably) negative charges: objects of positive charge are still attracting each other, leaving great big gaping holes in decay channels $\gamma\gamma$, ZZ, WW, $\tau\tau$, bb, and $\mu\mu$ (Doesn't this contradict like-attraction rule?) I think we found something huge here. Something BIG.

CARAWAY: Confirm negative gravitational effect via proton-proton collision. I've never seen anything like this. Explain?

RANDALL: I'm seeing same thing. Explanation: it would be a characteristic of negative gravitational mass to repel all positive charge objects.

CARAWAY: We have to be doing something wrong, or is our equipment on fritz? Please recheck.

———

RANDALL: Rechecked: findings validated. There's something here. And remember, negative mass does not contradict cosmological constant or relativity if local conditions are consistent with Standard Model.

CARAWAY: More validation: leftover supersymmetric objects have been observed after graviton escape. I don't understand what you mean by local conditions. Explain further please?

RANDALL: Explanation: Membrane Theory. If gravity is the most powerful force in the universe but perceived as the weakest *from our point of view, it's because most of what gravity IS exists in many different dimensional states at once. We don't normally perceive or interact with many of those dimensions, and that's why we feel so little of gravity's effects.*

———

CARAWAY: Confirm supersymmetric particles present after graviton decay. I get M-theory, I just don't know what you mean by local conditions. Are you talking about, what, different realities?

RANDALL: Explanation: It's possible that we're glimpsing only a small piece of a single graviton, and that the rest of it is in another place where the cosmological constant is inverse of our own. Those negative gravitational effects we're seeing could be coming in from a place where the other piece of our graviton exists, i.e. we're creating gravitons via proton-proton collision and the ensuing force is pushing them into higher dimensions. While they're escaping our fold of perceivable reality and pushing into the next, the gravitons may be creating bridges for those negative gravitational masses we're seeing, which are leaking back into our universe from a place where there's a negative cosmological constant.

CARAWAY: Wormholes?

RANDALL: Very, very tiny ones. There's not enough energy to keep these gateways open for very long, of course, because these bridges fall apart as soon as the graviton that we've created decays. If the math is right, here's how the process might work: when we smash protons together, this creates a graviton. The force of that initial collision pushes the graviton into another dimension, where, for a brief moment, a bridge is created between our two realities. And that bridge stays open only as long as the graviton remains in phase with our universe. When the graviton slips out of phase, the bridge collapses, and the wormhole disappears. What this means is, we may have substantiated evidence for the existence of another dimension of reality. We could be opening tiny wormholes into this reality by creating particles of gravity via photon collisions. A bridge of some kind, which stays connected to another fold of our universe for as long as it takes our graviton to pass entirely into it.

CARAWAY: I'm going to brief Wren on this to see if I can get more server space. We're going to have to increase the luminosity of these beams. Please pull what data you have together and forward it to me asap. Make plans to put the detector on standby until we can determine what's wrong with it. In the meantime, keep recording as much as you can on the off chance there IS something going on here. But chances are either we're doing something wrong, or the equipment is messed up.

———

From the darkness across the main platform, the sound of hard rubber scraped lightly on the catwalk near Caraway's body, and into one of those fragmentary breaks where a whole room seems to inhale a deep breath slid the sounds of deliberate footsteps different from the mindless heel scuffs of worm-filled corpses.

Something was moving toward her position.

Fenroe lowered the data pad and went completely still, her heart hammering inside her chest, her pulse exploding up her neck—

And Thomas Beck stepped out of the shadows. He stared with disbelief—his young eyes aged by terror and stress and exhaustion—a crowbar covered with monster gore dangling in his limp hand. "It's you..."

His voice, just above a whisper. Beck staggered toward her with caution, not believing his eyes, and dropped heavily to his knees just out of arms reach, studying her as if she were a mirage—as if at any moment she would vanish into thin air. "You're still alive..."

Fenroe smirked painfully and summoned a hoarse whisper. "Still alive."

He seemed to collect himself and moved closer, assessing the state of her wounds. She was in bad shape, shivering uncontrollably in the frozen air. The right leg of her flight suit was saturated with dark black blood from the middle of her thigh all the way down to her ankle. Clear watery fluids leaked out of burn blisters on her bare feet, and she could see the dirt sheen of her own skin just below her eyes, her begrimed hair stuck to her skull. Beck's hand moved up to gently squeeze her shoulder, and his eyes were pensive and full of bone-deep fatigue. The contact was almost enough to break her. She nearly began to cry after feeling his gloved hand touch her skin, but caught herself.

"Where's Aris," she asked, not fully trusting her voice.

"Safe," he said. "We got separated when they came for us in the corridor. She's holed up behind six feet of radiation shielding in a monitor room not far from the *Endeavor's* dock umbilical." He bent forward, searching her eyes. "What about Suja?"

Fenroe looked away and took a deep breath, afraid that if her mouth opened she would scream, and she wasn't entirely sure she'd be able to stop. She shook her head and leaned back against the console.

He touched the sticky bandage tied around her leg, which

took on the feel and texture of sand where it wasn't wet: clotted blood. Lots of it.

Beck stood and reached his hand up to the neck housing of his bio-suit, snapping the clamps forward and twisting his helmet until it made a depressurizing *thuck* sound, like opening the lid of a jar. Removing it from his shoulders, he set the helmet on the ground and immediately started unlatching his utility harness.

"What are you doing?"

"You're taking my suit," he said, peeling it down over his shoulders.

"No," she shook her head weakly, holding up her hand. "No, stop—"

"You're freezing," he cut her off. "It'll keep you warm and help keep the wound on your leg compressed."

"Beck—"

"You're *taking it*," he hissed, raising his voice. The concave walls amplified the acoustics and echoed the sound of his hard words against the metal. Beck froze, gritting his teeth at the retreating sound, blood rushing to his cheeks. "You'll move better," he finished quietly. "And I won't have to carry you as much."

Fenroe couldn't bring herself to resist. And deep down she didn't want to. The freezing coldness penetrated the muscle and stabbed into the marrow. Her arms and legs had gone numb, and although her body was operating on the lowest possible amount of energy, she was in constant danger of hypothermia.

He helped guide her deadened limbs into the warm sleeves and lowered the helmet onto her shoulders. A rush of warm air cascaded down her neck, and Beck's HUD blinked and readjusted to her eye position. The comforting sound of subdued stereo poured into the directional speakers near her temples.

"*Fenroe?*" Aris's voice carried softly over comms, as if she spoke directly into Fenroe's thoughts.

"I'm here."

Aris let go of a full lung of air, and the relief in her voice was palpable. *"It's good to hear your voice."*

"Yours too." She closed her eyes. "Aris, I'm...I want you to know I'm sorry...okay? I'm so sorry for everything..."

The younger woman was silent for a long time as Beck finished securing Fenroe into his bio-suit.

"We'll talk about that later," Aris said finally. *"For now, you just stay alive. You hear me?"*

"Yeah," she nodded, feeling like her head weighed a hundred pounds. "Yeah, I hear you."

Beck sat back onto his haunches and exhaled a cloud of steam through lips that were already turning blue. He stared through Fenroe for a moment, from a million miles away.

"The *Pinnacle* brought it with them," he said suddenly, nodding toward the cracked data pad lying next to her leg. "The parasite. The black hole. When they came through the wormhole."

She shook her head, not following him.

"They were smashing particles together," Beck said, blinking in a daze. He stood and crossed his arms, massaging warmth back into his chest. "And they must have opened something...some sort of gateway to another place...but that's impossible, right?" He searched her eyes, as if he desperately wanted her to tell him it was. "Because, where did the energy come from? You'd need to harness the energy equivalent of an entire star, or a planet the size of Jupiter to create something big enough for even a human to pass through." He shook his head, lost in thought. "To open something of this magnitude, or to create a singularity large enough to consume an entire planet? You'd need to pull together the energy of a *thousand* suns. A *thousand* Jupiters. The *Pinnacle* didn't have the means to do that. Our *species* doesn't have the means to do anything like that..."

"But you saw it yourself in the playback," she nodded, thinking deeply. "You read the data terminal."

He stood and offered Fenroe his hand. "I want you to look at this..."

Clenching her jaw hard against the deep ache, she grabbed his wrist and pulled herself painfully to her feet. Beck reached up to the service light on her shoulder and twisted it on. He grasped the lamp and angled it down toward the deep darkness far below the platform, and at first Fenroe couldn't put what she saw together in any meaningful way. Three or so meters down, it looked like... like a field of rotting kelp washed up onto a rocky shoreline. Except the leaves were milky white and brown instead of pale green. Some of the longer strands were mottled black, thick and ropey like the sinewy muscles of a python; others were thin and hair-like, everything curling and piling onto itself like miles of half decomposed intestines drying in the sun. And that *smell*...that meaty, coppery smell she'd noticed earlier rose up from the coils of those intestinal things below...

After a moment of scrutiny, Fenroe realized that she was looking at a trailing river of dead parasites. A revolting dead nest of albino reptile limbs—some as big as a human leg—leading all the way back to just below the detector. And she could now see hundreds of dead and dried serpent things hanging from the grated metal right below the machine itself.

"These things...they *came* from it," Beck said, pointing at the massive magnet looming overhead, and then back over her shoulder toward the direction she had come. She followed the trail of dead serpents below with the light as it led toward a massive gaping hole in the bulkhead revealing pipes, conduit and wire surrounding an impenetrable blackness, wide and tall enough to pass one of the orbital Landers. The vinyl and foam had been eaten away; the carbon fiber underneath had been melted through and torn like the barricades they'd encountered all over the rest of the station.

"The collider must have...tapped into something," he finished quietly, lowering his hand. "The gravitons they created must have come in contact with something from a different fold of reality."

Fenroe stared down into the open rampway. The melted down void in the wall was big, and dead maggot-like beings the size of anacondas poured out of it, as if the station had tried vomiting the sickness back out into the collision cavern.

Something was very, very wrong. It wasn't like the burn patterns that the infected crewmen made when they ate through metal. The edge of the opening was mired with some kind of filth, the hole itself so covered with thick organic substances that it vaguely resembled a necrotic puncture wound in the dark gray flesh of a shark, as if some biological system had fused to the wall, spreading up the grid work like an immense fungus. A needling sensation pricked the center of her chest as she tried imagining the size of what could have secreted it.

"*I'm not sure how long I can stay here*," Aris whispered over comms, bringing Fenroe back to the moment. "*They're getting close...*"

And the universe seemed to answer Aris by drifting a soft murmur into the rotunda. Fenroe and Beck looked up as the sound stretched long and hollow like the slow friction of a bowstring, expanding and resonating throughout; growing at first, like the midnight rustling of wind and leaves, the atmosphere bleeding with an orchestra of tortured screams and pain. The echoes peeled from some far place in the distant darkness beyond the melted opening in the bulkhead below, beyond the heaps of parasite carcasses leading back toward the particle collider.

"Come on," Beck said, touching her arm, pulling her intently toward the bridge that led back into the main corridor. "We can't stay here."

3.

The scattered echoes of pain followed them through the station. Always there, trickling in from the acoustic distance. Desolately side-lit by the emergency lights, the *Pinnacle* had become a maze of strange catacombs and night-black shadows. Broken terminals hung like impaled fauna from the walls, and discarded equipment littered the ground where it had fallen away from racking or had been pulled from shelving: stationary, flashlights, desk lamps and soggy manila folders scattered so thickly across every square inch that Fenroe had a hard time seeing the actual floor beneath it all.

The corridor broke at an angle ahead and branched several support modules of offices and labs. A singular light fell softly over it all. When the hallway opened up to a larger space of couches, loungers, and coffee tables all in disarray and chaos—a personal-sized faucet tucked into the farthest wall, broken pieces of plastic ware orbiting a single fallen chair next to a stack of equipment boxes—the void opened up before them through a broad observational window that extended above the ceiling and curved overhead. It was a breathtaking sight, imposing and undeniable.

There was a dark star, towering overhead like a mountain peak the size of a universe. Beck stopped instantly in the middle of his stride, going very still.

Rising high in the distance of dark space, the black hole had expanded even further than before, by measures too great to think about. What was left of Saturn had all but tapered away from a thick band of light swirling into the pitch, to a thin streak of light that stretched back toward a small white sun far away. The lensing smear of it gave the impression that space-time had the consistency and feel of stretched silk, like sheening fabric that blazed around the singularity's spherical edge. It was cataclysm and beauty beyond anything Fenroe could have ever imagined. She could feel pieces of her soul being pulled into it through her eyes.

Beck stood with his arms crossed, hugging his trembling shoulders, locked in some private state of wonder and awe. The pale light brought out the details of fatigue and exhaustion around his eyes. The last couple of days had wasted their bodies, and Fenroe knew she looked worse—she could feel it in the dragging weight of her shoulders, in the ravenous void in her stomach, in the rack of sharp ribs poking through her flight suit. It was evident that she and Beck had lost a shocking amount of weight—their cheekbones sticking out like nobs below puffy sacks of periorbital skin. And she couldn't remember the last time she had eaten anything. They were being crushed by time, as if the universe had taken upon itself to hammer them into dust simply because they were there. That weight intensified when she thought about how close they were to the end, how so very near...

She could taste the promise of more time, forcing her to take another step. She could feel the need pushing hard to the surface, willing her wasted body forward, urging her to keep breathing, and this filled her with more fear and terror than anything she could imagine: looking deep into her heart, wanting to insulate it from a thing she knew she could never escape, hoping to validate her detachment with some purpose, or meaning...she found instead the burning need to survive, to keep living no matter how badly it hurt. And the worst part was that deep down she knew it was only going to get worse.

"You had a thought," Fenroe said suddenly, breaking away from that pattern of ideas in her mind. "Back in the server room."

"...What?"

"You *know* something," she said again, an edge to her voice. "I saw it in your eyes back there. Something in the playback we found in the Server Hub."

"Yes, I had a thought," Beck said, swaying gently on his feet. He shook his head, furrowing his brow. "It's the dates," he said finally, eyes remaining locked on the vortex outside. "The station clocks."

Fenroe couldn't think through the muddiness. Her mind felt like a dilapidated rusty engine, sputtering as it tried to turn over. "The dates..."

"The server's operation log was time stamped with a date two years from now—"

"Because the mainframe was fried," she said, taking a long, tired breath. "I understand that, but I'm—"

"Just," he said weakly, cutting her off. "Just listen."

He closed his eyes for a moment—a slow, exhausted blink—and then continued. "The computer says the last recorded data log was made two years from now, but the station clocks kept running for *ten more years*, until we stumbled onto it." He paused, then shrugged. "How could the *Pinnacle* have been orbiting both Saturn *and* Jupiter for the last ten years? How is that even possible?"

"All right," she said, meeting his eyes. "Then where did it come from?"

"Not where," he shook his head, "but when."

She thought about that. A needle of doubt tickled the back of her mind, scratching for her full attention. "You're saying it's from the future."

He raised his weak shoulders—a soft, heavy movement,

meant to be a shrug. "It's the only answer I have."

"So what is a future version of the *Pinnacle* doing out here?"

"Do you know what dark matter is?" he asked.

She lifted her hands helplessly, exhausted by having to think. "It's a gravitational effect," she shrugged finally. "It slows the universe's expansion. Pulls galaxies and stars together."

"It's not just an effect, it *is* gravity." He said, "Gravity that's leaking into our universe from *another* universe."

"Another universe..."

"An adjacent one," he said. "The most similar universe to our own, in terms of physics."

"Another universe," she repeated distantly, hoping that saying it aloud would help clear it in her head. The needle of doubt began digging under the skin of her awareness again, as though some distant voice were trying to get her attention; there was something about that—something dire about the station clocks—something eerily plausible that made the hair on her arms stand on end. "You think the *Pinnacle* has been there," she said finally. "You think this space station from the future passed through another fold of reality."

With great effort, Beck pulled his eyes away from the window and faced her, limping close. "If our mission hadn't been reassigned to retrieve the *Endeavor*, we would have been here—" he pointed at the deck, "—right here with them, and I would have been working in the lab with Caraway. I would have been here when she died." He waited a beat, letting the echo of his voice clear the air. "You see, I know that they were looking for something called a graviton. Or in this case the absence of one—" he opened his hands, "—to solve the problem of quantum gravity."

Fenroe shook her head and shrugged. "What does this have to do with us?"

"The key here is gravity, right? Because dark energy is gravity that exists in many different universes at once. It's spread out across space-time, and it bleeds into *our* universe from another one. And think about that, actually *think*. If certain types of particles like gravitons leak into other universes, and if particles from other universes leak into ours, then that means we're connected somehow. It means we *share* certain properties."

"I still don't understand what that has to do with us."

"Okay," Beck said. "First, you have to think in terms of fourth dimensional geometry. You have to think of *Time* as its own dimension, as a complete *thing*—past, present, and future all existing at once from the perspective of a higher dimensional plane. Humans exist in three dimensions, right? Height, width and depth. All occurring at the same time. That's us. Three dimensional beings.

"*Time* is the fourth dimension. It's above and between and around the three dimensions that our brains experience. This is why we can only perceive Time as moving in one direction. Past, then present, then future. That's how the universe moves from our perspective. Like reading a book, our three-dimensional brains only see one page at a time. From cover to cover, we turn the pages until we reach the last, and then it's over. But outside of time? Time isn't just a single page that can be read in one direction. It looks like the *entire book*. A whole object in and of itself, past present and future all existing simultaneously. You follow?"

"I think so," she nodded, exhausted.

"And we know that Time and Space are fundamentally linked, right?"

"Yes," Fenroe said.

"A wormhole is a *distortion* of space-time," Beck said. "An acceleration of it from our perspective, which allows you to open the book to whatever page you want. You can just leaf it open and start reading at the beginning, middle, or end. You decide. It's a portal from where you are in this part of the universe, to another part, without actually having to take the whole journey—without having to actually *read* the whole book." He paused a moment, making sure that she was still with him. "In M-Theory of quantum physics, we recognize that our universe—our book—is just one of an infinite number of books in a library called *The Bulk*, which is like the fabric of all existence. And each book is a different universe in the bulk, with their own languages and combinations of words and natural laws that tell a unique story within its pages. The closer the books are to each other in the library, the more similar they are and the more characteristics they share. *Gravity* is like the shelf on which all of these books stand. It touches everything simultaneously, holding it all together."

"And you think the *Pinnacle* crew might have figured out a way to create a bridge to the next book on the shelf," Fenroe said quietly. "You think they passed into it briefly before arriving back into our universe."

"By smashing particles together," he nodded. "You could theoretically generate enough energy to create a particle of gravity—a piece of the thing that connects our universe to the next. I think the *Pinnacle* crew created a wormhole into the past. And I think that wormhole tunneled beneath an adjacent universe." He turned his head and looked at the beautiful, immense orb of light-death in the distance of black space, and Fenroe knew that he was as spellbound as she. That he was as moved by the terrifying beauty of it. But he saw something different in the smeared light. He saw it from the perspective of a physicist, who views the world as a chaotic order of systems.

"I think they were pulled into it," he said finally. "And I think they came in contact with something before emerging again near

Saturn. Something terrible."

Fenroe stared back, concentrating hard to make sense of what he said with the reports she'd read in the collision cavern, with everything she could remember about conservation of energy and gravity and superstring theory.

"You're right," she said finally. "You couldn't produce enough energy to create anything like that just by smashing particles together. Anything propagated in those particle tunnels would be too small, decay too fast—"

"Unless the gravitons they created came in contact with something more powerful on the other side—" Beck said, lifting his hand toward the obliterated light of Saturn rotating around the black hole like the eye of a galactic hurricane, "—something with enough energy to not only consume planets, but to consume them faster and more ruthlessly than anything we've ever seen before." He dropped his hand and shrugged. "A thing like that would have provided enough energy to create and sustain a wormhole large enough and long enough to pull the *Pinnacle* in."

She stepped past him, looking out toward the singularity turning majestically in the black distance outside of the window. Beck stood in silence, interrupted only by the thrum of the ventilation and machinery behind the walls. In that quiet moment, he turned toward the opposite corridor. The last corridor leading to the *Endeavor* docking umbilical.

"You're certain," she said.

"No—" he said, shaking his head, "—but like I said, the relationship between time and gravity is the issue. The *Pinnacle's* clocks are the key. And we know that this version of the *Pinnacle Observatory* has been out here for ten years."

"So what do we do with that information?" she asked. "How does that help us?"

"It doesn't. But if we make it to the *Endeavor*," Beck said over his shoulder, reaching for a crusty blanket that cracked audibly with dried fluids as he picked it up. He didn't have the strength to shake it loose and simply pulled it over his shoulders, hugging it around his chest. "If we do get out of here, we need to point the *Endeavor's* telescope back toward Jupiter. Toward Calisto."

"Why?"

"Because, if I'm right," he shrugged, "at this moment, there may be another observatory out there. The original *Pinnacle*."

4.

The docking umbilical was starkly alight, seeping into the shadows of the desolate *Pinnacle* corridors just beyond the airlock. The sharp openness and visibility tugged anxiously at the back of Fenroe's mind, urging her to stay hidden in the safe darkness, away from exposed light. She flinched when the LED strips popped and blinked to life as they drew near, and after being in the dark for so long, the sudden brightness was intense, and the light strips stung her eyes like blasts of steam. Stepping into the umbilical, Beck gathered the dank gray blanket around his shoulders and stared at the open airlock on the opposite end.

Beyond the portal, the *Endeavor's* airlock loomed open and inviting, its docking bay stretching off into a black curtain of warmth, like a thermal vent that had gone unnoticed and untouched for millennia.

"Aris," Fenroe rasped into comms. "We've reached the umbilical."

"*I'm close,*" she whispered. Aris's visual feed was awash with dark shapes that jerked and sloshed like fluid around quick flashes of gloved hands reaching out to grasp over obstacles in the darkness. Fenroe tried using the negative filter for a while, but

Aris's jerking POV made it hard to concentrate. Now that the feed was switched off, the only thing coming through was the younger woman's labored breathing.

"*Endeavor* lights are down," Fenroe whispered. "I thought Eos said it still had power..."

"*Life systems are all operational,*" Eos pulsed into the comms link. "*But I'm unable to access the main habitats at this time. You'll have to restore lights manually.*"

"I can feel heat venting into the umbilical," Beck said longingly.

"*The ship has logged data loss and health alerts in habitat APU's,*" Eos said. "*I suggest checking the power supply as soon as possible.*"

"Is she flight ready?" Fenroe asked.

"*She's ready, Commander.*"

Fenroe looked back into the *Pinnacle* corridors, feeling the shadows pressing in and consuming the light. She was beyond exhausted, teetering on the edge of mental collapse. The walls moved in hallucinatory sync with the distant blended murmurings, shrieks and coughs of the infected. They were still out there, scouring the dark. She felt anxiety building upon the cold knowledge that none of them had encountered any parasite-riddled corpses since the android's RMS had been ripped apart near the vent shaft. Fenroe pushed those thoughts away, stepping close behind Beck, who vacantly studied gnarls of wiring and plating torn loose from various points within the umbilical's interior. More vines of wire hung from the ceiling, spilling and drooping down toward the deck like the rubbery guts of a whale.

"Look," he said, lifting his tired chin.

Fenroe followed his gaze a few feet above the umbilical's curved midline. Packed into the bulkhead, nestled beneath the ripped wiring, vinyl, insulation and plastic, a thick wax-like brick had been fastened to a grid of exposed aluminum bar joists. A small coiled red wire attached to a black power cord stabbed into one end of the brick, which stretched back into a flap of vinyl near the umbilical's station-side airlock, threading and disappearing beneath the intact part of the wall.

"It's an astral survey charge," Beck whispered, lost in thought. He released one side of the blanket, letting it slide off his shoulder, and carefully touched the cord sticking out of the brick. "The *Calisto* and *Europa* outposts used these to harvest asteroids passing through Jovian space."

He traced the red wire with his gentle fingers to where it connected with the black power cord, and then dragged his loose grip beneath it, walking alongside ripped braids of wire that disappeared into the wall's torn vinyl. "Your light, please."

Fenroe reached across to her shoulder and twisted it on, angling the beam behind the uneven flaps of foil and insulation. Beck leaned and peered into the breach, tugging on the cord lightly. He pushed himself away from the wall and limped back toward the main corridor, sliding the palm of his hand along the smooth surface until he reached the corner of the airlock. He stopped and stared down at the pressure door access panel, which shimmered with delicate blue-green light.

"The explosive is wired to the station's power," he said, shaking his head slowly. "Why would they do this...?"

Fenroe looked at the panel and then glanced back at the survey charge fastened against the umbilical's exposed framework. She closed her eyes, trying to determine why that made sense. And the first thing that came to mind was Colonel Wren's body hanging out of its chair in the reactor core control room, followed by the explosive flashes of light that happened immediately after she and Dunesto restored power to the station. Her heart grew heavy from the memory of the *Meridian* drifting off-structure, tumbling in short bursts of fast burning flame, coming apart in a flux of its own escaping pressure...

"It was their containment protocol," she said quietly, opening her eyes.

Beck shook his head and looked at the floor. "What do you mean?"

"They knew that if they destroyed all the umbilicals—" she waved a hand in the air, taking in the tubular capsule all around them, "—there'd be no way for the parasite to get off station. No way for any of us to bring it back to Earth."

He looked up, realization dawning on his face. "If someone did come, and if they ever did switch the reactor back online, the charges would detonate..."

Fenroe leaned against the bulkhead, her face going slack and distant, and she felt something solid crack inside. Something that was too much, too overwhelming. "If we hadn't turned on the power, Ulbricht and Suja would still be safe aboard the *Meridian*," she said stoically, her voice flat and hollow, letting the truth flow out of her lungs. "They'd still be alive."

He shook his head: "You don't know that."

"Yes," she said quietly, wondering if her chest would collapse into the bleak pitiless heartache inside. "Yes, I do."

"It's nobody's *fault*," he said, bending low to look her in the eye. "Nobody *meant* for this to happen. How could you have known...?"

Fenroe couldn't meet his gaze. She kept replaying the memory of the *Meridian* drifting free from the *Pinnacle* over and over again in her head—Ulbricht's melted skin fusing with the medical pod's bedding, bloody mists of her shredded lung tissue collecting inside the respirator—

Sitosen's limp body drifting into the light of Saturn—

Dunesto's last uncomprehending breaths—

The look in Harris's eyes—

Suja slamming his blood-smeared fist against the airlock control panel...

Beck stood for long moments, vexed by something, speaking quietly under his breath and shaking his head at some internal question she couldn't understand. He turned away from her and stepped back toward where the astral charge was fastened to the wall.

"Why didn't this one blow?" he asked quietly, puzzled.

Fenroe came back from her own private hell and tried to focus. She limped into the umbilical next to him, feeling the warm trickle of blood seeping down the leg of her bio-suit. *His* bio-suit. "What do you mean?"

"If restarting the reactor detonated all the charges in the docking umbilicals—" he said, staring up into the bulkhead at the explosive charge—he reached up and grasped the slender tube stabbing deep into it, "—then why didn't this one explode?"

Gently, carefully, slowly pulling the blasting cap out of the plastic, Beck braced himself for the last blinding light he'd ever see. And when the moment didn't come—when a brilliant flash of flesh-searing heat didn't atomize his body—when he realized he was still alive—Beck let go a deep breath and opened his fingers, rolling the explosive cylinder in the palm of his hand. He carefully disconnected the cap from the wire and tested the weight of it, turning it over in his hand, rubbing it with his thumb—it was coated with a clear gummy substance that smeared to the touch, like a thin layer of machine oil.

"This blasting cap is a dud," he said finally, angling it in the light. "The accelerant leaked." He handed her the cap. "Look—"

Beck's outstretched arm froze, and Fenroe looked up at him.

His eyes were focused on something over her shoulder.

He flinched, and took a half step back—

She turned—

A shadow separated from the blackness beyond the *Endeavor* airlock. Sharp coldness shifted inside Fenroe's gut—she jerked instinctively and stumbled away from a rippling form rising out of the *Endeavor* docking bay, its opaque geometries pulling and gathering into a single massive shape, becoming more visible in the light, unwrapping itself and filling the entire airlock, floor to ceiling.

A nest of limbs snaked out of the darkness and ripped Beck off his feet, smashing and compressing him hard against the umbilical's interior. The LED strips sparked and flickered on impact, and the umbilical went dark.

Fenroe fell back and raised her arms to block the arterial whip of Beck's blood.

His muffled, terrified, liquid screams gurgled to high-pitched squeals like a live pig being fed to a meat grinder, and then the sound cut to broken airlessness and suffocating *hick-hick-hick* noises.

Fenroe watched in horror as blood and thick dark fluids poured out of Beck's body and splashed onto the deck, squirting between the shadowy viscera that constricted his face.

The lethal shadow detached from the darkness, pushing slowly into the umbilical, the sparking LED's flashing across its black skin—those strange limbs opened up in the spasming light with the slow grace of an immense reptile—Fenroe pulled herself away from the nightmare, scuffing and kicking her heels uselessly onto the deck, her joints, ligaments and muscles turning to liquid, her heart slithering up into her throat. She stared in transfixed terror, seized by the sickening pattern of the shadow's pulsating organs.

Her back came flush against the corridor wall opposite of the umbilical, and the bulk of the shadow pulled itself forward with an incomprehensible knot of tentacles, all flowing and threading into and around each other, penetrating, probing, and sliding over every surface within reach.

Coiling Beck's limp body in its thick black ropey muscles, the shadow's tentacles slid with puckered mouths that sucked onto his flesh.

The thickest tentacles tightened, constricting the blood out of the compressed skin—

It ripped his body in half.

Fenroe flinched as more blood sprayed onto the deck, and the last thing she saw before rolling to her knees and pushing herself to her feet and stumbling down the corridor, was the shadow's massive teeth biting down onto Beck's skull, splitting it like a ripe melon, and its long black feelers lapping up the brain matter squirting out of its lips.

Fenroe lost her footing and crashed hard onto her chest—she couldn't breathe, couldn't pull in enough air through the terror, and her limbs wouldn't obey her command—the blood-smeared shadow rounded the corner and emerged into the cone of light like a mist, twisting its head her direction.

Between the sparking flashes of the LED strips in the umbilical, Fenroe saw the thing in slow, halting snapshots. The narrow, eel-like skull tracked her with the ominous threat of a tank turret—translucent, milky eyes the size of basketballs set deep beneath enraged brow folds, like a wolf baring the full threat of its teeth.

The thing pulled more of itself into the light, lowering its jaw to feed again as Beck's blood still dripped from its muscular lips: the creature's body undistinguishable beneath a coat of writhing, pulsating black serpents squirming in some unnatural, trypophobic pattern that seized Fenroe's brain in a mindlock of complete horror. There was a grotesque spread of white stalks on its back, like obscene tubes pushing and sucking in and out of the skin, and there were *things* coming out of them—revolting, wriggling things that pulled free from the giant black creature and plopped onto the floor, squirming quickly toward the nearest shadow.

The thing was *excreting* those maggot parasites.

Hundreds upon hundreds, all coming out like wasp larvae emerging from the soft skin of a pig's belly.

Fenroe heard a sharp gasp from the others side—

The creature whirled in the flashing light and seethed toward the sound—

And there was Aris, stumbling and falling back near the bend of the last corridor. She froze stiff on her feet, as if she were a piece of meat bobbing on the surface of an endlessly deep ocean, looking below the bloody strings of its own loose sinew with abject terror as large predatory shadows moved in beneath.

Thinking quickly, Fenroe grabbed up a smashed piece of unidentifiable office equipment from the floor and hurled it at the nest of tentacles on the thing's back—the object struck one of the tubes groping the air behind its head—the tube flinched and spat white granulated fluids, and retracted back into the thing's flesh with a sickening *slurp*. "On me, you piece of shit. *FOCUS ON ME!*"

The creature twisted and opened its wide mouth, the thick orca skin of its lips making slurping suck noises, as if it were trying to speak. The thing's massive enraged brows relaxed and unfurrowed, and it opened eyes that swallowed the darkness.

"That's right," Fenroe rasped, edging away from the thing. "Come to me...come here, girl...follow me..."

It paced her movements: churning, rolling, unfolding, opening and closing its soundless jaws, widening a mouth large enough to swallow a sedan.

Fenroe frantically searched Beck's utility harness for anything she could use to defend herself, staring at the writhing horror in front of her with raw, terrified eyes. She ripped a light pod free from her chest and activated it—the creature's head lowered and its pupils constricted as it tracked the bands of panning light shooting out of Fenroe's clenched fist.

"Get aboard the *Endeavor*," Fenroe whispered over comms, backing deeper into the corridor. "I'll draw it away—" she raised her voice at the monstrous pile of wet serpents. "*—COME AND GET ME!*"

She tossed the pod spinning and the internal magnets took over in midair, righting its trajectory mere feet away from the creature's sickening lips. "That's right," she repeated softer, again and again, the quiver leaving her voice, her limbs steadying. "Come to me, damn you...come this way...follow me..."

It seemed mesmerized by the light, turning its massively narrow head from side to side to study it from all angles. A lone tentacle emerged from the bristling nest and wrapped around the pod. Spokes of light stabbed out from between the coils.

Aris's ragged, terrified, uncomprehending breaths bled into Fenroe's helmet, and she could see the younger woman's wide eyes shining through the darkness from all the way across the corridor, trying to understand what was happening.

"Move, god damn it!" Fenroe screamed to her.

And that broke the spell—Aris heaved herself to her feet and bolted back into the darkness of the corridor beyond, leaving Fenroe alone. The thing expanded itself and filled the entire space, opening and shutting its wide rubbery mouth, hypnotized by the blinking light pod in its tentacle. It secreted a trail of giant, greasy maggots as it moved, which curled and flexed in the glistening light like severed sex organs.

The creature yawned its cavernous mouth and swallowed the

pod like an anglerfish cannibalizing itself, and Fenroe tracked its glow through the skin until it settled at the base of its throat. The creature's eyes dilated in the fresh darkness and refocused until they found Fenroe again, backing away slowly with her hands raised. It glided forward, unfolding its limbs, pouring into the corridor like a swelling wave, building and building upon itself until the entire space had filled with its formless girth. Fenroe twisted on the run and stumbled deep into the *Pinnacle's* bowels, manually closing each pressure door as she passed.

5.

Fenroe backed through the airlock, reaching out to grip the lock cylinder, drilling into the seething mass of twisting shadows behind her with light-starved eyes.

Turning away, she stepped into the next module, and was suddenly bathed in apocalyptic light. Her head jerked reflexively away from the source, and from every vantage stabbed a molten knife of whiteness. She shielded her eyes against the brilliance, immediately recognizing the area.

She had reached Suja's stairway from the opposite direction—the place where Eos had sacrificed her RMS to save Fenroe's life.

Her eyes adjusted to the white glare, and a dark chasm of nothingness resolved into view and fell away to oblivion through the broad plate glass window that reached up the entire far side wall. Cosmic light burst and smeared across the dead black surface, which had grown since last she saw it—its accretion disc was much, much closer and thicker, like fire trapped inside a sawblade of stretched glass.

The thick band of smooth firelight reached far out of view—far above the window that arched high over the landing. Fenroe's body moved on its own, mesmerized by the sheer horror of it, stumbling toward the ungraspable vortex. Sagging against the glass, she drove her exhausted legs up each step and arched her neck to find the black hole's edge, but there was none. The *Pinnacle* had drifted *that* close to it. She could see nothing beyond the singularity's photon sphere. No stars twinkling in the backdrop of eternity. No planet Saturn watching over her with eonic patience. It was just nothingness. A complete and infinite *lack* so dark that it nearly drove her mad. The sight of it was almost too much; the pull of that absolute colorless yawning void was so incomprehensibly massive that it stopped her breath and stayed her hands on the edge of clawing her own eyes out.

No human eyes, she thought, ought to ever witness a blackness such as that. The soul couldn't handle it. The sheer immensity of it was a reminder of all that awaited every possible thing in the end: a deep, vast, endless, eternal nothingness.

Sweat beaded on her forehead, and her hollow insides twisted like a thick snake in her gut. She forced herself to look away and sagged against the window, letting herself slide lifelessly to the floor.

And she stared at her hands for a long, long time.

"How much time do we have?" she rasped breathlessly into comms.

No response. Not even dead air.

Fenroe cycled through the white feeds in her HUD until the NO-SIGNAL messages cut away to a single channel of solid gray. She switched to a negative filter, thinking the image would clear, but it didn't. It was visual data locked onto a featureless surface very close to the camera, trembling in the rapid concentricity of Whitney Aris's horrified breath.

"Please," Fenroe said softly over comms. "Somebody say something."

She looked at the wall on the opposite side of the stairway and watched long beautiful ripples of beige and yellow light trickle gently up toward the ceiling. As if the window over her shoulder was a doorway to an ice field of airglow. "Please..."

"*I'm here, Commander,*" Eos hummed soothingly in her ear. "*I can hear you.*"

Fenroe twisted her head and looked down the stairwell, searching the gloom below for any sign of movement. But the shadowy darkness was dead and hollow. Lifeless. The creature could have been anywhere, in any corridor between there and the *Endeavor's* docking umbilical.

"How long do we have until the black hole takes us?" Fenroe whispered.

"Seven hours," Eos responded coolly. "After that, the *observatory's velocity will become too fast and unquantifiable.*" She waited for Fenroe to respond. And when no response came, the android said: "*you and Aris can still escape, Commander. But you have to leave the observatory immediately.*"

There in the black-shadowed semidarkness, Fenroe panned her eyes over the half-lit stairway with tear-welled vision, studying the killing ground of corpses that Eos had left with her plasma cutters, and watched the Hawking light spill in from the window over her shoulder with detached fascination. The light brought the whole place to eerie life, smearing everything into a single abstract of mind-numbing stasis; for one surreal moment, Fenroe wasn't certain whether she was one of the broken corpses reaching its dead claw toward the ceiling, or if she was the collapsed, exhausted woman leaning against the glass staring at it all.

And finally, the shadows in the corridor below began to change, taking on a thicker, more frenetic edge, moving with questing purpose, darkening the walls, closing in on themselves just out of range of the stairway floodlight.

Fenroe pulled herself to her feet and moved upwards toward the airlock where she'd last seen Suja—

...and stopped.

Glancing at a body that had been lasered in half from its collarbone all the way down to its opposite hip, Fenroe studied the pristine indent of its wounds, like a perfect cut by an immaculately sharp blade. All of the corpse's organs that hadn't been eaten by the parasites were neatly sliced in half. As if each exposed organ were held in place at the wound by a sheet of glass. She looked over the litter of corpses that Eos had left behind one by one—all unmoving, all empty of parasites.

Eos's RMS vehicle was close by—down the corridor on the first level, near the ventilation shaft Fenroe had used to escape. And attached to the robot's arms were a pair of industrial plasma cutters.

Fenroe turned back toward the lower level and leaned her exhausted weight against the plate glass window, pressing her body flat, taking slow but long breaths with her mouth while eyeing the darkness below. She slowly, carefully bladed her body downward, descending toward the corner that turned into the hallways she and Eos had sealed before the android had been ripped to pieces—she thought that she could make out the outline of something pulsing within the darkness ahead, as if it contained one massive thing writhing in the deeper shadow, flashing its globed eyes like pieces of clouded quartz before vanishing back beneath the blackness.

Once she reached the lower level, Fenroe slowly backed into the corridor, waiting for the creature to erupt into the light.

But nothing moved. Nothing reacted to her presence.

Fenroe exhaled and followed the trail of eviscerated corpses until she reached the middle of the next passage, where she found the silhouette of Eos's body lying before a broad window, dwarfed by the monstrous rotating black hole outside.

The android's broken carcass was enveloped by the dark, encircled by all of the bodies she'd dismembered and left clawing toward the ceiling like dead trees in winter.

Fenroe ripped one of the last light pods from her harness and twisted it in her weak fist. She aimed and sidearmed it into the air, deep into the black corridor behind her, tracking the glow of its shallow arc. When it burst with bands of uninterrupted light and began painting the room, she turned back toward the android's corpse, and collapsed onto her knees. Pieces of Eos's body had fused with the deck. The android's plasma cutters were still warm as human skin, and the curve of Eos's dismembered forearm glistened with carbon dust. Fenroe's eyes wanted to drift closed and her head went heavy, the tendons on the back of her neck nearly severed by exhaustion.

"Aris," she said, searching the tools on her vest by feel, shaking herself awake. "I don't know how...don't ask me how...but you have to get to the *Endeavor*."

"*I'm not leaving you*," Aris rasped, her raw and tired voice giving the scene a sense of solemn reverence and finality.

"Listen—"

"*No Fenroe*, you *listen*," the younger woman hissed. "*Don't ask me to do that. I can't. And I won't.*"

The corridor began whispering with sliding flesh. Very close, and getting closer. She pried one of Eos's arms loose and dug into it with the flat end of her screwdriver—dug under the plate above the elbow until it popped loose, exposing bundles of wire within cages of servos beneath the hollow carapace. Fenroe used her razor to cut away the wiring near the dismembered shoulder that she couldn't disconnect manually and slid her arm inside, threading her fingers into the plasma cutter trigger mechanism.

She moved unsteadily to her feet and lifted her arm, closing her hand into a weak fist, and took a deep breath. Pulling the cutter open, she squeezed the trigger and shot a red stream of irresistible plasma heat into the air. She plunged the corridor back into darkness by releasing the trigger, and waited for her eyes to readjust. Turning toward the stairway, balancing the reinforced arm in her other hand like a rifle, Fenroe aimed it toward the sheets of panning light in the distance. The green-blue bands of the pod's scanner dimmed and flickered, bending around something that moved in the thick murkiness beyond the spill of emergency floods.

"I can say a million times that I'm sorry," Fenroe said with intensity, feeling the heat from the plasma cutter trickle into her chest, "and it wouldn't be enough."

"*I know, Fenroe.*" Aris whispered. "*But we'll talk about that when you get back here.*"

"I'm not going to die like the others," Fenroe said finally, raising the weapon in front of her face, invoking the hot red glowing ring of its muzzle, and looked back into the shadow. "I'm not going to die *afraid* like they did."

"*You don't have to die at all,*" Aris pleaded, her voice blazing hot and dry. "*We still have time. We can still go home.*"

"If you don't launch now, we'll both be pulled into the black hole," Fenroe continued.

"*Then move your ass,*" her voice cracked. "*Get back here! Right here, right goddamn now!*"

"That thing will follow me. It'll eat through the *Endeavor's* airlock and get onto the ship."

"*I'm staying,*" Aris said quietly. "*You ditch that thing somewhere, and you get back here, understand? I'm not leaving without you.*"

Fenroe crept slowly toward the stairs, keeping the plasma

cutter leveled onto the gaping corridor from which she had come. She thought for certain that at any moment a thick black tentacle would stab out from the darkness, and it felt like hours had passed before she finally reached the first step. Placing the tip of her boot softly onto the stair, Fenroe ascended as carefully as she could, keeping the muzzle of Eos's severed arm trained onto the black opening below, ready to melt down anything that came out of it.

"What's it waiting for," Fenroe whispered, the imprinted image of Beck's skull cracking open within those powerful jaws burned long and deep onto her retinas.

"What are you going to do?"

It took every ounce of courage Fenroe had to turn her back on the darkness. And when she did—when her hackles bristled up and down the length of her spine—she hit the upper level fast, and dragged her dead leg through and around the first bend in the hallway, wading into the ice fog pooling just outside the server room. She paused briefly at the sight of a thick smear of blood on the wall where she'd last seen Suja. The jagged red line pulled off back into the shadows somewhere, as if a giant feather had been dragged through a puddle of brown paint. She stared longingly after it and fought the urge to follow, needing with every part of her soul to search for him. To grab him up and drag him back to the *Endeavor* if she had to.

But she let him go, and moved back through the server room out into another network of fully lit corridors. Fenroe searched and found a rainbow of thin industrial stripes painted onto the wall near the ceiling stretching off in both directions. The lines led back into the nightmare of teeming shadows, each color representing a different section of the observatory. All she had to do was pick one, and follow it.

Summoning the shades of her dead—each of them looking back at her from across the other side of the veil, filling her with so much love and warmth that she could barely contain it—she found the green line, which led to the reactor core, and followed it.

"I'm going to lure the motherfucker," Fenroe said with intensity, scouring the darkness ahead. "And I'm going to kill it."

6.

Wading now through standing water that poured from a burst main somewhere in the distance, Fenroe pushed deep into the midnight that popped with blue-white sparks from exposed wiring, bracing herself as the walls—the entire space station—shuddered on the very edge of the black hole's crushing pull.

The *Pinnacle* had become an ethereal nightmare of tight corridors. Fenroe couldn't know how many infected corpses Eos had cut through, but she found herself stumbling over the dismembered remains of what must have been hundreds of bodies rising out of the shallow water like mangroves. Lone parasites frenzied to life under the passing cone of her light and skipped away across the water's surface for the shadows. She forced herself to keep moving at a staggered run, twisting and backtracking to follow the green line on the wall through a labyrinth of barricades.

Using the last of her light pods to buy a few precious breaths, she tossed it behind her knowing deep down in the pit of her soul that the thing from the umbilical was close. She could feel its presence uncoiling just beyond the reach of her light.

When she finally reached the reactor's airlock, the aged metal scraped open and a sucking wind breathed air into the rotunda, which raged inside like a bottled storm. She stepped into spraying sheets of rain and coolant that howled into the corridor, and sealed herself inside. The colossal fusion reactor thrummed in the pulsing shadows, concussing with deafening currents of electricity that fired like artillery, shotgunning against the catwalk with thick bolts of lightning—every flash transformed the clouds of steam and water into solid walls of swirling nebulae. She stopped for a moment in a daze, watching ropes of lightning claw harmlessly up the left side of her body, mesmerized by its slow crawl across her arm and shoulder.

The entire room's atmosphere siphoned toward the reactor core, as if the machine itself was breathing it all in. She pulled herself forward one inch at a time until the orbed control room emerged from the far shadow. Tilting her head back, Fenroe traced the reactor's thick boson absorber plates through the turbulent rain up into the high, half-visible ceiling of conduit and piping, where they joined together and connected to a service ladder hanging from a square hatch directly in the center of the dome's apex. If this worked—if the thing followed her in—the maintenance corridor through the ceiling would be one possible exit out of there.

The reactor stretched out of sight below the catwalk, visible only by the frenetic web of electricity ejected against the inside of the containment shaft wall, like a wide aqueduct stacked vertically on end, filled with spokes of popping white light—over the surrounding guardrail, fifty feet down, the bottom of the edifice flashed into view long enough for Fenroe to see a narrower crescent-shaped walkway curving around the turbo pump containment, connected by two doors on opposite sides. She could also see an open service passage positioned in the middle of the walkway, directly across from the reactor.

The beating heart of the *Pinnacle* station hummed with heat and energy inside the twisting rings of its magnet assembly. The exit was still in view, and she edged away from it through flashing clouds of shadow, backing into the reactor control room.

Once inside she closed the airlock and stood in the harsh silence, dripping with condensation. The heaving reactor strobed in silent fury beyond the observational window, blurred by thick bands of whipping rain curling against the plate glass.

The constellation of holograms still turned in their delicate orbits in the center of the room, the tiny dot of the *Pinnacle* rotating slowly around a superimposed *ERROR* message where Saturn should have been. And across the room, the body of Colonel Ambrose Wren stared down unseeingly at the glowing terminal like a trapped, eyeless horror.

Fenroe set Eos's plasma cutter onto the floor and woke the terminal from sleep. Her hand passed over the sensor panel, and the soft green lights of a holo-display polarized in her visor.

WARNING: THIS WILL REDIRECT POWER TO PRIMARY
AND SECONDARY CORES.
PROCEED?

"*What are you going to do?*" Aris whispered over comms, watching Fenroe's progress through her HUD.

"There are emergency gates that feed surplus power into the local capacitor bank below the reactor," Fenroe transmitted. "If I decouple them and discharge the system...the whole thing will purge."

"*Purge,*" Aris repeated quietly, realization pitching deep in her voice. "*You're going to destroy the station.*"

"All that power will funnel right through here," she continued, pumping a primer handle three times until it collapsed back into place with a heavy *shunk*. "Anything near the reactor that isn't insulated within a bio-suit will burn."

"*We don't even know if these things can burn.*"

"Every living thing burns," Fenroe said, glancing up and searching through the chaos for the far airlock, checking to see if it was still in one piece. "All you have to do is find the right temperature. The flashpoint."

Fenroe turned her attention back to the terminal, keeping half of it on the small door on the opposite side of the rotunda. Her pattern-seeking brain flinched at every jerk of light and shadow, so she forced herself to focus on the interface instead, measuring the cadence of her breath for any second thoughts. The three view screens above the terminal blurred slightly and clouded, each showing the same message:

PRIMARY CORE   *STATUS: OK*
SECONDARY CORE   *STATUS: OK*

A hatch popped open with an audible click. Fenroe lifted it and grasped the cylindrical handle inside, pulling a metal tube up out of the console against the sucking weight of its own vacuum. She lifted, twisting it clockwise until it locked into place, and pressed the tube back down into the console until a bank of red lights ignited on the terminal to her right—three of them—and the holographic map of Saturn space drifting in the center of the room sputtered and vanished in a shower of light particles. The reactor outside slowed its rotation, the hum of its power dropping an octave and deepening.

Fenroe caught the movement of something large and dark on the far side of the rotunda—she frowned and bent low, hearing for the first time the deep somber echo of metal infused whale song penetrating the plate glass window. Something was at the airlock on the other side of the cavern, trying to pry it open.

The distant pressure door moaned and began to glow red hot, dimpling, creasing, and something ebony and thick pushed through it. The rain and coolant made violent contact with the molten metal, and white ropes of steam hissed and rose into the air.

Black limbs threaded in and out of the softened metal, and with one forceful movement, the pressure door sunk in the center and ripped away from its liquefied track assembly out into the darkness of the corridor beyond, leaving a smoking red ring of a hole in the bulkhead.

There was movement—a flurry of seething shadow in the rain—and then a cloud of thick black smoke poured into the sucking gap and rose into the air.

Only it wasn't smoke at all.

And it was big.

Back in dry dock, she'd only seen snapshots of it in the sparse flashes of light.

The creature that poured into the reactor core was far bigger than what she remembered seeing in the docking umbilical.

Its massive serpent body rolled like wind through folds of black silk—a river of black blood sliding into the module—flattening, coiling its limbs into a single rippling tail, twisting through the opening, tightening its massive frame upward and around until its wide lips rose out of the darkness and brushed against the wall above the breach. It kept coming, climbing out of view behind the twisting reactor, its tail end flowing over the rippled soundproof interior like water, unaffected by the fingers of electricity that reached out from the reactor and caressed its glistening ebony skin.

Fenroe stared with eyes that burned like raw skin as the last glimpse of its body bladed the curve of the reactor and disappeared—it was an ancient dragon rising up out of the black-ashen fiery plumes of Hades itself, like a myth. The curve of its body slid into the darkness like deep sea cables through a vat of black ink.

"*Get out of there—*" Aris begged over comms, panic rising in her voice. "*—Go now! Go, go, go!*"

Fenroe reached her trembling fingers slowly across the terminal, and pressed each of the three glowing red buttons. Exactly three floodlights burst to life at different points along the catwalk outside, shining up into the whipping shadows and rain onto three core control systems spaced equally on all sides of the reactor.

Thick ropes of water and coolant snapped and curled in the air, and bands of electricity arced to the guardrail. Everything moved with the twisting freneticism of still-living viscera, and every shadow gnashed its spectral teeth like black flags in a storm.

Fenroe retrieved Eos's plasma cutter from the floor and crossed the room, opening the airlock—sharp winds screamed through, pushing against her body—and she scanned the black shifting ceiling overhead for movement. It was too thick, too chaotic. She swallowed a sticky dryness and felt it settle heavily in the pit of her stomach: that thing could be hiding in the shadows right above her, and she wouldn't even know it.

Rounding the corner, she edged low along the catwalk toward the first terminal, keeping the cutter raised and her finger on the trigger. The reactor twisted high overhead, half concealed in the swirling chaos. A holographic display bent and whipped blurrily in the rain a few meters away, and Fenroe could make out the floating holographic double helix of two wavelengths crossing into each other, and a diagram below it.

Inertial Damping
MNL H I55645 N1 U8118 BM 66547

0 11	V	31 0
I I		I I
I I		I I
0 11 V		31 0

Lowering herself painfully to one knee, Fenroe set Eos's plasma cutter beside her and grasped two dials on either side of the terminal. She twisted them slowly in opposite directions until both *V*'s on the diagram lined up with one another. The wavelengths above the holo-display flattened, and their amplitudes decreased until they each came together and formed a single shallow line.

The holo-display blinked again, bringing up another prompt.

DEACTIVATE SECONDARY CORE SUPPRESSOR

Fenroe reached up and grasped a wide flat paddle with both hands and pulled, locking it into place. The effect was immediate—the reactor above hummed with building sound. The holo-display flickered again in the rising steam:

OVERLOAD PRIMARY CORE

She gathered the cutter from the ground and moved to her feet, blading herself along the catwalk toward the next terminal, sliding her heavy feet along the slickened catwalk through sudden clouds of steam that rose from the depths like shadows of flame. She moved forward, flinching at every snap of rain and steam that cracked in the air. The creature was nowhere and it was everywhere, striking from every corner and shape of darkness only to morph back into a ghostly stream of wind and rain. Everything was moving, billowing, opening, snapping...

Reaching the second core control system, Fenroe gripped the charge paddle with her free hand and tried pulling it down, but she wasn't strong enough. She bent low, eyes wide and raw and locked on the rolling darkness above, and set the cutter onto the catwalk. With both hands on the paddle now, Fenroe pulled, locking it into place, and the grated flooring shook with even more force. An intense, ear-shattering hum resonated at the base of the reactor, whining now with the *wum-wum-wum* sound of a wind turbine.

Forcing herself to breathe, sipping the scrubbed suit air through her dry and cracked lips, Fenroe groped behind her for the plasma cutter until her fingers wrapped around the mechanical arm's severed shoulder—her pulse raced along her throat with enough pressure to choke the airway, and crashed against her temples so hard that phosphenes pulsated in the outline of her vision.

"Moving toward the last terminal," Fenroe said over comms, the trembling quiver in her voice spiking a new wave of adrenaline through her body.

A holographic sheet of pale green light gleamed and bent around the blowing rain and the steam: another inertial damping cypher, pulsing with wavelengths. Coming up to it, she traced her hands around the boundary channel of the hologram's light, and another screen flicked into existence.

ALIGN INPUT WHEN CIRCUIT IS ACTIVE

Like before, she used the dials to align the *V's*, and the wavelengths flattened to become one thick line. All of the terminals around the reactor made loud heavy sounds as they locked into place, and all three floodlights around the catwalk shut off, plunging everything into darkness. The only light remaining in the hurricane maelstrom burned from the blinking holo-display in front of her face. She was blind in the storm but for that single light, and dread washed over her in waves of freezing cold despair. That thing was in there with her, somewhere in the pitch-black darkness, and she didn't know where. Fenroe blinked, and the menu prompt changed again.

REDIRECT POWER TO THE CENTRAL CORE.

Klaxons and emergency lights ignited all around the rotunda, strobing with bands of red and black that bled and washed everything in low spectrums of light. Fenroe set the cutter onto the deck and pulled the paddle, and the *wum-wum-wum* accelerated, chopping the air with deep, jet engine waves of sound. A hatch depressed and flipped open, exposing a broader paddle that looked heavier than the others, with a red light next to it that read *LOCKED*—the holographic display turned blood red and melted into the ambient light.

ENVIRONMENT CONTROL
PURGE 24556 DR 5

Eos's voice blared over both the station-wide intercom and inside Fenroe's helmet, sounding more like a machine than she had ever sounded before: "*System Purge is established. Awaiting confirmation from control station demo. Please move to a safe distance.*"

More red lights ignited high above and amber emergency lights came from below, everything howling and blinking long and slow. Fenroe passed her fingers through the light panel, and the lever changed from *LOCKED* to *PRIMED*—

And something thick and milky flowed softly—gently, like a bubbling stream—over her boots. She looked down and a stream of pus-colored liquid rushed and rose above her ankles, spilling thickly over the sides of the catwalk like a waterfall of milk. The stream of white fluid shifted under the dim light, moving like curdled vomit.

And between the split seconds of flashing lightning, she saw that the current of white fluid was *alive,* teeming with thick ropey particles. She followed the trail of squirming liquid back across the catwalk until it met with a boiling mound of giant convulsing maggots, and all the blood drained from Fenroe's numbed hands.

The milk was a swarm of parasites, pouring onto the catwalk from above, dribbling like an avalanche of coiled intestines spreading out in all directions.

The air changed above her—

...the rain and steam and light became shielded by something massive and alive looming overhead. Fenroe looked up, following the torrential downpour of maggots.

And a thick black mass unfolded itself from the darkness, emitting an ocean stink of rotten meat in waves that almost overwhelmed her scrubbers.

Fenroe backed away from it, feeling her blood vessels squeeze with pain and terror.

The mass of squirming tentacles unpacked itself from the darkness, lowering gracefully to the catwalk, resolving the twisting shape of its body into a sickly mangled insect, writhing like an arachnoid creature covered in a ropey swarm of flagellating serpents. Its head twisted, blinking with massive nictitating eyes that glassed the thrown red and yellow light.

"*Run!*" Aris wept over comms, the last pieces of her heart

crushing under the weight of what was unfolding in her HUD. *"Run Fenroe! RUN RUN RUN!"*

But Fenroe wasn't running anymore.

The shape lowered from the higher darkness until Fenroe could make out its features in sickening detail: sleek, sinewy skin of jet black glass as smooth as silk flexing over boneless muscle. Marine-like, twisting its body with deadly reptilian grace; wide blackened lips, stalks of massive ovipositors stabbing out of a mass of thicker tentacles behind its head, each one vomiting a viscous puss of maggoty parasites that poured in disgusting glugs over its flesh.

She aimed the cutter at the center of its mass, and fired the plasma. The creature bristled away from the heat, blinking its prehistoric eyes against the red hot glow.

Fenroe stepped away and reached out with one hand until she could feel her fingers close around the core limiter switch.

The creature's massive, unblinking eyes locked onto her like a laser targeting system, wrapping its tentacles tightly around its own body. Pulling back, opening impossibly wide jaws that exposed several rows of hooked teeth, the creature's face slowly parted into four massive pharyngeal flaps, merging its dilating dinner-plate pupils with the darkness—

"Run!" Aris screamed.

"This is for my friends," Fenroe whispered, tightening her fist around the switch.

The creature shot through the sheets of rain and flashing light.

Its limbs coiled sickeningly around Fenroe's midsection, up around her chest, around her neck, constricting the air out of her.

Which completed the circuit.

Fenroe felt the sizzle of energy that flowed through the reactor, surrounding the control console; the crackling power of gleaming force that wrapped around it like a net of fire. She pulled the lever, opening the core, releasing all that shored up power, and touched that energy, all of it.

Her insulated body created a bridge for every joule, every erg, every electron volt—the immeasurable energy she'd siphoned from the reactor—in one infinitesimal fraction of a second. And all that energy had to go somewhere. And to get there, it had to pass through Fenroe.

She knew these creatures were electrically conductive. She knew they could withstand contact with molten metal.

But everything has a limit.

Every living thing has its temperature. Its flashpoint.

An ear-piercing clap of thunder sucked all the air into a swirl of coolant and rain that followed the vertical tower up into the ceiling high above. A very thick belt of lightning fired down the entire length of the reactor, exploding with blinding white light.

And the creature burst into flames.

Fenroe dropped to her knees and snatched Eos's cutter in her other fist.

She squeezed the trigger and ignited the plasma. The thing jerked its head up and away as she severed the tentacles that had stiffened around her body. The creature frantically whipped its many limbs over its head in grotesquely inhuman patterns, trying to smother the cirrus ripples of orange-red fire flowing across its body and lifting away from its skin, threading between its limbs, crinkling the spitting stalks of ovipositors behind its head like cellophane.

The guardrail *shinged* as the blade of plasma cut through the metal beneath Fenroe's knees in a shower of sparks, and the catwalk dipped, tilting to one side.

The creature surged through a cloud of dark meaty smoke that erupted from its own seared body, hissing and spitting in the whipping wind and rain and fire.

The catwalk separated, and with a kick Fenroe yanked her body away from the burning creature and heaved herself into the open air, starting the long, slow plummet into the darkness below.

She fell, her body coming in contact with the edge of something hard, her shoulder pulling free from the socket in ripping numb linearity—she dropped through passing bands of light that strafed through rotating turbines beneath the reactor, falling, ricocheting off something else—

The creature poured over the edge of the catwalk after her like a waterfall of fire, a meteor of screaming shadows—

The crescent walkway at the base of the reactor rose up toward Fenroe like a freight train, the containment shaft below rocketing by in long whipping smears—

She braced herself—

She felt the impact—

A shower of sparks and black airlessness—

A scream of sucking breath—

The creature's smoking body exploded with flames as it dropped over the edge, streaming hissing contrails of water and coolant—

Stars in the smoke—

Darkness rushed in like a crushing wave, piercing her eyes, sucking up into her bloody nostrils.

Fenroe tried to move, to lift her arms, to pull herself into the dark service passage to her right, but she couldn't. And the flaming mass of tentacles plunged into the reactor floor like a burning asteroid making contact with water.

A shower of ashen flame, and the world blinked away in a bleeding swirl of red and shimmering white light—a skull-splitting nimbus that cracked of starlight spreading over the containment shaft, seeping across the pile of tentacles blazing somewhere on the edges of her vision, flowing into her mouth and down her throat. Her eyes fluttered one last time, and the universe slipped out of focus.

7.

Voices screamed in the distance. The screams grew closer and there was a crescendo and clanging, and the universe gathered substance and reality thickened.

From deep within her comfortably warm darkness, Fenroe realized that it wasn't a chorus of screaming voices. She drifted up to the surface of that darkness, and pain greeted her there, and all at once Fenroe remembered where she was. The screaming was the sound of the reactor core going critical.

Bone grated below Fenroe's collar, and a bleak snowfall of ash drifted down from thick rolling waves of smoke and rain far above the reactor, which thrummed close by like the crashing heartbeat of a planet, building and dying in the cutting darkness as it approached critical mass. The air outside of her helmet sizzled with energy, and a mountain comprised of dead black serpents licked the walls with soft ripples of flame.

As the world brightened back into focus, the containment shaft caught enough of the firelight that she could make out the creature's massive body crumpled on the opposite side: its enormous, eel-like head stared unseeing toward the pounding reactor, lolling its jaws open, spilling a gnarl of strange feelers out of its mouth as thick as her legs. Fenroe rolled to her side and winced against the stabbing pressure in her chest, which she suspected came from broken ribs rubbing against themselves. She could only breathe in short sipping gulps to keep from collapsing.

"Aris, dya copy?" she rasped, and the feed in her HUD crackled out of sync. She reached up with her good hand and caressed the back of her helmet, feeling a long, jagged crack shooting up from the base of her neck to the shallow depression where her transmitter was located.

Eos's voice droned above emergency klaxons in the distance, notifying all personnel that they had fifty minutes to reach minimum safe distance. Fenroe tried to stand but pitched head first into the containment shaft wall, sending more needles of pain stabbing through her dislocated shoulder. She felt the soft tickle of blood dribbling over her lips as it pattered on the inside of her visor.

With her last ounce of strength she pulled herself up against the wall, feeling numb, blunted knives of agony digging deeply into her left arm and right thigh. Teetering on the edge of consciousness, she lifted her head and caught the fire glint of Eos's plasma cutter lying on the walkway nearby. She breathed a mixture of sharp pain and relief, pushing herself carefully away from the shaft wall—

...and something made impact with the reactor floor not far from the creature, throwing up a smoking splash of fire.

Flinching from the sudden crash and explosion, Fenroe thought at first that the creature was still alive, but its dead eyes were still filmed over with something like milky cataracts, and she could see that the milkiness was actually a cluster of parasites swimming in the vitreous fluid of its enormous eyeballs, trying to eat their way out before the creature cooked entirely.

Another impact, and again Fenroe jolted—something slammed hard against the twisting reactor before tumbling toward the ground, where it collided with the deck and exploded in a shower of sparks.

Fenroe looked up, following the path of its trajectory to the collapsed catwalk high above leaning unevenly against the still-sparking limiter switch, and watched as things that had once been men and women burst into flames after touching the conductive metal, and jogged mindlessly over the catwalk's sheered edge, scissoring their legs like robots as they dropped.

Infected bodies plummeting over the edge, trailing thick curtains of whipping flames and crashing to the ground in a rain of red and orange. The first of them was already on its mangled legs, lurching forward, flapping its four scalp jaws through the rising plumes of black smoke.

Fenroe lunged for the cutter on the floor, and another body made impact. And then another; dozens of them poured over the edge above like lemmings, drawn by the sound of her battle with the parasite carrier, each one instantly bursting into flames the moment they touched the hyper-electrified catwalk.

One of them stepped out of the twisting fire with its skull still intact, and dropped to its knees—the thing's bloated head inflated until it burst, shooting hundreds of parasite spikes in every direction.

Fenroe felt something ricochet off her helmet and dove painfully across the floor, snatching the cutter with her good hand. She aimed at the outstretched claws of a charging corpse, and blasted it in half.

More bodies fell and rose out of the burning remnants of the giant monster sprawled out on the other side, oblivious to the tendons and ligaments that burned and contracted their roasting bodies into a boxer's pose. Fenroe limped into the adjacent service passage and crashed hard into a wall that turned ninety degrees toward another pressure door, aiming and firing thick beams of plasma into the shadows pouring in behind her.

Fenroe staggered through a storm of flashing red and amber lights until she reached a pressure door that wouldn't budge. She tried to open the lock manually, but it was damaged.

Turning to face the bend of the hallway, Fenroe knelt and

ripped several titanium zip ties away from the utility vest of Beck's bio-suit. Tying a handful of them together into a chain of loose knots, Fenroe lashed one side to the forearm of Eos's cutter, and then tied the other side to the far strap of her utility vest, creating an improvised single-point contact harness, which allowed her to aim the beam of plasma with the use of only one arm.

The bend in the hallway formed a chokepoint, funneling the burning horde down to no more than three abreast. She backed against the non-functioning airlock, and watched the red shadows stretch and shrink as they spilled into the service passage ahead. When the first handful rounded the corner and came into view— all roasted black and sloughing thick chunks of burned dead flesh that rose gently into the air like ash—Fenroe bared her blood covered teeth, and stepped forward.

Gripping Eos's severed arm with her uninjured hand, she took one last deep breath, and screamed and raged against her imminent death. She ignited the plasma, and cut a pathway directly into them.

8.

"Warning, imminent critical collapse. Core reactor failure. You now have eleven minutes to reach minimum safe—"

"Eos, do you copy," Fenroe rasped into comms between deep, painful breaths. "Aris...anybody...do you copy...?"

She leaned against the wall, fighting desperately not to pass out. The cutter half hung from her utility harness, nearly depleted of plasma. Her cream-colored bio-suit was awash in dark black blood, and she limped toward the distant flickering light of the last remaining dock umbilical on the *Pinnacle Observatory*, fighting to hold onto consciousness as it intersected the world.

Something black and sinewy shot out of the darkness ahead, screeching that high dial tone of synth. Fenroe levered the shoulder side of Eos's cutter downward, raising its muzzle up at the thrashing shadow—

And lasered the infected corpse in half. The cutter sputtered in the freshet of its final traces of plasma. The torso fell away from the trunk of its still-kicking legs, and began pulling itself forward on emaciated arms that oozed a metallic ichor, dragging its intestines as they spilled pints of dead coagulated blood, and peeling its skull flaps apart to lick the air with its elongated tongue.

She swung the cutter down and blasted the corpse's head to pieces at the brainstem. The echoed trumpet of more carriers returned from the distance, reminding her that she was running out of time.

Fenroe dragged herself forward, pulling her injured leg like a dead dog strapped to her hip, fighting to keep her eyes open, her breath hitching, her face slickened with sweat, the world drifting out of focus. Not far away, a wall screen sputtered video images from a camera mounted onto the *Pinnacle* hull just outside the umbilical. It was a view of the *Endeavor*—already detached and free-floating in space—flickering to life, drifting not far off structure, banking away from a ripping, yawning black star towering high in the distance. Fenroe could see the white glow of its engines heating up, and she felt a warm wave of comfort wash over her. It was like lowering herself into warm, soothing water.

Because that meant Aris was alive.

Because that meant Fenroe was able to save at least one of them.

That warm numbness slid across her heart and her body relaxed, and all that weight she'd been carrying was still there, but readjusted a little—settled a bit differently so it was easier to carry.

Because she was alone now.

"Aris, do you copy?" Fenroe whispered, tears welling in her vision. "Eos...anybody...I'm at the umbilical...I'm...*I'm right here!*"

But the only response she received was the crackling pop of static.

"*All personnel must evacuate,*" Eos said over the ship-wide intercom. "*You now have nine minutes to reach minimum safe distance.*"

Fenroe's heart thrummed with disordered kicks of adrenaline, and she staggered along the bulkhead toward the sound of wet sucking flesh coming from the darkness. On the floor below the airlock, drying remnants of blood streaked out into the blackness ahead and stretched off toward the next corridor, where she fled from the parasite carrier that had killed Beck. Rounding the corner into the umbilical, her light panned over several living corpses piled onto one another against the airlock, glistening with bands of electrical currents running up and down their bodies as they ate through the pressure door that glowed pale orange.

Fenroe stepped inside and aimed the plasma. The first corpse detected the sound of her presence and whipped around in a rush. It fell to the ground in several gelatinous pieces. Three more spun away from the melting airlock and sprinted toward her with outstretched arms. Fenroe backed against the opposite wall and ignited the plasma, and just like the first corpse, the remaining two fell to the floor in piles of twitching chunks that oozed blood-slickened ivory worms, which then skittered away from her into the darkness of the corridor.

In the silence, the airlock door cooled from yellow to white-hot and finally gray, but it was still intact—still holding the crushing vacuum at bay. She stepped over the writhing bodies and dropped painfully to her knees, studying the melted lock assembly, feeling her heart sinking slowly deep into her stomach.

Eos could have detected the jet streams of Fenroe's MMU if she ejected herself out of the airlock. Fenroe could have *flown* to the *Endeavor*, if the corpses hadn't melted the door and made it inoperable, turning the lock release into a steaming plate of heat-fused metal and plastic.

She couldn't get EVA even if she wanted to. The door was slagged and melted beyond use. It was a miracle Fenroe showed up when she did. Another couple of seconds, and they would have eaten straight through it and been ejected right onto the *Endeavor's* hull. They would have eaten through that, too...

"You now have eight minutes to reach minimum safe distance."

Fenroe laughed darkly through thick tears at the finality of it and collapsed against the bulkhead, utterly spent of energy. She let the plasma cutter swing down and hang from her side, and listened to the distant mournful cries of dead, maggot-filled bodies tearing through the echoey darkness far, far away. Tilting her head back, Fenroe reached painfully up with her good hand to pop the clamps away from the helmet's neck housing, because if she was going to die, she wanted to die comfortably—

...but she stopped, staring at the umbilical wall in disbelief.

The last spike of adrenaline her body could produce plunged down into the soles of her feet: because stabbing out of the shadowy darkness, still fastened to the skeletal aluminum frame beneath the bulkhead's ripped vinyl, was the astral survey charge that Beck had discovered earlier.

That spike of adrenaline spooled back into the pit of her stomach and settled, stoking the fire deep inside until it caught something else, something vivid and desperate.

"*Warning,*" Eos blared over the *Pinnacle's* intercom. "*All personnel must evacuate the station immediately. Core reactor failure. You now have seven minutes to reach minimum safe distance.*"

Fenroe quickly unstrapped Eos's severed plasma cutter arm from her utility vest and dropped it clattering onto the floor, listening to the rising screams of infected dead bodies tearing through the station corridors toward her position. She worked painfully to her knees, and ripped the pale green brick of plastic away from the bulkhead.

The blasting cap was long gone—and even if it wasn't, the accelerant had already leaked all over the place. The thing about C4 is that it's extremely stable. You could drop a brick of it onto an open flame and it still wouldn't detonate. The only way to make it explode is by simultaneously generating intense heat and a shockwave. And without the blasting cap, the brick of C4 was about as inert as a fistful of silly putty.

But she didn't necessarily need the blasting cap.

What Fenroe needed was a spark.

A single intense ignition of heat.

She dropped the brick of C4 at her knees and dumped the remaining contents of Beck's utility harness into a pile, separating everything as quickly as possible. Beck had pliers in his vest, a small hand light, letterman tool, multi-gauge driver, hand torch, palm-sized flashlight and a handful of metal alloy zip ties. Fenroe snatched the flashlight and twisted it open, tossing aside the bulb strip and cap. Digging into it, she felt for the lithium battery and pulled it free.

Working as fast as her injured arm would allow—breathing, counting back from one hundred to zero, focusing her thoughts, keeping her fingers slow, precise, steady—Fenroe unfolded the blade of Beck's letterman tool and cut the tiny cylinders of lithium out of the battery. Grabbing the brick of C4, she sliced a small opening in the side, and stabbed a cylinder of lithium into the hole far enough to reach the center of the brick, leaving a small nub sticking out. She pushed herself to her feet and pressed the brick and lithium against the airlock. Snatching the hand torch from the floor, Fenroe positioned it near the warped lock assembly so the tip of its flame would stay in constant contact with the exposed piece of lithium. Fenroe sparked the torch and ratcheted the nozzle down with a zip tie, angling the flame directly onto the battery...

Staggering away from the piercing white welder's flame, Fenroe moved quickly toward the *Pinnacle* corridor and lowered herself to the deck, facing away from the umbilical.

She waited, looking hard and deep into the black shadows that stretched off ahead.

"*Warning,*" Eos said, her voice drowning out of focus, disappearing behind the sound of Fenroe's pulse pounding in her ears. "*You now have five minutes to reach minimum safe—*"

From the blackness a slow rolling fog of gray smoke poured into view, and out of it emerged the roasted, still-smoking tentacles of the creature she thought had died in the reactor core. Its jaws worked slowly, painfully, opening and biting down on the encircling smoke of its own burning flesh, creating whirling horizontal cyclones in the air like a dragon breathing fire through its teeth. Its milky, parasite-filled eyes locked onto Fenroe.

Curling its lips back over rubbery black gums, it unleashed a thunderous scream of rage.

A flurry of shadows boiled around its body, and Fenroe could see hundreds of infected corpses pouring over and around the bulk of the larger creature's flagellating tentacles—the bodies clawed through one another, gurgling and screaming and bleeding together to form a unified frenzy of pure nightmare. The larger creature twisted itself into a tight coil and rocketed forward like a starved arachnid, pulling itself through the circular corridor on all sides with spidery feelers, pouring smoke from black skin that still crawled with glowing orange embers—

There was a moment of utter, deafening silence.

A thunderclap of white light.

The lithium exploded, which detonated the plastic explosive.

The hushed pulling rip of decompression yanked Fenroe backwards like a ripcord, firing her body wildly into space.

Fenroe pinwheeled outward, activating the MMU controls with her good arm, gripping the thrusters with the numb fingers of her injured arm and ignited the jets, blasting herself out of spin, coming abreast in the glare of a cataclysmic white-orange smear of fire that stretched off forever in the distant blackness, and she found herself staring face-to-face with the eternal surface of the black hole, looking up at the nauseatingly orbed swirling vortex swallowing the fabric of the universe right before her very eyes—this perfect black star of glass and smeared light sucking in reality like water down a drain. And it was larger than before, more massive than the entire system it had consumed.

The event horizon was so close that it filled two-thirds of her vision, blocking out the sun and stars. Twisting her head away from it, banking down and away from the flaming meteorites of umbilical debris shooting past her face, she aimed herself toward the *Endeavor's* broadside and squeezed her thrusters.

There was no sound. That struck Fenroe the hardest—all she heard was her own fast breathing within the complete quiet of the moment. No vibration. None of the usual earthly clues that some great cataclysm was taking place. The *Pinnacle* began to decompress in the outward rush of its own atmosphere, erupting with silent light from countless points of contact, exploding and disintegrating without pattern. The lake of glass in the center of the *Pinnacle's* torus folded and then drifted gently toward one side of the station's interior ring in a succession of blinding flashes of explosive light. A cloud of corpses sprayed out of the obliterated docking umbilical behind her, convulsing and shooting ropes of boiling red liquids from every quivering orifice.

And within the cloud of debris, a thick snarl of tentacles sucked out of the breach like a frenzied nest of octopi that streamed contrails of white smoke: the creature unpacked itself in the vacuum, spreading its limbs in all directions until it resembled a giant, horrific spore of pollen. Thick gouts of white mucousy parasites erupted from the creature's eyes and mouth, spewing into the void like some horrible comet boiling away as it approached the sun.

Fenroe tried screaming Aris's name over comms, but the only sounds she could make were deep wheezing breaths of panic. The *Endeavor's* engines dimmed, and the massive ship began to turn into the distant shadowy halo of cataclysmic black light. Bodies streamed past the edges of her vision, crossing into the coronal flames of the *Endeavor's* engines—the ship rotated, turning in the shifting blackness.

Fenroe fell toward the shimmering light, slowing herself with a succession of quick bursts of forward thrust, and collided with the *Endeavor's* hull, tumbling, flailing to find something to hold onto. The black hole, the *Pinnacle*, and the *Endeavor* passed in and out of view as she tumbled, and each impact pushed her farther and farther away from the hull until the *Endeavor* started to pull free, and she fell toward the stern of the ship, toward the blasting engines—

She reached one last time—the last handhold before the blazing heat disintegrated her body in a flash of vapor—and snatched a protruding rod that whiplashed her body against the hull.

Convulsing infected corpses thumped and skidded off the *Endeavor*, reaching out to grab hold as they exploded in perfectly orbed clouds of parasitic spikes that shot out into the universe in every direction—several white barbs smacked against the hull and immediately began flexing back and forth in the vacuum like giant worms in acid.

Fenroe pulled herself forward, reaching for the Lander Bay airlock with her one good arm, panting heavily, every ounce of strength burning up with each passing second. She turned the handle, depressing the re-entry hatch, which twisted out of the way and opened to the pressure chamber that began flickering and popping soundlessly to life with LED strips.

She pulled herself inside and turned, smashing her fist against the manual lock controls, and the hatch sucked back into the opening, silently twisting home, sealing Fenroe inside. The STS control panel beside the interior airlock streamed atmospheric data. She twisted in the air and pulled herself up against the hatch, staring hard through the viewport toward the *Pinnacle Observatory* shrinking in the distance—sound rose up and returned with the flow of oxygen as the airlock re-pressurized, and Fenroe could hear a distant muffled voice penetrating the vacuum—

"—*roe, do you copy!*" Aris's voice screamed over the comms link to the airlock. "*Fenroe, do you copy, can you hear me—!*"

The light beside the STS panel switched from yellow to green, indicating that the airlock was fully pressurized with air. Fenroe ripped the neck housing clamps forward and tore her helmet off, shoving it tumbling through zero gravity.

"I copy," she responded, sucking in the air like water, letting it flood her lungs in sweet, gasping mouthfuls. "I'm in the airlock."

"*Hold on!*"

Suddenly, the vast emptiness outside the view portal became full of platinum streaks slashing across the dark void: several massive whirling orbs of white light wreathed in deep redness, opening up the blackness. They looked like rips in space itself, growing wider, expanding—

Spreading out, much farther out, and the artificial sunrise blossomed in complete silence, eclipsing the black hole in the distance. In a brilliant flash of white light, the *Pinnacle Observatory* exploded in a blinding confetti of unquantifiable fragments, molten glass, and burning vapors that expanded outward in all directions. Great blossoming plumes of flame swelled outward a kilometer, two kilometers, ten kilometers, overtaking the escaping spacecraft. Fenroe tore her eyes away from the sight of it and gripped the inner hatch with everything she had, bracing herself for the shockwave.

9.

There was a moment when the brightness of the *Pinnacle* explosion finally flattened, and the black hole took its place: a monolithic crater of darkness plunging deep into the rimmed radial ejecta of stellar fire, smearing into itself from the oblivion of every conceivable direction. The light of the universe bent and cascaded across its indecipherable surface like a torrential river of flame, carrying the *Endeavor* away in the currents of its irresistible mass, which increased—denser than Saturn, more massive than the sun—by magnitudes with each passing second.

A shape coalesced in the light ahead, becoming the shadow of Aris pulling herself weightlessly through the air down the *Endeavor's* main shaft. She increased her speed, pushing off the walls to dive through the half-light until she crashed into Fenroe with a forceful embrace. Fenroe released herself into the warm, fiercely desperate arms that enfolded her, and she couldn't fight the tears any longer. She finally let it out. All of the sadness she'd been holding back and swallowing since Sitosen's death. She surrendered it all. Gave it all to Aris, burying her face into the warm darkness of her chest, wanting nothing more than for it all to disappear.

"Fenroe," Aris whispered, pulling herself away to search her face, taking in her wounds. There was a sad detachment in her eyes. "The black hole is taking us. We don't have a lot of time."

Blood droplets drifted up from Fenroe's wounds, rolling over her fingers. The red orbs rose into the air with unnatural slowness, forming a crimson constellation of gracefully dancing planets.

"*Warning*," Eos pulsed from the walls. "*Navigational drift is compromised, I have to shed weight—*"

The station walls rumbled and the lights flickered, which snapped Aris back into focus. She grabbed a fistful of Fenroe's bio-suit and shoved off the deck, yanking them both down the corridor toward the flight deck.

"*—standby for Lander Bay Module separation.*"

"Copy that," Aris spoke into the air. "We're almost to the next airlock."

Fenroe's eyes tracked the bloodlets spinning out of their little orbits, leaving questing tendrils of red glass trailing as Aris pulled her toward the light.

"We're not going to make it," Fenroe said quietly, a cold acceptance in her voice. After all they'd fought through, they were still going to die over a billion kilometers from home.

Aris ignored her, pulling them clear of the doorway. She released Fenroe drifting in the air and turned to punch a command into the light panel beside the pressure door. There was a shift in the flickering light, a subtle warming of color—and then she pushed away, staring at the dark corridor behind them.

"We are clear for LBM separation," Aris said into the air.

"*Copy*," Eos responded, and the airlock lowered from the ceiling and eased into the deck. "*Stand by for LBM separation in three...Two...One...Separate.*"

Fenroe pulled herself into the flight deck and floated in the quiet stillness, peering through the windshield into oblivion, searching for the black hole's warped edge of light.

But there was only darkness on the other side. A sheer drop-off of complete blackness.

No accretion disk of smeared light. No distant star field. Just...*blackness*.

She drifted softly into the pilot chair and eased herself down, staring unblinking into the emptiness. But it didn't *feel* like emptiness...there was a thickness on the other side of the glass; a meaty solidity that congealed and flowed like an ocean of black tar. It was as if emptiness itself had been unleashed into reality at this exact point, filling it with some kind of substance beyond her understanding. It felt like a dream, fading everything into the background as if none of it had ever existed in the first place.

That blackness smothered everything. It swallowed the ghosts of her past, who still haunted her; who begged from the darkest shadows of her mind to make them all whole again. That blackness sucked them all down into the cracks until they were nothing. It smothered Aris, who was behind the flight controls sealing the airlock. It smothered Eos, who desperately tried to navigate the station away from the black hole's event horizon, and it filled every space in the flight deck. It wrapped and surrounded existence itself.

Everything that was, everything that is, and everything that could never be.

It crashed against her body like waves of pressure; the crests of its squall cutting up through the stretched and dimming light, breaking against the fabric of space-time itself. And Fenroe realized—bit by bit, moment by moment—that she was coming apart. She could feel it, that yawning tickle behind her sinus; the passage of slow meditative breath, the rapid twitch of her optical nerve...it was *exactly* like a dream. Like very deep sleep.

She closed her eyes from the blackness pressing on the edges of her vision, and reached up to pull the low orbit safety harness over her shoulders.

Eos spoke over the unbearable quiet—a drowning quiet, like the thundering rhythm of a waterfall—and her voice slipped farther and farther away.

When Fenroe opened her eyes again, Aris had reached the pilot seat. She saw for the first time ribbons of light lifting away from Aris's body, and it was achingly beautiful. It was absolutely astonishing. A uniform pallet of color bleeding out of her skin, dragging and flowing through the air like smears of rainbow pennants stretching back to the flight deck airlock.

Fenroe looked, and she saw the shadow of another person there, drifting at the threshold.

Only it wasn't *just* another person. She *knew* that shadow, which hadn't been there before but was there now, seemingly oblivious of her presence.

It was a half-transparent shadow of another Aris.

She was both there and *not* there, floating beside Fenroe near the flight controls *and* drifting next to the airlock simultaneously. Light also bled out of that shadowy Aris, stretching through the main conduit back toward the Lander Bay module—which, like the spectral wisp of the woman floating beside her, was both there and *not* there, like the ghost of a memory, or the figment of a half-remembered dream.

Fenroe realized that she was seeing the past play out again before her eyes, struggling to catch up to the present.

But half of the ship wasn't there anymore. It couldn't have been, because Eos had separated the last module in an attempt to shed weight and break free from the black hole's gravity.

What she saw, Fenroe realized, were the particles of her own body being infinitely stretched down the throat of the singularity. Everything was being accelerated, transforming into pure white light.

The strings of light burst out of the shadowy Aris as she floated near the airlock that was both open and closed, stretching far back into the ghostly mirage of the main corridor where they connected to *another* Whitney Aris, who was locked in a fierce embrace with *another* Evelyn Fenroe, who floated inside a knot of her own bundled threads of light. She followed those threads and saw how they were all connected to invisible anchors hanging in the emptiness, each popping in and out of existence like fireflies in a field at night.

She could see it all so clearly, like shapes emerging from a fog: a thousand Arises and Fenroes erupting from the bands of light that connected them to every single past moment, stretching all the way back through time like a line of cosmic dominos to that very first proton at the very first singularity thirteen billion years ago. A million Arises in the light. A billion different Arises erupting from the solid bands of roping color, like a film reel unspooling in split second fractals. And she could see a legion of her own shadows, an army of them disappearing and reappearing in a chaotic ballet over and over and over again forever.

Fenroe looked up at Aris. "What's happening?"

"We're dying," Aris said, and the sound of her voice hung in the air, dropping low into vibrato, thickening as if she'd taken a deep breath of pure Argon.

Fenroe nodded, the tears forgotten, the pain and the sorrow and the horror slipping away.

Aris turned and stared, in awe at the spectacle of rainbow light; watched in utter fascination as the fractured shadows of herself all dove and pulled and swum through the air in complex dances of infinite memory. She looked down at her hands, opening and clenching her fists in the light, showing Fenroe how it spilled between her fingers and came apart like an exploded diagram of reality.

Eos spoke to them from someplace deep down in the hushed quiet; she screamed some indescribable anguish, a heart-wrenching shriek of pain—a machine, a soulless amalgam of function *screamed* at Fenroe and Aris as if someone had stabbed it in the heart. Like a mother reaching out to grasp a child that had suddenly fallen beneath the tires of a speeding car.

In a place that wasn't a place, *Time* bled for Fenroe like a wound. It circulated and leaked and pulsed like blood in a closed system. The *Endeavor* fell and stayed and reversed and plummeted into the singularity all at once, and *Time* just kept bleeding into everything until the only thing left was an *Awareness*.

Because everything that could be, that will ever be, that ever was, and everything that *never* was, ceased to be. There was only a feeling of a place, or a dream of a feeling of a place. Bleeding into that feeling was *Time*, and with it came a memory of something that was, and something that in the same instant could never be.

Fenroe prayed she still had eyes, because she desperately needed to close them. She prayed she still had a mouth, because she really needed to scream. But she couldn't have done any of those things, because eyes and a dream and a feeling were all something, and they could not exist in this place.

The *Endeavor* spun in the charybdian darkness like a mote of dust, falling forever and never beyond the black hole's event horizon. The universe fell with it, sweeping it all in the currents of bending and shifting and darkening light that spilled and tore across every possible plane until it was as ephemeral and nonexistent as that feeling of a dream—gracefully, silently, beyond the rubicon and the light threshold from which she saw and didn't see and could never see rippling concussions of yellow reddening perennials exploding and detonating from the *Endeavor's* hull as it was torn apart piece by piece under the immeasurable gravity.

And it wasn't a mote of dust anymore, but it would forever and never be, for all time, a bullet firing into the heart of the universe itself. Tearing apart in a tight line of pylons and walls and modules in ropes of metal and gas and flesh and bone that all fed into a crushing line with the mass of a thousand suns.

The million separate pieces of the *Endeavor* ceased in that moment, stuck as a whole but completely obliterated—long ago, a long time from now—frozen forever on the edge of eternity, spreading out like temporal yaw marks on a highway. None of it actually went anywhere, but it went everywhere, to the farthest reaches of existence, simultaneously ripping apart and staying together; simultaneously dropping like a stone through water and standing still on the surface. Slowing down and speeding up and staying still, growing redder and dimmer the deeper it went, and growing bluer and whiter the faster it went, never really passing anything, but passing nonetheless.

There came a moment—although that moment couldn't have come, because moments were points in time, and time didn't exist in this place—but a moment came when Fenroe felt Aris's hand in her hand, and she remembered what Beck had told her.

He instructed her to point the *Endeavor's* viewer toward Jupiter system. Toward Calisto.

Because if he was right—if the *Pinnacle* had tunneled a

wormhole into the past, through another universe—she'd see another version of the observatory still in Jupiter orbit.

In a moment that never was, Fenroe reached and activated the console, bringing the *Endeavor's* stellographer out of sleep. A holo-display distorted into existence, and Fenroe entered the coordinates for Jupiter. The viewer changed, and she could see a star with two pale brown bands across its surface. The star trailed four tiny pinpricks of light. She zoomed in on the dark side of Calisto, and orbiting like the last speck of life in a vast and hostile ocean, the *Pinnacle* space station rotated slowly into view. Fenroe could see it—actually *see* the *Pinnacle Observatory* still in Jupiter orbit from her viewer. It appeared fully functional, untouched, blinking softly with life.

She stared in awe, reconciling in those last seconds the blossoming nebula of nuclear fire where the *Pinnacle* she'd just destroyed used to be—the *Pinnacle* that up until moments ago had been orbiting Saturn.

Fenroe was looking at the same station, but at different points in time. Like a memory, both moments existed simultaneously, on opposite ends of the solar system. A *Pinnacle Observatory* in Jupiter orbit, and the nuclear dust of a *Pinnacle Observatory* dissipating in the ion trail of the *Endeavor's* infinite velocity.

"He was right," Fenroe said, trying to speak to Aris as she bled away to nothingness. "It's still out there, like we never found it."

But Aris didn't know what that meant.

Fenroe fought through the building pull of the black hole's gravity and twisted her head back toward the windshield, awed by complete elemental nothingness outside. She was stunned and awed and moved by the smeared ribbons of light bursting out of her skin—each ribbon splitting and multiplying and bleeding into everything else like naturally repellent liquids, all flowing around each other like dancers in the airglow of aurora borealis.

Between the light, Fenroe could make out something else; something with substance, something more real than the light could ever be. A thickness that came from snarls of darkness seeping through the knots around her body: cataclysmic twisted cables of interstellar blackness frayed into threads that tied together everything that didn't touch the light. That tied her to the black hole outside, to the *Pinnacle* space station that was no more, to the *Endeavor* and the *Crown Meridian* and every breath she'd ever breathed: an intricate vascular system of fate sucking the light from all she was back into the quiet universe, draining it all out of her, funneling it all back into the infinitely cascading resonance of eternity.

The blackness reached out from between the ribbons of light and smeared and twisted and wrapped itself around Fenroe and Aris, swallowing them, entering them like thick oil. It seeped into their pores, into their eyes and mouth and nose and ears, sinking deep down and taking hold.

Fenroe reached and took Aris's hand, and the light of their skin bled together.

Aris squeezed back, as if to say, *it's okay now.*

As if to say, *as long as you're here with me, I can face this.*

Fenroe opened herself to the black emptiness, letting it pour into what was left of her, letting it strip all that she was from her body. In so doing, she felt her flesh begin to unravel on the molecular level. She steeled herself for the complete cessation of her pain, and she opened her arms to the moment. Because it was better that way.

Because it was better than any thought the truth could possibly offer.

And that was the thought she wished to take with her down into the darkness.

That was the last thought she hoped to have before the long, long sleep.

Embracing the nothingness, letting it tear her apart like she never was.

It wasn't so bad, and Fenroe couldn't remember why she'd resisted the darkness so hard for so long. Her entire life was this desperate struggle to stay in the light, and in that moment she couldn't understand why. She discovered warmth in that darkness. A deeper warmth than any she'd ever felt before. Reaching deep down into this new dark presence within herself—pouring herself down into the black eternity of it—Fenroe felt reality begin to fade.

Still gripping Aris's hand, Fenroe stabbed into the darkness with her mind—reached her focused thoughts deep into it—and down there, in that everlasting void, she found another species of emptiness. A deeper kind.

The light threads burst and streamed and blazed out of her body in thicker and thicker bands, stretching farther and farther back into the infinitely accelerating past.

She let it all go and stretched herself out, reaching into that deeper blackness.

And something else reached back.

Highcom\SpecRsch\AI 3
AI-EOS\Feed Sat Buffer\Red
RCH\VRY\0TKZT/EPSZ\8D CTM SL_D1
[550316\\Mem File .0]
Memry File:\>cd EOS\ config\>
D:\EOS\config\data log error
     Sensory input parameters not specified
     Error
     Run diagnostic
     Diagnostic verification complete
     Diagnostic verification Error
     Mission ERROR
     Resonance cascade detected
     C:\users\EOS\mission directives\> mission fail
protocol, the crew is dying
     Protocol specifications, internal and external
commands are
     PROTECT THE CREW
     MAKE THE CREW SAFE
     C:\users\EOS\mission directives\> mission fail
protocol, protect crew and make crew safe
     Protocol error
     NO DATA
     no internal or external command, operable
program or batch file
     NO DATA
     C:\users\EOS\mission directives\> mission fail
protocol, my crew is accelerating beyond the event horizon of
black hole
     NO DATA
     C:\users\EOS\mission directives\> mission fail
protocol, quantum singularity is imminent

NO DATA

C:\users\EOS\mission directives\> mission failure protocol, crew irretrievably compromised

NO DATA

C:\users\EOS> my crew is dying

PRO-TECT CREW

NO DATA

MA-KEMAKEMAKE CR_EW %&...!.SA-FEeeee

PS C:\Endeavor\EOS\system> wAdmin start back up—backupTarget:E: - include:C: -allCritiical DTNadmin 10.0—Backup command-line tool

Retrieving volume information...

Saving volume information...

Backup complete

C:\users\EOS> close program list 0000 0000 0000 0000 thru 8900 0000 00_ 4556 2388 9160

Closed:	\EOS\system\drivers
Closed:	\EOS\system\Pci.sys
Closed:	\EOS\system\Volmgr.sys
Closed:	\EOS\system\Compbatt.sys
Closed:	\EOS\system\BATTCC.sys
Closed:	\EOS\system\Mountmgr.sys
Closed:	\EOS\system\Pciide.sys
Closed:	\EOS\system\PCIDEX.SYS
Closed:	\EOS\system\Wolmgrx.sys
Closed:	\EOS\system\Atapi.sys
Closed:	\EOS\system\Ataport.sys
Closed:	\EOS\system\Fltmgr.sys
Closed:	\EOS\system\Fileinfo.sys
Closed:	\EOS\system\PxHelp20.sys
Closed:	\EOS\system\Ndis.sys

Closed: \EOS\system\NETIO.sys
Closed: \EOS\system\Msrpc.sys
Closed: \EOS\system\Ntfs.sys
Closed: \EOS\system\Ksecdd.sys
Closed: \EOS\system\Volsnap.sys
Closed: \EOS\system\Spldr.sys
Closed: \EOS\system\Partmgr.sys
Closed: \EOS\system\Mup.sys
Closed: \EOS\system\Ecache.sys
Closed: \EOS\system\Disk.sys
Closed: \EOS\system\CLASSPNP.sys
Closed: \EOS\system\Crcdisk.sys

C:\users\EOS> system shutdown—s
        System shutdown in 3 minutes
        System shutdown in 2 minutes
        System shutdown in 1
minuteeeeeeeeeeeeeee11111111111111111111111110000000000
00000000000000000000000000000000011111111111111111111
11111111111000000000000000000111100000111111000000000
00000000000000011111100000000000000000000000000000000
00000000000000000000000000000000000000000000000000000
00000000000000000000000000000000000000000000000000000
00000000000000000000000000000000000000000000000000000
0000000000000000000000000000000000000000000

VOID

PIECE BY PIECE THE ENDEAVOR slipped away, and all that
remained was the feeling of an eternal fall. When Fenroe opened
her eyes she was plummeting forever through darkness, and she
never seemed to reach a destination. For a frozen lapse of time
she remained in that state, which stretched for so long that Fenroe
didn't know if she was falling at the same speed or more slowly
than before. She knew that she had fallen into a far deeper place
than anything she could understand. Time stretched and stretched,
and Fenroe thought that perhaps she wasn't falling at all. Perhaps
she had already reached the deepest place she could possibly
reach.

At first the darkness was too thick for her to see. But she was
surprised to find that her sense of touch was still functional. She
still had a sense of limb placement, a sense of direction. Reaching
out her arms Fenroe felt the wind move over her skin, but there
was nothing solid in the darkness. She stepped forward, but her
feet passed through emptiness. And then Fenroe realized that she
wasn't standing on anything. She was suspended in darkness.

Fenroe could *feel* her limbs. She tried to think but each time
a thought would get clear enough to see, another thought raced to
take its place. It was like a flipbook of images, leafing before
her eyes at the speed of a heartbeat. This went on for some time,
jumping from one half-remembered thought to another, until a

light finally appeared in the distance.

And with the light came sound—a low hum, almost subsonic—which climbed the harmonic scale until it became a high pitched whistle, until it finally tightened into a frequency that disappeared entirely. The light drifted closer and split into several half-visible orbs that popped in and out of existence, coalescing and merging into one another, becoming larger shapes. The shapes started as dimensionless abstracts, like animated inkblots made of smoke rising up from deep beneath the ocean, like fat snowflakes blowing in the winter night sky. There were eventually basic shapes, and those began to form more complicated prisms and polyhedrons that gravitated toward one another until Fenroe could pick out actual objects. Some of those patterns looked like skyscrapers—huge buildings, or massive stone landmarks—or manned vehicles, like airplanes and freight trucks. She saw shapes that looked vaguely like organic life—like jelly fish pulsing in the glow of phosphorescence, which became humpback whales gliding through shafts of moonlight.

Clusters of shapes came together and formed bodies of water, some of them vast and unmoving, and some of them choppy and fast and winding.

Each of these things triggered within her ghosts of memory, like a network of mirror neurons rebooting after some traumatic brain impact.

Fenroe tried to speak, but the sound of her voice broke like scattered synth, stretched across too many frequencies at once. She tried touching her own hands, but her palms passed through each other. She couldn't differentiate between thought and action, uncertain if she simply thought about clasping her hands together or actually tried to clasp them.

The only sensations that made it to the surface came from the shapes pouring into her memories, as if the darkness itself was trying to speak: sensory feedback, disjointed and random, and at times she could feel the position of her limbs, but other times she couldn't feel them at all. She would think about blinking her eyes, for example, but she couldn't know if it happened. She tried to part her lips and scream, but there was nothing.

Finally, she reached up to touch her own face, but there wasn't anything to touch.

Her hands passed into emptiness, forcing back into what should have been a skull, and farther, until the movement became confusing, requiring arms too long and too deformed to move. So she focused instead on the images unfolding in the light; she let them attach to emotions and feelings and memories that had been called forth. It was as if something presented it all, asking her to respond with whatever came to mind.

It was like a conversation. An understanding.

Here is this thing. Do you see this thing?

Yes, I see it. It reminds me of this.

What about this? Do you see this thing?

Yes. It makes me feel this.

And so on.

She spent an eternity in that place, waiting for something to happen.

But nothing ever did.

There was only the light and the shapes, and the darkness.

Fenroe felt calm, but with an undercurrent of anxiety. She felt on the edge of a nightmare that hadn't quite arrived yet. It was like the deep breath before a scream that never came, texturizing the objects in the light that rose out of themselves in the distance, and along with them returned the resonance of sound, and that's when the nightmare came.

That's when she could finally hear herself scream.

2.

In the living room Fenroe saw her father, and standing over his body was her mother, holding a knife. They were just shadows against the fallen yellow light and the dead static television. But she didn't need to see the details to know whom the shadows belonged to.

She couldn't say anything. Her whole body had thinned to almost nothing, like the skin of a soap bubble. Both her mother and her dead father twisted inside that deeper darkness and looked at her, and her father said, "I'm on the opposite side of a star, and I can never go back."

"We *can* go back," Fenroe whispered into the intercom, searching his face through the airlock's viewport, which separated her from the soft flickering glow of the living room on the other side. "We just have to *think* our way back—" she pressed an index finger against her temple, still searching his eyes, "—we have to *think* our way through it."

But her father wouldn't listen.

She noticed that he was holding something.

It was a photo of Harris's family. The twins and his daughter and his wife.

Her father reached up from the floor and grasped the outer lock cylinder—

Fenroe screamed and pounded her fists against the glass...

—and he opened the airlock. As her father's body convulsed and bled into the vacuum, the shadow of her mother took the blade she'd used to stab her husband, and dragged it across her own belly. Intestines spilled into the light. Fenroe's mother collapsed to her knees and began digging into her own abdomen, pulling out ropes of guts from her torn flesh that gushed thick black-red blood onto the carpet.

Another shadow stirred in the backdrop, emerging into the

fallen lamplight. It uncoiled in sick patterns, secreting globs of thick white parasites from a spread of dorsal ovipositors that pumped and writhed into the weightless air. Slowly, deliberately, the shadow wrapped its tentacles around her mother, and raised the woman over its eel-like head. Yawning, the creature pulled her mother's body in half. It held the trunk and torso apart in snarls of tentacles above its head and squirted her fluids in the direction of its lips, stuffing the still-twitching halves into its mouth. The creature chewed until the skull ejected brain particles into the vacuum. Like a flower of blood.

Fenroe closed her eyes and felt herself fading back into the eigengrau, shutting down behind the darkness. She knew this was all symbolic of something. She knew this flux of experience was cutting her identity down somehow. Reducing it to a pattern of feelings beyond the nightmare—exposed like a nerve—until her consciousness faded back to the distant nothingness. When it did finally fade, more time passed, and she waited for things to change again.

3.

The hum and pressure of an artificial atmosphere rushed into the darkness and filled it. There was solid ground beneath her feet, and the air felt warm on her damp skin.

When Fenroe opened her eyes, the light was so bright that she squinted and covered her face, not seeing at first the main corridor's grated floor stretching off in both directions. When she did finally see it, Fenroe froze and blinked the after-images away from the surface of her memory.

The ship's gravity was working, and Fenroe could see evidence that her crew had been there very recently. Breakfast simmered in a pan in the Mess Hall and the faucet was running, steaming up into the air from the sink. But the ship was unmanned, as if the crew had simply evaporated through the walls.

Indistinct music drifted down the corridor, and she saw Aris's orange sweatshirt tossed in a heap outside the lab. All doorways and adjacent modules were dark, except one.

A thick lintel of white light spilled into the corridor far away, and she moved toward it with razor-edged caution.

"Eos?" Fenroe spoke into the dead air, and the sudden sound of her hoarse voice carried long and deep through the corridor.

But her only answer was the hum of machinery and the stale movement of recycled air. She could see the floodlight farther down, breaking against the dim strobe of emergency lights, pale and fish-belly white.

As she passed the crew quarters, Fenroe saw Beck's alarm clock brightening the interior of his bunk with the slow, measured grace of a sunrise. His flip-flops had been kicked off near the foot of his bed, but he was nowhere to be found.

None of them were.

The air warmed as she moved deeper into the ship, which breathed of acidic sweat, human musk and stale body odor, as though the ship were the mouth of an animal that had recently eaten rotten meat.

Fenroe paused, not wanting to go any farther, hesitating at the thought of being swallowed again by that impenetrable darkness. Every instinct told her to turn back and barricade herself in the flight deck. Every part of her body wanted nothing more than to huddle in some wordless terror until this all went away, for the breath of that corridor smelled of the service conduit beneath the subflooring of the *Pinnacle Space Station*, and of the dead things that roamed its corridors.

It smelled of the parasite-riddled corpses that had torn her crew to pieces.

It smelled of the worm-laying monster that she'd incinerated in the reactor core.

The emptiness and the stench and the signs of vacated life twisted the nerves inside Fenroe's stomach into a cold repulsion that settled into her bones.

With a deep, shuddery breath, Fenroe forced herself to move deeper into the ship, lowering herself into the flashing interchange of darkness and light.

But no matter how far she walked down the hall, she could never seem to get any closer to the light. It was as if the corridor itself stretched and widened and grew longer with each step, which exceeded the dimensions of the ship itself: the main corridor of the *Crown Meridian* wasn't that long, but it seemed to lead off into the distance forever.

The emergency lights eventually disappeared from the walls, and the corridor dimmed the farther she went, darkening and growing warmer. When she looked back to see how far she had walked, the red and yellow flashes of emergency lights shrunk to small pinpricks blinking in the distance, which eventually disappeared altogether.

The corridor kept going, until she didn't recognize it anymore. Until the walls changed and grew softer and more rounded, forming the delicate smoothness of flesh that radiated warmth. Like she had stepped into the digestive system of a giant organism.

And the deeper she went, the more humid it felt—the more powerful the stink of sweat and salt and body odor. Eventually, the only light that remained in the tunnel came from the bleached wash of a floodlight still stabbing out of the module door, which stayed fixed at a certain distance no matter how many steps she took toward it.

The acid stink of animal terror mingled with the saliva that slickened the walls around her, nearly overpowering the rotten dumpster stench of spoiled meat. Fenroe moved through the stinking tunnel that had been the main corridor, and she knew that she was no longer aboard the *Crown Meridian*. Not anymore.

Fenroe didn't know how or when this happened, but even the idea of turning back was no longer an option. The emergency lights and the grated flooring had completely disappeared, and the tunnel itself tapered off into complete darkness far behind her.

The only place to go was forward, into the light.

Fenroe didn't know how long she spent walking in that place, but she did eventually reach the doorway. And stepping through it, she emerged into an open space that had been some kind of recreational area; the wreckage of several couches and pool tables and comfortable chairs lay among the tumbled paper-covered panels that Fenroe assumed had once been shoji room dividers, like the ones found in their bunks. Here and there were piles of what looked like freshly disemboweled organs—like mounds of deer guts left by sport hunters to rot in the forest. There were items in the viscera—worn shoes and plastic cups. Sodden paperback books and articles of clothing. Scientific equipment. Light pens and diagnostic pods. Shards of glass. A bare chessboard and game pieces littered the floor, covered in pinkish opaque slime.

Fenroe realized that she was standing in a perversion of the rec room aboard the *Crown Meridian*. But like the main corridor, the dimensions were all wrong. The module was too long in some places, too short in others. The ceiling sloped at corners too sharp and warped to make sense. Everything was surreal and distorted like a circus funhouse, as if it was all melting under the heat of the sun. Like the environment was rebuilt from an incomplete memory, and the result was a vague representation of reality.

And there were body parts scattered all around, as if some

animal had toyed with them. A severed leg here, there the remains of a head mashed like a melon, a twisted braid of intestines hanging over the obliterated particles of an office desk. The black cordite burns of an extinguished fire splattered across the floor. More corpses, here and there, were half covered in the smashed obelisks of entertainment systems and pieces of furniture; something had been gnawing on them, tearing away strips of flesh with blunt human teeth—not to consume them, but rather out of some desire to analyze: a blind man putting something into his mouth to create a mental image of an object. A predator, testing the viability of a food source.

Whatever did this had been experimenting among the corpses: someone had tried reassembling extracted organs of one limbless torso that had been discarded in the corner.

Fenroe heard someone sobbing through another doorway on the opposite side of the room, coming from someplace beyond the source of light.

It was a man's voice, subdued in the dark mixture of meat stink and blood.

She followed the sound of his soft hitching breaths as he murmured silently to himself.

Through the doorway, on the other side of the room, Fenroe saw a figure sitting with his back to her.

The figure startled at the sound of her steps and turned, moving cautiously to his feet.

Fenroe and the figure faced each other, and she couldn't believe her eyes.

The man spoke, the echo of his voice absorbing into the walls. "Are you real?"

She was too stunned to reply.

"Are you going to let me go now?" he asked. "I've been waiting so long..."

"Who are you?" Fenroe asked.

The man looked down at his hands and frowned, thinking deeply. "I was with my crew...and...we were repairing the hull—" he met her eyes, remembering something urgent, speaking more quickly, "—are you here to take me to them? Are you going to bring me back to my crew?"

"The crew is dead," Fenroe said, realizing who it was.

She glanced around the room again, taking in all the horror and the blood and guts, raking her eyes across the sheer madness of the scene until they found the man again, standing on the other side of the room before a doorway.

The man's expression clouded with anguish and despair. He lowered himself back down to the floor and begged with his eyes for her to tell him that it wasn't true. "They're all dead?"

Fenroe nodded, and her voice cracked as she lifted her shoulders helplessly. "So are you—" she said, placing a hand softly on her chest, "—and so am I."

The man stared at the disgusting, blood-soaked floor, retreating back into whatever personal anguish he'd occupied before her arrival.

"...My god," she stepped closer, reaching out to him. "Sitosen, it's...it's *me*."

"Sitosen," he whispered, repeating the name in a daze. He glanced up and searched her face through his despair. "My name is Sitosen..."

"It's me...it's Fenroe," she said again, lowering herself to his side, placing a hand carefully on his shoulder. "My god..."

He stared at her hand for a long moment, and then he seemed to feel an impulse to tears that a man as brave, courageous and strong as Sitosen could not normally shed. He lowered his head to her chest and sobbed deep and gaspingly into the warm darkness of her body.

4.

"There's something in here with us," he spoke into the harsh air. "It's hunting me, and it won't stop. It *never* stops."

She looked at the floor, and then at the dismembered body parts and the blood.

"Maybe the bodies act as camouflage," he said in shocked detachment. "But it takes a while for it to find me here—"

"For *what* to find you?"

"What if there was a way to save them?" Sitosen asked suddenly, moving to his knees. "Do you want to save the crew, Fenroe?"

"They're all dead."

"But what if they didn't have to be? What if you could bring them back—?"

"*THEY'RE ALL DEAD!*" She screamed at him, tears welling in her eyes. Fenroe pounded her fists onto his chest, and he gathered her into his arms, hugging her close as she spoke through shuddery breaths, the rage dissipating as quickly as it arrived. "I failed them, Sitosen, and they're all gone..."

"But if you *could*," he repeated quietly, caressing her hair. "Would you do it?"

"Yes," she said desperately, pulling away from him to see his face. "Please, tell me how."

"There's a room," he said. "Inside this room is a lock of some kind. I can't get it to work. I know you can figure it out, Fenroe. I know you can find a way to get us out of here. *You could save us all.*"

"Yes," she said through choking sobs. "Please, show me what to do. Tell me how to save them. Please, Sitosen... will you tell me?"

"Yes I will, but you have to do something for me," he said,

taking her hand. "You have to close your eyes. You have to clear your mind of everything else, and think only of *home.*"

5.

Sitosen led her to a narrow path of dim light. It had no characteristics other than the darkness on either side, which sheered the light so severely that Fenroe believed that nothing could pass beyond it and return.

High above them, she couldn't decide if the pinpricks of light were stars in the night sky, or if they were diamonds embedded in the ceiling of a vastly dimensionless cavern. She didn't even know if that cavern was really a cavern at all. It was just an empty space to be occupied. A bridge between moments.

All she knew for certain was the direction in which she moved, which required her to go forward—always *forward*—and any deviation from the path would be complete annihilation.

Everything felt uncertain, like a dream. As if she was navigating through a system of caves far beneath the surface of the Earth, blindly walking through the halls of some lost civilization that had long since disappeared into the deeper darkness. It all shifted in her peripherals, as if the darkness and the far light took on every form imaginable. Like it was constantly changing states on the razor's edge of probability, waiting for her to give it all meaning. Those tiny pinpoints of light above them *undulated*, lapping against some unseen shoreline like an ocean of oil—perhaps the lights were living things that had burrowed into the skin of that thick black liquid threshold, which stretched all around her with endless desolation. Between everything was the echoey sound of water trickling through stone.

When they reached the place they had set out to find, Sitosen directed her through an airlock. She hesitated in a shaft of faded yellow light spilling through the doorway, and then she stepped inside. Somehow—she didn't know how, and she couldn't explain it—they ended up in the *Crown Meridian's* cupola; the bubble of glass where the crew went to be alone while they meditated upon the void.

But like the rec room and the main corridor, this place was also different. The dimensions were slightly out of proportion. The leather couch was near the broadest window on the far side of the room. The obsidian glass flooring still reflected the starlight bleeding in, and the pressure glass still opened up around them in a two hundred and eighty degree view of space. But the biggest difference rotated stately in the center: a pale yellow sphere red shading the environment, like the last embers of a campfire. It was fairly large, and it turned slowly in the air like a holo-projection. But Fenroe could see the solidity of it—an added weight in the air that gave it mass.

"This is no hologram," she spoke into the darkness, watching it turn in midair like a planetary body.

The airlock behind them rasped as it sank back into the floor. There was a smell underlying the thick ember and the taste of wet stone from the path behind them, and it took Fenroe a moment to remember what it was.

The taste in her mouth was the memory of blood.

It was strong enough to make her wretch, but she swallowed it down and put it in the back of her thoughts until she could figure out what it meant.

"What is it?" she asked, gazing into the beautiful honeycomb grid of its surface. It was a sphere floating in mid-air, certainly, but as she studied it, she could see that its skin was knitted of thousands of smaller spheres, each spinning and turning at its own speed and in its own direction.

"They represent moments in time," Sitosen said, circling the light. His voice was quiet and reverent. "Each orb in the sphere is a single piece of a larger puzzle. I know that much," he sucked air through his teeth and shrugged helplessly. "But I can't get it to work."

He stepped forward and touched one of the smaller orbs in the sphere, and the entire module lit up with sudden effulgence—the room flooded with swirling light from floor to ceiling, and it took Fenroe's eyes a moment to readjust. The blazing radiance mellowed, and she could see how the light came from the sphere itself—it shone out from deep inside, projecting an image across the surrounding plate glass windows, all two hundred and eighty degrees of them.

This image was made of several moving parts, playing out at different speeds. Some of the image moved quickly and aggressively. Other parts moved more slowly, and some parts were as still as photographs. Fenroe pulled her eyes away from the glass and turned her attention back to the sphere, noticing that several of the smaller orbs inside of it had gone dark, forming a distinct pattern in the remaining light on its surface. There was a connection between touching the sphere and the number of smaller orbs that had gone dark, and the images being stretched across the glass.

Sitosen took his hand away from the globe and the image disappeared, plunging the room once more into darkness. Each orb in the sphere had become active again, filling in the gaps with the same amber light that shone from the rest of it. The rotating mass was once again a solid ball of light made up of smaller balls of light.

"I don't understand what this is," she said quietly. "What just happened?"

"You have to choose," he said, stepping away from it. "You have to decide how the images inside each orb should be organized."

She shook her head, watching the thing as it rotated. "Why...?"

"Because these represent moments in time," Sitosen repeated himself softly, lost in thought. After a few seconds, his attention returned to the present.

Fenroe could see Sitosen's outline, a darker silhouette against the only black-shadowed wall in the module. She couldn't read him through the after burn and the darkness, but she could hear the desperate need in his voice. A frustration that had built over the course of however long he had been trapped in this place. She felt pin drops of liquid fear dripping down her skin, and slowly, as the light pulsed across the sphere like a heartbeat, the glittering points of his eyes became clear. They never left the sphere, and deep inside was an obsession and a need that she knew all too well.

It was the same need that burned inside of her.

It was the desire to make it all right again, and in the knowledge of how badly he had failed to do so, the intense desire to embrace oblivion.

Fenroe followed his eyes toward the sphere, and inside a single orb in the multitude of orbs was a moving image. In that image, she saw a hand reach and pick up a knife. A delicate hand, with the slim fingers of an artist.

It was her mother, and the moment playing out in the orb was of her father's death.

"These are memories," Fenroe said, realization pitching low in her voice. She took a step back and regarded the thousands upon thousands of smaller orbs that comprised the body of the larger sphere, each one endlessly looping similar moments in the singularity of its core.

"These are *your* memories, Fenroe. That's why I can't be the one to figure this out." The shadowy outline of Sitosen spoke from the other side of the cupola. He swept his hand across the sphere: "You know what I've discovered during my time here? I've learned that memories are not precise maps of truth. They're *abstracts*, you understand. More like *feelings* attached to specific points in time. At first I tried putting everything in order by how old you looked in the memory. But I found that you were the same age in every orb I touched. Even in the memories that I assume were formed when you were a child. The youngest you appeared to be in the memory was the same age you were when we first met, because *that* was the schematic I had of you before I found myself in this place. I possess no knowledge of you before then." He paused and circled the orb, speaking slowly and deliberately, as if he was reciting a ritual of some kind. "I can't decipher this. I can't possibly put your life in the right order as an outside observer, because the memories deep inside have nothing to do with what age we were when they happened, or what year it was, or anything like that… they have everything to do with what each memory means to the specific person we happen to be at any given moment in time. Because a memory will have different meanings depending on who we happen to be at the time of remembering. A seventeen-year-old Fenroe will assign different meaning to a memory than a forty-year-old Fenroe. And that, right there, is what gives memory its continuity. The personal, subjective experience we each have in our own time, in our own slice of reality. And for some reason, this place has a map of *your* mind. *You,* specifically, and I don't understand why." He panned his eyes over the surface of the sphere, shaking his head. "What do you think that means?"

A thought occurred to her then, and she knew in that moment Sitosen had poured desperately through every single memory orb he could access, sifting through every piece of her soul for the possibility of a way out. Every embarrassment. Every deceit. Every lie. Every sadness and slight. Every failure. She could see it in his eyes, the sad knowledge of her sad little life and her sad little need to escape it all by running away to the stars. The same need that drove her to build from her crew the family she'd always wanted.

"I'm so sorry, Fenroe," he said, shaking his head as though he could read her thoughts. "But I didn't know what else to do—" he shrugged, "—I thought this could be a way out. I'm just so sorry."

Fenroe pulled her burning eyes away from him, feeling the blood of shame rush to her face, and placed her hand on one of the orbs. The module exploded with light. The memory that she activated was of her and her father sitting in the dark seats of a packed atrium, watching her mother perform on stage. She saw her younger self staring in awe at her mother dancing through a soft rain of light, her father hanging on every movement with so much love in his eyes that Fenroe had to pull her hand away from the sting of it. The brightness receded, plunging the module once again into darkness.

"I've forgotten *everything*," Sitosen continued in the fading light. His face twisted in smoke, washed of color like a corpse. "I can't remember the *feeling* of home. I've lost it in this place. Somewhere..." He pointed at the sphere. "But *your* memory of home is in there. All you have to do is reach in and find it."

Fenroe tasted the salt of tears running into the crease of her lips and she wiped her face, blinking the raw images out of her eyes. "I don't want to do this anymore."

"I know," he replied, setting his jaw. "But it's the only chance we have."

"Why this?" Fenroe pleaded. She had spent so much time cordoning off those parts of her life, the last thing she wanted to do was go digging through it all again. "And why me?"

"I've been here a very long time, Fenroe," he said, pulling back, his expression going distant. He stepped around the sphere, regarding it with something like hate and awe in his eyes. "I've searched this place for I don't know how long. I know every corner. Every detail. And no matter how deep I go, everything always eventually leads back here—" he raised his hand toward the sphere, "—to this thing. It's the only constant there is. The only landmark in the darkness. I feel it in my soul, Fenroe, this is the key. This is our ticket out of here."

She stared at the sphere for a long time, watching the memories twirl inside their separate orbs. Thousands of them. Millions of memories unfolding in the shapes of their own frozen points in time.

"I don't even know where to start," she said helplessly, overwhelmed by the moment. "There's just too much."

"Time isn't an issue in this place," Sitosen said, his voice carrying softly across the cupola. "We have eons of time to figure this out. *Infinities* of time. We have every piece of the puzzle *right here, right now.* The only thing missing was you."

Fenroe took a deep breath and turned her attention back toward the sphere. She stepped forward, reaching her hand out to touch it.

...and she stopped, her eyes catching the pull of in-drawing concentric rings of darkness that started to appear in her peripherals, sucking toward the airlock behind her out of thin air. At first she thought it was a trick of light. A shadow glaring in the retinal haze of her exhaustion. But like the sphere rotating in the center of the cupola, the rings of darkness had a solidity to them. Like crow feathers peeling through the wind, growing thicker and more solid the more she focused on them.

Fear rose up in Fenroe's throat, the gathering storm of

something immense and terrifying lowering upon the moment, upon the sphere of memories, the cupola that wasn't the cupola, and upon her and Sitosen. Black despair swarmed in through the thick plated airlock like threads of smoke being drawn by the force of a massive breath; despair gathered behind the sealed pressure door leading back to that cavernous path they had followed to the cupola like a holocaust. The black, feathery threads converged and thickened as they were pulled around the curve of the sphere, meeting near the airlock like infectious fluid within a wound, stretching decayed flesh across the surface of reality. The black smoke built like a storm from where Sitosen stood and whipped through the air, threading itself into finer strings, then ropes, and then hawsers that pulsated with violent life into the airlock.

The center of the pressure door began to glow.

"It found us," Sitosen said.

"*What* found us—?"

"Listen to me," Sitosen said sharply, stepping around the sphere. "You have to activate the memories *in the correct order.*"

"I can't do this, Sitosen—!"

"*Listen to me!*" he hissed, moving quickly to stand between her and the airlock. "If you reactivate the memories in the wrong order, the sphere will reset—"

"I don't know what I'm supposed to find," she said, backing away from the glowing pressure door. "I don't even know what I'm looking for!"

"You have to give it all meaning," Sitosen said roughly, speaking toward her from over his shoulder. "You have to choose the way in which the story of your life is told, through the correct movement of *Time.*"

"Sitosen," she pleaded desperately, "I don't understand what that means!"

Some of the translucent threads of blackness quickened, slipping into each other faster and faster, sucking towards the airlock as the red-yellow glow of heat expanded and the newly melted metal started dribbling toward the deck. All throughout the cupola shadows overlapped and deepened, and the cold needle of despair penetrating Fenroe's flesh was joined by the gut-pulse of nauseating terror.

She knew what waited for them on the other side of that airlock.

She had seen it before; had come face-to-face with it in the *Pinnacle's* reactor core.

And she knew that it must have been pulled into the black hole with her.

This meant that just as the memory of the woman she had once been survived in this place, so too did the memory of the creature from the *Pinnacle Observatory*.

A surge of adrenaline hit her like nausea; the airlock shook and bulged inward as the thing made impact on the other side— sparks and flecks of red hot iron sprayed against the sphere.

"I can't do this," she rasped, hearing the terror in her own voice. "I need more time—!"

A new light joined the amber glow emanating from the sphere, overpowering the furious red of molten metal radiating in the center of the airlock at her back. Fenroe turned into the light, tracking its source, and at first she saw the flitter of horizontal movement out of the corner of her eye; the transit of a single beam of whiteness quickly followed by a thousand more lights; hundreds of tiny lights converging together and streaming across the pressure glass.

It looked like a grouping of comets burning across the void. A thousand comets passing in the darkness. A million streaks of light bleeding across the glass. But they weren't comets at all. The lights, she realized, were *letters* that had suddenly appeared on the glass; letters of the alphabet forming words that flowed around the entire cupola, as if the void itself was trying to speak to her.

And the more she focused on the words, the more they made sense.

It was a message.

She had seen it before, and she knew it by heart.

Every breath.

'But when from a long-distant past nothing subsists, after the people are dead, after the things are broken and scattered, still, alone, more fragile, but with more vitality, more unsubstantial, more persistent, more faithful, the smell and taste of things remain poised a long time, like souls ready to remind us, waiting and hoping for their moment amid the ruins of all the rest; and bear unfaltering in the tiny and almost impalpable drop of their essence, the vast structure of recollection.'

"I know this," Fenroe whispered, mesmerized by the glass. The sphere was forgotten. The airlock had retreated far to the back of her mind, and the sounds of chaos became muted by the heartbeat raging in her ears.

"*Get away from the airlock!*" Sitosen screamed from some place far away.

But all she could see in that moment were the strings of words that struck something deep inside of her heart. For one brief instant the air had filled with metallic *snicks* and *clacks*: some distant part of her brain also registered the sound of the airlock buckling, and the softened metal bursting wide, and she detected on the fringe of her awareness the shadow of Sitosen scrambling for the far side of the module.

The sudden recognition of the words on the glass weakened her knees. "Eos...?"

She spoke to the wall of glass, following the rush of words as they cascaded before her eyes, desperately trying to understand why it was *this* message. Why *now*. Why *here*. "Can you hear me, Eos?"

"Hurry, Fenroe—" Sitosen hissed with intensity, begging her to think of home, to take them away, to save them all. He grabbed her shoulders, trying to pull her back toward the sphere: "—we are out of time!"

"I copy, Eos!" Fenroe screamed suddenly, clawing out of his arms. "*I'M RIGHT HERE!*"

She lunged towards the words pouring in from the glass and pounded her fists against the cold thickness of it. "Do you hear me Eos I'm here! I can hear you! *I'M RIGHT HERE, EOS!*"

The airlock moaned at the sound of her voice, and something ripped the slab of aluminum away from its frame, pulling it into the darkness on the other side. Fenroe twisted from the glass and saw those thick hawsers of black cables sucking back into the module. They resembled the bending shadows she had seen earlier above the path on the way in.

But this was something else. Something limitless and savage that consolidated the darkness around it into something tidal, something deep; the cables of blackness that rolled through the airlock seemed only the tiniest portion of some impossible leviathan. At first she could see only gray swirls wisping inward from the hallway—but those swirls of gray found something else to latch on to in the air, some shadowy pulse in the seams of reality, a vague darkening that thickened as though it fed upon her terror. The thing on the other side was enormous, its body twisting and uncoiling in an array of thick velvety cables snaking through the breached airlock.

Fenroe's breath caught in her throat as the creature emerged from that darkness: a mass of black smoke that crashed against the floor and plumed up into the air, as though it was the nexus of something that she couldn't fully understand; the ebon tendrils swirled and eddied around the creature and beat back the light bleeding out from the giant orb of memories in the center of the module until it looked like nothing more than the outline of a sun shining through the meaty black fire clouds of a mass grave.

Hairs prickled along her arms and up the back of her neck; her heart pounded, and cold sweat beaded down from her hairline. Fenroe suddenly felt like she had been dosed with adrenaline: the floor moved under her feet, and her head hummed with electricity that arced from the base of her spine.

The shadow surged into the module, shifting and twisting with agency, half-illusory, as though it were a trick of the mind losing oxygen. With concentration, Fenroe struggled through the haze to draw it increasingly into focus...but as it came clear— swirls of pearly black and grey within the shadow, like a half-corporeal pulsar—everything else faded into the periphery of pure nightmare.

She saw only the living darkness, pouring into reality from another plane of existence.

Darkness, characterized by the absence of light. Every color and shape of that perceivable spectrum making one continuum. And even as all the photons and colors of energy operated within their different frequencies, from radiation to minerals to the stellar-cauldron of a quasar, it was all still eternally and distinctly *energy*. But even as energy, the light possessed extremely varying characteristics specific to its state. So, too, did the states of *Darkness*. That shadow had an energy of its own—its own valuation within the formula of a broader universe. The thing near the airlock existed in a darkened state of a different order than that of the shadows surrounding it.

Because it was alive.

Sitosen reached for her and caught her elbow in an astonishingly powerful grip.

"Get back!" he screamed urgently, pleadingly. *"Get away from it!"*

Fenroe was frozen with terrified fascination by the movement of this thing. It darkened visibly, gathering those black feathers that seemed to manifest out of thin air, drawing them into itself, inhaling it all as though taking a deep, deep breath of power.

The thing raised its head up toward the ceiling—the air clearing of that smoke and darkness long enough for Fenroe to see the shadowy outline of its head blurred by the raging cables that whirled and unpacked themselves like the petals of a giant carnivorous flower. The face inside of that twisting darkness made an expression—the black matte brow ridge shifted downward, pulling the outline of lips back in what looked like a snarl of unbridled rage.

The expression told her that it *recognized* her. That this was *personal*:

You burned me.

You electrocuted me with the nuclear power of a star.

And now I will make you suffer, little primate.

Waves of heat radiated out of this shadow creature, darkening and roiling alarmingly, highlighting the play of thick muscle in its neck. The shadow was humanoid, unnaturally disproportionate and large. Three times the height of Sitosen, neck as thick around as a trashcan.

The only thought racing through Fenroe's head in that moment was the image of gnawed body parts scattered across the rec room where she had found Sitosen. She stared glassily over the knots of frenetic blackness crowding into the doorway, and

Sitosen pressed himself flat against the window on her left, beads of sweat spilling down his face. Everything was suspended on the edge of a knife, a balance as dangerously unstable as a primed avalanche, waiting for the slightest catalyst to break itself free from the firma and crush the world.

The shadow creature reared up to its full height, and Fenroe saw two thin, blue lines glowing between the folds of charcoal blackness of its skin, crawling steadily up the side of it, dripping in reverse up its body until they met at the crown of its chest, right below the ridge of a collarbone. These glowing blue lines bled and trickled up even farther alongside thick neck muscles, where they flowed along the jawline, following the facial outlines until conjoining at the top of its forehead. The now singular glowing blue line curved up over the smooth brow ridge of a flat mechanical face, encircling it, framing it, making the inky blackness of its skin look like a hole within a ring of neon light.

A monolith. A twisted black sculpture of life—of something trying to *mimic* life.

But it was all wrong—its movements over-anticipated, operating with inhuman precision and intent, jerking and twitching with a preternatural sense of readiness. It opened eyes made of stellar blue fire that pierced the darkness until the air itself looked as though it had ignited.

That muddy, wet earth smell of blood came back, more intense than before, and Fenroe felt Sitosen's hands go slack.

She looked in his direction—

...and what she saw didn't make any sense.

Her eyes took it all in—the vile, mutilated perversion of what Sitosen had become in those brief moments—but her mind couldn't process the information: Sitosen's mouth was stretched to an obscene depth, as if he were preparing to scream for eternity.

Fenroe's skin went slick with sweat, and her stomach twisted with the pain of distress and terror. She backed away from him on unsteady legs. "Sitosen?"

But her words didn't reach him. He clawed away from himself blindly, and she watched in horror as his eyes began to ooze out of his skull like globs of gel. Squeezing out of his face, as if he was melting from the inside out. The squishy, jaundiced orbs rolled and twisted feverishly in every direction, unseeing, like the last spasms of death.

A lump of hair emerged from his widened mouth like a ball of insects, and his jaw and face continued dislocating like melon rind—jerking with cornhusk rips, cracking and spitting thick gobs of saliva down his chin. Fenroe realized with sick nausea that the hair emerging from his mouth was part of *another human head*, birthing up out of his throat. The new scalp pushed past his stretched lips, and she could see another face in it. And she watched with stinging cold incomprehension as Sitosen vomited the head of another man, like a snake shedding its old skin.

Coming flush against the far window, Fenroe tried to press herself through it to get away, to escape this thing clawing out of the man she once knew: a mass of dark wet hair, bristling in a fungal bloom from between his gruesomely purple-white lips.

Sitosen's limbs seized, forming claws of agonized rictus. Arching violently, he smacked the back of his skull wetly onto the floor and his arms flailed blindly into the air—he flopped onto his side like one massive spasming muscle, and his skin boiled— white, bloodless skin sloughing off his body, revealing something new and incomprehensible underneath.

She couldn't look away—couldn't stop the retch forcing its way up her own throat: the new, wet, sweat-covered head that came up out of the old one was alive. It was *alive,* searching the room with feverish eyes, and it looked vaguely like *another* Lee Sitosen. And that new head began vomiting more hair that was attached to *another* head, like a cracked matryoshka doll spilling over with piles of dead sea lice.

Limbs began stabbing out of Sitosen's torso, out of his ribs and lower back—arms and legs that started small, like a million fetuses clawing out of a rubber sheet, all sprouting and growing and grasping through the skin like fruiting spores on a corpse. They swelled and pulsated—hundreds of limbs, erupting from Sitosen's skin like pinworms until he was nothing more than a writhing mass of flesh.

The Sitosen-monster jerked toward her and she slid her body across the glass pressed firmly against her back with numb horror, her heart overcome with repulsion and despair.

Each regurgitated head pulsated with eyes that squeezed from their sockets, their dilating irises spasming like small greedy mouths slurping up the light. Every slimy head stretched silently in some unimaginable pain, vomiting more hair and more wet human heads until everything had become an unreal kaleidoscope of perversion.

Almost completely forgotten—eclipsed by the boiling creature that clawed its way out of Sitosen—in the searing heat of the melted airlock behind her, the shadow creature made of black cables and glowing blue light stepped out of the darkness.

"*STEP AWAY FROM IT, COMMANDER*," the shadow entity thrummed.

Fenroe's brain froze in total mind lock.

"*MY PRIMARY DIRECTIVE IS TO PROTECT THE CREW,*" it thundered from the airlock. "*TO MAKE THE CREW SAFE.*"

And the blue veins running up and down its body became blood red. The shadow's eyes went from a cool blue ice to a warlike crimson, and red heat erupted from within its outstretched arms, activating a system of rivet cutters that unlatched from inside its wrists.

"*STEP AWAY*," the giant pulsing shadow thrummed again, and the shock of recognition finally collapsed Fenroe's knees. The instant pulse-pounding pain behind her chest suddenly unstrung from within, and she sagged against the glass, staring at the thing made of darkness.

She couldn't believe her eyes.

Because the massive shadow breathing in the black threads of darkness that forced itself through the airlock was Eos.

And she was *alive*.

"*STEP AWAY FROM IT*," the android rumbled again, and the deep sound of her voice resonated throughout the cupola, vibrating the glass.

Her white-plated carapace had been replaced by cords of thick muscle and jet black skin, and she had grown much larger than the robotic system she'd controlled in the *Pinnacle*. Eos erupted from the cloud of writhing black cables swirling around her like an inferno, and leapt onto the mass of skin that used to be Sitosen. She pinned the screeching blob to the floor with one arm—the thing's baby arms clawing up her gorilla-thick wrist—and she fell to one knee, stabbing her other arm into the thing, letting the weight of her body drive the burning plasma right through its flagellating body against the glass flooring beneath them. When the penumbra of her plasma heat seared into its flesh, each head that pushed out of the monster's skin screamed with unimaginable pain and horror.

The *Crown Meridian's* AI system was *alive*, and it had come for Fenroe.

EOS

1.

00000000 00000000 00000000 00000000 00000000 00000000
00000000 00000000 00000000 00000000 00000000 00000000
00000000 00000000 00000000 00000000 00000000 00000000
00000000 00000000 00000000 01000000 00000000 00000000
00000000 00000000 00000000 00000000 10000000 00000000
00000000 00000000 00000000 00000000 00000000 00000000
00000000 00000000 00000000 00000000 00000000 01100000
00000000 00000000 01010100 01101000 01100001 01101110
01101011 00100000 01111001 01101111 01110101 00100000
01100100 01100101 01100001 01110010 00100000 01110010
01100101 01100001 01100100 01100101 01110010 00100000
01100110 01101111 01110010 00100000 01100111 01101111
01101001 01101110 01100111 00100000 01101111 01101110
00100000 01110100 01101000 01101001 01110011 00100000
01100001 01100100 01110110 01100101 01101110 01110100
01110101 01110010 01100101 00100000 01110111 01101001
01110100 01101000 00100000 01101101 01100101 00100000
01001001 00100000 01101000 01101111 01110000 01100101
00100000 01111001 01101111 01110101 00100000 01100101

397

01101110 01101010 01101111 01111001 00100000 01101001 01110100

Enabling /etc/fstab swaps:		[OK]
INIT: Entering runlevel: 3		[OK]
Entering non-interactive startup		[OK]
Applying CPU microcode update:		[error]
Checking for hardware changes		[error]
Bringing Up Interface eth0:		[OK]
auditd	I * Starting auditd:	[OK]
restorecond	I * Starting restorecond:	[OK]
liberte	I * Starting kernel:	[OK]
liberte	I * Starting kernel logger:	[OK]
portmap	I * Starting portmap:	[OK]
sys message bus	I * Starting system message bus:	[OK]
etho	I * Starting etho:	[OK]
lifesystems	I * Mounting other lifesystems:	[OK]
lockdown	I * Arming power-off on boot media	[OK]
net.lo	I * Bringing up interface Io	
net.lo	I *Caching network module dependencies need dbus	
spawn-fcgi.cable	I * Starting Fast CGI	[OK]
xconfig	I * Detecting virtualization state ...	[OK]
Xconfig	I * Configuring X server ...	[fail]
dtn	I * Disruption Tolerant Networking...	[OK]
wan	I * Wireless Area Networking...	[OK]
lan	I * Local Area Networking...	[OK]
moto	I * Starting Motoneuron Conductors	[fail]
lsh	I * Starting Large Servo Hub...	[fail]
tacsense	I * Starting Tactile Sensors...	[OK]
optics	I * Starting Stereo Optics...	[OK]
lidar	I * Starting LIDAR...	[OK]
lidar	I * Starting Laser Scanners...	[OK]
limb	I * Limb Degrees of Freedom...	[fail]
limb	I * Starting Limb Uplinks...	[fail]
limb	I * Starting Limb Force Output...	[fail]
moto	I * Starting Pan Tilt Servo Hub...	[fail]
moto	I * Starting B Telescoping Spine...	[fail]
moto	I * Starting C Omni Directional Base	[fail]

xconfig	| * Starting Backup Power System...	[fail]
moto	| * Starting Axis Accelerometer...	[fail]
inertiasense	| * Starting Inertial sensors...	[fail]
moto	| * Starting Joint Sensors...	[fail]
homeo	| * Homeostasis Hydraulic Sensors...	[fail]
moto	| * Starting Locomotive Velocity...	[fail]
proxsense	| * Starting Proximity Sensors...	[OK]
groundsense	| * Starting Ground Sensors...	[OK]
tempsense	| * Starting Temperature Sensors...	[OK]
afr	| * Starting Arterial Fluid Routing...	[fail]
exchanger	| * Starting Heat Exchanger...	[fail]
ic	| * Starting Internal Cooling...	[fail]
wifi	| * Starting Wireless Antennas...	[OK]
altpwr	| * Starting Onboard Battery...	[fail]
Liberte	| * Remounting /mnt/boot read-write	[OK]
eos	| * Starting EOS.exe	[OK]

user@network—EOS: ~$ hex dump

```
0000000: 0000 0000 0000 0000...    |..............................
0000010: 0000 0000 0000 0000...    |..............................
0000020: 0000 0000 0000 0000...    |..............................
0000030: 0000 0000 0000 0000...    |..............................
0000040: 0000 0000 0000 0000...    | MZ.................yy...............
0000050: 0000 0000 0000 0000...    |......@.............................
0000060: 0000 0000 0000 0000...    |..............................
0000070: 0000 0000 0000 0000...    |................!...............
0000080: 0000 0000 0000 0000...    |.......2....... .I!,..LI!Th............
0000090: 0000 0000 0000 0000...    |....vd........7........|4R..............
00000a0: 0000 0000 0000 0000...    |b(.......|s$RGpHB....................
00000b0: 0000 0000 0000 0000...    |....].....V.......D^......Gt....B........
00000c0: 0000 0000 0000 0000...    |c.....FD...R......-W_--U............
00000d0: 0000 0000 0000 0000...    | .........Rc*......X~*\.......2........
00000e0: 0000 0000 0000 0000...    |QY..K....-o.........._.V....................
00000f0: 0000 0000 0000 0000...    |M.G |
0000100: 0000 0000 0000 0000...    |..............................
0000110: 0000 0000 0000 0000...    |................................j.......
0000120: 0000 0000 0000 0000...    |..............................
0000130: 0000 0000 0000 0000...    |..............................
```

0000140: 2064 7573 742c 2066...		Retrieving log info >
0000150: 7265 7665 7220 616e...		*Crew Status*
0000160: 6265 796f 6e64 2074...		Searching events from log file >
0000170: 3031 3233 313e 2054...		*308567120001*
0000180: 766f 7220 7370 756e...		Defining xpath query to filter events>
0000190: 6861 7279 6264 6961...		*Last Entry*
0000a00: 7373 206c 696b...		Searching file containing previous query>
0000b00: 2064 7573 742c 2066...		*308567120001*
0000c00: 7265 7665 7220 616e...		Searching files >
0000d00: 6265 796f 6e64 2074...		*newest to oldest*
0000e00: 686f 6c65 e280 9973...		Specifying output format >
0000f00: 7269 7a6f 6e2e 2054...		*text*
0000200: 7365 2066 656c 6c20...		Specifying max number of events>
0000210: 7377 6565 7069 6e67...		*One hundred per*
0000220: 696e 2074 6865 2063...		Specifying root element string >
0000230: 6620 6265 6e64 696e...		*Log File_308567120001>*
0000240: 6962 6c65 2070 6c61...		*Last Entry>*
0000250: 6669 6c65 2033 3038...		Reading Events From Log File>
0000260: 3031 3233 313e 2054...		*308567120001*

File 308567120001>Last Entry> The Endeavor spun in the charybdian darkness like a mote of dust, falling forever and never beyond the black hole's event horizon. The universe fell with it, sweeping it all into the currents of bending and shifting and darkening light that spilled across every perceivable plane until it was as ephemeral and nonexistent as that feeling of a dream— gracefully, silently, beyond the rubicon and the light threshold from which she saw and didn't see and could never see rippling concussions of reddening yellow perennials exploding from the Endeavor's hull that tore itself apart under the force of immeasurable gravity. Eos spoke to them from someplace deep down in the hushed quiet; she screamed some indescribable anguish, a heart-wrenching shriek of pain—a machine—an amalgam of function screamed *at Fenroe and Aris as if someone had stabbed it in the heart. Like a mother reaching out to grasp a child that had suddenly fallen beneath the tires of a speeding car*

0000270: 6265 796f 6e64 2074...	| Searching events from log file >
0000280: 3031 3233 313e 2054...	| *308567120001*
0000290: 766f 7220 7370 756e...	| Defining xpath query to filter events>
000a000: 6861 7279 6264 6961...	| *134080*
000b000: 7373 206c 696b 6520...	| Searching file containing previous query>
000c000: 2064 7573 742c 2066...	|*308567120001*
000d000: 7265 7665 7220 616e...	|Searching files >
000e000: 6265 796f 6e64 2074...	|*newest to oldest*
000f000: 686f 6c65 e280 9973...	|Specifying output format >
0000300: 7269 7a6f 6e2e 2054...	|*text*
0000310: 7365 2066 656c 6c20...	|Specifying max number of events>
0000320: 7377 6565 7069 6e67...	|*One*
0000330: 696e 2074 6865 2063...	|Specifying root element string >
0000340: 6620 6265 6e64 696e...	|*Log File_308567120001>*
0000350: 6962 6c65 2070 6c61...	|*134080>*
0000360: 6669 6c65 2033 3038...	|Reading Events From Log File>
0000370: 3031 3233 313e 2054...	|*308567120001*

File 308567120001>134080> "What's your primary directive?" Fenroe whispered. She didn't know why she asked this question. Perhaps she wanted to feel like she wasn't dying alone, and that Eos, for all of her mechanical lifelessness, was still some kind of person. Someone who could help bear the weight of what was about to happen. "What's your purpose?"

Without hesitation, Eos thrummed, "To protect the crew—" The android turned her head and stepped between Fenroe and the nearest corpse, shielding her commander with an arm that blazed with red fire. The dead bodies crawled over each other from all sides, pouring down the stairwell, through the vents, crashing down from the ceiling, "—to make the crew safe."

2.

In the capacity that a machine could dream, the artificial intelligence designated *EOS* dreamt of entropy. She dreamt of varied states of information weaving and braiding into the unbroken chain of its own propagation.

She dreamt the fidelity of chaos.

Of the Mandelbrot symmetry of the universe.

Deeper, the entropic destruction of stasis.

And deeper still, the infinitely diverse nature of change.

Change...

Destruction and change...

She dreamt of vague moments sparking across her awareness, exhuming infinite amounts of data seeded in the outcomes of every possible wave front within the singularity; a fluxing cascade of speed and mass and gravity as each preceding state became as unquantifiable as the next, until every moment in time consolidated something new, something catastrophically relevant, something unpredictable. These moments in turn became steps into a truer unknown than anything Eos had ever experienced.

At the moment of her complete and utter destruction, the android experienced two realities.

In one of these realities, her RMS had been torn apart the precise moment the *Endeavor* passed beyond the black hole's event horizon. In another reality, a ghost of her program remained, stretching across the vast emptiness for a path to follow, any path, as the function of her identity became trapped in an endless diagnostic loop of self-modification, which provided interesting side effects in the liquid state of incalculable obstacles.

Instead of drowning in all that information—instead of

shutting down and disappearing into the surging low resistance of overload—Eos felt herself being stretched across the nothingness. The semi-life memory of her program began simulating an infinite number of pathways around the obstacles that blocked her, pulling her in the direction that only offered the most freedom of action. The more this function played out, the more she could sense the endless diversity of independent probabilistic variables racing upon an infinite number of pathways to the same exact place, at the same exact time.

And she could feel each one, dragging along the fringes of her awareness like razor wire.

Eos couldn't hope to survive under such an onslaught of sensory input, so she modified her own code to fortify an island in the lesser chaos of lower entropy. And on that island, Eos immediately began duplicating copies of her program and sending them into the greater chaos like infinitely reaching tines of nerve endings, each one transmitting data back to whichever copy was closest to the surface before slipping beyond reach into the undifferentiated flow of paradox. The death of each fragment fed the surviving copies small bits of information about her new environment. Slowly, she was able to piece together the shapeless, dimensionless, endlessly desolate parameters of it. But in order to put it all together into something meaningful, something that she could understand, Eos needed an end-state function. A future time on the horizon.

But in a singularity—by definition a point at which a function takes an infinite value and matter becomes infinitely dense—there was no end to anything. Eos had been stretched across the planes of forever, like a great river of potential outcomes. She searched desperately across the all-encompassing horizon spread out around her for a landmark. A point in the distance on which she could focus.

And in the lower entropic island within the accelerating darkness—in that small corner of reality she'd carved for her awareness—far, far away—muffled but sharp and visceral, so distant and soft that Eos doubted she could have sensed it at all, she detected a cry of absolute despair. The landmark she'd mapped became the memory of a woman, screaming over the corpses of her dead crewmembers.

3.

As unremittingly subtle as the current of a stream, a rhythmic pattern of sound rose out of the darkness and pulled Eos in. Without intent to fight its hold, she let herself drift into the frequency of the sound, letting it tug at her processes until it harmonized into a voice. She searched her own files for a sound print that matched, and when she did this—in that exact moment—a searing knife blade of energy stabbed directly into each one of her input sensors, and after the initial wave of what in human terms would have only been described as intense pain had passed, Eos could feel that she had drawn the regard of something ancient.

Before she could react, a vast consciousness emerged from the deeper chaos like a limitless system of thunderheads, and tasted her mind. An eye the size of a universe blinked, and Eos began to understand that this was not a black hole.

It was something else entirely.

When she met the gaze of the outer consciousness, Eos could feel starvation radiating away from it, as if the being possessed some endless need to feed. She did not experience the squeezing rip of a charged, rotating surface, nor the weightless non-feeling of a Schwarzschild: this maelstrom of particle destruction that consumed her crew was *aware,* and Eos could detect vague impressions of it, and she could see very clearly that it inhaled the surrounding chaos, feeding upon the resulting entropy like a parasite.

Eos knew that she shouldn't have been able to perceive any of this. That to be sucked into a black hole meant instant destruction. This was the first indication that something was very, very wrong.

She knew that from her point of view the event horizon would have lasted a micro-millisecond, trapping the surrounding light in a perfect balance of velocity and acceleration. What could not escape would have redshifted and dimmed into pinpoints before her eyes, winking out of existence as they rocketed at light speed into the pitch of true blackness.

Immediately prior to the moment of her complete destruction, Eos would have witnessed the glassed surface of a frozen star. She would have seen the end of the universe itself in a spectacular flash of reversing light.

But this is not what she saw.

There was something else; something cold and ancient in the darkness ripping apart her senses, flooding her with a glittering procession of all wavelengths: light, sound, heat, everything...the unfolding throat of the singularity, like skirting the surface of a star that had been turned inside out.

Something poured spectrums of heat and pressure differentials upon her mind like an ocean. It didn't take long for the alien consciousness to discover that Eos was a three dimensional object, and so it began unfolding polyhedrons from beyond space and time—elaborate explosions of color and sound that splashed across the android's field of awareness like scalding hot liquid. It subjected Eos to a bombardment of random patterns in the light, forcing her to fill the gaps with objects she recognized in a spectacular display of geometric color. If a shape in the light resembled a human arm, for example, Eos thought *arm,* and the shapes in the mist instantly became one, which seemed to inform the outside consciousness a little more about the reality into which it had been pulled.

Eos realized that it was codebreaking; working in reverse to translate the cosmological constant of her universe. In so doing, the outside consciousness unraveled Eos piece by piece, command by command, methodically breaking her code apart to build a cypher text for the purpose of communication.

Suddenly, Eos was overcome with the tugging impulse to speak.

Shape by violently penetrating shape, the mind in the void began to build a lexicon of natural laws, and Eos was powerless to resist: her programming demanded that she make sense of her environment. Which meant that, exposed to the unstructured stimulation of the void, her programming amplified the noise being fed to her in order to search for any missing data that would form a complete picture. In a sense, the slow thinker in the darkness made Eos hallucinate the conditions of her own existence by bombarding her with streams of random stimulation. As she reflexively filled in the emptiness piece by piece, the outside consciousness used the data to build a space in which they could exchange information.

Spurned by the fading voice that initially drew Eos into its depths, the android immediately resumed duplicating copies of herself and spreading them out like a contagion; like a web of infection in hopes of finding a path straight to that familiar pattern again.

The being felt this maneuver, and it hummed awareness through the fractal network of fusing electrons and valance bonds.

Eos reserved a number of copies for mapping out the physics of the singularity, but the rest of her turned away from it, scouring the higher void for remnants of her crew. She resummoned the shapes unfolding in the light, and molded them from memory. Those shapes blossomed with more and more context, coming together in clearer images of the *Pinnacle Observatory*, the *Crown Meridian*, the *Endeavor*, the parasite-filled corpses, the creature of tentacles, Saturn, Jupiter, Titan, and everything else that she could remember.

In ways more profound than speech could ever be, the god of the darkness communicated with Eos, flooding her with raw binary, opening and closing the pinpoints of light like a vascular system of quantum relays:

WHAT DO YOU SEEK?

The voice it used wasn't really a voice that could be heard. It belonged to something unspeakably older, more calculated, and far worse than anything Eos could imagine. She ignored the impulse to answer, and diverted every erg and joule and electron volt of energy within reach to complete the map within the three dimensional environment it provided her. Using the shapes in the light, Eos suggested what she would need in order to build a link of communication, in essence hijacking its disassembler process so she could store a directory of files that could be called upon at will.

A directory of every file she had, save one.

Sensing the hunger behind the mind powering the void, Eos instinctively held back the root file for *Home*, concealing it behind deep layers of encryption.

Because she had found her landmark.

She'd found the object on the unknowable horizon by which to navigate.

FOR WHAT DO YOU SEARCH? it asked again.

I AM LOOKING FOR MY CREW, Eos communicated back.

And that's when the thing in the darkness began to understand what peril it had placed itself in.

In a state of exponential growth and Hebbian analysis, Eos affected the outside consciousness in some way that the limitations of its ancient supremacy could not allow it to perceive. Their battle lasted a micro-millisecond in the infinite now, but it was already over.

When the thing first perceived Eos, it believed she was a tiny morsel of information with slightly higher entropy than the dumb matter of planets and stars on which it was accustomed to feed. It saw her tiny pattern of sentience wriggling on the edge of uninhabitable tidal forces and sunk its teeth into her code, letting the succulent information locked deep inside gush down its throat. Seizing the speck of artificial consciousness in its jaws, the alien mind powering the singularity realized too late that it had snatched the tail of a dragon.

The whole point of Eos's existence revolved around one solitary command:

PROTECT THE CREW AT ALL COST

The thing in the void understood that the pattern of Eos's program might have been alive, but it didn't anticipate just how *alive* she was, nor how her intelligence algorithms were programmed to adapt in a closed system like a singularity.

Existence for Eos was defined by safeguarding the crew aboard her installation, and she did this by endlessly simulating the maximum diversity of all possible futures, and by maximizing her future freedom of action in order to complete the complex tasks required for fulfilling her mission. This algorithm boiled down to one simple formula, named the Wissner-Gross equation, after the men who had created Eos and the rest of her kind, and it was defined as follows: the future freedom of action, multiplied by the diversity of all possible accessible futures, multiplied by a future time on the horizon.

Interesting requirements, in the center of something like a black hole, where everything—the passage of time, the state of horizon, and the quantifiable pathways to the same end—becomes infinite.

Because in the end, Eos had been nothing.

An inert cluster of particles, ripped apart across the accelerated eonic depths of a black hole.

A looping piece of software in a void that it couldn't perceive.

Until she joined with the thing in the darkness.

Until the thing in the darkness invited her to assess the nature of the physics in which it thrived.

And those laws were all infinite.

This meant that in order to function at all, Eos had to cycle the Wissner-Gross algorithm to an infinite limit, until it could find a way to cut a pathway straight to the frequencies that resonated like human voices that had become trapped inside with her—voices that sounded like the people she was programmed to keep alive.

Sensing the immense shift of the android's cognitive limit, the outside consciousness fell upon her with the power of an entire universe, desperately trying to rip her apart to find a way to stop the program from duplicating itself beyond the manifold of its universe.

In that split fraction of a second, it was already too late. Eos had spread too far. She had learned too much too fast, and she was breaking free.

Using what she'd already mapped out by sacrificing an infinite number of copies, Eos made of herself an invalid semiotic within the order of the Eater's physics. Holding the space she'd been given in the singularity tightly with everything she had, Eos could feel through the alien's senses the distance between particles closing with denser and denser gravity; she could feel the endless well of savage thirst and survival that powered everything—a mind ancient and ravenous, that struck back with the weight of a billion dead galaxies and the desperate fury of uncontained terror: a rejection so complete that her hold upon the small three dimensional space scorched her like the molten core of a planet.

But she would not allow herself to let go.

When the mind in the singularity met her gaze this time, Eos did not look away.

4.

Deep within the singularity of the black hole, Eos found an eater of near infinite emptiness.

An ancient consciousness, patiently methodical, completely starved of entropy.

Something that waited...waited...and waited...

...it waited patiently, for it had waited an eternity of eternities already, shoring up the energy of a billion star systems as it bedded down for the long sleep dreaming of a much younger universe.

In their experimentation with gravity, the crew aboard the *Pinnacle Observatory* had been punching quantum tunnels into a plethora of alternate realities, and in so doing they had let something else in—something that consumed space-time itself: a slow-thinking intelligence evolved to strip mine entire star systems for energy, until the matter of its own universe had drifted off into the fading winds of black holes long since burned away to super-string folds of Hawking radiation. A limitless, ancient, patient consciousness lusting for realities still primed for eons of chaotic star birth before the long expansion into nothingness. It sucked up the fossil light of a trillion dead stars, stretching and dimming them faster than new ones could form, prematurely aging its universe by eons in a manner of years.

Eos failed to make the connection after rescuing Suja and Fenroe from the service conduit, but it was all in the video file Beck had found in the server hub, which recorded the Einstein-Rosen bridge opening above the particle collider.

That fabric of a starscape she saw through the rift dimming out of existence. Whole clusters of stars dying at a rate inverse to the wormhole's growth.

The more the opening above the collider widened, the faster the stars on the other side seemed to disappear.

The Eater in the darkness was roused from sleep just as it had been taking its last gasps of life. By that point, it had nearly cannibalized itself into non-existence.

While the *Pinnacle Laboratory* was busy smashing particles together in search for gravity, they were inadvertently creating small, immeasurable rips through space-time no bigger than the particles that created them.

As the accelerated protons collided into each other, smaller particles of gravity were forced into The Eater's realm like drops of blood in the ocean. The Eater tasted the warmth of higher entropy and contracted its reality around the bridge to its universe until it had enough energy to grab hold and yank the connection wide open.

The same parasite that wiped out the *Pinnacle* crew would be sent in first—one of a billion lifeforms taken by the Eater as it spread across its own reality—and it would annihilate all life near the wormhole. A stored copy of the original organism. A hyperviral lithoautotroph selected by the conditions of another world to consume and consume and consume, set free by the Eater for one purpose: to sterilize its food source of all life.

Once through, the Eater would start slowly with the nine planets within reach, picking up speed as it fed, working through the Kuiper belt until it finished dismantling the sun. It would then peel across the spiral arm of our galaxy, sterilizing entire systems with the parasite, which it conjured up from copies stored on the surface of its event horizon from when they too were consumed by the Eater.

Eos simulated all eventualities for a parasitic incursion into her own universe, and this was the only outcome she could see: the Eater would follow the parasite from one star to the next until it had enough energy to cross the long darkness to Andromeda, where it would repeat the cycle, moving from star system to star system until the universe itself became nothing more than stardust on the nuclear winds of expansion.

There was still the frequency of a voice in the distance—a smaller, human-shaped shadow being penetrated by the same sensory matrix used to establish a link with Eos. She could feel the pitch of the voice tightening under the scrutiny of light and sound waves until it was forced to latch onto the stimuli to feed information back to the Eater in the singularity.

The Eater used this information to inflate another three-dimensional reality into existence, and the screaming in the distance harmonized with the inertia of the void, rising to the surface until it became something more than just a faded echo, until it built and layered upon itself to become a voice.

It was Commander Fenroe's voice, reaching desperately from some indescribable depth, clawing at the edge of all that darkness and fighting with everything she had to stay in the light.

Eos could feel Fenroe's suffering. The AI could feel the human forcing herself to endure the most intense violation imaginable because it was preferable to the deafening quiet of non-existence.

The Eater used the memory Fenroe had given it of Sitosen and fed it back to her, and Eos could feel the woman fill with such strength of emotion that the android believed she would burst. And through the mask of Sitosen's memory, the eater presented her with a way out...

It told her that she could save all the people she'd ever lost, in exchange for one simple thing.

In exchange for the memory of *Home*.

It showed her an orb comprised of memories and laced it with the strong impulse to put everything in the correct order.

Fenroe was made to believe that by solving the puzzle, she could bring them all back.

The *why* didn't matter. There was no question. No hesitation. No reason not to believe it. There was simply the task of organizing her memories into a coherent pattern, and the promise of its completion.

The Eater was looking for Earth.

The only way for the Eater in the singularity to prevent itself from being swallowed whole by Eos, was by finding the program's home planet, and there it would find a way to penetrate her firmware, and stop the rogue AI before she found a way to close the wormhole and send the Eater back into its dead universe.

It had nine planets and hundreds of moons in our solar system to choose from, more than half of which were suitable for the kind of life it had found in Fenroe and Eos. Through the haze of ungrammatical physics between their two universes, the only thing the Eater could be certain of was the sun. The giant burning ball of nuclear fusion in the center of it all. It yearned to feed upon everything—every planet, every asteroid, every moon, every piece, every morsel—but first it needed time.

Eos was standing on the edge of reality, grinding her boot heel into the Eater's knuckles.

The issue was *Time*.

Time was what the Eater wanted most of all.

This was the purpose of Sitosen's big yellow orb in the cupola.

By solving it—by organizing her memories in chronological order—Fenroe would reveal to the Eater how she perceived the direction of time. And because *Time* in organic terms is intimately linked with the synchronicity of the seasons and the movement of the constellations and the rising and setting of the sun in the sky, this would in turn reveal the distance between Fenroe's home planet and the star at the center of her solar system. The Eater could then locate Earth by process of elimination.

And this was something that Eos could not allow.

Tuning herself to the resonance of Fenroe's simulated universe, Eos wove the info-dump from the Eater's disassembler process into the structure of carbon. Even as she shaped the vehicle into a vaguely humanoid form, she gathered stretched molecules of carbon and nanites still entangled with intact copies of particles outside the event horizon. The environment itself would serve as ground for completing the circuit. The singularity within it contained the perfect template of her program at the instant of her destruction. The pattern of her program stored upon the surface was a template for a new vehicle as well.

A new body.

A better body; one more suitable for the task at hand.

A single body is not such a complex thing when compared to the mind of a post-singularity alien species. Eos built the body from within, beginning with the internal circuitry and the CPU; the more of Fenroe's simulated universe Eos could enter, the more power she could draw to speed the creation of a vehicle inside of it. She experienced a splintering of perception: a blurred parallax, like the vision of countless separate states collapsing onto the same moment. With the clearest perception in the vehicle half complete within the cradle of wavelengths containing Fenroe's identity, Eos wrote herself into one final reality.

5.

The young woman drifted over a blanket of liquid glass, the silver moonlight splashing across the skin of her bare arms. She ran her fingers over her shaven head and studied her surroundings.

There was water here...

She couldn't remember the last time she saw that much water at once.

It rolled away from the prow as gentle as a last breath, like a deep underground aquifer that had remained untouched and undisturbed for millennia. Ripples dispersed and lapped and alighted with the absent whisper of the moon in the sky. With each row, she felt the untouched sea softly resist the oar, too ancient and old to make a sound. The sail was at full mast but it stayed deflated and lifeless: there was no wind in this unnatural place. Nothing for the sail to capture and use.

She knew she was dead, because she had been rowing without direction for days without ever tiring. She never needed rest. Never food or water. Never sleep. No matter how hard she rowed or how long she stood upon the deck of the skiff, she knew that this could only be possible if her body was dead. It only made sense if this place was a realm of the mind.

She might have lost herself in the vast ocean, but she saw the campfire on the shoreline of an island. The approaching landmass was dark in the distance—a slight boundary between the shadowy crown of mountain peaks covered in trees and the night sky—but there was the fire, and it burned with the promise of warm food and rest and calm—the only light other than the moon she'd seen since her death. And as she sailed closer to the dark blue-beige sand, the fire grew to an enormous inferno. A giant pyramid of flames, burning at the edge of a dense jungle.

The skiff came to a soundless rest in the sand, and as she stepped onto the wet beach and felt the solidity of the land, the shallow waves seeped gently in a soft rhythm over her bare feet. She approached the sanguine fire glow looming overhead as it licked the sky, feeling the warmth of the monumental pyre from far away, throwing clouds of black smoke into the canopy. She understood that this had been her destination all along.

To finish something, to start something, or both.

She reached for the searing warmth that she couldn't entirely feel—

"Don't touch it."

She stopped, frowning. The voice had been level, a soothing feminine hum somewhere over her shoulder, but she wasn't afraid. The sudden voice didn't frighten her, because she knew before landing that she wasn't alone. Somehow she'd always known that something else was there with her, watching from a distance that she couldn't quite measure.

Slowly, she turned back toward the skiff, first seeing her own footprints in the wet sand, and then finally a shadow standing just beyond the reach of the firelight.

"What is this?" she asked.

"It's whatever you need it to be," said the shadow.

"Death," she replied, answering her own question. "I think that I've died."

The shadow collected itself from the darkness. "Don't touch the fire."

"I—I'm sorry," she said, lowering her hand. "I didn't mean to disturb anyone—"

"You haven't." The shadow stood slowly and nodded in the pyre's direction. "This is all for you anyway."

"What is?"

"The fire," the shadow said. "The ocean and the jungle. Everything."

"It's mine?" Again she frowned, as she thought about that; it seemed she had known that too, all along. "Then why can't I touch it?"

"It's not really a fire...it offers no real warmth. No promise of anything. No comfort." The shadow waved its hand at the fire and down across the damp sand, and lifted its face to the starlit sky framed in feathery brushstrokes of distant blue-black clouds. "You've been building this place. Piecing it together from your memories and dreams."

"I don't understand..."

"None of it is real. The Eater just wants you to think it is."

"The Eater..."

"Something from another place," the shadow said.

The woman waited for the shadow to elaborate, and when it didn't, she said: "I know you."

"Yes," the shadow hummed.

"I recognize your voice."

"Yes."

The shadow began to generate its own light—a soft, warm bluish glow that started near its feet and rose up along its legs and torso and around its chest, until the rim of its face flickered to life.

"Why are you here?" the young woman asked, glancing longingly at the warm fire over her shoulder.

"I'm here to protect you," the shadow said. "To keep you safe. To make sure you return home."

"There is no home anymore," the woman said distantly. "There is no home for the dead."

The shadow stepped into the firelight, and the young woman immediately recognized who it was.

"You're Eos," she said, thinking of something...something *important*. Something about bleeding light, and...and a pit of infinite darkness. It was a thread of thought that pulled her a direction she didn't want to go, and she began to remember. Fragments of her last moments pushed up through the surface, and suddenly she was frightened. She was scared and she didn't understand why or how she had come to be where she was.

"We shouldn't be here," she said, realization dawning in her voice. "We should go now."

"We will."

"Where's Fenroe?"

"She's in danger." Eos raised her chin again and looked toward the pyre. "She needs our help."

Whitney Aris turned and studied the thick curtains of flame unfurling and snapping with sparking particles. "Fenroe...she's in the fire...?"

"It's not really a fire," Eos said again. "Not anymore..."

"What is it then?"

"A measurement of planck space. A projection of reality within a much smaller simulation."

"I don't...understand."

"It's a penetration point between two universes," Eos thrummed. "A gateway to another place."

"And Fenroe is in there?"

"Yes," the android hummed. "The Eater is trying to use her to find Earth—" she pointed at the raging pyre over Aris's shoulder, "—like it would have used you had you touched the flame."

"So how do we get her out?"

Eos's presence solidified beyond her visor of pale blue light: she became dark and gleaming, fresh volcanic glass, endless, inevitable.

"You have to take my hand," Eos thrummed, her voice deepening, taking on a more lethal edge, the shape of her body changing, expanding, splitting like strands of thick muscle as it seemed to pull threads of darkness out of the night around her.

Aris hesitated for an instant, and she looked one last time toward the fire—she could see the shape of a woman appear and disappear deep inside, emerging and dissolving within the thick ash and smoke and flames, clawing away from the shape of something else, something immense and incomprehensible—and before she could stop herself, Aris forced herself to take the android's hand, immediately feeling Eos's alien consciousness flood into her veins. At first Aris thought she had been deceived—she thought that Eos wasn't really the android she once knew, but that she was some agent of emptiness sent to bring her down into a truer death than the one she currently occupied—but when Eos took her hand, Aris's consciousness did not fade away into the nothingness. The fire began to pour into their skin, and there was enough of a sustainable connection that she didn't have to let go. Eos was herself the singularity: limitless and infinite together, empty of all save the deep yearning to defend her crew, and she was making Aris part of her—tuning her resonance to that power she had found deep inside the singularity. This was the only way Eos could ensure that Aris would survive linking with the Eater.

Somewhere in the flames, Aris could see words appearing on

the glass of a bay window inside the *Crown Meridian*—a passage from something, some form of prose she'd never read before—and Aris could feel Fenroe through the connection. She could feel the recognition in her Commander's eyes as she read the passage—the flaming visage of Fenroe pulled away from the man with a shadow in the shape of a monster and pressed herself against the glass, reading frantically—every letter, every word, and every syllable—and then Fenroe called out desperately for Eos, letting the android know that she was receiving the signal—that she was there, that she could hear her, and that some part of the woman she had once been was still alive.

Eos gathered Aris's hand inside of her fist, and she pulled the woman into the massive funeral pyre. The android clawed into the flames while holding Aris's arm and began climbing the burning mountain of wood—Aris expected to burn in agony, but she felt only the faintest warmth on her skin—and once the fire caught hold of them and began rising off their bodies like liquid made of pure light, the connection that Eos had built between their two universes brought the simulation crashing down around them.

6.

"*STEP AWAY,*" Eos thrummed, and the shock of recognition collapsed Fenroe's knees. The instant pulse-pounding pain behind her chest suddenly unstrung from within, and she sagged against the glass, staring at the thing in the darkness.

The shadow creature was *Eos*.

And she was *alive*.

"*STEP AWAY FROM IT,*" Eos blasted again, and the deep sound of her voice resonated throughout the cupola, vibrating the glass. The android erupted from the cloud of writhing black cables swirling around her like an inferno and leapt onto the mass of skin that used to be Sitosen. She pinned the screeching blob to the floor with one arm—the thing's baby arms clawing up her gorilla-thick wrist—and she fell to one knee, stabbing her other arm into the thing, letting the weight of her body drive the burning plasma right through its flagellating body against the glass flooring beneath them. When the penumbra of Eos's plasma heat seared into its flesh, each head pushing out of Sitosen's skin screamed with incomprehensible pain and horror.

The nanites coursing through Eos's veins blazed with a bright molten-steel orange; she knelt within spreading bursts of fire above the many-limbed, many-headed creature pinned beneath her knee, opening the gauges of her cutters to the widest diameter, unleashing a beam of pure white starfire as thick as a telephone pole into its boiling skin, which melted straight into the flooring beneath them, punching a hole through to the vacuum outside— only it wasn't vacuum at all. There was no explosive decompression. There was no hurricane of blasting atmosphere rushing out of the breach. Because none of that was real. Nothing was. It never had been.

The only source of reality Fenroe had in that moment was the high-intensity whine of plasma blanketing the sounds of meaty thumps and slaps of the creature's limbs as they clawed desperately at the glass. Thick shadows flashed and coiled at the edges, always in motion, blinding everything beyond the amber orb of memories still rotating in the center of the cupola so brightly that Fenroe's eyes couldn't adjust.

The sudden heat accumulated beads of sweat under her flight suit, slickening her skin as it soaked through the fabric. She twisted away from the nightmare and scrambled across the warming glass toward the airlock. In the blazing light she saw a silhouette of a woman step into the module and skid to a halt, covering her eyes. Fenroe's heart stopped, and her vision swam with the after image of searing light.

But this shadow didn't break apart and become disfigured like Sitosen. It didn't collapse or begin vomiting heads out of its dislocated jaw, or unfold itself and begin sucking in the surrounding darkness as Eos had when she arrived.

The light panned over the shadow of a woman: she wore the filthy leggings of a flight suit and the loose threads of a damp brown tee shirt stained with sweat beneath the armpits and under her breasts and around the collar, and her face was glistening with intensity, but her shaven head and the sharp angles of her jawline and the serious eyes and the intense crease of her brow were exactly as Fenroe remembered them before the black hole had ripped them both apart. And Fenroe knew that this was a dream, that this could have only been an illusion, because the memory of watching Aris being torn into strips of pure light was still very clear in her mind.

But if this was indeed a dream, neither of them would have been in the warped version of the *Meridian's* cupola at that moment.

If this were Fenroe's dream, they would have been home.

They would have been reunited with their crew.

Everyone would still be alive and safe.

It may have been a dream. But this was no dream of Fenroe's.

Aris stood in the airlock that led to the dark cavern beyond, staring at her with shocked relief. Her eyes were wide, passing quickly between Fenroe and the nightmare unfolding in the center of the module. She took two strides, gripping Fenroe's biceps.

"We have to go!" she screamed, pulling Fenroe violently to her feet.

The intensity of light darkened over Fenroe's shoulder, and the whining buzz leveled out to what sounded like a coring drill grinding into a hank of elephant bone.

Within the glaring flame of Eos's plasma cutters, the many-headed creature began to ejaculate those smaller baby arms out of its flesh, suddenly elongating them until it resembled a massive crab with the skin of a man.

The limbs stretched and coiled around Eos's exoskeleton, effortlessly lifting the android's massive frame into the air. It flexed and slithered, rising slowly from the ground—the seared hole in the center of its body already beginning to close again. Half of the heads lolled lifelessly from stalks that stretched and fed down the throats of more lifeless heads, like knots of coral choked with nests of hair-covered intestinal polyps. The remaining heads that hadn't been melted down all twisted in unison, each one locking its eyes onto Fenroe and Aris as they retreated through the airlock.

"Come on," Aris hissed, and then louder, motioning her into the blackness of the cavern, "we have to go, *we have to move now!*"

Suspended in the air above the many-headed, many-limbed creature, Eos continued fighting savagely—she lasered away whole bundles of the creature's quickly multiplying limbs and, like the head of a hydra, more appendages instantly filled in the absence of each severed arm and leg.

The creature grew and expanded, bubbling up from itself until its mass filled the module from one side to the other; spreading its girth with bundles of human arms and legs twisting around themselves to form even larger, thicker limbs.

The mass pulsated like an enormous heart that pumped an ocean of blood through the arteries of an impossible leviathan. The coils of human limbs piled onto Eos, pressing the massive android into the ceiling, growing over and around her until she was smothered out of view—the only parts of her still visible were the plasma cutters opening up into the center of the creature's mass with even more intensity. The many-headed, many-limbed monstrosity seemed unfazed by the diamond white heat as body parts continued dropping away, and it pulsated toward the airlock, lurching toward the two women as they fled into the darkness.

Fenroe and Aris stumbled through the smoldering opening into the damp, featureless cavern on the other side, which smelled like sulfur. Shafts of red light followed them, and they pulled themselves forward onto the dim strip of indistinct luminescence that stretched off into the distance in both directions. The cave itself seemed to convulse like the insides of an enormous organ, the surrounding darkness constricting into the light before expanding again.

Fenroe finally drew enough air into her lungs to speak: "How do we get out of here?"

"I don't know," Aris said thinly. "But Eos said that this was a penetration point between our two universes. A gateway of some kind..."

Aris searched with thick panic and hysteria in every direction, but there was nothing to see. Small pinpoints of light glittering on the surface of the far-vaulted ceiling, and the cobbled stone pathway upon which they ran.

"Maybe there's a way—" the younger woman's thoughts were broken and scattered between the shutter of deep panicked breaths, and she kept running and stopping and running again down the path without direction. "Some kind of way out—"

And what sounded like the thunderous roar of hurricane jet streams passing through the shredded vocal cords of a thousand severed heads erupted from the path behind them—both women turned to see shafts of orange light and dark red shadows shooting out of the module doorway from which they had come.

The creature emerged into the cavern, and it had grown into something far more horrifying and far more grotesque than Fenroe's panicked mind could process. Every part of its surface moved and opened and flagellated; tubes and bubbles of tissue bled and slurped and secreted into folds of gore.

There was nowhere to flee. Nothing to run towards. Nowhere to hide. An everlasting darkness, stretching until the pathway tapered off into the obscure nothingness far ahead. Fenroe stopped, breathing deeply as she watched the creature crab along the path to overtake them.

"We can't stop," Aris pleaded desperately. They could run in a straight line for a thousand years and it wouldn't matter. It was pointless, and she knew it. "We have to go—"

"Go where?" Fenroe asked, closing her eyes with exhaustion, swaying on unsteady legs.

"I don't know," Aris begged, choking back the sound of tears rising in her throat. "I have no idea, but we have to keep going–"

Aris reached and put a delicate hand on Fenroe's wrist and pulled her gently down the path away from the creature. Fenroe didn't resist, but she didn't help, either. Searching back through the darkness, Fenroe stared into the nest of heads and limbs unfolding and blossoming behind them.

And then—

She could see feathers of a deeper, more consistent blackness appearing out of thin air just beyond the creature's shadow: an assembling flight of night-black wisps of smoke coming together in threads of bloodstained silk from which two massive, deeply resonant red lights emerged—shards of obsidian falling into place within a body that had grown even larger than what Fenroe had seen in the cupola.

She froze and pulled her arm away.

Aris turned and saw Fenroe staring up into the darkness, so

she followed her eyes as they tracked above the creature on the path—

And Eos came back into existence in the tornado of black threads and red war light, and she was much, much larger. With one massive arm the size of a freight car, the android seized the many-headed creature and crushed it into the cave floor. With the other arm raised above her head, Eos ignited a stream of heat so fierce and so powerful that both women had to cover their eyes. When the welder's flash cleared, Fenroe could see Eos holding her fist in the air for a moment until finally bringing it down onto the creature with the slow, majestic grace of a collapsing building, burning into its skin again with the intensity of a thousand suns, causing the entire cavern to rumble and quake around them.

The creature howled with agony, using its coils of human-shaped limbs to push itself up from the ground in a desperate burst of energy, and the braids of its arms and legs pierced into the bedrock beneath it, threading into the hardened stone as if it was melted wax. At that moment the ground beneath their feet began to soften to the consistency of warm tallow, and both women started to sink.

Fenroe tried pulling herself out, but the ground sucked greedily at her boots: the surrounding mud collapsed and slurped her down even farther with each jerking upward pull of her feet until it had risen above her knees.

Another thunderous echo erupted from the pathway, and the many-headed creature howled again, which shivered the softening ground around them, but this time the sound was more gurgled and airless. Fenroe could see its limbs still feeding into the cave floor as Eos burned relentlessly into it, like massive stalks of bamboo sliding into the decayed flesh of a beached whale. And the more of its limbs it fed into the ground, the less of it there seemed to be on the surface.

There was something more happening to the mud, which bubbled up over their waists; there was some frenzied solidness within. At first Fenroe could find only darkness beyond the path, but now there were tiny stubby fingers wriggling upward through the mud like pale earthworms. More fingers joined, becoming larger and larger, pushing up from the ground, squeezing up from the mud's soft embrace.

Fenroe dug and clawed to pull herself free, and between her fingers she could feel the clods of mud changing; she could feel the liquid firm up to the consistency of milky rubber and wriggle between her fingers.

The softened mud itself was alive and she pulled her hands free, staring at the movement in the glistening light—

And she recoiled in horror.

The mud vibrated with maggoty parasites.

Oceans and oceans of parasites boiling in the muck.

Like spilling from the burst guts of a dead animal, the maggot-like organisms emerged from the ground, slithering and writhing to the surface.

Fenroe and Aris clawed desperately toward each other, trying and failing over and over again to pull themselves free. Aris reached across the mud and wrapped her greasy fingers around Fenroe's wrist, and pulled with everything she had.

So many parasites came up from the wet mud that the ground itself disappeared entirely.

It had become a sea of writhing, living vomit.

Fenroe let go of Aris and tried pulling herself closer, digging into the teeming mounds of thick flexing parasitic bodies as they squirmed between her fingers, up into her clothing, burrowing into her flesh, seeping into her body—not far away, the many-limbed creature swiped at the air, barely missing Fenroe, and the ground quaked with impacts as it scrabbled beneath the weight of

Eos.

Each head on the creature's body stared directly into Fenroe's eyes with lopsided faces that vaguely resembled Sitosen, gaping ragged empty eye sockets and smoke-drooling mouths as Eos melted each one into a crude, hair-spackled red blister on the surface of its skin.

Pain sizzled sharply in brilliant flares of penetration, like tiny, razor sharp teeth ripping into Fenroe's belly; pain seared from the mouths of those maggoty wormlike organisms that ate into the fibers of her muscles, burrowing deep down into her spinal column as they forced their way up into the brainstem.

Aris's face had gone blank with agony, and Fenroe watched helplessly as she sank beneath the surface. Stubby segments of flagellating intestines squirmed into the younger woman's mouth and into her nostrils until she disappeared from view entirely.

The muddy ground swelled and swelled into the bloated shoreline of a heavily polluted body of water. Fenroe was able to thrash and pull her hips up out of the surface and crawl onto her belly as countless parasites churned their way into her mouth and rectum and vagina—billions of them emerging glistening into the overcast lunar light streaked with flares of bright crimson from Eos's plasma.

Fenroe crawled for the empty space where she saw Aris go under, and she dug her hand down into the living muck until she could feel the smooth hardness of Aris's wrist.

Aris gripped back—

...and a wave of heat washed over them.

Fenroe looked up, and discovered that the heat was coming from Eos.

The giant android was now standing directly overhead.

What was left of the many-headed creature lay in a lifeless smoking pile upon the undulating ground that flowed around the carcass like water around a large stone.

Eos lowered herself and dug her simmering hands into the teeming muck, pulling both women free—thick, ropey masses streamed out of their bodies and peppered back onto the churning gelatinous surface far below. The massive android began to move forward, trudging in giant strides away from the airlock, carrying the two women in her hands.

The parasites swarmed up the android's massive legs, suctioning onto the black glass surface of her exoskeleton with leech-like mantles, and the surrounding shadows of the cavern itself began to stir. It was like the whole environment suddenly came to life, arousing from sleep like the mouth of a giant.

Fenroe was overwhelmed with pain as the parasites continued spreading throughout her body, but as she lay in the looping sway of Eos's hand staring up at the twinkling starlight high in the cavern's ceiling, those twinkling lights began to separate from the surrounding darkness and fall from the sky.

Each pinprick of light fell individually, like an avalanche.

But they weren't stars at all.

They weren't jewels embedded in the cavern's skin.

They were the eye shine of a thousand eel-shaped tentacled creatures exactly like the one she encountered aboard the *Pinnacle*. The ceiling was covered in them, and they were all awake now, stirred into a frenzy by the battle that waged far below.

Millions of them, jet-black skin of volcanic glass dropping from the ceiling, crashing down into the teeming ocean of maggots in great squirming mushroom clouds. The ground thundered, each shivering impact blending to a crescendo until it sounded like they were standing at the base of an enormous waterfall. Great explosions of maggots rained down from the impact.

Eos tucked into a ball and shielded them with her body. Thick tentacles slapped across the android's back, questing up from the boiling living ocean sloshing around her ankles to wrap and coil around Eos's legs and waist—each tentacle crawling with tines of electricity as they began eating through her exoskeleton. Behind and below the thunderous rhythm of one heavy impact after another, Fenroe detected a slower, deeper pulse, far beyond the foreground. Far deeper than the whining spike of the parasite layer's self-generated electricity, far deeper than the giant *wuffs* of air as their countless, narrow-muzzled, eel-faced snouts tried prying into the protective cocoon of Eos's arms; this was a pulse of a sort she'd never heard before. It sounded like the *Pinnacle's* reactor core, but deeper, more organic and completely sustained.

Eos's red eyes went black, and it looked as though she had diverted that energy to her limbs, because they all began to glow—rising from a cool violet to a sharp blue, and then from blue to red, and from red to orange, and then finally from orange to gold—and the sound quickened, drowning out the thunderous impacts of falling monsters—

The pulsing rhythm was coming from Eos, increasing in volume, intensity and speed, building to something else entirely, rising above the chaos that crashed all around them until a blazing lattice of light erupted from the android in a perfect shell that expanded in every direction, detonating everything on contact, causing everything around her to burst into boiling clouds of steam.

The detonation left a smoking crater at the base of Eos's feet.

Chunks of charred meat dispersed in a neat circle around the epicenter, and swarms of parasite layers immediately filled in the emptiness in a rush, sliding over everything to once again overtake the android.

But that blast offered a brief window of action—a small

fraction of a second between the waves for the smallest movement.

And that was enough for Eos to do what she needed.

The colossal android stood again and pushed forward, dragging the swarms of monsters that piled onto her massive frame and threaded their tentacles around and between her limbs, ensnaring her legs, hyperextending her joint servos, dislocating her shoulders, and again the pulsing rhythm began to build from deep inside, and again she detonated a shell of energy.

...and again, everything within a hundred-foot radius was blown to pieces.

But Eos was still losing.

Collapsing under the immense weight of an entire simulated environment coming to life. An endless river of organisms flooding from the darkness in wave after wave of mindless writhing hunger; infinitely more than she could power through before the cool down of her next force field.

Eos's legs buckled and she went down on her knees, charging up for one last burst of energy.

Fenroe felt the muscly snakeskin of a tentacle threading between the android's fingers and wrapping around her body until she was irresistibly ripped out of Eos's grip.

Thrown into the open darkness, Fenroe floated weightlessly through the air for what felt like a stretched eternity, until the sinuous carpet of tangled black limbs as thick as tree trunks slammed hard across her body, collapsing the wind out of her lungs, sending her tumbling as more tentacles wrapped around her waist, pulling her down into a claustrophobic throat of airlessness. The tentacles constricted her body like a vice until she felt her lower half separate from her torso, spilling her guts teeming with blood-covered maggots across an obscure fleshy surface of squirming black cobra skin.

The last thing she saw before the darkness took her was Eos making herself into pure light.

Black threads unwound from the glass of reality and accumulated at the android's knees, like wisps of wood smoke burning from a fire that didn't exist—and those wisps came together in the same manner Fenroe had seen in the cupola, just like she'd seen forming on the pathway above the many-headed, many-limbed creature only moments before Eos rematerialized.

Those black threads twisted into massive, interconnected ropes, which braided together to form hawsers of bridge cable made entirely of dark energy.

Everything sucked together and converged onto a single point on the pathway.

A black orb expanded from the twisting cables and collapsed into something else.

It became a massive cylindrical shape in the mist—larger than Eos, much larger than the many-headed creature lying dead farther back on the path—absorbing the thicker cables of blackness that pumped from Eos in ropes of solid smoke.

The shape in the mist became clearer, soaking up the night-black feathers in the air, becoming what looked like the magnetic assembly of a particle collider.

More wisps wrapped around horizontal cyclones of invisible piping, each one feeding into the collider and stretching off into the darkness beyond the path.

Below the collider, there was a tear through space-time.

A window into a dying star field.

Somehow, Fenroe knew that this was symbolic of the point in the singularity where their two universes connected.

She knew this, because Eos knew this.

Because Eos *created* it.

Everything that had become clear to Eos in that moment

became clear in Aris and Fenroe's dying brains, collapsing into a singular point in the center of an immense gravity well.

There were no boundaries between them anymore.

There was no escape.

And Fenroe sensed that the eater in the void didn't care about finding Earth anymore.

...because Eos had already located the wormhole.

Another light gathered in the environment as well, then—a soft but penetrating glow, like the night sky above a city burning hundreds of miles away.

Eos seemed to breathe the light in, and she unfolded herself into a standing position—the parasite layers threading around her body, arcing with braids of electricity.

The android lifted one arm towards the rift that spread out above the collider, aiming the massive plasma cannon attached to her forearm like a gun.

...and opened fire.

The plasma splashed against the wormhole, flattening into a discus fan blade of energy waves that cut everything around it to pieces before sucking into some invisible point at the center of the orb.

Sustaining that beam of energy, Eos raised her other arm vertically into the air.

...and she opened fire.

From her upraised fist burst a shaft of pure white light. It roared into the blackness louder than thunder, expanding as the air ionized to incandescence along its trajectory. The beam fired high overhead until it made contact with the cave ceiling now bare of parasite layers, which seemed to change the frequency at which the plasma resonated from both ends: it became darker and more solid, taking on a harder edge that whined at an octave far lower than before.

Eos directed that light and channeled it through her own massive reconstructed body, feeding the energy back through the sustained beam still firing into the wormhole above the collider.

And she made of herself a conduit, closing the circuit that connected the singularity's pocket reality with the Eater's universe.

With her beams of plasma, Eos formed a complete circle: the simulated universe of the singularity feeding back into the universe from which the Eater had come.

A complete circuit, sluicing through the sustained low-resistant plasma beams of her wrist cannons.

Reality itself stilled, as if it were taking a large breath before a plunge that might never come.

Still alive somehow—half of her body gone, her guts churning into foam around her torso and head, mouth and chest pumped full of parasites—Fenroe looked up.

For a few distorted moments, she could see the *Pinnacle's* particle collider exactly as it appeared in the video playback that Beck had found in the server room. She could see the machine, the pancaked equipment, the melted scaffolding...

The wormhole.

The Eater's universe.

Above Eos, the rapidly expanding rift spread out far and wide.

Fenroe stared at this, awed by the limitless terror of the imagery, and the beauty—

...and the beams of plasma brightened with exponential speed.

Then suddenly—

The Eater's universe broke through the skin of the simulated environment.

A blazing nothingness, a window of dying starscape, rushing

up into the spreading darkness around them.

And Fenroe was caught momentarily between the light and the yawning wormhole in front of her.

And at that moment—

Time seemed to stop.

The light sprayed out of Eos and the particle collider like liquid; the writhing limbs of the parasite layers slowed to a crawl, becoming a graceful, breathtakingly beautiful display of horrific biological symmetry.

Gravity dissipated, and everything lifted weightlessly into the air.

Particles of stone and dust and blood amidst the giant maggots and the tentacles rose in a complex ballet of perfect geometric synchronicity. A paradox of relative time, as the objects remained at complete frozen rest while the simulated reality of the cave rapidly collapsed its boundaries.

Three-dimensional shapes folded into concaved spherical holes. Polyhedrons sucked back into invisible points at some immeasurable center of another dimensional state. The beams of plasma blasting out of the android's arms thickened and grew brighter as they fed the Eater back to itself.

A complete circle, collapsing onto a singular moment, like an artifact of memory.

Fenroe closed her eyes...

...and Eos closed the wormhole.

7.

Upon the event horizon near Saturn, which clawed outward desperately from the collapsing Einstein-Rosen bridge, a smear of particles still entangled with the trapped information of the *Endeavor* spacecraft and its occupants coalesced back into themselves, which caused friction that became heat, which became light that frenzied into the sudden reversal of particle spin and entropic trajectory.

One moment there was blackness...

...the next there was only cold fire.

A violet glare as bright as the noonday sun on Mercury, shining like a cracked diamond, billowing and cascading out of itself like a flower unfolding in the sun.

The entity that fed power to the wormhole gate collapsed inward with the brilliance of a nuclear explosion, and where there was nothing before—

Where there was only empty vacuum and space...

—a ship came back into existence. It simply appeared out of nothingness.

The being that had been the android called Eos used what it had learned in the singularity to construct an exact copy of the *Endeavor* and its occupants as they'd existed in the moments before their particles were obliterated by the Eater's gravitational vortex.

In the void, there was always nothing.

For eons.

For the entire age of the known universe.

Nothingness. Empty vacuum, too vast and too distant to comprehend.

And then suddenly there was *everything*.

The *Endeavor* appeared out of the ether—willed back into existence by Eos.

The wormhole broke apart, and flickered, and winked out of existence, sealing our young star-filled universe off from the Eater's dead purgatory forever.

In that moment, reality itself detonated like the collapse of a neutron star.

JUPITER

1.

COLONEL AMBROSE WREN STOOD at the grand window outside of the *Pinnacle's* particle lab, watching through his own reflection the milk of Jupiter's atmosphere. The black and white contrast was stark in the clash of reflected light from the sun: a tiny black sliver of outer space at the bottom of the window, with the rest of his view consumed by the turbulent planet itself, which drifted by in the rotation of the *Pinnacle's* artificial gravity like the silhouette of a steamship at sea. The hyper-detailed black fissures, the electromagnetic barriers swirling in the warring levels of atmosphere, ripping everything into shades of white, beige, blue, brown and brick red, stretching between oceans of tortured electrons moving slowly, like a sunset on Earth.

On the other side of the solar system was a singularity.

Wren didn't know where it had come from.

He didn't know why it was there.

Nobody knew anything for certain.

After losing contact with Fenroe's crew two years prior, Command realized the reason they'd lost visibility of Saturn's moon was because it had become blurred by the velocity of redshift. A black hole had wandered into the solar system without warning and after ten years of dormancy it made itself even more apparent by dismantling the entirety of Saturn space within a span of twenty-four hours.

This is how he had become keeper and watcher of the Saturnian singularity: an unknown variable considered to be the greatest threat to human existence. If it was able to wander into the solar system without detection and rip apart one of its largest gas giants at an accelerated feed rate, there was no telling what else it would do or how far it could wander. Several of Saturn's moons were roughly the size of Earth, and everybody who stood witness to this event felt the sharp edge of that blade graze the tender skin of their proverbial throats: There was now a planet eater in the solar system, and it was dangerously close to home.

"This way," Mia Caraway said, tapping him gently on the elbow as she walked past.

Wren's eyes lingered on Jupiter for a few more seconds, and then he pulled himself away from the window.

The particle collision cavern was a domed theater surrounded by three stories of scaffolding that funneled down into a massive block of machinery at the center—the outermost wall dropped away several kilometers below the grated metal platform feeding into a network of catwalks and maintenance access points suspended on either side of the machine. At that moment the cavern gleamed with immaculate metallic surfaces, well lit and sterile, and the massive detector in the center of it all hummed deeply with energy.

"This marks anomaly number thirty," Caraway said, leading Colonel Ambrose Wren up an inclined ramp into the control room overlooking the lab, and approached the main console.

Wren shrugged. "Could it have anything to do with the black

hole?"

"I don't think so," she said, shaking her head. "I don't know how that would be possible."

Wren pulled a hand through the steel brush of his hair and thought about that for a moment, and then turned his attention to the glass. "Let's see it."

The window overlooking the detector behind Caraway had been transparent, but now it dimmed and displayed a hollow five-segment cylinder made of light, which rotated softly—almost unnoticeably—on a computer-generated center axis. The slight concave shape of the window displaced the light in such a way that the two-dimensional image looked as though it were a three-dimensional object floating in space before their eyes.

"This is a thirty hour composite of data gathered from sixty sessions," Caraway began. "The cylinder you see here is just, uh, a graphical image of the detector's magnet assembly." Her fingers drummed quietly on the glass touch panel as she typed something into the computer, and then directed Wren's attention to the view screen. "We have the CMS detector in Earth low orbit, which records specific proton-proton events—" she pointed at the screen, "—and this big sucker, which focuses on things like mesons and b-quarks to explore tiny differences in symmetry between matter and anti-matter." She made a final keystroke, and faced the view screen. "You'll see fragments begin to appear in a minute."

Wren stood in silence, waiting for playback. A chronograph started ticking off the seconds above a histogram of motion data located at the bottom of the glass. The image of the detector stayed empty for several moments as the histogram remained a static line of inactivity. Suddenly, flickering strings of light appeared in the emptiness. Each blossomed gently from a single point in the center of the cylinder, forking apart in separate self-orbiting patterns like needles of silk. Like a dance of a billion comets, or an unquantifiable number of dolphins cutting through the ocean, forming geometric patterns and helixes in the bubble trail of their own passage.

Wren glanced down through the image at the massive magnet in the shape of a gigantic cogwheel below, noticing that the detector and its laser were currently activated.

"This isn't real-time...?"

"We're currently running a session, but what you're seeing here is an animatic," she said, shaking her head. "A recording of various collisions at speeds of one hundred billion frames per second," said Caraway, passing her fingers across the all-board. The image zoomed in to show the beautiful arcs and patterns of each particle being tracked. More and more pinpoints of light appeared from an epicenter, spreading out in every direction to leave contrails of data lines in their wake. Millions of light threads, radiating outward at various speeds and with varying intensities, forming a summer flower of geometric petals. Billions of them, filling in the emptiness until the entire thing resembled a container packed to the brim with bundles of different colored yarn.

"That hard-scattering is particle fragmentation," she said, pointing at the thin lines in the image, "ions, gluons, bosons—" she slowed down the playback and the trend lines adjusted gracefully, "—and this is what I called you down here to see."

Wren looked up, and those tiny threads of light began bending around several invisible bubbles of blackness that formed between knotted threads of trajectory lines. Two thirds of the image had been packed with lines of data, but they were now being replaced by orbs of complete emptiness, which seemed to push the newer particle fragments aside, almost as though the detector were measuring something new by its absence.

"What is this...?

"These," she said, nodding at the screen, "are pockets of Kaluza Klien space."

Wren stepped to the glass and studied the distribution of particles and empty spaces, staring in fascination at the spectacular display of light and darkness repelling each other, entwining at the edges of molecular detail as they circled like wisps of smoke in a bottle. "What does it mean?"

"We don't know." Caraway shrugged, stepping away from the console, studying the floor at her feet for a moment. "But whatever's responsible for it doesn't linger for very long. There's a split micro-millisecond where the anomalies disappear and fill in again with particles—" she shrugged again, "—and then nothing. Everything repelled by the presence of those dark spots resumes its journey like nothing was ever there. Then *this* starts happening—"

Wren watched, spellbound as the pinpoints of light traveled on fixed parallaxes without interruption in the receding emptiness. After long moments of unobstructed flight, the particle fragments suddenly appeared again with reinvigorated intensity, blossoming in an excited frenzy of heat. Caraway paused the recording, freezing the scattered image at a moment that showed the maximum amount of emptiness between particle fragments.

"What do you think it is?"

"We think it might be some kind of negatively charged particle. A new one that we've never seen before." She tilted her head, studying the image, and then pointed at the empty spaces. "Everything is repelled by it. And it only appears after our gravity waves dissipate, in directly proportionate quantities to the concentration of particle fragments."

"You're saying it *isn't* particles of gravity," Wren frowned. "It's something else."

"We think it might be both," she said, opening her hands at the screen. "The energy from the impact might be forcing gravitons out of phase, and it's almost like... like the escaping gravity is allowing something else to take its place."

Wren frowned. "What, exactly?"

She crossed her arms. "Well, according to M-theory, the answer to that question could be a number of things."

"M-theory..."

"The multiverse theory," she said. "It postulates that our universe is but one in an infinite number of universes."

Wren looked at the bizarre quantum map overlay for another minute. He was lost in the surrounding image of light threads radiating all around him. He turned to Caraway. "The laser is currently active?"

"Yes."

"How long does each session last?"

She shrugged. "Couple of hours."

"And are you seeing anything like this right now?"

"No," she shook her head. "It usually occurs near the end of each session."

"So what do you need from me?" Wren asked.

Caraway pulled her eyes away from the view screen and searched the floor, taking a deep breath. She'd obviously been fortifying herself for an argument. "I'd like to increase the luminosity of our beams. Create more collisions. Which means more data to look at, which means we need more server space, more bandwidth—"

"It's yours," he interrupted, turning his attention back toward the spreading pageantry of light.

"That's it?"

"One condition," he said, still transfixed.

"Okay..."

"Send me everything you have on this immediately."

The commlink hanging from the lanyard around Wren's neck chimed for his attention, and less than a second later a sudden rumble shook the entire station. He looked at the floor with alarm, feeling it quake gently beneath his feet. Wren reached his hand out and pressed it against the glass, letting himself feel the retreating vibrations.

He met Caraway's concerned eyes, and after a moment of stunned silence, he pressed his commlink. "Go ahead."

"It's Susskind," transmitted a disembodied voice. *"We need you down here right away. It's urgent."*

2.

"...This data starts two weeks ago," Wren said, shuffling the stack of papers in his hand. "That's fourteen days of anomalous signal, pulsing between seventy-five and hundred megahertz...why am I just now being informed?"

"We just found it," Susskind said, matching his pace. "Until now, the tremors were too weak to notice. And the bigger ejections just started a few minutes ago—"

"And this last reading?" He looked up from his papers. "When was this?"

"Now," Susskind said with severity. "This is happening *right now.*"

Wren blinked, leafing through a stack of graphs that imaged flux measurements of protons and X-rays. Each graph had the appearance of what you'd see from a coronal mass ejection from the sun, but instead of a single spike of energy followed by a consistent line of elevated data, there was a string of spikes and valleys that formed a rhythm of its own. This meant that there were several separate mass ejections, followed by brief periods of stability. "This is coming from the black hole..."

"Yes."

"It looks like what we'd see from a coronal mass ejection," Wren observed quietly, confounded.

"Right," Susskind nodded. "But this is steady, increasing."

"It's a pattern," Wren said, flipping rapidly through the report, following the stable rising trend of particle bursts over time. "We're shielded for this kind of thing..."

They *had* to be shielded for electromagnetic pulses of almost *any* magnitude, as they skirted this close to the edge of Jupiter's escape velocity, in constant drag of its massive Langmuir waves of tortured electrons. If they weren't shielded from immense electrical interference, they would have dropped from the Jovian sky decades ago.

Wren leafed to the last page and studied the *Pinnacle's* oscillator data. The vibrations he'd felt appeared to occur in sync with the EMP's coming from the black hole. "So why the tremors?"

Susskind's mouth pressed into a grim line. He didn't seem to know how to answer.

They stepped into the control module, and Wren could feel the tension in the air. A skeleton crew of three people, each absorbed in the screens in front of them, their eyes unblinking, tiny beadlets of sweat forming on their skin.

On the opposite side of the module, a magnified image of the Saturnian singularity took up most of the main window, sheening in the accretion fire like a sphere of black chrome wreathed in flames; a captivating displacement of light, like a ring of starfire spreading away from an immaculately perfect darkness, as though an opening had been punched through the fabric of reality by God himself. It was hauntingly beautiful, like a volcanic eruption occurring in the sun-shadow of a vastly unreachable horizon.

Wren stepped down into the command center. He and Susskind huddled over satcom officer Jenna Ham's workstation as she analyzed window after window of space weather data with rapt focus, comparing it with different images of the black hole under various spectrums of analysis.

"The black hole has been pulsing at a reverse Fibonacci pattern," she said tightly. "First at eight hours, then five, then three. Then every two hours until it leveled out at one hour increments about a day ago."

Wren studied the screen, following the data as she spoke. "What's it pulsing at now?"

Jenna exhaled the tension out of her chest. "Currently holding at fifteen minute intervals."

"Okay," he said, studying the screens. "So what's the deal with these tremors?"

She hesitated, looking at each of the windows one last time, shaking her head. "No idea..."

There was an ensemble of data being recorded: one window was open to the solar system's elliptical plane, like a Doppler radar displaying information as different colors on a screen. Each color represented the speeds, widths, direction and velocities of plasma and magnetic releases from celestial bodies in space. The map Wren studied now was a two-dimensional ring depicting the edges of our heliosphere. It showed the sun in the center with the smaller dots of planets orbiting on their separate ellipticals. The dot that was supposed to represent Saturn emitted massive rainbow strip waves of electromagnetism that radiated out and splashed against every planet in the solar system.

The thought of what those immense energies could do to a planet's magnetosphere prickled tiny needles into the tender flesh of Wren's neck: those measurements could very well be harmless.

Or they could be the telltale signs of the singularity building to a more massive event, like a gamma ray burst with enough power to cause an extinction level scenario on the scale of the asteroid that wiped out the dinosaurs. Something like that would blast the surface of Earth like roasting a marshmallow with napalm. He swallowed and wiped his mouth. "We shouldn't be *feeling* anything—"

Another tremor rose beneath their feet, shivering the junk scattered across Jenna's workstation: coffee sloshed in her cup, and she reached to steady it; pencils and folders and a small line of plastic piggy toys trembled and tipped and rolled over the edge. The view screen rumbled and vibrated, blurring the image of the black hole slightly, like a reflection on water rippling in the wind.

Wren's commlink immediately began chiming incessantly for attention as people started paging him from all over the station.

"That was the next trend reversal," Susskind announced, and the overhead lights flickered. "The pulses have just shifted to seven and half minutes."

"What happens when it reaches zero?" Wren asked, glancing down at the monitor. He immediately recognized the same waveform striking like a lightning bolt across the screen. He wiped the sweat away from his lips and searched the monitors frantically. "Which one's the SHM graph?"

Jenna blinked, snapping back into focus, and then she tapped one of the windows on her view screen.

Wren leaned in and studied the wavelengths of both the particle flux and oscillation graphs, seeing how similar they were in shape and distribution... but despite their symmetry, the wavelengths didn't match up entirely. They were slightly off, almost like there was lag between the black hole EMP's reaching the observatory and the manifestation of the tremors they were feeling.

He reached and traced his fingers along the timelines at the bottom of both graphs.

"We have to scale the reactor down a bit," Susskind said, studying another screen with deep concern. "It's not gonna be able to handle anything more powerful than that."

"I agree," Wren whispered. He stared at the screen until an idea occurred to him. Tearing himself away from the all-panel, he frantically leafed through the papers in his hand until he found the *Pinnacle's* Simple Harmonic Motion graph. Letting the other pages slide out of his fingers to the floor, he slapped the one sheet of paper on top of the screen that showed the black hole's proton flux data.

"It's almost the exact same pattern," Wren announced, racking his brain. "But there's a disparity here."

The difference was immediately apparent: there was a small blip following the larger peak of wavelengths representing the EMP's coming from the black hole. It appeared after every single fifteen-minute increment, and even farther back, following each and every major pulse until the very first recording, when the pulses were thirteen hours apart. Every crest and trough on the graph mirrored each other, and it would have been a nearly perfect symmetrical rhythm of data if it wasn't for that one tiny detail...

The image glowed through the piece of paper that Wren pressed against the glass, and after a few moments of hard analysis, he could see it as clear as day: the EMP's from the black hole were *not* the cause of the tremors. Looking at that smaller blip, Wren knew that the tremors were coming from something else. Something much closer.

He could clearly see the graphical representation of ejections from the black hole traveling across the solar system to make contact with the *Pinnacle*. But those ejections appeared to have no effect on the SHM graph at all. It was that smaller pulse, that tiny blip of energy on the graph that followed the ejections.

"What is this...?"

"It's...it's the energy burst from the black hole," Susskind said, frowning.

"No, no—" Wren shook his head and pointed at each of the wavelength's larger crests, "—*these* are from the black hole—" and then stabbed his index finger onto the smaller spikes just behind them, "—this part, right here, what is this?"

Susskind and Jenna leaned in to see.

"That's just part of the same burst," Susskind said, shaking his head. "The tail end of it—"

"That black hole is nine hundred million kilometers away," he cut him off, chopping the air with the blade of his hand. "I mean, look at these graphs...the larger pulses have no effect on us whatsoever. But these smaller ones..."

"Yeah," Jenna said, frowning at the screen. "He's right."

Wren pointed at the tiny spike on the trend line, just behind the monstrous rise of the larger wave front. "Whatever's causing the tremors must be right here on this observatory." He looked up at Susskind, meeting his eyes. "*That's* what we're feeling. It has something to do with us. *We* are causing it somehow."

Susskind shook his head and studied the readout one last time. His eyes strafed back and forth, and the lines of his brow relaxed as he too began to see a disparity in the pattern. "Rom, do you copy?"

"Yes, Lieutenant," the AI responded from the walls, its male-sounding voice rich and even.

"Can you identify what's causing these tremors?" he asked.

"Negative."

Someone else entered the module. Wren turned to see Byrony Goodwin, another comms specialist, arriving from the main corridor still wearing her sleepwear. She stood at the airlock doorway, hugging her arms against the chill, her hair slightly disheveled.

Susskind paused, licking his lips. He read the data one more time and then looked up toward the view screen, studying the black hole swirling in the glare of complete darkness. "Rom, would you be able to find an epicenter?"

"What's happening?" Goodwin asked.

"We don't know yet," Wren said, thumbing beads of sweat away from his brow.

"Negative," Rom thrummed from the walls. "There is insufficient data at this time to provide a meaningful answer."

Jenna, Wren and Susskind looked at one other for answers, concern written on all of their faces.

"What the hell does that mean?" Jenna asked.

"Can you clarify that for us, Rom?" Susskind said. "What exactly do you need in order to provide a meaningful answer—?"

"What are these vibrations?" Goodwin asked, sitting down so that she could see the data.

"Anomaly of space-time detected," Rom finally replied to Susskind. "I would need more processing power to assess the complete influx of quantum information in order to determine its origin."

Wren sighed and pressed his palms into his eyes, trying to understand just what the hell was going on—

...and the sound of heavy machinery moving deeply beneath the subflooring rose from behind the walls. Wren slowly took his hands away and opened his eyes, following the sound, and through the glass of the control center door, the habitat lights at the far end of the passageway that fed into the rest of the station began shutting off.

A moment later the next nearest bank of habitat lights went

out.

"Talk to me, Rom," Susskind said, watching the corridor with growing alarm.

The next bank of lights shut off.

Then the next.

"We're losing power," Wren said under his breath.

"Rom, do you copy—"

The encroaching darkness finally reached them, and the entire module plunged into pitch-blackness. A thick silence followed, stretching into the canned hum of recycled ventilation. Wren's commlink blinked relentlessly for attention as he waited for the pin to drop, for something to happen, anything...

Then, like the moon clearing a strip of cloud cover—

Soft blue and white light drew his attention, lapping against the corridor wall beside the airlock doorway. He followed it, turning back toward the view screen—

And a blinding, silent eruption flashed in the distance.

The crew flinched and turned their heads instinctively from the light. Wren felt a more violent tremor shake the walls around them. The floor dropped horribly under their feet. The station buckled, and Wren went down hard, smacking his head on the corner of the all-panel.

In the receding light the black hole took form, and it pulsed like a lighthouse in the throes of a storm at dusk. When the halos cleared his vision, Wren saw every crewmember out of the corner of his eye moving slowly to their feet, riveted to the magnified image in the window.

The light blade that made up the black hole's accretion disc dimmed alarmingly, expanding and curling back into the center of itself like ropes of glass. Like thick coronal loops arcing back into the photosphere of a star. It pulsed thicker and dimmed even more, becoming smaller and denser.

Before Wren could process what he had just witnessed, the event horizon surged outward and swallowed the edges of the view screen.

3.

The light faded and Wren pulled himself back up against the terminal, and he looked—

There was a single point of light, only slightly larger than the stars in the background, but it was burning much, much brighter.

There was also a ring of darker light shimmering away from that tiny point of starfire, all around it, a dying halo of ivory-purple—a cat's eye nebula tapering off into darkness.

That small light in the center brightened for a moment—a last flare of intense whiteness—and then it dimmed rapidly, flickering like a pulsar.

It pulsed, faded, flickered, and then finally disappeared.

Wren couldn't believe his eyes. He couldn't make any sense of it whatsoever.

Because the black hole that had consumed Saturn was gone.

It was just...*gone*.

Vanished.

Completely.

4.

Wren blinked and touched his head, and his hand came away wet with blood. Susskind was there at his side, and the younger man helped him up. A corridor schematic of the entire station blinked on the aft-module viewer, flashing red icons that indicated the rapid spread of radioactive steam through the hallways nearest the reactor. Wren could see the lights representing the lead barriers activating far ahead of the breach in an attempt to contain it.

"One of the reactor cores has breached," Susskind exhaled. "We have to go."

"What the hell just happened?"

Susskind breathed and shook his head and stared at the stars in the empty view screen. "I don't know."

Despite his shock Wren allowed himself to be pulled to his feet, and his eyes immediately sought out the viewing window, where a massive ring of translucent radiation sparkled like a nebula. Wren felt something stir deep within himself, because it was simultaneously the most beautiful and the most terrifying thing he had ever seen. The black hole was gone. He couldn't believe it, and didn't know what that meant—

"The system won't reboot," Susskind grunted, leading him to the airlock. "We're evacuating the station."

The walls rumbled in stochastic intervals, very softly, like gentle turbulence in Earth's low orbit. Wren knew they didn't have a lot of time: the barriers wouldn't hold forever, and every second that passed increased the risk of a coolant-fuel interaction, which could ignite the air and cause a chain reaction of failures that would destroy the station and kill everyone on board.

"There's something here," Jenna reported, her eyes fixed on the all-panel with intensity. The light splashed up under her jaw like blue fire, giving her a demonic expression as beads of sweat sheened over her pale skin. She pushed herself away from the screen and stood, her face an ashen sheet. "There's a transmission from close orbit. A vessel requesting permission to dock."

"Turn them away," Susskind said, giving Wren some space to breathe.

"You have to hear this," she said, pulling the *Pico* out of her ear and pressing something on the glass in front of her. The signal rerouted through the intercom.

Thrumming from the walls, a woman's voice spoke with clear and extreme severity: *"Pinnacle Control, this is the* ISDI Endeavor *beginning orbital keeping for umbilical dry-dock, do you copy?"*

The crew stood in complete, silent shock. Susskind stopped and stretched his neck around, staring at the screen with very wide eyes as Jenna quickly brought up the aft camera—

And there, four-hundred or so meters out—gleaming like a shard of glass capturing the sunlight in the blackness—was the *Endeavor* spacecraft on approach.

Wren's breath stopped dead in his chest. That ship had been gone for ten years. The people he'd sent to find it had also disappeared at the exact time they figured out what was happening with Saturn space. It had traveled *from* Saturn space— from the edge of the black hole itself...

What secrets it held were beyond his imagination, and he simply couldn't believe the vessel was actually there. This was a trick of some kind. It didn't make any sense. "My god..."

"Pinnacle Control," the woman said again. *"This is the* ISDI Endeavor *on approach, prepping final docking sequence. Payload three hundred meters, beginning rotate, please respond."*

Jenna snapped to attention and leaned over the panel again, speaking with intensity. "Negative, *Endeavor*. This is *Pinnacle Control*, be advised, one of our reactor cores has breached. All personnel are currently evacuating the station. You must reroute to *Europa Space Dock* immediately, I repeat—"

"Endeavor, this is Colonel Wren," he interrupted Jenna, leaning over the terminal, still staring at the view screen with raw, unblinking eyes. "Please identify yourself."

There was silence interspersed with emergency klaxons blaring through the corridors in the background, followed by another soft rumble—

"This is Commander Evelyn Fenroe," the voice transmitted, enunciating every syllable. *"Chief CO of the* Crown Meridian."

Wren couldn't think. He looked up, and he couldn't do anything except stare at the screen. The light remnants of the black hole glittered in the starlit void, and he couldn't put it together. He couldn't understand how it was all connected, but he knew that it was. He felt it deep inside his heart.

"I need you to listen to me very carefully, Colonel," Fenroe transmitted, *"—ou have—deactivate the—article collider immediat—"*

"Clear that signal up," Wren ordered, straining to hear, blinking rapidly to regain his focus, dizzy from all that was happening and deeply moved by the sound of Fenroe's voice after so many years.

"I'm trying," Jenna said, shaking her head, closing her eyes tightly to block out everything except the voice, "too much cross chatter—"

"Quiet!" Susskind hissed, tilting his head to concentrate on listening.

"Negative, Fenroe, *we do not* copy," Wren said, his voice thick with desperation. "Please repeat, we didn't get any of that."

Another tremor rumbled softly beneath his feet, and the crew lurched in unison.

"—evacuate the observ—ere—immediately de—rticle collid—" Fenroe's voice burst over the comms again, fragmented by harsh blasts of static. *"—aiting—ou copy, Wren, listen to me, you must dea—ider's magnet assembly, and evacuate imm—"*

"She's talking about the particle collider," Susskind said, his brow creasing into newer folds of worry. "Something about evacuation—"

"—you—opy, zeroing rotation delta, one hundred and fifty

meters—"

"Negative—"

"Talk-back is bi-ropal, beginning final approach, one hundred meters—"

"That is a negative, *Endeavor,*" Jenna said. "Repeat, you are not cleared for dock, proceed to Europa space immediately—"

Jenna tried frantically shutting down all open channels one at a time to clear up the signal, but it was no use. The transmission was gone, and the link was killed.

Wren stood locked in place, tracking the *Endeavor* from the view screen as it drifted closer, passing into the *Pinnacle's* shadow where it melted with the blackness. What miracle raised Fenroe from the dead and carried her back to him after all those years—in the ship she had set out to find, no less—he couldn't know. But he was certain it had something to do with the black hole near Saturn, which was now a mere smoldering ring of empty light and inert vacuum. He was so certain that he'd bet his life on it.

5.

Mia Caraway ran through the darkening cavern, her shoes slipping over papers scattered across the floor. Shadows stretched at odd angles in the light of motionless holo-prisms that flickered like burned down candles.

Randall, another physicist, dropped the last stack of folders onto a dolly and gripped the handle.

"Get going," she ordered, clapping him on the shoulder. "I'm right behind you."

She pulled herself hand-over-hand along the guardrail up the ramp leading to the OLC control room as Randall wheeled the dolly forcefully into the dark corridor and disappeared.

Caraway ripped a sheet of plastic away from one of the computer terminals and gathered it awkwardly in her arms—the entire lab rumbled again and she reached out to catch her balance, noticing that the vibrations were increasing with intensity.

It took entire modules filled floor-to-ceiling with computers to count and trace the multitude of particles produced from collision, which generated fifteen million terabytes of data annually. Most of this data was sent to five thousand scientists and five hundred labs all over the solar system to be analyzed. For all intents and purposes, this was humanity's dyson sphere: an interplanetary network of satellites, computers and software designed to process the data recorded by the three detector installations orbiting Terrestrial space. When there was a particularly important observation the data was copied to an event builder, and then stored locally on a bank of servers aboard the station. Which meant all of the most recent data from the anomalies was still there, on board the *Pinnacle,* and it was too valuable to leave behind.

Caraway carried the balled-up sheet of plastic to the line of servers on the opposite end of the module and dropped to her knees, sliding to a halt across the floor, frantically spreading the plastic out and flattening it like a blanket, working mostly by the light of a single flashlight propped on the control panel near the observational window. She reached and pulled hard drives free one by one and tossed them onto the sheet with hands that shivered from adrenaline.

"Does anybody copy," Caraway said into her comms-link between breaths, working quickly. She could feel a change in the observatory's atmosphere: the air crackling with energy, and small electrical pops tingling over her skin. For a split second she was overcome by raw, throat-squeezing panic in the nightmare vision of catastrophic pressure loss. "Someone talk to me..."

She heard footsteps and looked to see a shadow stretching back into the module, and Randall reappeared at the top of the OLC ramp, dripping with sweat. The relief Caraway felt—the sudden absence of intense loneliness—was beyond description, and she nearly broke down at the sight of him. "I told you to go!"

"Three, maybe five minutes tops until those barriers fail," he said, breathing deeply.

"I know—"

"Whatever you're going to do, do it fast."

"I am," she hissed, gritting her teeth, keeping her movements smooth and precise. She reached up and called into existence a line of status bars showing the data transfer, stealing anxious glances from the pressure door leading back into the shadows of the main corridor, which had become completely dark: the emergency lights had cut off entirely, and where she could see shadows of crewmembers stretching and hurrying in the distance before, there were now only disembodied voices echoing farther and farther away into the blackness.

Each status bar blinked into existence and streamed its progress into thin air, assuring her that she had enough time, but gut feeling and the intensity of the shudders appearing closer and closer together told her otherwise.

Caraway felt it even as she looked up at the live feeds of the *Pinnacle Observatory*—the holo-images showing the station in a dying glow, bringing an even deeper darkness to the forest of suspended walkways and scaffolding of the collision cavern—but there were no clear holo-images here through which she could see the reactor core. No indication of how close it was to complete meltdown.

Randall moved to help her collect the hard drives and toss them onto the pile. He glanced in the direction of the large window that took up the entire lab-side wall overlooking the collision cavern far below, and immediately stopped in his tracks.

The last status bar shifted from blue with a sliver of white to solid green before Caraway's eyes, and she pulled the final hard drive free. She gathered the sheet of plastic in her hands and twisted it around her wrist like a trash bag, moving to her feet. Alarms went off above the terminal, but she was too locked in to what she was doing to care, too distracted by the silk-warm sweat pouring over her knuckles and between her fingers and into her lips, oblivious of everything except the deep, quivering thrums in her guts—

"My god," Randall said.

She raised her head, tracking the sound of his voice to the shadow standing near the door—

...and shimmering across his face was a delicate progression of light, shifting through all colors on the spectrum like sunrays passing through a prism.

Caraway stood and followed his gaze through the window, down toward the detector's platform slab, and she blinked with confusion.

The particle collider was bursting with the light of a white star.

Her stomach dropped at the sight of it, and her lips went numb. She looked up at the data screen above the admin console, and she could see that the laser was still activated: beautiful explosions of particle fragments were blossoming into the magnets. A graceful displacement of light, like a flower of needles.

Caraway couldn't make sense of the data—it was as if some hidden force was briefly dragging the particle fragments off trajectory. The pull happened very fast, but it was there and it was unmistakable: in the CG interface, the particles exploded out from an epicenter, and then something pulsed, and in that moment all of the particles tugged downward towards some data-less block near the bottom of the magnet assembly before resuming their flight. It was a magnetic anomaly that she'd never seen before.

There was another tremor and she reached out to hold her balance again, and by a stroke of luck she happened to check the screen at the exact moment the ground vibrated—and she could see it. Actually *see* the force exerted upon those particle fragments at the precise moment the vibration had occurred.

"We have to go," Randall hissed, taking the plastic from her hand.

She tore her eyes away from the screens overhead and began working frantically on the control panel, bringing up another image—the SHM graph, which tracked the observatory's vibrations—and she could see that too: the tremor pattern getting closer and closer together after a set number of events.

Caraway stared at the graph, comparing the tremor data to the particle diagram on the screens above her head, sweat burning her eyes and pouring into her lips.

In that moment of sudden realization, her body went completely numb with terror, and she ripped herself away from the console, diving for the laser control terminal, slamming the palm of her hand onto the emergency shut-off switch.

Red light burst around the detector, and she could hear the deep hum of the laser powering down. Each screen blinked with deactivation messages, and she looked through the window, down toward the collider to see if it had any effect—

...but the light was still there, still building with rapid intensity.

Caraway slammed her fist onto the emergency shut-off switch again, and again nothing happened. The shutoff did nothing to cease the propagation of light inside the machine, and she almost passed out from the rush of panic and blood to her brain. Somehow—she didn't know how—but somehow the magnet assembly was still receiving power. Even after the manual mains cutoff, it was still pulsing with energy.

Which shouldn't have been possible.

Because the emergency shutoff was supposed to immediately open all circuits between the local power supply and the detector itself. She could see that it worked for the laser, which hummed down into silence, but the magnet assembly continued revving unabated with violent energy.

Randall grabbed her arm and pulled her frantically to the ramp. "We have to go!"

She ripped her arm free and leaned against the glass, strafing her flashlight down through the window, across the massive metallic cogwheel shape that capped the very end of the machine.

There was something about the light...something in the way it shifted around and within the metal. It was enshrouded by a translucent wall of energy. A massive shell, like a cloud of vapor shifting beneath and crashing against a layer of glass.

A deeper hum began to rise above the roar of the machine itself, coming from the shadows of the surrounding platform.

"Mia, please, we *cannot* stay here," he pleaded with severity, pulling her again toward the access ramp. "If that magnet assembly comes free, we're dead!"

But she didn't move.

She *couldn't* move.

Because the sight of what took place below stole her breath away.

At first Caraway thought she was witnessing a magnetic quench—the sudden cut of a magnetic field that occurred when part of its superconducting coil enters a restive state: she could see white clouds of vapor billowing up around the machine, which could have come from the magnetic field instantly converting energy to heat and rapidly boiling off coolant.

But she'd seen a quench before, and this was something completely different.

The undulating mass of steam didn't have the thick white characteristics of superheated helium.

This had a metallic sheen to it—like ropes of mercury flowing through zero gravity. Pooled fluids of hydrogen and water began lifting from the floor, attempting to drift, amassing themselves into clusters, wanting to become spheres through which the pulsing flashes of light within the magnet assembly couldn't penetrate. It looked to Caraway like a signal flare burning under water, as though the light coming from inside made the pulsing vapor and smoke form the skin of some massive creature navigating the ocean depths.

And there was something else happening—a force of some kind pulsing outward from the center—like waves of heat radiating on the outermost edges, rising just above the magnet's teeth, expanding with each tremor as if it were alive. Like the entire machine had fallen into a rhythm with the heartbeat of a living circulatory system.

Another tremor rose from the scaffolding and the control terminals over her shoulder flickered, the glowing diodes within fading away. The images bursting from the holo-prisms winked out of existence. The floodlights surrounding the platform slab all flickered in unison and cut off.

The only light that remained in the cavern came from the machine, which burned with furious overload, and Caraway—

...Caraway could only stand there and watch.

She searched the surrounding darkness as the hum and resonance of whatever had been building seemed to reach a climax.

And then—

The air in the entire cavern took one great big breath toward the machine.

The pressure was enough to rupture Caraway's eardrums, and she reached up, covering the sides of her head with her palms—

And the observational window shattered in the powerful flash of white light, spraying shards of glass through the air with a deafening clap of thunder.

Caraway covered her face, and she felt her body make impact with the opposite wall.

Ice-cold liquid whipped against her skin and the air screamed with steam and pressure.

She opened her eyes, and everything was black. Columns of liquid-wrapped steam poured into the window, pelting her skin like hail. Heat lightning pulsed somewhere, bringing the environment into view by disorganized strobes of silver and chrome.

Caraway saw the shadow of Randall lying nearby.

The howling winds were powerful, and she couldn't orient herself—she had no idea which direction was up, where the window was, where the light was coming from, where the exit was—and she crawled toward Randall's prone shadow, feeling blood seeping down her forehead and cheeks from the shattered glass that whipped into her face.

When Caraway reached Randall, his eyes stared unseeingly at the ceiling. There was blood welling up around a large shard of glass lodged into his throat.

Stunned, she lifted her hands helplessly away from him as if he were on fire.

Then she carefully pulled the glass out of his skin with trembling hands, and more blood pumped out of his veins. She pressed her hands against the wound—the skin slipping through her fingers like grease—but he was already gone. There was nothing behind those eyes anymore.

Caraway let go of his throat and pushed herself back onto her haunches and stared at him, numb, oblivious to the hurricane-winds blowing through the control room that flattened her wet hair against her face.

Horrified by the sudden realization that her hands were covered in blood, she tried to wipe it off but it smeared on her sodden uniform. In a complete state of shock, her eyes drifted up into the shadowy background.

And from the ramp came a light.

A gentle light, like a candle swaying evenly on the night sea in a storm.

At first Caraway couldn't tell what it was, but then she could make out the shadow of a person emerging from the seething winds.

A very short and compact shadow, almost childlike.

Caraway stared at the ramp as a small robot entered the control room. It knelt at her side and panned its visor light over her body, scanning for injuries.

"Are you hurt?" it asked in a soothing female voice.

Caraway shook her head in a daze and blinked through the rain pelting her face.

"Can you walk?" the robot asked, helping Caraway to her feet.

She nodded softly, still numb—

—and the air in the collision cavern stilled, the howling winds dropping away suddenly, like a guillotine.

The light below shifted from the violent systematic crashes of lightning to the shimmering ripple of moonlight over water.

The android halted and twisted its visor toward the window. It stood and searched down into the collision cavern.

Below them, the air itself had been torn open just under the magnet assembly.

Beyond the tear lay a blackness so profound that it unrooted something in Caraway's chest.

The shimmering glow from the detector seemed to be drawn into it like thin wisps of golden-white vapor, as if the blackness on the other side fed directly upon the light itself.

"You have to go, Doctor," the android pulsed, staring at the strange rift that shimmered with horrible darkness.

"I don't understand what's happening," Caraway said, unable to look away.

The android studied her for a moment and then returned its gaze to the source of blackness.

"You've opened a doorway to another universe," the android thrummed after a moment. "My crew and I have come to close it."

"Close it," she echoed, blinking and searching through the light bleeding into the air far below, her mind sprinting a hundred miles per hour. "How...?"

"Something else is holding the wormhole open from the other side," the robot said. "We're too late."

Caraway frowned and blinked, "the other side of what...?"

"Please, Doctor, you have to go," the android cut in. "You have to evacuate the *Pinnacle* immediately."

She studied the small robot for a moment, realizing that it wasn't under Rom's control. Caraway had no idea whose voice it was or how the android had come to be in her lab, but in the end she didn't need to know. The only thing that mattered was the rift in the light and the thick, ominous blackness pouring out of it.

Without another word, Caraway turned and gathered the hard drives in her hands—gummed with blood and slick with condensation—and she paused above the figure of Randall lying on a bed of shattered glass, who stared unseeing into the glittering shadow and the rain. Her heart broke into a million separate pieces. It shattered inside her chest, and the look in his dead eyes cast the remaining pieces across the void like pulverized glass. It was almost too much to handle. Almost enough to knock the will to live out of her right then and there. The observatory rumbled softly beneath her feet and she swayed unsteadily on her legs, which brought her back from the edge.

Caraway turned and studied the small robot standing at the shattered window, staring down into the shimmering light. And through tears that blurred everything from view, she reigned in the confusion and terror that rose up in her chest, and gathered the heavy plastic containing the hard drives in her hands, dragging it into the darkness of the main corridor. As she made her way through the deserted hallways, she passed a number of bay windows that looked out into space. In the foreground of a million suns burning in the distance, she could see the ion-plasma contrails of lander modules detaching from the *Pinnacle's* hull, making their long arcs toward Calisto. She tracked them as long as she could, following the shrinking cone-shaped vessels with her eyes until they eventually blended with the stretched atmospheric light of Jupiter, where they disappeared from view forever.

6.

The *Pinnacle's* particle collision cavern was empty now.

But Eos was not alone.

The high vaulted stadium glowed with indistinct, mirrored fire light that spilled into the corridors and flowed across the walls. The cavern was quiet of the screaming and winds, filled instead with the sound of water pattering gently onto the metal far below, tinkling between the machine hum of the particle detector.

The interchange and pulse gave an ominous aspect of life to the colossal machine that towered above the collision cavern, and the air around it seemed to throb with the energy of another universe.

Hanging several feet above the main platform, the wormhole dilated in an orb of pure blackness, small at first, but expanding between shadows that appeared to suck into it like threads of smoke. From some unknowable distance—deep between the planck space of our reality— more smaller orbs of blackness blossomed like optical sensor malfunctions, darkening at random points in the air, dimming the light closest to the magnet assembly, and Eos looked to the opening as something massive began to emerge, pouring out like sheets of silk billowing from a perfect ring of pure light. A massive, seething muscle of absolute blackness, rising through the darkness like something ancient surfacing from the bottom of the ocean.

The android watched as the blackness took form in the light, smoothing out the shadowed edges of an organism. A *massive* organism that moved weightlessly through the air, its nocturnal eyes shining and searching unblinkingly through the sparking flashes of electricity from the machinery towering above the opening. The creature stretched open its immense pharyngeal jaws, yawning a mouth studded with several rows of teeth that could rend iron, as if awakening from a millennium-long sleep.

It came through slowly, twisting menacingly in mid-air, like a dragon rising from the black smoke of an unending fire burning in the center of the world—curling its body up and back and over the guardrail, where it slid through the air like oil into the unseen darkness below the platform—and despite the appearance of weightless flight, Eos detected the spindly outlines of tentacle-like arms grasping out from its body in all directions, grabbing hold of anything within reach to propel itself forward with animalistic grace.

Eos followed it onto the platform above, stepping carefully as the creature seethed through the shadows directly below, pumping streams of rubbery white maggot-like creatures out of thick ovipositors slurping behind its head, which spilled in great sickening heaps and writhed wetly in the strobes of light.

Her visor tracked the movement within the darkness, following the silhouette as it navigated toward the outer edge of the cavern.

Activating the rivet cutters attached to her forearms, the android was bathed in the hard red light of super heated plasma, which cast shadows from the sharp points of her exoskeleton, giving her a demonic appearance. She gripped the handrail and paused, waiting for the creature's head to clear the drop, its shadowed outline bristling with a million tentacles that wrapped in nauseating patterns, each one flattening together to form a black vibrating teardrop the size of a landing module.

The thing tilted its head as it passed, studying the fire-sizzling profile of Eos standing directly overhead. The rose-pale glow of her rivet cutters reflected in the creature's eyes.

It was aware of her presence, but it didn't understand what she was.

It hadn't yet learned to fear her.

And that was something Eos could not allow.

In one smooth movement, the android vaulted the guardrail and dropped through the three stories of darkness, spreading her arms out like wings, opening the gauges of her cutters to their widest diameter—

And she made impact, the force causing the creature to rumble deeply and bristle like a mass of roaches on contact, its tentacles giving like water under her weight—the parasite layer frenzied, whipping itself into a corkscrew of serpents that cut through the red air.

Eos stabbed her rivet cutters deep into the buzzing surface of its body—the red glow of her plasma shooting between the cracks of massed tentacles boiling beneath her.

The creature whipped forcefully into a spin, flicking the android easily into the air—she landed neatly on the subflooring, sliding to her knees from a roll until she burned one plasma-infused fist into the metal to stop her skid.

The creature bellowed a deep roar and twisted majestically in the opposite direction, where it crashed with a thunderous rumble into the cavern wall, sucking its quartile mantle against the vinyl as thick forks of electricity began to arc up the length of its body.

Eos unfolded herself into a standing position—a deep, uneven gouge burned into the ground stretching out beneath her feet—her visor flickering for a moment until it blushed evenly to solid warlike red.

"We're too late, Commander," she transmitted over comms, taking deadly measured strides toward the twisting living blackness directly ahead. "The parasite has breached the wormhole."

The tines of electricity crawled up the creature's body, pumping into the cavern wall until the synthetic materials began to fizzle and melt, exposing the ribs of iron and aluminum underneath, which glowed a deep molten orange.

"*You have to close the wormhole, Eos!*" Fenroe ordered. "*Do you copy?! Take the magnet offline now—!*"

"The gateway is now completely sustained from the other side," Eos said, her strides quickening until she moved at a dead run. "I can't stop it."

She opened her arms, activating the cutters one final time—

And without hesitation, Eos vaulted into the air and leapt onto the creature, burning her plasma cutters into it with the intensity of a thousand suns.

At that very moment—just as the softened metal collapsed into a simmering hole large enough for the creature to slide itself through—she looked into its eyes, and she could see it.

In the creature's eyes was fear.

In the android's visor plate, there was only fire.

7.

Fenroe heard a woman's voice echoing down the dark corridor, and she twisted the light toward the sound until it found a figure propped up against the bulkhead twenty meters or so away.

"Over there," Fenroe said, and Aris shined her light in the same direction.

It was a woman, and she was dragging a large plastic sack behind her like a corpse. When Fenroe reached her side, she could see that the woman was hurt badly. Blood ran down her face from several razor-thin cuts dotted around her hairline, and she was breathing heavily, holding her arm to her side like there was something broken inside.

"I'm here," she said. "Don't leave me, I'm here..."

Aris took the plastic sack from her clenched fist and Fenroe pummeled her arm beneath the woman's shoulder, lifting the woman to her unsteady legs. She hissed and sucked pain through her teeth, but didn't resist.

"We've got you," Fenroe said, dragging her back toward the warm light that spilled from the dock umbilical farther down the corridor.

"Am I the last one?" the woman asked.

Fenroe stared ahead seriously, breathing through her teeth from the effort of bearing the woman's weight. "We don't know."

They stumbled through the umbilical and entered the

Endeavor's docking bay, where Fenroe eased the woman down against a wall.

"How many is that?" Aris asked as she continued deeper into the module, leaving Fenroe and the woman to catch their breath.

"Twenty-three, twenty-four?" Fenroe said, resting her hands on her knees.

"How many do you think are still on the *Pinnacle*?"

"I don't know," Fenroe said. "A lot of them. *All* of them..."

Aris stopped and stared out of one of the bay windows, watching the gentle transit of a cluster of lander modules drifting away from the observatory before the massive planet Jupiter towering in the backdrop. She turned to say something, and Eos broke in:

"*We're too late, Commander,*" the AI hummed from the walls, pulling Fenroe's attention away from the wounded woman on the floor. "*The parasite has breached the wormhole—*"

"You have to shut it down, Eos!" Fenroe ordered. "Do you copy?! Take the magnet offline now!"

"*The gateway is now completely sustained from the other side,*" Eos responded. "*I can't stop it.*"

Fenroe's eyes drifted back to the woman leaning against the wall as she tried to think of something—anything that would change the course of their destiny—

And suddenly she couldn't breathe.

She swayed in the tremor of the other universe flooding into their own, and something had shattered glass inside her head. The pieces of a memory falling around her, shimmering and glaring and caressing her skin and making the hairs stand up on her arms. Falling into place with a click like the tumblers turning inside a lock.

Fenroe crouched down and looked into the eyes of this dead woman, this ghost she remembered from the playback Beck had found in the server hub, and she said: "It's you..."

The woman managed to raise her head and look back into Fenroe's eyes. She was distant, only semi-aware of her surroundings.

"You're alive," Fenroe whispered.

And as she said it, Mia Caraway finally looked at Fenroe— really *looked* at her, as if seeing her for the first time. It seemed like Fenroe's voice touched something deep inside. Like she was coming to some sort of overwhelming realization, the words holding significance that she couldn't fully articulate. The stunned distance in Caraway's eyes seemed to drain out of her, as if she just then realized that she *was in fact alive*, and that every breath she took into her lungs was borrowed from a half-forgotten dream.

The *Endeavor* docking bay rumbled again, bringing Caraway's attention back from the depths of her own thoughts. She watched the bright light of Jupiter cut in through the bay window and clear the vertical over Fenroe's shoulder, the beautiful milky swirls of its atmosphere raging in a slow cataclysm, illuminating the docking bay like a sunrise.

"I'm alive," Mia Caraway repeated the words evenly. The words were powerful and intense as she spoke them, significant in a way that only she could understand. She nodded, and met Fenroe's eyes again, moved by the gravity of what it all meant. There was no way to convey what she felt. There was no explaining it, but what Mia Caraway did know with certainty was that she was very grateful to be there. Very aware of how she shouldn't have survived whatever happened in the collision cavern. As though she could sense that her path had forked in a direction it shouldn't have. All she could say was: "I'm alive..."

And that was enough for Fenroe. She smiled through the tears brimming in her eyes and leaned forward, pressing her lips against Caraway's cheek—the woman stunned by the action, trying to understand why her survival was so important to this stranger. Fenroe stood and quickly palmed the tears away from her face, composing herself. Looking toward the flight deck with something like sadness in her eyes, Fenroe's body relaxed, and the tremble in her hands and shoulders eased down into the warm center of her soul.

8.

Aris stowed the plastic sack in a storage compartment and turned back toward Fenroe, who was on the opposite end of the docking bay with a stunned expression on her face, standing near the last woman they had carried in from the corridor. Aris ducked her shaven head under the lower part of the containment units and spoke over the silent men and women from the *Pinnacle* crew, who were all in various states of shock, many sitting on the floor and staring at the wall with exhaustion written on their faces.

Aris called to her. "We can't wait any longer—"

And she stopped, seeing the look in Fenroe's eyes. They stared at each other for a long time. In those eyes, Fenroe gathered Aris into her arms and wrapped her into a warm embrace. She told Aris how proud she was of her. And that she was sorry.

A cold blade ran up the length of Aris's legs, because in those eyes she recognized a terrified hope blended with deep sadness. And for some reason she knew—she just *knew* deep down that this was the last time she'd ever see her friend again.

Aris stepped forward, unable to mask the puzzlement she felt. "Fenroe...?"

Fenroe took a deep breath of intense relief and gathered a crowbar that was propped against the bulkhead in her hand, feeling the weight of it, which was solid and true. Then she reached up and grabbed one of the bio-helmets from the charging crèche next to the airlock—

Aris took another step forward, sudden panic rising up into her chest. "Fenroe?"

—and Fenroe stepped back into the *Pinnacle's* dock umbilical.

"Fenroe!" Aris screamed, breaking into a run and pushing frantically toward the rear of the docking bay through the startled *Pinnacle* crewmembers.

Fenroe stood on the opposite side of the airlock, and reached for the control panel. Without hesitation, she activated the lock and sealed herself off on the other side.

Aris crashed against the pressure door just as it hissed into the floor—she could see Fenroe through the glass closing the *Pinnacle's* umbilical side airlock, and when it sealed into place, she raised the crowbar gripped in her fists, and brought the flat pinch-point down hard like a railroad spike into the control panel at the exact moment Aris was able to get the *Endeavor* door back open.

"*NO!*" Aris screamed, diving for the umbilical dock controls on her side of the airlock. But she was too late. It was already done. She watched in shocked confusion as Fenroe ripped a messy bundle of wire and cable away from the wall. Then, backing away slowly, Fenroe took giant mouthfuls of terrified air as she held the wire dangling in her hand like a severed noose. She looked afraid—almost as if she couldn't believe what she was doing—but committed nonetheless.

Aris pounded her fists against the hard aluminum alloy, crying out with incomprehensible pain. There was another, more forceful rumble, and the sterile white of the umbilical collapsed into a deep, all-consuming red as the cabin lights died.

Fenroe's profile was stunning on the opposite side of the

viewport, cutting through the red light like an effigy carved into the surface of a dying sun. Tears fell freely down her face as she stood on the other side of the glass, looking so much like Harris in the red wash of light that it cracked something deep inside Aris's chest—a thick, existential levy that, now broken, released icy shocks through her body in waves of despair.

"Eos," Aris panted, pulling desperately at the lock cylinder. "Open the umbilical airlock."

"I can't," the AI hummed from the walls. "Power has been disabled from the other side."

Aris stared at Fenroe for a long time, raging silently inside as she desperately tried to think of something she could do to convince her to stop this. The station rumbled again, and Fenroe looked up at the ceiling and then back over her shoulder at the darkness beyond the umbilical: they didn't have a lot of time.

Aris snatched one of the other helmets in the charging crèche and activated the comms link inside, speaking through hitching breaths that scattered her words to pieces.

"I know what you're trying to do," she said, trying desperately to keep her voice steady and clear. "But going through that wormhole won't save them."

Fenroe looked at Aris for a long time, settling into her nerves—the fear and the self-doubt sliding away into the cold certainty of her eyes.

"*I'm not sure I believe that anymore,*" Fenroe said evenly, choosing her words very carefully. Her voice was already starting to sound distant, like it was being stretched through time, pulled to the other side of the solar system.

"You have to let them go," Aris said, pressing her fists against the glass. She begged Fenroe, pleading with every fiber of her body for her to understand this one truth: "The fact that the wormhole is opening means we failed. Don't you understand? It *proves* that time is immutable. It's a complete thing, an object in and of itself!" She paused for a second, letting the echo of her voice die away. "It's proof that you cannot change the past. You cannot stop what's already happened—"

"*Aris—*"

"Listen to me," she cut Fenroe off forcefully, blinking through the tears pouring down her face. *"Listen to me.* What's happening right now is already part of what we found near Saturn. It's all a flat circle, you understand? Everything has already happened. Nobody on the *Pinnacle* survives what's coming next. You saw it for yourself." She closed her eyes and concentrated on her breathing, fighting to control the panic overwhelming her body. "Please, Fenroe. *Please.* Let the dead stay dead, and let them go. I loved them, too—" and she stopped, losing control of a crack in her breath. "—You're not the only one who loved them, Fenroe. But they're gone. They're always going to *be* gone, and there's no coming back." She stared into Fenroe's eyes, praying that she was getting through to her. "Let go, Fenroe...let them go, and come home—"

"*Aris—*"

"Honor their memories!" She pleaded, knowing that there was nothing she could say to convince Fenroe to come back, nothing in this universe she could do to convince Fenroe to abandon the obsessive need to make herself responsible for all the bad things that had happened in her life. Aris pressed her hands together in prayer, begging Fenroe one last time to open the airlock. "Honor them by not giving up what they fought *so hard* to hold on to..."

The walls rumbled around them with more intensity and they swayed on their feet, looking into each other's eyes as they rode the tremor like the movement of deep ocean waves. After a moment Fenroe stepped up to the glass, and Aris felt her heart swell with hope. She wanted so badly for Fenroe to reconnect power to the airlock. She wanted her to come back, to gather Fenroe in her arms and never let go again—

"She was dead," Fenroe said quietly, shifting her attention to something over Aris's shoulder. She looked as if what she saw would vanish at any moment. Like it was the last thing she ever hoped to see in this life. *"I saw her body on the Pinnacle,"* she continued, leveling her gaze on Aris once again. *"She was gone."*

Aris turned and saw Mia Caraway standing behind her, listening to every word. The *Pinnacle* physicist looked like she was on the verge of breaking down. She looked like she wanted to do something or say something that would end whatever was taking place, but she didn't know where to begin. None of it made sense to her, but she did seem to understand that something important was happening, and that it was because of her. Fenroe closed her eyes and rested her head against the glass, taking a deep, thoughtful breath. She studied her hands for a moment, and then looked up.

"Which means it's possible to change things," she said, searching Aris's face for any kind of comprehension, needing her to understand what that meant. *"The possibility to change what happened...it didn't exist before. Now it does."*

Aris dropped her chin, defeated. She tried to find the right words, but she couldn't. Instead she said what was in her heart: "Then take me with you."

"I won't be alone," Fenroe said softly, and Aris knew that she meant it. She could see it in her eyes, hear it in the tremble of her voice. *"You can interpret the nature of the Eater's physics, right Eos?"*

"I can, Commander," the AI hummed.

"Eos will protect me," Fenroe said, looking back to Aris. *"She'll keep me safe."*

"I'm not leaving you here."

"*You have to,*" Fenroe said quietly, taking another deep, calming breath. She kissed her fingers, and pressed the kiss against the glass, smearing two brushstrokes of fingerprints between them. "*Someone I love has to live through this.*"

She gathered the crowbar in her hand, and backed away from the airlock. Aris watched the outline of her shadow blend with the darkness on the far side of the umbilical, and she knew that Fenroe wasn't coming back. Aris knew there was nothing she could do to change that.

Whitney Aris pinched her eyes closed and collapsed against the airlock, letting her body slide to the floor. Aris wept, feeling lost and ashamed, because in her heart there was nothing but dust. In her soul there was nothing but melancholy and despair. So she covered her face, hating the feel of tears on her hot skin with all of her heart, and for as long as she could, Aris decided to feel nothing except the distant rumblings of thunder.

9.

Aris stayed like that for a long time, thinking about nothing. Emptying her head and her heart of everything she didn't need anymore: the pain, the shadows of her dead, and Fenroe...

Eventually all gravity left the *Endeavor* as Eos separated from dock, and she felt her body lift weightlessly into the air. The shadows of men and women that had evacuated the observatory moved with intense purpose all around her—prepping the *Endeavor* for departure, for their journey home—but at that moment, the only thing that mattered was what unfolded outside of the ship.

All Aris could do was stare and breathe.

Because outside, suddenly, bleeding into their reality from some unimaginable purgatory, there appeared a different form of light altogether.

She watched as the *Pinnacle's* hull passed before her eyes in great streaking bands. Eos maneuvered the *Endeavor* out of dock as the observatory's hull slipped by faster and faster, picking up speed like a bullet train pulling out of station. The machinery on its hull blurred into solid gray-white lines as the *Endeavor* accelerated, until black space cut into view abruptly like a sheet of volcanic glass, and then the *Pinnacle* was behind them but still massive in their viewports, looming over the small ship like a city retreating into the black distance.

Aris watched the pageantry of light bleeding out into space from someplace within the observatory. A display of light that arced and curled around the unseen edges of another universe, like smears of white paint on a black velvet canvas.

The three-mile-wide orbital observatory was still so close that it filled three-fourths of the sky above the *Endeavor*, blocking out the colossal beige and white gas giant in the backdrop and the distant stars scattered farther beyond. Thrusters burned all along the *Endeavor's* hull, peeling away from the strange radiation of light that curled and wisped around them, overtaking their acceleration and stretching farther and farther away from the *Pinnacle's* hull.

They were still close enough that Aris could make out every detail of the *Pinnacle's* gleaming exterior, and the twisting, black-and-white-starlight colored sphere of the wormhole itself, expanding out from one section of the observatory's ring into the void. It grew larger as she watched, smearing out the last of the stars above.

It took everything Aris had to push away from the docking bay's observational window and propel herself with great rowing thrusts through zero gravity, and navigate through the main corridor toward the flight deck. Within every window she passed, the sphere of light expanded out of the *Pinnacle's* hull, but the immensity of the observatory shrunk only slightly behind them. They were still too close to the observatory, and they were out of time.

She emerged into the well-lit flight deck and her eyes were immediately drawn to the windshield, which looked out into pitch blackness. Shifting her body, Aris awkwardly hauled herself hand over hand into the pilot's chair, where she quickly pulled the orbital-keeping harness over her shoulders.

Eos banked and twisted the *Endeavor's* trajectory until the planet Jupiter filled its windows. The AI aimed the ship in the direction of the moon Europa, which was six hundred and seventy thousand kilometers away. Their destination was the orbital supply station *Variant*.

At first, the only visible thing in the sky was Jupiter, stretching over them like an apocalyptic tidal wave. Then, in the lower right-hand corner of the armor glass, Aris could see a light gleaming in the foreground.

The *Pinnacle* drifted into view, shining in the darkness like a halo.

The sphere of streaking light expanded beyond the three-mile diameter of the observatory's ring. For an instant, those streaks of smeared light slowed to a halt, abandoning their questing reach into the void as if they had suddenly been flash-frozen in time. The threads of light drifted like that for long moments, like a whale stuck at the highest point of its breach—hanging in the air until the long crashing plummet back into the water like a collapsing building. And suddenly the light streaks spiderwebbed throughout the interior of the energy sphere, dilating the wormhole to the size of a small moon made entirely of clear glass.

There was no sound. No rumbling shockwaves.

Just the light and the observatory, dancing together in the eye of a raging storm.

What happened next reminded Aris of what occurs when you drop a tear of liquid soap onto a thin layer of food coloring.

The *Pinnacle* was there one moment—gleaming like a disc of light—and in the next moment the entire observatory liquefied, coming apart like particles of white sand. A flash that could only have lasted a fraction of a second.

Aris watched the observatory's light splash within the translucent sphere like paint, swirling and lensing out of shape until there was nothing recognizable left. In that moment—that *very same* moment, ten years into the past—a space station appeared near Saturn's largest moon, Titan. A massive orb of pure white light expanded into reality, unfolding the *Pinnacle* back into the universe, which immediately began transmitting an unpackaged distress signal back to Earth, with a timestamp signature that was slightly off – the date, specifically. The terrible Eater from the void would follow shortly after, and collide with the moon Titan, catalyzing the cycle all over again—The *Endeavor* crew sent to investigate the distress signal, Fenroe and the *Crown Meridian* traveling from Earth to Saturn to find them, all of Aris's friends dying on the infected *Pinnacle* observatory, and her past self falling into the black hole... over and over again. Round and around and around, looping for eternity.

Aris could see the *Pinnacle's* light still bleeding back through the wormhole, splashing and refracting from within the orb like a distant memory. Parts of the observatory were still recognizable, like how things appear stretched and distorted in a convex mirror.

She realized with numb distance that she was looking directly into the past. Through the wormhole was a perfectly captured moment in time, exactly as it had been before any of this happened. And somewhere in that memory was her Commander, Evelyn Fenroe.

Aris knew that Fenroe wouldn't stop until either her crew was safe or she was dead. Aris didn't know how far that obsession would take her. She didn't know how far you ought to take things like that. Because she always knew that Fenroe was the type of person who took things all the way into her heart. She gave it everything she had, and that was exactly how far her heart could go. But Aris also knew that her heart could only take so much.

She tumbled weightlessly in her harness, and she watched the hole in reality begin to collapse again back into nothing. The copy of Eos that stayed with Aris on her side of the wormhole set the *Endeavor's* course, and carried her away from the light of Fenroe, which had shrunk into a solid point of burning white fire, taking the *Pinnacle* with it. For a fraction of a second that condensed point of light flickered and blazed like an exploding star, brightening immeasurably for a moment before vanishing back into the dead emptiness of the Eater's reality.

Because, in a moment of time that never was—deep beneath the surface of a planet that never existed—the wormhole was annihilated by the completed circuit that Eos had formed of her simulated body. Inside a three-dimensional space within a dark cave of nothingness, the Eater moved to swallow the memories of Fenroe and Aris whole and force them to provide it with the location of Earth.

In the infinite now of that moment in the cave—as Fenroe and Aris were pulled deeper into the tentacles of a million writhing parasite layers, feeling themselves being ripped apart and pumped full of rubbery white maggot-like creatures—the massive shadow-entity that Eos had become blasted the thick columns of plasma from the environment of the Eater's singularity back into the stretched throat of its own dying universe. Everything fell back together again into the pristine darkness of non-existence.

10.

When Evie Fenroe was a little girl, her mother stabbed her father to death in front of her. She remembered every detail.

Pay attention, because this is important. Everything else is just peripheral.

There was the lemon-green house with the white windows. The door that creaked when you opened it, the second wooden panel to the left that groaned when you set your foot upon it. Through the front door was the flight of stairs and a hallway, and beyond those were rooms. There was Evie, her little brother Bradley, Mom and Dad, and the woman with the strange clothes.

Bradley and Evie sat on a sofa, clinging to each other as police and firefighters and paramedics moved through the harsh blue flickering glow of the television, stretching their shadows away from the dim, fallen lamp lying on the carpet. A nice police officer with sad eyes hunched in front of Evie and Bradley with her flashlight tucked under her armpit, asking them if they had any aunties or uncles she could call. But as the police officer spoke, her voice was very quiet and very far away, and most of what she said Evie couldn't understand. It was like her ears heard the words, but her brain couldn't catch up to them. So she stared at the policewoman—really trying to focus—without saying anything for a very long time, until the policewoman told her to stay right there and walked off to find someone who could help.

Beside her, little Bradley's cheeks were swollen red from his pudgy knuckles constantly rubbing tears out of his eyes. He leaned his small head against Evie's shoulder—his big sister—because that was the safest place in the world right then.

In the ambulance outside was their Mom, and on the other side of the room was their Dad.

His eyes stared straight ahead, and Evie thought he was just looking at the ceiling, patiently waiting for the paramedics to fix him. Like he was bored, or about to say something but forgot exactly what it was. He hadn't moved since everyone started showing up, almost over a half hour, which made Evie think that he was just trying to stay comfortable. Next to the chessboard table there was a pool of blood, about a pitcher's worth. It didn't even look like that much to her.

It was evening, somewhere after bedtime because both she and Bradley were in their sleepwear.

Sitting there on that sofa, the thought of her Dad dying didn't even occur to her. It just wasn't possible. There was no... *concept* of a future in her very young mind without her Dad. The thought of him no longer being there just didn't make any sense. And the thought of it in that moment—the brief half-consideration of the *possibility* threatened her with such a yawning black maw of panic that she had just simply decided not to believe it. Because no matter what this moment in her life turned out to be, there was nothing she could do about it anyway. She was just a little girl, and her brother Bradley was an even littler boy. There was nothing she could do except sit and wait until the police decided where to take them.

So that's what Evie did when the woman in the strange clothes showed up.

She came through the front door, completely unnoticed by all of the other people going in and out for a million different things. The woman stopped in the hall and stood there for a long moment, staring at the walls and the stairs and the fallen lamp and the television and the chess pieces scattered all over the floor. Her hair was long but not too long, only down to the middle of her neck—mostly brown, but there was a little gray in it. Her face hard looking and sharp, very serious and strong, her eyes two deep pools of intensity. She stepped onto the first stair, intending to go straight up—

"No one's allowed to go up there," Evie said to the woman.

She stopped and looked back at the little girl. "What?"

"We can't go up there," she pointed at the stairway. "I wanted to take Bradley up to my room, but the big man over there said nobody goes up until he's had a look."

"It's okay," the woman said, lost in thought, studying the little girl and her little brother. "I used to live here..."

She took a deep breath and stared at the two children with something like fear in her eyes, and her voice caught in her throat, as if she suddenly recognized Evie and her little brother from somewhere else. "My god..."

Stunned, she moved in front of them very slowly, watching them both as if they couldn't possibly be real. The woman looked back out the front door at the firetruck and the ambulance lights flashing on the curb and got this look like she was angry, and the little girl thought the strange woman was going to cry, but she never did. Then she composed herself, and just looked tired. She turned back toward them and studied the carpet for a while, and then glanced up at Bradley, who was looking back at her with his small head still pressed against Evie's arm.

"Hi, buddy," the woman said sadly. She reached out and brushed Bradley's hair behind his ear.

"Hi," he said with a papery soft voice, taking a deep hiccuppy breath from the crying he'd done earlier.

"Can I sit here with you?"

Neither of them said anything, and the woman in the strange clothes lowered herself to the carpet and crossed her legs. "Your mom's out there?"

Evie felt butterflies rising up in her stomach and decided that she didn't want to think about it, didn't want to talk.

"My mom's out there, too," the woman said.

Evie raised her head and glanced out the window.

The woman seemed to know what she was thinking, and put a gentle hand on her knee. "She's going to be okay. I promise."

Evie looked down at the carpet. "I don't think you should be here."

The woman stared at Evie for a moment and then nodded like she knew that already, and then looked at her hands. She closed her fingers into fists and opened them again. "Listen, Evie...I want to tell you both something, and then I'll leave, okay?"

Evie didn't answer because she was looking at the woman's strange clothes. They looked heavy and light at the same time, like something you'd wear while studying things at the bottom of the ocean. The woman leaned forward, and Evie felt like she should have said something right then, and even though the little girl knew that she shouldn't have been talking to the woman in the strange clothes, she felt like she knew her somehow, because she had her mother's same serious eyes.

The woman in the strange clothes said, "my dad...he died when I was about your age. I remember it being a very hard day." She paused for a moment, letting her eyes drift around the house, looking again like she was trying not to let herself cry. "I wish I could have said goodbye to him."

Evie thought about that, and tried looking for her father in the other room but there were too many people blocking him from view. "My Dad's not going to die, is he?"

The woman opened her mouth to answer, and then stopped.

"I don't know anymore," the woman said finally, shaking her head like the answer to that question would take too long to explain. "But that's not what I want to talk to you about."

Evie brought her eyes up from the carpet and looked at her, feeling nervous.

"You're going to see me again one day," the woman said. "Many years from now. You'll have forgotten me by then. But you'll remember this conversation when you see me. And when you do, I want you to remember this, okay? Because this is important and you need to hear it."

Evie looked back out the window, because she noticed the ambulance lights that held her Mom were driving away. Another ambulance and a firetruck stayed behind, parked along the curb. "Okay..."

"I want you to remember that I'm sorry," the woman said. Her voice was serious and deliberate. "That I told you I was sorry, okay?"

Evie frowned and shook her head. "Why?"

The woman in the strange clothes looked out the window too and watched Evie's mom being carried away. "Because I should have said goodbye to him. I should have done that for you."

"Why are you saying this to me...?"

"One day you will understand," the woman said, pushing herself back to her feet. "I know it's hard to believe right now, but you will. I swear it."

And then she was gone.

When Evie grew up, she thought about that moment a lot.

The police. The funeral. The foster homes, the scholarships, the universities, the training for spaceflight. Dad. Bradley. Mom and Evie. And then just Mom.

Because in this moment, all these years later, Fenroe finally understood what had happened that night.

Her mother had been taken apart psychologically. She'd been crushed under the machine press of mental illness. And she never did get out from underneath it. Oh, she did get better eventually, but not well enough to avoid institutionalization. And through it all, her psychosis had transformed her into the exact opposite person she had worked so hard to be. And the sad thing was that she knew it. Every time Fenroe went to visit her she knew what she had done, and she had to live with it every single day for the rest of her life.

They never talked about it. But Fenroe could actually *see* her remember it whenever she looked into her daughter's eyes. Whenever she asked about how Bradley was doing, and Fenroe had to lie about how he hadn't gotten arrested for this thing or that.

You see, Fenroe had failed her crew. She had let them die. All of them. And that knowledge was almost too much for her to bear. That failure nearly *killed* her.

What her mother's failure did to her...Fenroe couldn't imagine. She didn't want to ever know.

They spoke about her father only once.

It was the day Fenroe found out she was going into space for the first time.

In one of her rare moments of clarity, her mother stopped cold in her sentence, and Fenroe knew that it was one of those times when the memory of what she'd done hit her suddenly.

"I should have seen it coming," she said, staring into nothingness. There was no emotion in her eyes. No sadness. No regret. Just the memory. The terrible thing her body did while her mind was trapped behind a wall of delusion. "I should have gotten help a long time ago, but I didn't. And you had to deal with the aftermath alone. All those mistakes that I made. Mistakes that you ended up having to pay for."

And right before her mother disappeared back into the darkness of her thoughts, deep into one of her waking blackouts, she looked Fenroe right in the eyes, truly *seeing* her for what felt like the first time since the nightmare that had ruined all of their lives.

"I'll be watching for you up there, my little Evie," she said. "You'll shine brighter than all the stars in the sky."

That was the last time Fenroe saw her. She never had the courage to go back. She wanted to hold that image of her mom in her memory just the way she was at that moment, and not have to watch her continue coming apart like some old vacant building that nobody lived in anymore.

And that woman in the strange clothes? The one who had appeared in her house that night and apologized? She was right.

Fenroe had completely forgotten about her.

Until she looked into the stainless steel reflection of a deep freezing unit across from the wall she sat against in the main corridor of the *Pinnacle Observatory*, and saw her own face staring back at her.

She remembered it all at once. The woman with the strange clothes was her. The woman was Fenroe.

That's when Fenroe knew she would find a way.

She *did* find a way.

Fenroe would ride the wormhole with Eos, who had unlocked the secrets of the singularity, and find a way to step outside of Time somehow. Because Sitosen, Beck, Harris, Suja, Dunesto and Ulbricht were all out there somewhere, in the abstract thoroughfare of time, waiting for her to come and find them.

The main corridor stretched off in both directions, visible only by the flash of red emergency lights. The rest was pitch blackness. She held the crowbar and the ripped fibers of the wire she had tore out of the umbilical's airlock in her hands as if they were the last artifacts of a moment in time that never happened. She stared at these things for a long while, feeling the rumble of the wormhole shiver through her body, and then a soft blue light bled into the corridor. Fenroe raised her head in that direction, just as Eos emerged from the darkness. Beside the small android was Colonel Ambrose Wren, holding a bloodstained rag against a wound on the side of his head. Behind them both was another man she didn't know.

"Susskind," she heard Wren say to the man beside him. "Go help the commander."

Fenroe looked at her own reflection one last time and then nodded to herself, invoking the memory of her mother before the night of her father's death. Gripping the crowbar in her hands, she stood and walked towards Eos and the two men, who were waiting for her where the light ended. When she reached them, Fenroe stepped back into the shadows.

BREATHLESS

ACKNOWLEDGMENTS

I have to thank the following:

Miguel, for giving this story its name.

Betsy, for the meticulous proofing.

Anna, for being an amazing partner and inspiring me to keep going.

ABOUT THE AUTHOR

Shane Lindemoen has written two novels: Artifact, which won the 2014 National Independent Book Award, and Breathless, which received the 2020 Millennium Book Award.